PRAISE FOR
Hannah's Dream

"Irresistibly touching, delectably uplifting, Hammond's under-stated yet gargantuan tale of devotion and commitment poi-gnantly proves that love does indeed come in all shapes and sizes." —*Booklist* (starred review)

"Diane Hammond writes with heart, compassion, and humor. With subtle assurance, she invites you to fall in love with Sam and Winslow and Neva and Corinna and Truman and Max and, of course, Hannah, the beloved elephant that ties them all together. A generously told tale that will stick with you long after the last page is turned."

—Terry Gamble, author of
Good Family and *The Water Dancers*

"While it's easy to guess the outcome of *Hannah's Dream*, its predictability lends to its charm. It helps that Hammond's writing never becomes overly sappy. She treats each of her characters with a tenderness that draws sympathy rather than groans. And she's no stranger to the bond between humans and animals: In the mid–1990s she was part of the rehabilita-tion team of Keiko, the killer whale in the *Free Willy* movies, at the Oregon Coast Aquarium. . . . *Hannah's Dream* runs at a quick pace but feels substantial, and the humorous bits sprin-kled throughout make it a very satisfying read."

—*Portland Oregonian*

"A pleasure to read. *Hannah's Dream* is gently unpredictable. It's full of suspense—but not unbearable suspense. There's a missing document, a devoted pig, and a villain with a pith helmet and a riding crop. Most of all, there's an elephant and the people who really love her."

—Susan McCarthy, author of *Becoming a Tiger* and coauthor of *When Elephants Weep*

PRAISE FOR
Homesick Creek

"*Homesick Creek* follows two troubled marriages and an enduring friendship through some exceptionally difficult midlife straits, and does so with sensitivity and intelligence. Given the material, this could be a three-hankie job, but the story never turns maudlin, thanks to Hammond's clean prose, pitch-perfect dialogue, and keen eye for social detail. . . . *Homesick Creek* is an honest, finely nuanced, emotionally rich novel."

—*Boston Globe*

"Hammond digs into the past, revealing bad decisions and their consequences, desperate acts of courage, kindness that sometimes is not enough to save or redeem. And woven throughout are insights, sprinkled with humor, on marriage and friendship. *Homesick Creek* is an honest, beautifully written book."

—*Denver Post*

Seeing ⭐ Stars

Seeing Stars

A NOVEL

Diane Hammond

HARPER

NEW YORK · LONDON · TORONTO · SYDNEY

HarperCollins books may be purchased for educational, business, or sales promotional use. For information please write: Special Markets Department, HarperCollins Publishers, 10 East 53rd Street, New York, NY 10022.

FIRST EDITION

Designed by Betty Lew

Library of Congress Cataloging-in-Publication Data is available upon request.

ISBN 978-0-06-186315-8

10 11 12 13 14   OV/RRD   10 9 8 7 6 5 4 3 2 1

FOR KERRY

Acknowledgments

THIS BOOK WOULD NEVER HAVE BEEN POSSIBLE WITHOUT the generosity and support of family, friends, and colleagues. Special thanks go to Caryn Casey, whose abiding friendship I first lucked into on a TV set and who has ever since, with unfailing tact and patience, helped me chart and navigate the minefield that is Hollywood. Caryn: You, Jim, Siera, and Carlie have given me both psychic and physical shelter, and I only hope that one day I can repay the debt. Your willingness to slog through an early draft of *Seeing Stars* when it was in its gawky adolescence unquestionably made the grown-up version a better book.

To Delaney Andrews: I owe you boundless gratitude for the many insights that helped shape this book, as well as your keen sense of humor, your ever-ready shoulder, and, by turns, your unwavering faith and righteous indignation. You, Andrew, and Brandon were always a welcome reminder that even when the assault was on, we were all in the bunker together.

To Richard Liedle: I am deeply appreciative of your friendship, enthusiasm, and indefatigable good humor. Those LA dinners kept us sane.

To Donnajeanne Goheen and everyone at Young Performers Studio back in the day: We are indebted to you for giving us a community when we needed one most. To Judi O'Neill: A special thank-you for your sage words "Love the work." They hold every bit as true for writers as for actors.

To Kate Nintzel at Harper: I once again extend my most heartfelt thanks for believing in me and for turning an incisive editorial eye to immature drafts of this book. It would have been a very different and much diminished work without you. To my agent Erin Malone and to Jennifer Rudolph Walsh: Thanks, as ever, for your support and belief that good books will find good homes. And to Dawn Stuart and Brenda Ambrose: Thank you for helping me take my place in the world as a writer.

To my mother, Debbie Coplin, who supported us during the dark days: I have no words that adequately express my love and gratitude. To my sister, Laurie Coplin, who read draft after draft of this book with unflagging energy and insight: I am especially indebted to you. You may have missed your calling.

To my daughter, Kerry: I admire your talent, your courage, and your willingness to share your Hollywood experience with us on bad days as well as good ones.

And, as always, I have no words that adequately express my love and appreciation to my husband, Nolan Harvey. I would not have survived, never mind written about, the funhouse that is Hollywood without you. It was one hell of a ride.

The thing about Hollywood is it makes you doubt yourself—your identity, your judgment, your motivation, your parenting—because you are trafficking in children. Harsh but true: if you want to cast a Geisha-child in kimono, wig, whiteface, and tabi, fifty mothers will rush forward and offer you their daughters; if your taste is for a red-headed tomboy who looks like she could build the atom bomb with a pen, two rubber bands, and some baling wire, you can find her on any street corner. Baby dimples, Eurasian glamour, Chinese dolls with moving parts, black girls and Barbie dolls and boys as beautiful as angels—they can all be delivered right to your door, where you can make them up and feed them lines and they will do whatever you ask them to do, because their mommies and daddies and agents and managers and producers and directors have told them it's perfectly all right because they are going to be famous one day. Try your luck! Pull the lever, swing the hammer, throw the dart, shoot the gun, play any game you like, because you never know who's going to be a winner. And you'll not only allow your children to play, you'll hold the door open for them on their way through. You'll feed them and water them and dress them and coach them, and the fact is, you'd slap their latest headshots onto the backs of the benches where derelicts sleep, if you actually thought it might help.

—VEE VELMAN

Chapter One

RUTH RABINOWITZ HAD A WAKING NIGHTMARE THAT SHE had hit a transvestite crossing Highland at Hollywood Boulevard. In her mind the transvestite would be lying in the crosswalk surrounded by Shreks and Dorothys and Princess Fionas; Batman would call 911 while Japanese tourists took pictures of the fallen one with their cell phones. The transvestite would be fine, of course—it was a *waking* nightmare—and when s/he was set upright on his/her extremely tall platform shoes, s/he would look down on Ruth from six feet up and say kindly, *Go ahead, honey—you cry if you want to.* Ruth would break down right there, and the transvestite would take her gently in his/her arms—and his/her skin would be wonderfully silky and toned from hours at the gym—and smooth her hair from her face while she wept.

That's how much pressure she was under.

Driving into Hollywood was always harrowing, and though she and her thirteen-year-old daughter, Bethany, had been in Los Angeles for only three weeks, she had already learned that the smoothness of the trip to a casting studio was inversely proportionate to the importance of the audition. Right now it was three o'clock, Bethany's callback time had been two forty-five, and they were stuck in choking traffic on Highland near Santa Monica.

Admittedly, some of their tardiness—all right, most of it—was Ruth's fault. She had a tendency, even under routine circumstances, to dither. She'd changed clothes twice before they'd left, even though no one would care or even notice what she was wearing. She'd checked and rechecked an e-mail in which Mimi Roberts, Bethany's manager, had forwarded the callback's time and location. She'd printed out, misplaced, reprinted, and then found the original copy of the MapQuest directions she'd pulled up—even though they'd driven to the same casting studio just yesterday. Now she heard the same maddening refrain looping endlessly inside her head: *You should have left sooner, you should have left sooner, you should have left sooner.* Her blood pressure was so high she could feel her pulse in her feet. "I just can't believe there's this much traffic," she said.

"Mom," Bethany said with newfound world-weariness. "This is *LA*."

"Well, you can certainly see why it's the birthplace of road rage." They moved up a couple of car lengths and then stopped, still at least eight cars short of the intersection. Beside them a young man in a BMW cursed energetically into his Bluetooth. Ruth couldn't tell what he was saying, but she thought he looked very attractive in his nice suit and tie and tiny gold hoop earrings. She couldn't imagine her husband, Hugh, in earrings. He was only forty-six, but he could have belonged to their parents' generation. He was, conceivably, the last man in America to own Hush Puppies. "What?" he'd said when she'd pointed this out once. "They're very well-made and they're comfortable."

"You should try clogs," she'd offered. "Dansko ones, like your hygienists wear."

But he'd just made a dismissive sound and applied himself to tying his shoelaces so that the loops of the bows were the same size and the leftover lace lengths matched. Sometimes it took him three or four times to get it just right. Ruth would have just pulled the hem of her pants down lower so no one would see. Not that she wore oxfords. She'd been wearing the same style of Bass Weejuns loafers since 1973.

"Hold up the MapQuest directions again," she said. Bethany held the sheet of paper far enough away for Ruth to read without her glasses. She scanned the page and sighed deeply. "At least we're within five blocks. Do you have your script? Maybe you should run your lines."

"*Sides.* They're called sides. If you call it a script, people will think we're right off the boat."

"We are right off the boat."

Bethany crossed her arms tightly over her chest.

"No?"

The girl gave her a look.

"Don't sulk. I *know* we should have—"

"*Mom.*"

"*What?* Oh!" Ruth finally got it. "Right. You're in character."

"Duh."

Ruth sighed. She wished Bethy wasn't in character, because right now her daughter was the rapidly fraying line that connected Ruth to everything she loved and gained strength from. Still, everyone talked about how important it was for even the youngest actor to walk into every audition in character, even if she had just one line. Casting, as Mimi had told her and Bethy in their first week in LA and repeatedly ever since, began in the waiting room. Actors were sometimes cast on the spot, before they'd even read a line, they were *that* right. "Do you have the glasses?"

Bethany held up eyeglass frames without lenses. She was auditioning for a costar role—a part with fewer than five spoken lines—to play a nerdy sidekick on the Disney Channel sitcom *That's So Raven*. Ruth felt a little shiver of possibility. The casting director at yesterday's audition had called Bethy "adorable, just adorable," and specifically instructed her to bring a pair of glasses to the callback. According to Mimi, they weren't even supposed to *tell* you they were giving you a callback; they were supposed to call your agent, who called your manager, who called you. The point was that protocol had been violated, the casting director had been that enthusiastic. They'd gone to Target and found a pair of weird sunglasses and popped out the lenses. They'd also done her hair in a side ponytail and bought her a pair of strange knit pants.

This was her first callback. Mimi had told them that you had to get callbacks regularly because if you didn't, your agent (in Bethy's case, Holly Jensen at Big Talent) would lose interest in you, in which case you might as well pack up and go home. Mimi had amplified on this by telling a chilling story about one of her clients who hadn't been out on a single audition in *six months*, whereas when he was still in his agent's good graces he'd gone out two or three times a week. She'd then stated bluntly that the family was to blame. Not only had the boy not been enrolled in the acting classes Mimi had recommended, but his mother had insisted on using a terrible headshot that had been taken by a *relative*, for God's sake, and if you weren't willing to pay for professional materials, well then Mimi couldn't be responsible for the consequences. She had told the boy's parents to take him to Honey Schweitzer, a photographer who was red-hot right now. Four of the clients who'd had her take their headshots were series regulars now, three on sitcoms and one on a prime-time, hour-long drama. Honey charged five hundred dollars for a one-hour photo shoot and still clung to film instead of a digital format, but the point—at least as far as Ruth could follow it—was that people still used her, she was that good. If you did things on the cheap—and how many times now had Mimi already emphasized this—you might just as well take that money and shove it up a rat's ass. Some of her clients' mothers— the good mothers, Mimi implied; the ones who knew how to take direction—had commissioned as many as four different sets of headshots before they'd gotten the one in which the eyes reached out and spoke to you. If your headshot didn't do that, you could just forget about everything else.

Mimi made a lot of pronouncements.

Don't mumble. Own the room. Don't let your mother speak to anyone.

Never be late for an audition.

It was four fifteen. They were two cars from the intersection of Santa Monica and Highland. Ruth rested her forehead momentarily on the steering wheel and then took a strengthening breath. "You know you're going to have to walk into this callback like you own it. Do you need to use the bathroom?" Ruth asked because she did, and she and Bethy had always been in sync that way.

"I didn't, until you said that," Bethany said.

Ruth sighed and watched a transvestite—not a nice one like in her nightmare, but a haughty, faux-breasted person with an alarming blond wig—cross the street. S/he had a better figure than Ruth had ever had, never mind now. She'd never minded before; in Seattle, middle-aged women just spread and thickened and got on with it, but here you were supposed to look like you had when you were twenty, except for your hair, she gathered; you were supposed to be more sophisticated with your hair. But of course it was Bethy's appearance that mattered.

"If you're going to come all the way down here, you're going to have to do some things," Mimi had warned Ruth that first day in her office in Van Nuys. "For starters, there are her eyebrows. They're a little, hmmm, Anne Frank, aren't they? Plus we need to do something with the hair. If she's going to keep it long, you're going to have to get it straightened because, let's face it, it's nappy. The price has come way down—you can probably find a place that'll do it for less than five hundred dollars." When Ruth had gasped, Mimi just shrugged and said, "Given what we're starting with, we need the best. She'll still have an ethnic look, but she'll be able to play Arab, Jew, gypsy, whatever. You send her in the way she is now and the casting director's going to look for a prayer shawl." Ruth had feebly pointed out that only men wore prayer shawls—not that the Rabinowitzes were Orthodox or even practicing Jews—but of course that wasn't the point.

Last week they'd consulted with an orthodontist Mimi had recommended whose office in Beverly Hills required you to valet-park at forty dollars an hour and had a water feature in the parking garage lobby. He'd yanked Bethy's braces off on the spot, even though Dr. Probst, Bethy's Seattle orthodontist, had been very clear that she should wear them for at least another year before they could even talk about when to remove them. Next week they'd be getting Bethany's first set of clear plastic Invisalign braces for twice what they'd paid for her old braces and admittedly a poor therapeutic second. But on this, as on every other point, Mimi had been adamant. "Nothing says nerd like steel braces. Do you want her playing the kid in the closeup who represents the losers' group?"

So the braces were off, the hair and eyebrows had been done, and four days ago they'd finally had their emergency appointment with Honey Schweitzer, which had cost them almost six hundred dollars by the time they'd ordered fifty sets of one theatrical headshot (no smile) and one commercial headshot (smile).

If Mimi had told her that Bethy needed an eye transplant, Ruth would probably be out there right now trying to find a donor. She was that committed.

As it was, Bethany Rabinowitz was now Bethany Ann

Roosevelt, Mimi's creation. "Hmm . . . Rabinowitz. Let's go with something more mainstream. Does she have a middle name? Bethany Ann Roosevelt. That'll make it a little different." She'd punched the name into the Internet Movie Database to make sure there wasn't a Bethany Ann Roosevelt already, since two Screen Actors Guild members couldn't have the same one. Not that Bethany was a SAG member yet. But Mimi had made it plain that they would have to take some steps to get her union card as soon as possible. As she'd explained it to Ruth, SAG membership would not only give Bethy a much more competitive edge and establish her worth as an actor sanctioned by other producers and directors, but it would also give her access to auditions that, until she became SAG, were closed to her as a nonunion actor. It simply had to be done, and the sooner, the better; by implication, once she was a SAG actor, nothing would impede her from rocketing straight to the top. Ruth hadn't had the strength to ask exactly what that might entail, or how much it might cost. Hugh was very conservative when it came to money, and she had only so much courage.

"Roosevelt?" he'd said on the phone when Ruth told him. "Roosevelt is ridiculous."

"Mimi thought it would be a good idea," Ruth had said weakly. "Not so ethnic."

"Honey, she's clearly anti-Semitic. If Bethy has a manager who doesn't like Jews, she should get another manager."

"No one likes Jews," Ruth had pointed out. "Name one female star whose last name is Greenberg. You can't. No one can. Or Schwartz or Steinberg or—"

"Jeff Goldblum. Steve Guttenberg."

"They're men."

"They're Jews!"

At last Ruth surged through the intersection. It was now

four thirty. "Headshot?" she asked Bethany for the sixth time. Bethany held up the eight-by-ten photograph with her résumé stapled to the back and waggled it. The résumé was a work of near-genius. Mimi had assembled it from a string of school plays and summer theater camps at home in Seattle, going all the way back to when Bethy was six years old and had played the part of snow. Ruth and Bethy were both paranoid about the head-shot and résumé. During their first week here they'd shown up at an audition without them—Ruth had thought Bethany had them and Bethy had thought Ruth did—and the casting direc-tor had snapped at Bethany in front of the entire waiting room, "Oh, for God's sake," and then she'd seized the sign-in clip-board, scratched through Bethany's name, and yelled, "*Cecilia Planchard*," which was how they knew Bethany wouldn't even get to audition, and after they'd spent seventy-five dollars on a half-hour coaching session. Ruth had treated them to a ham-burger at Bob's Big Boy, but even so it had been a glum evening in their stunningly expensive, crappily furnished extended-stay studio apartment. After Bethany had fallen asleep, Ruth had closed herself in the bathroom and cried. "She's already old to be starting," Mimi had told them in the lobby of a La Quinta Inn in Seattle six weeks ago, when Bethany had taken Mimi's two-day intensive seminar on Acting for the Camera. "You know I don't make any promises." Yet here they were in Los Angeles, far from home and far from Hugh, who couldn't leave his dental practice and, anyway, believed that they'd been sold a bill of goods by a shyster talent manager who came to Seattle every three months to pick a little more fruit from the naïveté tree.

Ruth made a final right turn onto Las Palmas. They found a parking spot directly across from the studio lot's guard shack—who said there wasn't a God?—where they were checked in on the strength of a handwritten list and Bethany's headshot. It was four thirty-five. They raced past several soundstages, past reserved parking spaces for Disney directors and writers, past an open-hatched SUV with five identical bearded collies inside, animal actors for some movie or other, and then, at last, they were at Soundstage 33, home of *That's So Raven*—a show that, three weeks ago, Ruth had not even heard of.

Just inside the door, a second door led into the soundstage itself. A red light over the door was turned on, which Ruth had learned meant cameras were rolling. Even so, a gorgeous girl and a snotty-looking boy came out, laughing extravagantly. They brushed by Ruth and Bethany without so much as a flicker of acknowledgment or apology. Once they were past, Bethany clutched Ruth's upper arm and hissed, "Mom, they're on the show! I recognize them!"

"That could be you," Ruth whispered back, because it could; someone's career could be fast-tracked right now, at this callback. It made Ruth queasy with excitement to think about it. "You have to be patient," Mimi kept telling them, and Ruth knew that she really did, but in a secret part of her mind she was already smiling for the camera at the Oscars.

They climbed a flight of stairs and emerged in a hallway with the same messy, hand-printed paper sign as yesterday, which said simply, *Casting.*

"Hair," Ruth said.

Bethany smoothed her newly straight bangs, tightened the scrunchy around her ridiculous but beautifully straight side ponytail, and put on the lensless glasses. "Okay?" she said.

"Okay," said Ruth. "Breathe."

The waiting room was ringed with twenty or so folding plastic chairs, the kind that Ruth had seen for sale just last week at Costco. A clipboard was set out on an unmanned reception counter, which Bethany approached to sign in like an old hand. All but one of the seats was taken by either a girl or her mother, and every one of those girls and mothers seemed to regard Bethany and Ruth with something between mild indifference and withering contempt. None of the girls wore glasses or side ponytails. No one was wearing strange knit pants. Nothing about them said anything but Hip Southern California Tween Babe. Ruth had never seen so many beautiful heads of naturally straight hair in a single room.

She gave Bethany a little push toward the last empty chair, and Bethy sat on exactly one inch of the seat. Ruth, having learned her place in the first week, leaned against the wall behind her daughter, ready to serve. She could feel her stomach pooch out. None of the other mothers in the room looked like they had stomachs that pooched out. They looked like they ran for an hour every morning and then took Pilates until their late afternoon nail appointment. No doubt these were women who dared to wear bathing suits. Ruth should have had a grapefruit half for breakfast instead of Denny's Fabulous French Toast Platter. Menus always made things look delicious, and then they turned out to be just one more serving of lard on a bun, which you ate every bit of anyway because you'd paid for it and you didn't want to be a bad role model for your daughter, who could eat eight thousand calories a day without a single serving of fresh fruit or vegetables and wake up the next morning looking like a goddess.

A girl came down the hall from the casting room looking at the floor. Her mother rose, put an arm around her, and gently led her away. A minute later an elegant woman in an expensive leather ensemble clicked into the waiting room on perfectly coordinated heels: the casting director from yesterday. Ruth nudged Bethany with her elbow, but the casting director passed right by without acknowledgment or even recognition, picked up the sign-in clipboard, and scanned the room. Suddenly she was all smiles. "Hey!" she cried to a girl on the far side of the room with a twelve-year-old body and twenty-five-year-old makeup and hair. The girl jumped up as the woman click-click-clicked across the floor and pulled her in with a lavish one-armed hug. "How are you, sweetie? I didn't know you were reading for this." Which was specious, of course. Even as green as she was, Ruth knew that the casting director hand-picked the callbacks.

The girl ran her long fingers through her long hair and shot one skinny hip out. Ruth could identify her mother on the far side of the room because she was the only mother who was smiling.

"Where are you on the list?" the woman asked. The two of them consulted the clipboard, flipping back a few pages before the casting director gave up and said, "Oh, just c'mon back." She linked her arm through the girl's, and Ruth and Bethany and nearly everyone else in the waiting room watched them walk every step of the way down the long hall to the audition room.

"They do that to freak you out," said an amused, dry martini of a voice with underlying notes of old smoker. "It's one of the ways they see if your kid is tough enough—or if you are. Shake the trees a little."

The woman who'd spoken was sitting on Bethany's far side, watching them both with amusement. To Ruth's relief, she didn't look like she worked out at a gym or jogged. She looked more like someone with a pack-a-day habit and a weight problem. She wore clothes that were on a par with Ruth's—shapeless jeans, faded T-shirt, Costco sneakers.

"Well, it worked," Ruth said.

"Is this her first time auditioning for Evelyn?"

"Evelyn?"

"Flynn. The casting director."

"Oh! Yes. Plus it's her first callback ever. We're so nervous."

"I'm not," Bethany said. "I just have to pee."

A cheerful, blocky, red-haired girl came down the hallway toward them from the direction of the casting room and said, "Well, *that* was a joke."

"Clara, meet"—the woman picked up Bethany's head shot—"Bethany Ann Roosevelt."

Clara grinned. "No shit—is that your real name?"

"No," said Bethy. "My manager named me that. My real name is Bethany Rabinowitz."

"Jeez," the girl said sympathetically.

"Vee Velman," said the woman, and held out a hand to Ruth. The hand was warm and dry. Ruth's was cold and sticky with nerve-sweat.

"Vee?" she said.

"Technically, Virginia."

"Oh. Well, I'm Ruth. You were just joking when you said they do things to try and rattle the kids, right?"

"Are you kidding? They do it all the time. Evelyn Flynn's famous for it."

"But she couldn't have been nicer to Bethany yesterday," Ruth said doubtfully. Maybe this Clara was an awful actor, in which case you could understand the casting director's lack of interest. Bethy was a very good actor.

Clara and her mother exchanged a look. Clara grinned and said, "One time I went in and read and left and the whole time she never even got off the phone."

"Didn't it bother you?"

"Nah."

"But why would they do something like that? Especially to children."

Vee said, "There's your first mistake. They're not children. They're job applicants. You're new here, aren't you?"

"It shows that much?"

Vee reached over and patted Ruth's hand. "Yeah. But enjoy that naïveté, honey, because when it wears off you're going to want to start drinking."

"How long have you been here?" Ruth asked.

"Born and raised. My kids—Clara and her brother, Buster—have been in the industry since they were three. All the kids have. It's what LA kids do instead of 4-H."

"Uh oh. *Mom.*" Clara tapped her watch urgently.

"*Shit!*" Vee snatched up a purse big enough to comfortably accommodate a six-pack of beer. "It's three fifty-one and we're parked on Santa Monica. If you're not driving away by four on the dot they'll tow you, and let me tell you, *that* is a nightmare." She pulled out a piece of paper and a pen and scribbled her name and phone number. "If the girls want to get together sometime."

Ruth accepted the slip of paper gratefully. "Thank you. You're pretty much the first people we've met since we got here who've been friendly."

"Doesn't mean we're nice, though," Vee said, grinning. "Always watch your back. This is Hollywood."

Ruth looked after them as the door closed behind them. The room suddenly felt bigger and colder. She felt a pang of homesickness for Hugh. He didn't agree with their being here but he was a good, solid, sensible man, as well as a gifted dentist. They'd been married for twenty-two years, known each other for twenty-three. They'd met as graduate school students, she of ceramic arts, he of dentistry. She'd always been grimy with clay or glaze residue and he'd smelled of pulverized tooth enamel and amalgam.

Back then she'd told herself that Hugh, who was a model of measured words and earnestness, would be more passionate once he could take his attention away from dental school. He'd never become passionate, but by the time she realized that, she'd come to appreciate him all the more for his durability and even keel. And though he was frank with her, he didn't dwell on her shortcomings. In addition to being a ditherer, she was hopelessly transparent and gullible. She would ask Bethy about a friend at school who weighed no more than a bird, and Bethy would say, "It's fine, Mom, she just has a really high metabolism," and Ruth would *believe* that; and next thing she knew, some parent she'd run into in the aisles of Safeway was telling her that the child had just been checked into an eating disorder clinic. It came down to the fact that Ruth always thought people were better and nicer than they really were. Hugh had been gently telling her so for years—he was telling her that now about Mimi Roberts.

"You want the world to be a nice place, Ruthie, but sometimes it just isn't," he'd told her once. "Wanting something to be true doesn't make it true."

Maybe so, but you had to have conviction about some things, and Ruth believed utterly that Bethy would end up standing head and shoulders above other people—perfectly *nice* other people, Ruth would readily concede—who were simply less talented, less gifted, than Bethy. Fate had bestowed upon her daughter a great talent and the drive to put it to its highest use. Therefore, Bethy would be seen, would be discovered, here in LA. Her life would be one long string of successes and the occasional mention—*tasteful* mention—in *People* and on *Access Hollywood*, until it was time for her to attend Yale or Harvard like Jodie Foster and Natalie Portman had; and after that she would come back to a string of challenging, *thoughtful* projects as long as her arm—meaningful movies that would be discovered at Sundance or would premier at Cannes to critical acclaim and would go on to perform outstandingly at the box office.

Was it wrong to have dreams, to think big, to picture the best and head straight for it? Sure, the odds were long—Ruth wasn't an idiot—but consider the case of George Clooney, who'd been to network twenty times, *twenty times*, before he booked *ER*. And look at him now.

Another half hour crawled by. Girls and mothers departed in pairs, draining all the energy and breathable air from the room. Ruth finally let Bethy go to the bathroom but told her to hurry. She shouldn't have worried: it was another ten minutes before the casting director came for her at last, talking loudly on a cell phone. "Look," she was saying, "she's not booking because she's unstable, and she has that mother, you know exactly which one I'm talking about. *Christ*. So hear me when I tell you that we will *never*"—Ruth watched with appalled fascination as she grabbed Bethy's headshot, the only one left, and waved it in the air—"*ever* book that girl. On anything. All right, c'mon back." That last was to Bethany. The casting director clapped her phone shut and marched off down the hall with Bethy hurrying along behind her.

Ruth's heart leaped. Maybe she did remember Bethany but had just been keeping it a secret while all those other people had been in the waiting room, so it would seem like they had an equal chance of booking the part. If Bethany had last-minute nerves she certainly didn't show it. Ruth was so proud. This— *exactly* this—was why they were here.

WHAT BETHANY LOVED MOST ABOUT ACTING WAS THAT you could take yourself off like a coat and put on somebody else—usually someone you liked a lot better. No one else knew, not even her best friend, Rianne, but for years she had walked around as Courage Girl. Courage Girl hadn't been afraid of the coat closet when she was in first grade; Courage Girl answered any question boldly, her head held high. It had been Courage Girl who'd fended off her crazy uncle Billy when he kept plying her with Passover wine at last year's Seder; who'd told stupid Randy Maxwell to just go *screw* himself when he told her she looked like his mother's dog (though actually, the dog was a cocker spaniel and, in Bethy's opinion, very pretty). Courage Girl had taken swimming lessons when Bethy was afraid of drowning. Courage Girl was not afraid of Dumpsters or those kinds of cats with no hair. Not that she was always Courage Girl. A couple of years ago, in sixth grade, she had liked Billy Williams, but he'd never even noticed she was there until the day she came to school as the school's supremely confident seventh-grade bitch Cynthia Morgenstern—the clothes, the jewelry, the walk, the laugh—and all day kids told her she just seemed so much more fun than usual, so *out* there.

Now, here in LA, Bethany had lots of new alter egos: the geeky girl, the sidekick, the best friend, the brain. They, not Bethy, were the people who inhabited her skin in the casting studio waiting rooms. They were the ones who walked into every audition like she was, in Rianne's words, the Biggest Frickin' Deal on the Planet. That was her secret; that was why she just knew she'd be famous one day. It was what she dreamed about every night before she fell asleep; it was what she thought about when she first woke up in the morning. When she flipped through *People* magazine, she saw herself in the *Scoop* section; she'd already identified the place on Hollywood Boulevard where her star would be placed. She was going to live a wonderful, charmed life and when she won her first Oscar she would weep a little bit and thank her mother for standing by her all these years. She'd thank her father only at the very end, because he didn't share her dream.

Surprisingly, she wasn't bitter about Hugh's disapproval. She knew the reason he lacked enthusiasm was that her dreams took her away from him, plain and simple, and that was fair enough. When she made her second or third movie, or had become a regular on a television series, she'd pay for him to move down here and set up a new practice where all his patients would be starlets and stuntmen with teeth like jewels.

She donned her glasses frames and followed Evelyn Flynn into the same audition room as yesterday, where a video camera was set up on a tripod at the back. She waited for the casting director to step behind the camera and then she moved into its line of sight, the way Mimi had taught her. The casting director showed no sign of remembering her from yesterday, which was confusing. Worse, she looked irritated. She squinted at the camera, clicked it on, and said, "Go ahead and slate."

Bethy smiled at the lens and said very slowly and distinctly, as she'd been taught, "My name is Bethany Ann Roosevelt and my agent is Holly Jensen at Big Talent."

The casting director didn't even look up from the camera, just picked up a creased and dog-eared copy of the sides. "Okay. Go."

Bethy was confused. "But you have the first—"

"*Go,*" the casting director said.

Bethy raised her sides and said, "*Mom said she'd love me no matter what.*"

Evelyn Flynn read, in the flattest voice imaginable, "*But you're a loser, Sandy. You know that. Everyone knows that.*"

"*I'm not a loser,*" Bethy said without even having to consult the paper. She was off-book, like Mimi had told her to be for every audition.

"*I have lizards that are prettier than you.*"

"*I'm pretty. I know I am,*" Bethy said, giving her voice the slightest tremor.

"Okay," the casting director said, switching off the camera. "Thank you."

"But I—" They couldn't be done. Bethy had two more lines, and they were both laden with emotion. She'd worked with a coach on those two lines, *just* those two lines, for twenty minutes.

Evelyn Flynn crossed to the door and held it open for Bethy. "Thank you," she said again, and her eyes were flat. Bethy felt tears as she meekly passed in front of the casting director. Just as she was out the door, the woman said, "Oh, and honey?"

Bethy perked up.

"Don't bring props to an audition. Ever."

BETHANY CRIED MOST OF THE WAY HOME. "SHE TOLD ME to bring them. She *told* me to! And then she didn't recognize me. I didn't even get to read all my lines. If I could have read them, she'd have chosen me."

"Oh, honey," Ruth said, feeling the prick of tears behind her own eyelids.

Eventually Bethy subsided, looking out the window dully and gnawing a fingernail. Ruth was appalled, but what could she do? These people were in a position to change the future. They didn't play fair, but there it was: you could stay and take it, or you could go home. Thank God Hugh wasn't here to witness this. He'd have transported them both back to Seattle before they even knew what had happened. He was very protective, even sometimes when it wasn't necessary.

Ruth got off the 101 at the Barham Boulevard exit. They'd

driven this way for almost every audition Bethy had had, and it took them past the Oakwood every single time. The Oakwood was a tony apartment complex in Burbank that catered to actors, directors, and writers from out of town.

"I wish we were staying here," Bethy said wistfully as they drove by. "There are tons of kids. They have a pool and a hot tub and a game room and stuff."

"We have a pool."

Bethy just looked at her. This morning they'd heard that the pool man found a rat in the skimmer. "It's *green*."

"It is a little green," Ruth conceded. "But that's just paint, Bethy."

"No, it's not," Bethy said. "It's algae."

Ruth sighed. It might be algae.

"Plus the pool at the Oakwood has a diving board and a slide."

"Honey, last time we talked about this I told you it was too expensive for us, and unless they've lowered their rates in the last two days, it still is."

Their own crappy rental was a couple of miles away, at the Alameda Extended Stay Apartments. It cost four hundred dollars a month less than the Oakwood's cheapest studio because it was extremely basic: kitchenette corner; floor covered with shiny maroon industrial paint instead of carpeting; marshy beds that were more like cots; funky bedspreads that looked like, and quite conceivably *were*, cotton throw rugs; a bathroom that could, at the very least, benefit from a new surround and an application of Drano. Ruth insisted they wear flip-flops in the shower. And it *still* cost $1,198 a month. Their mortgage back home was only $852, and that included property taxes.

Instead of the triumphant dinner Ruth had planned for them to have at Bob's Big Boy—they'd seen Drew Carey there two

Tuesdays in a row, and God knew who else might stop in for a burger—Ruth decided they'd go to Paty's, instead. Paty's was a less popular coffee shop three blocks past Bob's on Riverside Drive, with a nearly identical menu, fewer people, and a manager who looked exactly, but *exactly*, like Neil Diamond. But when they were within a block of the restaurant Ruth could see there was a line of people waiting. She drove on. "Honey, maybe we should eat in tonight," she said. "I could make us spaghetti. Or we could go to Poquito Mas."

Normally, that cheered Bethy up. Poquito Mas was a Mexican patio restaurant just down the street. The first time they went there, they were thrilled to see a sign over the order window that said, NO PHOTOGRAPHS. WE RESPECT THE PRIVACY OF OUR PATRONS, which implied that at any minute you might see a star or two. So far, though, all they'd seen was a flamboyant blonde who was, Ruth was sure, a porn star. She'd heard that the San Fernando Valley was *the* place for porn production, and it was true that all up and down Magnolia Boulevard she'd noticed unmarked, windowless production buildings. Not that she'd ever mention this to Bethy, of course.

"Honey? Poquito Mas?"

"Whatever," Bethany said listlessly, so Ruth just drove to the apartment.

"Do you want to call Daddy?" Ruth asked as she led the way through the courtyard. Sometimes Hugh's sheer cluelessness could calm Bethy down, even cheer her up.

"I don't know," Bethany said. "No."

"Sure?"

"Yeah."

Ruth let them in and Bethany dropped her Mimi Roberts Talent Management audition bag on the foam-block sofa. The sofa was extra-compressed on one end, like someone huge had

sat there for much too long—in the dark, Ruth imagined, eating high-calorie, high-cholesterol takeout food with a spork.

"You could call Rianne."

"Mom. Rianne wouldn't understand."

"How about Clara?" Ruth suggested.

"Who's Clara?"

"The girl we just met at the callback."

"Oh. Nah."

Ruth waited until Bethany went to the bathroom before she
called Mimi to report on the audition. Mimi listened silently
until Ruth was done, and then she said, "Did Evelyn give her
any redirects?"

"Redirects?" Ruth said.

Mimi sighed. "Did she have Bethany do the scene a couple
of different ways?"

"I don't think so. She didn't even let Bethy get through the
whole thing. Are redirects good?"

"If they're serious about you at all, they're going to see if you
can take direction."

"Maybe she just thought Bethy did it right the first time."

She could hear—or at least she imagined she could hear—
Mimi's jaws clenching. "It has nothing to do with right or
wrong. If a kid's as green as Bethany, they're not going to book
her without making sure she can take direction. Is she coming
to class tonight?"

Ruth had forgotten all about the class. It was called Believability, and Mimi required that all her clients—and there had
been dozens and dozens of them—take it in their first month of
representation, at two hundred dollars apiece. "I don't know,"
Ruth said. "It's been a pretty emotional day."

"If you're going to get upset every time she blows an audition—"

"I don't think she *blew* the—"

"—then you might as well go home."

"We're not going home."

"Then I'll see her in class," Mimi said, and hung up.

AN HOUR LATER, RUTH PULLED INTO THE STUDIO PARKING lot. Mimi Roberts Talent Management occupied four shabby rooms in a strip mall in Van Nuys. The studio was the beating heart of Mimi's empire: office, classroom, parental gathering place, and venue for talent showcases in which actors performed scenes for invited talent agents and casting directors at $125 per actor per show. The largest room had a raised platform stage at one end and a seating capacity of thirty. Mimi's office—the inner sanctum—was furnished with a lumpy couch, sprung visitor's armchair, overflowing desk, grimy dog bed for Mimi's imperious rat terrier Tina Marie, an aged computer, and a door that closed and locked—the only one within the entire suite. The third room served as a greenroom when there was a show-case and as a waiting room for studio parents when there was not. The fourth room—actually a walk-in closet—was the private waiting room for visiting agents—whom, Ruth had no-ticed, Mimi liked to keep as far from the parents as possible.

Tonight the room was empty. The other parents must have dropped their children and run. Ruth heaved a sigh and sank into the stove-in cushions of the greenroom sofa. It was the first chance she'd had all day to just *sit*. Without the usual chaos of kids and parents, though, it was strangely barren. From the of-fice she could hear the chatter of Mimi's keyboard, the clink of dog tags as Tina Marie scratched, sighed mightily, and turned over in her basket. Whatever was going on in the classroom was silent—yoga? Tantric meditation?—until there was a guf-faw from someone, a sharp though indecipherable order, and then a low and steady noise that started up as the class shifted gears.

Across the room, one wall was covered with a corkboard, to which dozens of headshots had been pinned, most sporting Post-its announcing the client's latest bookings: Pizza Hut, *Zoey 101*, McDonald's, *The Closer*, *House*, *CSI: Miami*, a Red Cross industrial film. Bethany's headshot was stickerless. Ruth ached for her. Which brought her back to a troubling truth: Bethy wasn't auditioning as often as the other girls. She'd been sent on only four auditions since they'd arrived, and two of them had been for student films, which, though they offered good experience and introduced you to a student director who might conceivably be the next Steven Spielberg, didn't pay anything and were therefore less prestigious both in the studio and on the child's résumé.

With her heart hammering in her chest, Ruth had approached Mimi about this last week, and the conversation hadn't been at all reassuring. Mimi had sighed, taken off her glasses, and rubbed her eyes for several minutes—she made it clear that she was often exhausted from her ceaseless work on her clients' behalf—and said, "Look."

Ruth hated when people said *Look*, both because whatever was coming next was inevitably something you didn't want to hear, and because it implied that you were mentally incapable of grasping even the obvious on your own.

"First of all, there are three boys' parts in Hollywood for every one part for girls. It's always been that way and it always will be and no one knows exactly why, so stop comparing. Second, Bethany's never going to be going out as much as the other girls."

Ruth had been stunned. "Why?"

Mimi had sighed heavily and said, enunciating each word,

"Bethany's a niche actor. Her agent says so. I'm saying so. A showcase panel has said so. She's going to be the sidekick, the kooky friend, the kid that's slightly, hmmm, *off*. That's what she's going to be auditioning for, because that's what she looks like."

Mimi had gone on to make it very clear that this was final, and that if Ruth continued to harry her, she would drop Bethany as a client. Just as Ruth reached the doorway Mimi had said over her shoulder, as an afterthought, "I assume you understand that if she loses me as her manager, she'll lose her agent, too."

Ruth had given an involuntary gasp. Bethany's agent was the linchpin of their hopes. Without a good agent, Mimi had made clear, your child might just as well be in Sheboygan. The conversation had been very distressing, but what could they do? They didn't know anyone else. For now, right or wrong, they needed to stick with Mimi.

From the classroom, Ruth heard one of the students shrieking, *"You're just like my mother!"* Privately Ruth thought an inordinate amount of class time was devoted to scenes that were violent or ugly or inflammatory in some way. When she'd mentioned this to one of the other mothers, the woman had just shrugged, so it was possible that Ruth was overreacting. The class was taught by Donovan Meyer, a once-successful character actor whose career had reached its zenith in 1983 with a two-year stint as a recurring character on *Guiding Light*. He was spectrally tall and thin (the camera adds ten pounds, a factoid that everyone at the studio murmured like a mantra), with chiseled features and penetrating blue eyes that Ruth suspected were enhanced by tinted contact lenses she'd been able to make out very clearly the one time she'd seen him in daylight. The confident studio mothers, as well as all the kids, called him Dee. Ruth called him Donovan.

The classroom door opened and a tall, slender reed of a girl came out. This was Allison Addison, one of the children who lived with Mimi and who were known collectively around the studio as the Orphans, though they all had families someplace far, far away: Akron, Pittsburgh, and so on. Allison's family, as Ruth recalled, lived in Houston, but if she missed them or minded, Ruth had never seen or heard any sign of it. Allison had an astonishing, even an alarming, beauty, and though she was technically only a year older than Bethy—fourteen and a month to Bethy's thirteen and three weeks—she was light-years older in every other way; older, possibly, than Ruth herself. Ruth, frankly, was wary of the girl. Bethy had said on more than one occasion that she wasn't always nice.

Now she came right over and flung herself onto the sofa only a foot or so from Ruth, huffing and crossing her arms over her chest.

"What?" Ruth said.

Allison shrugged. "I don't know. I'm just not into it tonight. I told Dee I needed a time out."

"Oh."

Allison glanced over and then picked up the handle of Ruth's purse, which lay between them on the ratty sofa cushion. "This is nice leather," she said, rubbing it between her thumb and finger. "I'm guessing kid."

The purse was, in fact, Ruth's only quality accessory, bought at Nordstrom Rack for 50 percent off. She hardly ever used it at home, for fear of scuffing it. She'd brought it to LA only as an afterthought, but she was glad, now. When it came to her purse, at least, she had nothing to be ashamed of.

"Michael Kors," the girl said. "Am I right?"

Ruth was impressed in spite of herself.

"Mine's Coach," the girl said, gesturing to her bag and school things neatly stacked just inside Mimi's office door. "My mom's husband bought it for me. I won't even let anyone *touch* it." She sighed, crossed one long leg over the other, and bobbed her foot up and down.

"Do you like this class?" Ruth asked.

Allison shrugged. "Dee's cool."

"Bethy says he's a little intense."

"Well, of *course* he's intense. I mean, that's why his kids are series regulars."

"We'd kill for that," Ruth acknowledged.

"Everyone would kill for that," Allison said in a *duh* tone of voice.

Ruth could feel her face getting warm. "Why do you like acting?" she asked. She was always surprised at how much easier it was to have an intimate conversation when you were sitting beside someone and not facing them. She and her mother had had their frankest talks driving between Seattle and Tacoma to visit Ruth's aunt Vera.

Allison thought for a minute. "I don't know." She frowned. "I really don't know."

"Is it work for you? Is it hard?"

"Oh, sometimes, if I'm playing like an unpopular girl or someone who doesn't really get it. I don't go out for those much, though. Mimi gets mad when Holly sends me out on character roles."

Holly—Holly Jensen—was Bethy's agent, too. And those, Allison's reject roles, were the ones Bethy was sent on.

The girl had gotten up and was rummaging around in her bag, pulling out a can of Red Bull. Ruth didn't approve of energy drinks, especially for children. "We don't let Bethany drink those," she said, watching Allison bring the drink back to the sofa.

"Really?" The girl looked at her cheerfully. "God, we live

on them." She thought for a minute. "Last summer there was this kid at the Oakwood who had a nervous breakdown sort of thing. He was only sleeping like two hours a night for weeks, and then he started hallucinating, so his parents took him to this psychiatric clinic or something where they treat mentally ill people, and it turned out he'd been drinking like five Snapples *a day*. I mean, do you have any idea how much caffeine is in those things? Quinn Reilly—he's another client—used to drink them, too, until Mimi made him stop because they sort of canceled out his Ritalin." She fell back into the sofa cushions and sipped her Red Bull reflectively. "Anyway, we didn't see the Oakwood kid after that. I think his parents made him go back to San Francisco or someplace. Which is pretty stupid, if you think about it, because it was *Snapple*. I mean, it's not like it's illegal."

"Well," said Ruth.

Chairs started scraping in the classroom. Allison hopped up. "Time for improv. I love improv."

And just as suddenly as she'd arrived she skipped off again, leaving Ruth feeling strangely enervated. Mimi's current clients' headshots and résumés were stacked in labeled cubbies across the room and Ruth had originally thought about using her time alone to look through them, but the thought was suddenly repugnant. She put her head back and closed her eyes and thought about how talking with Allison had been like talking to another grown-up.

Ruth was exhausted by the time the Believability class ended. She got Bethany home and to bed, but of course once they *got* to bed, they were too tired and keyed up to fall asleep. It was eleven forty-five before Ruth heard Bethy's breathing settle. Only then did she mouth in the general direction of the heavens the same prayer she'd been saying every night since they arrived: *Please God, shine on my Bethany and make her a star.*

Chapter Two

ON ANY GIVEN DAY, MIMI ROBERTS TALENT MANAGE-ment represented anywhere from thirty-five to fifty child, teen-age, and young adult actors, depending on Mimi's mood and willingness to be pinned down. Her clients' abilities ranged from execrable to extraordinary. The ones who were darling but couldn't act auditioned for commercials and print; the ones who could act but weren't cute went out for student films, info-mercials, character roles, and lesser dramatic parts; the ones who were cute *and* could act were sent out for everything: commer-cials, infomercials, industrials, public service announcements, student films, TV episodics (both dramatic and comedic), indie shorts, and feature-length movies.

At the epicenter of Mimi Roberts Talent Management was Mimi herself. Sixty-one, childless, and unmarried, she was as tough and canny as an old cat in the night. A skilled campaigner, she drew her clients, helpmates, and resources out of thin air, making it all up as she went along. Because she was chroni-cally cash-strapped (though there were some who believed she had hundreds of thousands of dollars salted away), she lived in a never-ending state of barter, shilling for her poorer clients by digging a little more deeply into the pockets of her wealthy ones, though of course she'd flatly deny that, if pressed.

Mimi doubted there was a soul left in Hollywood who'd remember now, but she'd come to LA as a young actor her-self way back when, full of the certainty that the world was waiting just for her. She'd come to LA from upstate New York on a Greyhound bus with nothing but eighty-five dollars and four changes of clothes. What they didn't understand—what no one outside Hollywood ever understood—was that she'd *had* to come, to meet what she was sure was her future. She was plain now, and she'd been plain then, too, though quite a few pounds thinner. She'd also been realistic; she knew she would never become a leading lady, especially not in those days, when leading ladies had tidy hair and elegant hats and Daughters of the American Revolution credentials and just the right balance of self-confidence and sass. Her plan had been to become a character actor, a sidekick like Vivian Vance, who'd made a career out of being Ethel Mertz.

But of course it hadn't worked out that way. At any given moment there wasn't really much difference between a drifter and an actor looking for work. She'd gotten a few small roles, uttered the occasional line, delivered the odd voice-over, but her voice tended to be unmodulated and her acting, while serviceable, didn't have a thing to separate her from thousands of others. She couldn't pinpoint the precise day and moment when she realized she was screwed, but once she did, her next move had presented itself like pure kismet.

She'd been living in a West Hollywood apartment building as shabby as an old shoe, sharing a dank apartment with an unwed young mother out of Kansas named Susan, who modeled lingerie and turned the occasional trick while she waited for her big acting break. Her daughter was a three-year-old named Lucy, who had a high, clear voice, silky blond curls, and a darling space between her two front teeth. Mimi often took care of her while Susan was working, in return for which Susan cooked. One day, Mimi brought Lucy along with her to an audition. The audition itself—what had it been for? A digestive aid of some kind, she thought—had gone badly, but there had been another audition in the same casting suite for children Lucy's age. On a whim Mimi signed Lucy in, gave the name of her own agent as Lucy's, and said they'd forgotten her headshot but wouldn't the casting assistant's Polaroid shot do for now? With young children, then as now, rules were more bendable, and that time had been no exception. Mimi accompanied Lucy into the audition room and saw exactly what she'd expected: on camera, the child had the presence of an angel.

"Honey, is she yours?" the casting director had asked her.

"I manage her," Mimi had lied, and why not? Managers needed no credentials, no certification. All you had to do was say you *were* a manager to *be* a manager. Lucy had booked the commercial on the spot.

"Well, you've got a keeper there, but you probably know that already," the casting director had said, and he was right.

Susan had been thrilled, and Mimi had kept fifteen percent of everything Lucy earned—the standard manager's commission—which had turned out to be substantial. It turned out that Mimi had a talent for picking a child with star potential out of any crowd. In her experience, it was a rare parent who turned her away when she approached him or her at a mall or farmers' market with her card extended—

MIMI ROBERTS, OWNER
MIMI ROBERTS TALENT MANAGEMENT
MANAGING THE CAREERS OF
SUCCESSFUL YOUNG HOLLYWOOD ACTORS

—and said, "I couldn't help noticing your son. Has he ever acted or been in a commercial before?" By the end of the conversation Mimi had an appointment to see the parent and child in her studio. The parent was generally goofy with pride and Mimi had a new client with the looks for commercials, at least, and with a little luck and training, some went on to theatrical roles as well. Her own acting ambitions blew away before the winds of solvency and now, when she read the second character in scripts for her showcasing clients, she made no attempt to act at all, but used as flat a voice as possible, so that even a minimally talented child would shine by comparison.

But the children got older, whereupon they tended to outgrow their looks or their talent, or Mimi and the parents had a falling out, or the parents got cocky and believed they could manage the child's career, sending Mimi a terse handwritten note or e-mail informing her that the child would be moving on. A few of the kids went on to hit the big time and most did not; but either way, there were a hundred more waiting for Mimi in the provinces, especially once she started her now-famous boot camps for young actors, housing ten or twelve kids for a ten-day intensive course in auditioning and acting for the camera. And since her specialty was bringing in actors from out of town, the boot camps had inevitably led to longer-term housing for kids whose parents wanted them to stay on, until at any given time she had three or four living under her roof. She used to house boys and girls, but six months ago there had been an incident with Quinn Reilly, her boy resident, so now she housed only girls, and except during boot camps, she had a hard-and-fast cutoff age of thirteen.

Except, of course, for Allison Addison. Allison was a once-in-a-lifetime find, a child who had the looks, the strength, the talent, and the drive to go all the way to the top. Mimi had discovered her three and a half years ago at a seminar she'd given in Houston as a favor when the talent manager who'd put the event together had come down with the flu. Allison had been sitting in the back of the room, small for her age and delicately, even crushingly, beautiful. Mimi had held her breath all that morning while she taught the kids about slating and believability and cold reads and camera angles, until it was time for each one to receive a script from an actual commercial and be put in front of a video camera. One awful child after another got up to read and Mimi pretended to pay attention, but all she was doing was waiting, teasing herself by keeping Allison for the very end.

And the girl had stood up and smiled and given her name and read through her script fluently, comfortably, utterly believably, like she'd been born to it. Only then did Mimi exhale, feverishly plotting how she could get this child broken loose to come to LA. The mother had turned out to be a back-combed, skinny-hipped, big-busted, leathery-tanned woman with the eyes of a drinker, whom Mimi felt sure had put the girl in the seminar just to keep her out of the way for the weekend. And she hadn't been far off the mark in her assessment. When Mimi had taken her aside the woman had drifted all over the place, her attention on the quality of her manicure, the size of her diamond, the smoothness of her recently waxed legs. Which had all been fine with Mimi. In the old days, women like this had given their kids up to the circus for a song. By the end of the weekend she had gotten the mother to agree to fly Allison out to LA the following week for a meeting with a couple of talent agents. Three weeks later, Allison was ensconced in Mimi's back bedroom, and for the most part she'd been there ever since.

It was possible—and Mimi hated to admit this, even in the privacy of her own head—that when it came to Allison, her judgment was cloudy. Mimi had never had a child of her own. Many years ago she'd thought about it, but she hadn't wanted to bring up a child alone, and there hadn't been a man in her life—or a woman, for that matter—in years and years. Her own mother had raised Mimi on her own, and although Mimi was grateful to her, of course, she'd always thought her mother would have been much better off without her. It was bad enough to be poor alone, but how much worse to drag a child along with you. That was a whole different shade of awful: the yearly struggle to put something under the Christmas tree and make it look like the gift came from you and not a charity; birthdays that were undercelebrated; pretty clothes and music lessons you couldn't afford, not to mention regular dental care and meals that were more protein than starch. Those were the colors of the poverty rainbow, at the end of which there was nothing but an empty pot because somebody had gotten to the gold long before you showed up.

ALLISON KNEW SHE WAS BEAUTIFUL; SHE'D LEARNED IT early from her mother, Denise, who was, like God's final rough draft, nearly beautiful but still flawed—her eyes were a little too close together; her cheekbones were flatter, even crushed-looking in a certain light. "You've got looks, baby," she'd told Allison when Allison was nine years old. "Work it, because it's your ticket out." That had been before her mother had met Chet-the-Oilman. After Chet, whom she'd met when Allison was not quite eleven, her mother had treated Allison like the competition. She'd been apologetic about it, too: "Honey, I know you can't understand this but I've got to keep him because he's my last chance." Allison did understand, at least in a way, because she could feel Chet's eyes on her all the time. Maybe her mother could feel it, too. In any event, her mother drank a lot more once he was in the picture, and she had this new laugh that sounded like it could turn any minute into a long, thin scream. *You've got looks, baby. Work it.* Allison guessed her mother was working it, too, only she was playing for higher stakes. *It's your ticket out.*

Allison hadn't been sure what her looks were her ticket *to* until she came to LA to live with Mimi. Now she knew. She was going to be a star, someone even parking lot attendants would recognize and get nervous around. She was going to be not just famous but *ultra*famous—she'd be the face of Revlon or Chanel or whoever it was that Nicole Kidman or Drew Barrymore worked for. She would wear pearls as big as marbles and pose in front of a fan that would blow her hair back in glamorous slow motion, and the whole world would admire her because she'd be exquisite and privileged and could rent a yacht in Cannes or the Caribbean any time she felt like it. She'd go to the best spas and fashion shows and premieres, and doormen would fall over themselves to help her and she'd laugh all the time because she wouldn't have a single worry in the world, *that's* how famous she'd be. *Vanity Fair* would want her on its cover, and Annie Leibovitz would take her picture.

Allison knew that Mimi knew she was going to be famous, because Mimi was the one who was going to make that happen. She told Allison all the time that Allison had what it took, and that that was rare. Allison knew Mimi was serious because when Allison's mom was late with the monthly check, which she was almost all the time, and Mimi had to threaten to send Allison home, she made a point of telling Allison she wouldn't really do it, it was just her way of shaking loose what she had coming to her—though Allison knew there was no reason for her mom being late with a check, now that she'd landed Chet. Mimi celebrated Allison's birthdays with cake and a party, which Allison's mother had hardly ever done because she could never get organized, and she took Allison shopping if she needed something for an audition and let her try on things even if they weren't on the sale rack. She got her to the dentist every six months like clockwork, because when Allison first got to LA she'd had fifteen cavities and hadn't seen a dentist since she was eight. Allison and Mimi fought all the time about homework and chores and having to share her room with other kids, but when it came down to it, Allison was pretty sure that Mimi loved her, and she was pretty sure she loved her back.

AT NINE FORTY-FIVE ON MONDAY MORNING, MIMI PULLED out of her driveway in her Honda Civic. The car was the latest in a line of junkers Mimi traded as freely as baseball cards. A lifelong asthmatic, she turned up the car's feeble air-conditioning and pulled an inhaler out of her bag. There was a smog inversion—again—throughout the San Fernando Valley. Mimi puffed the inhaler into her lungs, breathed deeply, and felt no relief whatsoever. She looked at the prescription on the side of the canister. Its use-by date was eight months ago. She threw it on the passenger seat, where it hit a small can of Cheez Whiz, rolled onto the floor, and disappeared under the seat.

In the studio parking lot Mimi pulled into her usual spot by the Dumpster and extricated herself with some difficulty from behind the wheel. She was fat and she was tired. She'd been carving a living out of the granite face of Hollywood for nearly forty years, and they'd taken their toll. A long time ago she'd been mentored by a talent manager who'd told Mimi if she wanted to succeed, she needed to develop, above all else, the sensibilities of a killer. "You're at war, honey, and don't ever forget it. A talent manager is in a constant battle between goods and services, where you're the services and your client's the goods, and neither one can stand without the other, which is why they are going to hate you so much and you're going to hate them. Regrettable but true. And if you're smart, you won't get attached to anyone and you won't let them get attached to you. Otherwise when they go down in flames—and believe me, they will go down in flames—it's only a question of when and whether they'll take you with them."

From down the block Mimi's two other current boarders, Hillary Constable and Reba Melvin, waved to her before disappearing into the 7-Eleven. She could probably buy herself a new car for the amount of money those two spent on snacks. Hillary was from Columbus, Ohio, and Reba was from San Francisco; both were twelve and a half, and they didn't have enough talent between them to fill a thimble. Hillary was wearing one of Allison's hand-me-down outfits that was about a year away from fitting properly and five years away from being appropriate, and Reba was wearing a sundress that she shouldn't—the smocked elastic top had migrated up her Tweedledee belly, leaving the hem about four inches shorter in front than in back. God knew when she'd last washed her hair. Mimi sighed. She really should insist that the girls go back to their homes, but the mothers were adamant that their daughters would be stars, and anyway Mimi would miss the combined six thousand dollars a month.

She pushed through the studio door, which was covered with little handprints and had a tendency to stick, and trudged past the vacant reception desk that one of her young-adult students should have been manning. Waiting for her in the greenroom were Laurel Buehl, one of her newest clients, and her mother, Angie. As usual, both were immaculately dressed and made up. They came from outside Atlanta and favored floral print purses and intricately coordinated outfits. Mimi had found them at an International Modeling and Talent Association meeting in LA nine months ago. At sixteen, Laurel was one of her oldest girls. Normally Mimi didn't take on child clients older than fourteen because finding them work was so hard, especially when they lacked screen and TV credits. The midteen years, in Mimi's vast experience, were the Hollywood landscape's valley of the shadow of death. They were too old to play preteen and too young to play late teen, and no one wrote parts for midteens anyway, so the best they could do was hunker down, do their schoolwork, keep up with as many acting classes as they could afford, and wait it out. She'd explained all this to the Buehls, but they'd been unusually focused and utterly determined to come to Hollywood, with or without Mimi's help, so what was there for Mimi to do but hop onboard?

And the girl did have some talent, which, coupled with her obvious drive and focus, might be enough to carry her. She also had flawless skin, so fair it was almost translucent. After Mimi had mentioned almost offhandedly to Angie that Laurel's hair, though platinum, was relatively limp, the two of them had compensated with hundreds of dollars' worth of extensions at a Rodeo Drive salon. The girl's eyes were a striking, true cornflower blue and her figure was trim, though big-boned. She'd have to work very hard to keep her weight down when she entered her thirties, but for now she simply looked athletic and healthy—so much so that whenever Mimi saw the mother, she was struck anew by how *off* she looked in comparison. Even through her immaculate makeup Mimi could see dark, almost bruised-looking circles under her eyes, and though she was slender, it was in a bony, slack way, as though she'd lost a lot of weight recently and her skin hadn't sprung back. Mimi had never seen Angie eat, not even at the studio potlucks one or another of the parents convened from time to time—though the Buehls didn't attend studio social functions very often. Angie did carry energy drinks with her everywhere, which Mimi supposed could account for her pallor and the waxy quality of her skin.

"We were hoping you'd have a minute," said Angie now, jumping up from the greenroom sofa when she saw Mimi.

"I haven't worked out the order of the showcase yet, but I still want her to do the *Marbles* monologue," Mimi said, because everyone always wanted to know the order of the scenes to be performed in her showcases, despite the fact that Mimi said over and *over* that she didn't make up the schedule until that morning, when she had a final tally of who was participating and what scenes they would present. *Clear Glass Marbles*, the monologue she'd chosen for Laurel, was about a young woman recalling her mother's very recent death from cancer. When it was performed well it gave the actor a chance to cry, which could bring down the house. Mimi had seen parents and even an agent or two weep by the end, and there was almost always a snuffle or two in the house even if actual tears weren't produced.

"That's what we wanted to talk to you about," Angie said. "We don't want her to do that one."

"Why?"

Angie and Laurel exchanged quick glances. "We just think another monologue might be better," Angie said.

"Can she cry on cue?"

"Yes."

"Then that's the one I want her to do. It's the toughest piece I have, and if she can pull it off, Evelyn Flynn, the casting director who's coming, will remember her. I've been trying to get that woman to come to one of my showcases for years, so don't blow it."

The two sighed as one, but acquiesced. "All right," Angie said. Probably thinking Mimi couldn't see, she took Laurel's wrist in her hand and pressed. Laurel nodded: *All right*.

"And I want to see her do it before the showcase." To Laurel, Mimi said, "Are you off-book?"

"Yes," Laurel said faintly.

"Well, I want you to work on it with Dee before class. I mean that."

Angie and Laurel both nodded and turned to go.

"EYES ON THE PRIZE, DARLING," SAID ANGIE UNDER HER BREATH.

Laurel nodded. "I know, but—"

Angie just shook her head and said firmly, "Eyes on the prize."

"TINA MARIE!"

As Mimi came into her office she caught the little dog squatting in the corner. Bullet-proof Tina Marie simply looked at Mimi over her narrow shoulders and shrugged, as though to say, *So? I'm undisciplined. It's my nature. What can you do?* Knowing a lost cause when she saw one, Mimi just sighed, pulled a gallon jug of Nature's Miracle from the top drawer of her file cabinet, and dumped some on the spot, where it mingled with urine of yore. It was true that the dog, like the rest of Mimi's operation, was undisciplined. Go to the house at two o'clock in the morning on any given day and you might find Mimi popping Orville Redenbacher's in the kitchen, or Allison cleaning out a closet. And what was wrong with that? Mimi had gone to San Francisco during the Summer of Love, had seen Janis Joplin in concert. She was an old rebel, messy as much by philosophy as by her nature. Allison was the tidy one, an island of order amid the chaos. She did her own laundry and often Mimi's laundry, too; kept her cosmetics in a musical jewelry box with a dancing ballerina that her mother had bought for her, evidently, when Allison was young, and in which she also kept a surprisingly extensive inventory of earrings, inexpensive bracelets, pendants, and charms.

Allison imposed some of that order on Mimi, as well. Mimi remembered to color her thinning hair only because Allison reminded her. Sometimes she'd tease the girl by telling her she'd decided to just say to hell with it and let it grow out, as lusterless and gray as a cardboard egg carton. As it was, whenever she let it go too long Allison would take it upon herself to buy Mimi's L'Oréal hair color and dye Mimi's hair in the kitchen sink. Mimi loved the feel of the girl's long fingers working around her scalp, making sure the chemicals were evenly distributed so they'd take the way they were supposed to. They'd had a disaster or two before Allison coaxed Mimi into buying a timer. When Mimi argued that they could just as easily use the timer on the stove, Allison said it had been broken for as long as Allison had lived there—didn't Mimi know? But, of course, Mimi didn't know, because she didn't cook very often and when she did, as a point of pride, she followed no recipe or instructions, which made their rare at-home dinners unpredictable and, as often as not, featuring a dessert course of takeout Chinese.

In the three and a half years that Allison had been living with her, Mimi had seen the girl grow a foot and test her wings on some of the younger girls to see what power she could exert over them, getting them to tell her each other's secrets. On the whole, Mimi was not averse to this. Good girls—and she'd seen this time after time—rarely had staying power. Bethany Rabinowitz was one of those, a mama's girl, a pleaser. Allison, on the other hand, had a talent for forming strategic friendships and playing her looks like a high poker hand—which was not to say that all the girl's qualities were good, merely that they were useful. Mimi wasn't blind to the flip side. She knew, for example, that Allison was a notorious classroom cheat. She'd been outed by any number of tutors and proctors whom Mimi had hired to monitor her boarders' homeschool work. Allison looked up answers in the backs of her textbooks and brazenly copied the other girls' homework assignments, and when she was caught—and she never made much effort to disguise what she was doing—she and Mimi had terrible arguments, brawls, really. Mimi knew better than anyone that Allison might need to find an alternate career one day; and if so, she'd need at least a basic education. Allison did not agree. "I don't care about algebra!" she'd scream. "I don't give a shit where in Europe you can find Mongolia! That's what librarians are for, to answer stupid questions like that. You just call the Los Angeles Public Library and you ask for the reference desk and you say where is Mongolia and they tell you Spain or whatever!"

But the fact was, Mimi was tired. Now, when it was all but too late, what she dreamed of—the only thing she still dreamed of—was a client who loved her. In Allison Addison—beautiful, beautiful child—she knew she'd found what she was looking for: the one who would have her. Mimi wasn't a fool; she'd seen the furtive cuts running up Allison's arms like needle marks. But in her line of work you accepted as normal a certain degree of damage, and cutting wouldn't kill the girl. Chances were, she'd outgrow it. In the meantime they fought about school, and their arguments generally ended with one of them storming out of the house or the studio. The farthest Mimi had ever gone was San Francisco; Allison, who had more limited resources, had gotten as far as Tarzana. But their reciprocal abandonment was pure show. By now she and Allison were bound together as tightly as if there'd been chains.

Chapter Three

AS RUTH UNDERSTOOD IT, THERE EXISTED A DICHOTOMY of opinions about the relative merits of working as a television or movie extra if you were an unemployed actor. There were the *Once an extra, always an extra* ideologues on the one hand, and the *Anything to become a SAG member* pragmatists on the other. Mimi belonged to the latter camp, explaining to Ruth that sending Bethany to work as an extra on a Screen Actors Guild feature film was the first in a two-step strategy by which Bethany would become eligible for SAG membership as soon as possible. A SAG membership, as she described it, would open up worlds.

So three days after the disastrous *Raven* callback, Ruth was back on Barham Boulevard, fighting the morning rush-hour traffic on the way to Hollywood's old Rialto Theatre. Bethany sat beside her and packed into the backseat of the car were the Orphans. The four girls would be working as extras on a union feature film called *High Fivin' the House*. Ruth strongly suspected that Mimi had signed the Orphans up not so much to keep Bethany company or for the work experience, but to keep the girls busy and out of her hair for the day.

The Rialto was being used as a location for the tween/teen Disney film about a close-knit, interracial, interethnic, socio-economically diverse group of kids in an experimental high school who form an alternative cheering squad. It starred Zac Efron and Ashley Tisdale—of course—and Mimi had said if they were lucky the extras might catch a glimpse of them on set. Now, from the front seat, Bethany was telling the girls in the back, "My mom brought her camera, so if we see anyone we can get our pictures taken. Rianne, my BFF back home, would just *die*. She thinks Zac Efron is so cute."

"You're not going to get within eighty feet of them, you know," said Allison. "Mimi just told you that so you'd sign up. One time she made us work on a movie with Ashley Tisdale in it for a *week* and we never saw her once, just her stand-in."

"Wow," said Bethany.

"Her what?" said Ruth.

"Her stand-in—her double. Boy, you guys really *are* new. Big stars aren't going to just stand there for half the day while the tech guys work on lighting and camera angles and stuff, so they hire someone who's about the same age and size to stand there for them. I knew a girl who was Keke Palmer's stand-in for *Akeelah and the Bee*, and she said it was the worst job *ever*. She had rickets or shingles or something by the time the movie wrapped."

"You could probably be Ellen Page's stand-in. You're as good an actor as her," said Hillary loyally. She was Allison's self-appointed sidekick, an elfin, precocious child who made it known that she'd gladly put her entire future in jeopardy for just one Victoria's Secret push-up bra and something to put in it. "We saw *Juno*, and she was awesome," she explained to Ruth.

Allison elbowed her in the ribs. "Ellen Page is like four foot ten and she has really bad hair. She should get extensions. I'm serious."

"Well, you have nice hair," Hillary reassured her.

"Well, yeah, compared to Ellen Page." Allison sank back in her seat, crossed her arms, and looked out the window. Ruth suddenly recalled a comment Angie Buehl had made about Allison: "She'll either be famous or pregnant by the time she's seventeen."

"I hated that set," Reba was saying from the backseat. The third Orphan was the most unfortunate of them; she was sallow, sullen, overweight, and numbingly untalented. "It was *so boring.* You couldn't go to craft services unless they told you to, plus even once you could, the food sucked. The union extras got like a Hawaiian luau and *we* got a couple of hot dogs and some Jell-O."

"Yeah," echoed Bethy in a chorus of aggrievement.

"Craft services?" said Ruth.

"The *food* caterers," said Allison. "Man, you guys."

"Then why aren't they just called caterers?" Ruth asked.

Allison shrugged. "Anyways, we told Mimi we didn't want to do this stupid movie but she's making us, anyway."

And so there they were, sitting in Ruth's car and benefiting from Ruth's services free of charge. Ruth still couldn't figure out how, exactly, Mimi had talked her into driving these girls and chaperoning them once they were on-site—but then, it was widely acknowledged that Mimi had a special genius for pawning the Orphans onto new, hapless studio moms. "Bethany's audition is at two o'clock," Mimi would warble, "and please take Hillary with you, too, because I know you'll have room in your car and she's going in for the same part." You could always tell who'd been conned because of the trapped, glassy-eyed look the women developed at finding themselves saddled with girls as unruly as magpies.

They were making no progress in the stalled traffic. Ruth was sweating lightly. Out of habit she glanced in the rearview mirror and was appalled to see fat Reba drinking a Slurpee and eating a Hostess Ho Ho. It was eight fifteen in the morning.

"Honey," she said, "why don't you save that until lunch? You could have it for dessert."

"That's okay," Reba said, chewing complacently. "I can eat it now. They always feed us on set."

"I know, but what I meant—"

"Don't worry about it," Allison said. "She has them every morning. That, or those cupcakes with the white squiggle."

"They're really not good for you," Ruth said. Reba shrugged. The other girls just looked out the windows, bored.

"What do you eat for lunch?" Ruth pressed.

"Funyuns," Allison answered for her. "She lives on Funyuns."

"I do not," Reba protested.

"Yeah, you do."

"I eat other stuff, too."

"Oh, right, I forgot. Nachos," Allison said. "And pizza. She eats a *lot* of pizza. Papa John's is right down the street from the studio."

"We all eat pizza," Hillary pointed out. Ruth could corroborate that. Every time she'd been in the studio there were pizza boxes scattered around like C-rations.

"Plus she never has fruit or vegetables," said Allison.

"Oh, and like you do?" said Reba, wiping her mouth on her Mimi Roberts Talent Management tote bag.

"I have an apple or a fruit beverage every day," Allison said primly. "Especially when I can get someone to drive me to Jamba Juice."

Ruth's blood was pounding in her ears. "Do you girls have *any idea* how many calories are in some of those drinks? Not to mention how expensive they are."

Allison shrugged. "It's no big deal. I get two hundred and twenty-five dollars a week from Chet. Plus I weigh like eighty pounds and I'm already five foot six."

"Well, not everyone is as lucky as you," Ruth said, and then subsided. "Anyway, Mimi must cook for you at night."

Allison just shrugged and looked out the window, clearly bored.

"Mom," Bethany said. "*Nobody* cooks in LA."

RUTH BELIEVED THAT HER STRENGTHS AS A PERSON AND as a woman did not necessarily include parenting. Unable to conceive almost nine years into their marriage, she and Hugh had made their peace with being childless. As middle age approached, Ruth assumed that she and Hugh would gradually, *gently*, fill the void by developing an unhealthy attachment to some neighborhood child or pet. Then one morning she'd woken up and vomited. When it happened twice more, she'd picked up a home pregnancy test and stared at the pink strip as though it were stamped with hieroglyphics. She'd made herself read the box several times just to make sure she wasn't taking a no as a yes, because sometimes she got flustered, but there it was: she was pregnant.

Her first trimester had passed in a state of sleepy astonishment, which was gradually replaced in the second and third trimesters by an unsubstantiated but nagging certainty that she would give birth to a child with terrible birth defects. In the delivery room her first question, once Bethany had been born, was "Is she normal?" She thought the delivery nurse had given her a disapproving look, though it might have been her imagination—yes, she'd opted for narcotics during labor, even though it wasn't the best thing for the baby; *that* was the kind of mother she was. When the news came that Bethy was perfect, Ruth believed with all her heart that she'd gotten away with it only because God had been momentarily distracted.

Sometimes even now, when she looked at Bethany, her ears

began to ring, actually *ring*, with amazement that this exuberant, smart, talented child was hers. She stood in awe: Bethany was a doer, not a watcher like Ruth. To *do* meant to risk acts of poor judgment, faulty thinking, weak-mindedness, and lack of conviction, all qualities in which Ruth believed she herself abounded. Not so Bethany; which was why, when Mimi Roberts had come to Seattle to give her Acting for the Camera weekend seminar and it had coincided exactly with Bethy's decision that she wouldn't pursue musical theater after all—and what stage productions *weren't* musical, these days?—Ruth had signed her up immediately. The child had no neuroses, abundant dreams, and significant talent. What could Ruth do but trot along a half-step ahead of her, scattering rose petals in her path?

And so here they were, tracking a series of yellow plastic signs with *High Fivin'* printed both right side up and upside down, with an arrow telling them where and in which direction to turn. Ruth and Bethany had been seeing signs like these nailed to power poles all over LA: *CSI: Miami*, *Ghost Whisperer*, *Numb3rs*, *The Closer*. Ruth had assumed that the signs, with their upside-down names, were someone's colossal mistake but that the shows used them anyway rather than waste them. It was Bethany who'd figured them out: with the name of the show printed both right side up and upside down, the sign could be used to point either left or right, as needed. It wasn't the first time Ruth had thought Bethy *got* this place in a way that Ruth clearly didn't. Every time they turned a corner and found a street barricaded by a chaos of white semi trucks and light arrays, *every single time*, Ruth assumed they'd stumbled onto a catastrophe—a car accident, a fatal stabbing, a drug bust. And every time, Bethy said, "Mom, they're filming something! It's so cool. Those trailers are dressing rooms, some of them. There's probably someone famous in there right now."

Ruth turned into a parking lot that was already nearly full and set the parking brake—she was a cautious driver, even when they were on a flat surface—and turned around in her seat. The three girls looked back.

"Do you all have your work permits?" Ruth asked. Entertainment industry permits were required for all children under sixteen, with no exceptions. Producers took this very seriously; their sets could be shut down if a child was allowed in without a current Department of Labor–issued original. No permit, no work, no exceptions. Ruth had heard that Mimi routinely made color photocopies of all the Orphans' work permits—the official stamp was done in red ink and photocopied beautifully—and sent the girls with those whenever they lost their originals.

Now nods: yes, they had their permits.

"Schoolwork?"

Two nods, and a shifty little smile from Allison. Like all Mimi's clients, the Orphans were homeschooled. As Mimi had explained it to Hugh, you couldn't be available for auditions, coaching, work (God willing), and acting classes any other way; you just couldn't. But the good news was, so many kids were in the same boat that the Burbank school system had what Ruth thought of as their "school in a bag" program. You were assigned a coordinator, received your curriculum, and were issued all the necessary textbooks, worksheets, lab materials, and handouts that normal kids got in "real" school. You worked on the material on your own schedule and met with your coordinator every three weeks, when your progress and work were reviewed. There were no teachers, no classrooms, and no group activities.

"Don't you need to show the set teacher you have something to do?" Ruth asked Allison now.

"Nah. I usually just tell them I have to write an essay on my family tree or the Civil War or Chrysler or something. They leave you alone as long as you sound like you mean it."

"But you have to spend three hours in the classroom," Ruth said. "What are you going to do that whole time?"

Allison dipped into her Coach tote and produced a leather-bound manicure set. "Your nails?" Ruth said. "You're going to do your nails for *three hours*?"

The girl looked at Ruth like she was an idiot. "Well, I'm not going to fake-write an essay that whole time."

"But that can't possibly work," Ruth said.

"No, it does," Hillary piped up. "She just tells them she's studying cosmetology."

"And they actually buy that?"

"Usually," Allison said. "Think about it. Mimi said there were going to be about seventy-five kids on set today. They have to put us in school for three hours and give us a set teacher because that's the law, but they don't have to actually *do* anything with us except make sure we stay quiet and stuff and sign us in and out. I mean, it's not like they teach you or anything. They're more like lunch ladies."

"Mom, we need to go," Bethany broke in urgently. "They told us to be there by nine, and it's nine ten already."

Ruth looked down the street at a crowd of kids milling around outside what must be the theater.

"All right. You do all have your work permits, right, and your Coogan account information?"

"*Yes!*" the girls huffed at her in a chorus. Every child was required to have a special bank account—named after Jackie Coogan, whose childhood earnings had been squandered by his parents or manager, Ruth could never remember which—into which fifteen percent of the child's gross earnings were deposited directly and couldn't be touched by anyone except the child himself upon turning eighteen. Like work permits, the lack of Coogan account information meant you couldn't work, though some kind production assistants—PAs—had been known to allow you a day to produce it.

"All right, go," Ruth said, releasing them. "I'll catch up."

Bethany looked at her doubtfully. "You, too," Ruth said, giving her permission to be part of that most delectable thing, a girl group. Bethany raised her eyebrows: *Are you sure? I can stay with you.* "Go," said Ruth. "*Go!*"

THE RIALTO WAS AN UNPROMISING OLD PILE, WITH NONE of the showstopping, gilded art deco splendor of the nearby Pantages. It reminded Ruth more of a cross between an old movie theater and a civic auditorium. Once they were checked in and had run the gauntlet of Bagel Alley, a cheap buffet that craft services had set up to cater to the doughnut-eating, carb-addicted, caffeine-dependent extras, the parents and chaperones were directed to one location, the actors to another. Ruth could see that Bethany was vibrating, actually *vibrating*, with excitement. Her first movie set! Her first step toward becoming a professional actor! Even Ruth fell under the spell as they moved inside, intimidated by the sheer mass of cables, light arrays, cameras, mikes, flats, PAs, makeup artists, wardrobe fitters, and grown-up extras dressed as teachers, parents, and school administrators.

The actual parents and other set-sitters were relegated to their own area and a production assistant barked through a portable sound system that they had to stay put; those found wandering would be invited to leave the set permanently, along with their wards and children. Thus chastened, the grownups—easily twelve women to every man—busied themselves establishing camps in the gulag of the mezzanine, which Ruth felt could have been worse because at least you could see all the action from up there, even if you couldn't hear much. Like a flurry of birds, children kept appearing, alighting, and flying away with retrieved notebooks, pens, iPods, water bottles, and light snacks. They had been divided into three groups and assigned to makeshift classrooms in the costume shop and two rehearsal rooms. To Ruth's relief, Bethany had been separated from the Orphans. Reba and Hillary had been assigned to one room, Allison to another, and Bethy to the third.

Once the girls had made what Ruth hoped was their final exit, she pulled out the copy of *Seabiscuit* she'd been meaning to read for forever, but she was too nervous to settle down; she read the first page nine times and gave up. All around her were little islands of adults surrounded by laptop computers, picnic coolers, DVD players, knitting, crocheting, even a pillow and blanket or two for the toddlers and preschoolers who'd been dragged along. (Now *that* would be a nightmare, Ruth thought; how did you keep a tiny child busy, happy, *and* quiet while sitting in theater seats all day?) The women and handful of men weren't nearly as well-heeled as the mothers at Bethy's *That's So Raven* callback. There were a lot of elastic-waisted pants here, and plus-size shirts from Target.

"Well, *that's* a load of crap," Ruth heard a raspy voice announce from several rows down. Ruth thought it sounded familiar, and by moving just one seat over she confirmed that it was Vee Velman from Bethy's callback the other day. Her hair, which was refreshingly shot with gray, was pulled back and piled up and pinned indifferently, and Ruth thought she looked wonderfully tough and capable. "Do you need me to come down there?" she was saying into her cell phone. "No? Look, just tell her it's your epilepsy medication—don't say medicine, say *medication*—and that you'll have a grand-mal seizure any minute if you don't take it. Honey, I don't—" A pause, a loud sigh, and then, "Hi. Yup, this is Clara's mom. Look, my daughter has epilepsy, though she was probably too ashamed to tell you, *severe* epilepsy, and if she doesn't take those meds *right on schedule*, which means five minutes ago, she's going to start seizing. I know she should have a note. She *did* have a note when we left home, but God only—" A beat. "Have you ever *seen* a grand-mal seizure? Because I can tell you, it's not pretty. A lot of times it involves vomit, and sometimes feces, and then there's the tongue-swallow— All right. *Thank* you." She snicked her cell phone shut.

Ruth made her way down and touched Vee on the shoulder in what she hoped was a supportive way. "Ruth Rabinowitz. We met at the—"

Vee turned around. "Hey—sure, how are you?"

"Fine! Well, a little overwhelmed." She gestured at the chaos around them, then asked as delicately as she could, "Is everything all right?"

"What? Oh, that was Clara. She's got hay fever, and the Nazi set teacher wouldn't let her take a Sudafed. It's ridiculous, because you know they're not going to want her on set if she's sneezing every two minutes, which is pretty much the way it's been going this morning."

Ruth was nonplussed. "She's not epileptic?"

Vee looked amused. "You heard that?"

"I didn't mean to, but —"

"Pretty good, huh?"

"So she's not?"

"Nah."

"Are the teachers always obstinate like that?"

"Not all of them. Sit!" Vee said, patting the seat beside her. Ruth sat, taking in Vee's minimal camp: a laptop, two paperback books with broken spines, and a water bottle filled with what looked like beer.

"Actually it depends," Vee was saying. "Sometimes they're fascists and sometimes they're okay, and you never know which one it's going to be until you get there. They're supposed to be the kids' on-set advocates, making sure they get enough breaks and have water and stuff. Technically, they're social workers. Some of them are totally worthless, though. Those who can't do teach, and those who can't teach teach on sets. And on big sets like this, with tons of kids, you're lucky if they just keep the room quiet. One time, Clara said there was a kid who spent the whole three hours rolling doobies inside a lunch box."

"You're kidding."

"You'll see. How's your girl, did she book *Raven*?"

Ruth sighed. "No. Frankly, it was a disaster. The woman didn't even recognize her, and then she yelled at her for bringing glasses that she'd specifically *told* her to bring the day before."

"Well, like I said, Evelyn Flynn's a piece of work."

"Poor Bethy was so upset."

Vee looked at her shrewdly. "I bet you took it harder than she did."

"Probably," Ruth admitted. By her estimation, she'd gotten four and a half hours' sleep that night.

"Yeah, well, the parents usually do."

"Really? You go through that?"

Vee shrugged. "Not so much anymore, but when the kids were little it was hard. Now they kind of don't give a shit. If they book something, fine; if they don't book something, fine."

"So is Clara one of the extras, too?"

"God, no," Vee said. "She's Girl Number Three. She has seven lines, not one of which has more than four words in it."

"Still," said Ruth. "That's wonderful."

Vee smiled at her fondly. "You're *so* new."

"Does it really show that much?"

"Honey, like neon paint on a stripper. Not that that's always a bad thing. A lot of casting directors like the kids right out of Kansas or wherever."

"Seattle," said Ruth.

"Like I said. Sometimes those are the kids who give the freshest reads. They have that clean, unspoiled, *real* quality directors love."

"Speaking of strippers," and here Ruth lowered her voice, "is it true that the porn industry is headquartered here? Because I think we've seen some places where they film. On Magnolia in North Hollywood there are these big buildings that don't have windows or signs, and all the parking's around back. I mean, we've seen some *people*, too. Well, women."

"You bet," Vee said cheerfully. "Porn's big business, baby. If you ever want a real hoot, watch the Adult Movie Awards on TV. It'll blow your mind."

"I don't think I'm that strong," said Ruth.

"Just wait. Once you've been here a few years you'll not only watch, you'll see that some of your neighbors are nominees. We had a porn queen once who used to walk her dogs all the time—pugs, Peachy and Butch, neither of them could breathe worth a damn, dumber than clams—and whenever she walked, men up and down the whole damned street suddenly remembered they had to go out and check the mail. My husband, Herb, kept a pair of binoculars in the front window. Her name was Honey von Buns or something. I am not making this up. Buster used to call her the Implant Lady, and that was when he was only ten. We used to marvel that she didn't just topple over from the weight. When she put her house on the market, every single person within a quarter-mile radius went to the open house. You would not *believe* what you can do with a little feng shui and faux painting. I'm not kidding, the whole place was like a Roman grotto where someone had killed a couple of tigers. There were olive branches, stone columns, togas in the coat closet, tiger-striped towels, drapes, toilet seats, the whole deal. You could smell the strawberry massage oil from the front lawn." Vee sighed, a faraway look in her eye. "Now an entertainment lawyer lives there, and he's *such* a bastard. If we'd known, we'd have tried harder to get her to stay. She probably lives in the West Hills now, in some house that Spartacus built. You think I'm kidding?"

Ruth was laughing so hard her eyes were tearing. Vee subsided, taking a swig from her water bottle.

"I've got to ask," Ruth said.

"I know—you think it's beer. Everybody does. It's this special apple juice Clara makes me buy at Trader Joe's. Organic, which I keep trying to tell her just means there's probably a couple of ground-up worms in it. She loves Trader Joe's. I figured out once that we pay their monthly electrical bill."

"We were so glad when we found one near our apartment," Ruth said. "We love that place."

"You and everybody else."

Downstairs, kids were suddenly filing in from three different doorways and being directed to seats in the center section of the orchestra until every single one was taken.

"Oh!" Ruth said, leaning forward in excitement.

"They're packing them in, so they must be shooting tight," Vee said. "No cardboard cutouts for this guy."

"What do you mean?"

"You don't know about that? You know how in a sports movie the superdome or wherever looks completely filled? They use cardboard cutouts of people up in the high seats."

"You're kidding."

"Think about it. They're not going to pay ten thousand extras. Cardboard's a lot cheaper, and from a distance you can't tell the difference. *You* never noticed it, right?"

"So there's a company somewhere that makes a million cardboard cutouts of people?" Ruth said incredulously.

"Yup."

Ruth shook her head. In another minute she saw Bethany come in, look up for her, and wave. Ruth waved back. A production assistant was giving each row of kids a number. Ruth was thrilled to see that Bethy's row was number four. Based on where the cameras were placed, she might get a close-up. By Ruth's calculation, the kids in row twenty didn't stand a chance.

Once everyone was seated, a young man in a ratty sweatshirt, high-tops, and a baseball cap turned around backward hopped up on the stage. "He can't possibly be the director," Ruth said. "He's twelve years old."

"That's him, all right. Dick Fiori. He's pretty new, but his last movie, *Winning Proposition*, made a ton of money, so now he's one of Hollywood's golden boys."

"I remember that movie," Ruth said. "Wasn't it about a soccer team or something in Proposition, Ohio?"

"Yep."

On the stage, a PA offered Dick Fiori a portable mike, but he waved it away and shouted, "Can you all hear me?"

The kids hollered, "*Yeah!*"

"Cool." He made a settle-down motion with his hands and said, "Okay, hey, thanks for being here today, first of all. How many of you have done this before?"

About half the kids put up their hands.

"How many of you want to be in the movies?"

Almost everyone raised a hand.

"Groovy." In a mock-confidential tone he said, "How many of you are only here because your parents made you?"

About eighteen of the kids raised their hands. The director turned to the mezzanine with a boyish grin that Ruth suspected he'd been perfecting for years and said, "Thanks, all you stage moms and dads!"

A feeble ripple of laughter went through the gulag.

The director turned back to the kids. "No, but seriously, guys, you're going to be part of one of the movie's most important scenes. LaTisha and Brian have been working with the squad on this popping-krumping kind of cheer for a couple of months. No one's ever seen anything like it before, and they're getting a ton of static, including from Mr. Wong, the principal. So they're worried about that. Plus—and don't tell anyone this—they're falling in love."

In a united chorus, the kids all said, "*Awwwwww.*" Dick Fiori gave them a minute before saying, "Seriously, though, if they don't at least place in this competition they're going to have to go home and the squad's going to be disbanded because even the school board doesn't like them and they're just looking for any excuse, so how they do is super important. Okay? So here's what we're going to do. We need you guys to react—that's what you're going to be doing for me today—and I'm going to *tell* you what you're reacting to, which means you're going to have to use your imaginations, because nothing's actually going to be happening up here on the stage, even though in the movie we'll be cutting back and forth to the squad performing. Okay? So the first thing is, we're going to boo"—and here he made a booing noise like a moose call—"because you're thinking these kids are just freaks and spoilers and they should step aside and let the regular squads win. Okay? Let me hear it."

The kids all booed with gusto. "Great! Now I want you to do exactly that same thing, only this time you all need to be looking at me, because the camera has to see *you* seeing these kids that you hate. Are we ready, Harvey? Yeah? Okay, we're going to roll this time. You ready? Here's your chance to get famous."

The kids booed and cheered and shouted and catcalled and when, after an hour, they began to flag, the director dismissed them for a quick sugar break. "Okay, guys, craft services has put out some more doughnuts and I think we've even got some Cinnabons—Paulie, do we have Cinnabons? Yup, we've got Cinnabons—and we want you to stretch your legs and eat and drink some juice for energy, and after that, rows one through eight, you're going back to your classroom." Loud booing broke out, which the director rewarded with a rueful look. "Yeah, I know it's a bummer, but I promise we'll bring you back out pretty soon. Rows nine through seventeen, you're going to come back here, and the rest of you, you get to go to your classroom, too, because Disney loves educated actors."

From the tangle of kids, Ruth saw Bethany seek her out with a look of adoration. And Ruth knew exactly why, because she could feel it, too: here they were, in Los Angeles, making a movie that all Bethy's friends were going to see, starring kids she revered, on an honest-to-God movie set. Any lingering disappointment from the *Raven* callback had been washed away by the awesome magic of Hollywood.

DICK FIORI WRAPPED THE MORNING SHOOT AT TWELVE o'clock exactly and announced that the actors had one hour for lunch. Everyone, including parents and set-sitters, was required to leave the set, so Ruth picked up her purse and headed outside to meet the girls. They'd already lined up in the theater parking lot, where two tents had been pitched, one for the union and the other for the nonunion extras. Reba had been right: from what Ruth could see, the extras got boxed lunches consisting of a thin and unadorned turkey sandwich, potato chips, and an apple. From the aroma wafting out of the other tent, the union actors were getting an assortment of Thai dishes with a salad bar and dessert buffet.

Once they'd made it through the lunch line, which moved at roughly the same glacial speed as rush-hour traffic, Ruth found a spot of shade beneath a tired and spindly oak tree. There were no chairs anywhere, so she and the girls sat on the cement.

"See?" Reba said balefully, poking around inside her lunch box. "I told you."

"Did you see Clara at all?" Ruth asked Bethany. "I sat with her mom this morning, up in the gallery."

"Was she the girl at the *Raven* callback? Yeah, she was in my classroom. She started out in a different room that was just for the actors with speaking parts, but the teacher had a nervous breakdown or something. Clara said she kept staring at her and asking how she was feeling and stuff, if she felt light-headed or weird or anything. Then she sent her to our room."

Ruth suppressed a smile. Bethany bit into her sandwich. "We talked a lot," she said through a mouth full of gummy white bread and turkey. "I like her—she's funny."

"I thought you were supposed to be doing schoolwork," Ruth said.

Bethany gave Ruth her *duh* look. "No one did schoolwork, Mom."

"Well, *somebody* must have."

Bethany shrugged. "Anyway, the teacher and this other woman just sat outside the room and let us do whatever we wanted."

Vindicated, Allison said, "I told you they don't care."

Bethany started waving at someone. Ruth looked around and saw Clara emerge from the union tent with an overflowing plate. She came over and sat down beside Bethany.

"Where's your mom?" Ruth asked, looking for Vee.

"She had to go pick up my little brother. You're not supposed to leave a minor on the set unaccompanied, but she does it all the time when there are a ton of people. It's not like anyone's keeping track."

"Well, if anyone asks, you just say you're with me," Ruth offered. She stood up with effort—she really had to lose thirty pounds—and asked who wanted something to drink.

"Diet Coke," said Allison.

"Milk," said Bethany. "Chocolate. Please."

"Coke," said Reba. "*Regular* Coke."

"Orange juice," Hillary said primly. "I haven't had a fruit or a vegetable yet."

Clara just hoisted her can of soda and said, "I'm good."

Ruth threaded her way among the little camps of kids and parents and snuck in the wrong side of the nonunion tent, grabbing cans and cartons. When she got back the girls were deep in conversation.

"My mom thinks I'm going to be famous," she heard Bethany say.

"Everyone's mom thinks they're going to be famous," said Hillary.

"Not mine," Clara said cheerfully. "My mom thinks me and my brother are going to get little piddly-ass jobs until high school and then tank."

Ruth sat down with a grunt. "What do you mean, tank?"

"Stop booking. Which it pretty much doesn't take a genius to figure out, because *everyone* stops booking in high school.

You're too old to play younger than fourteen, and you're too young to play older than fifteen, and there aren't breakdowns for fourteen or fifteen *ever*. They're always for twelve, sixteen, or eighteen, so you're pretty much screwed. Plus, you know, I'm a redhead."

"Does that matter?" said Ruth.

"Name a redhead besides Marcia Cross, Kate Walsh, or Juli-anne Moore. You can't."

"But that can't possibly be true," Ruth said. "Especially what you were saying about getting too old or young or whatever it was."

"Bet?" Clara offered cheerfully.

"Some kids, like David Henrie, just go back home for a year," Allison told her, "and go to high school like normal kids until they're legal eighteen."

"Who's David Henrie?" Bethany said.

"You guys are going to *have* to watch more TV," said Al-lison. "He's been on *That's So Raven* and *How I Met Your Mother* and a bunch of other stuff since forever. He's friends with some kids I know."

"He's really cute," Hillary offered. "I mean, he's pretty old and stuff now, but he was cute when he was younger, and he's still kind of hot."

"What did you mean about being legal?" Ruth asked.

"Legal eighteen? It means once you're sixteen and you either have a high school diploma or you've passed this killer profi-ciency test, you can work as a legal eighteen."

Ruth frowned. "But why does that matter?"

"Because if you're a legal eighteen they don't have to give you three hours of school every day on set. So producers like you, because they save money on the set teacher *and* make you work for those three hours, plus you can stay on the set for twelve hours instead of only eight. So of course if it's between taking a regular kid and a legal eighteen, they're going to book the legal eighteen."

"Or they could Taft-Hartley you," Reba piped up.

"Taft-Hartley?"

"If you're nonunion, sometimes a producer will like you so much he'll tell the union there's no union actor who can possibly play that role, only you, and if the union gives them permission, then they can hire you."

"But that has nothing to do with being legal eighteen or not," Hillary pointed out. "That's if you're nonunion and the show is SAG."

"Or AFTRA," Clara said. "I think."

"The American Federation of Television and Radio Actors," Reba told Ruth.

"Artists," Hillary corrected her.

"*God*, you guys," said Allison. "It's not like she's going to remember it anyway. Whatever."

Ruth assumed that she was the *she* in question, but it was hard to be offended because Allison was right.

"You'll probably figure it out soon," Hillary reassured her. "I mean, everyone thinks it's kind of confusing when they first get here. The first couple of months, my mom used to lock herself in the bathroom every night and cry after she thought I was asleep. Plus she'd sneak in shots of vodka. That was when we were staying at the Oakwood, before she went back to Columbus and I went to Mimi's."

"The Oakwood," Bethany said reverently. "You stayed there? You're so lucky."

"Yeah. I never told her I could hear her. Then my dad came down for a couple of weeks before she went back home, so that was better. He's really good with directions and stuff. My mom just got us lost every time. I never made it to a single audition when I was supposed to the whole time she was here."

"Yeah," Bethany said pointedly to Ruth.

"Ten minutes!" A PA walked through the crowd, shouting. "You've got ten minutes, people! Use the restroom, tidy up, and be ready."

Ruth sighed. "Did everyone get enough to eat?"

"*Yes*," Bethany, Clara, Allison, and Hillary shouted in a chorus.

"No," said Reba.

THE CAR RIDE HOME AT THE END OF THE DAY WAS CONSID-erably more subdued than the outbound journey. By the time they were dismissed, Ruth had gas and the girls were in ad-vanced states of nervous exhaustion. They'd booed and cheered and mugged and held their breath over and over and over, and by four o'clock, when they were released, they were *done*, de-spite a mid-afternoon sugar extravaganza of nondiet sodas, fruit juices, energy drinks, Hershey bars, Three Musketeers, Snick-ers, Milky Ways, Paydays, Rolos, Baby Ruths, and chocolate chip cookies the size of hubcaps. Not only had the girls not seen Zac Efron or Ashley Tisdale, they hadn't been included in a single close-up or offered the chance to deliver a line, a privilege that had gone to a dweeby little black kid who, in their estimation, in no way deserved it. Worse, both Hillary and Reba had been completely hidden behind columns for the en-tire afternoon. Ruth kept an eye out for Vee, but when she came back she was talking to another woman, and Ruth decided to keep to herself. Ominous deep disturbances in her upper colon announced that the evening was likely to be unpleasant. On the bright side, Bethy got a SAG voucher and $150, which meant that her brand-new Coogan account was worth $22.50.

"So much for glamour, huh?" Allison said to Bethany once the girls had collected all their stuff and Ruth had loaded them into the SUV.

"It was okay," Bethany said loyally.

Hillary did a perfect impression of Dick Fiori. *"Okay, guys, we're going to make this one a big cheer, biggest of the day!"* Even Ruth had to admit that what had seemed chummy and hip early in the day had become, by the end, almost unendurable.

"Well, he was a little smarmy," Bethany allowed.

"A *little*?"

Bethany settled lower in her seat and stared out the window. The traffic was crawling up Highland toward the 101.

"I don't know," Allison said. "He was actually kind of cute, in a way."

"Oh, ick," said Hillary. "In an *old* way."

"He wasn't that old."

"What do you consider old?" Ruth asked.

"I don't know—forty, maybe. I mean, he was probably only thirty-one or something."

"Only?" At Allison's age, Ruth had thought *nineteen* was old.

In the rearview mirror Allison just shrugged.

AFTER THEY'D DROPPED OFF THE ORPHANS AT THE STUDIO, Ruth and Bethany went back to their apartment. "Let's just rest," Ruth suggested hopefully. "I'm exhausted. Aren't you?"

"No. I was for a little while, but now I'm okay."

"Why don't you go for a swim?"

Bethany gave her a look. "I wish I had my bike."

Ruth wasn't sure she'd want Bethy biking by herself around Burbank, though there were some excellent neighborhoods relatively nearby. At home in Seattle she never worried about her being out alone even though Ruth realized, intellectually, that her daughter was every bit as much at risk there as here. But somehow the children she'd met in LA seemed more vulnerable to the madness of adults, and not just child molesters and deviants. Just look at poor dumpy Reba, who was about as likely to land an acting career as Ruth was. God only knew Hillary's story, or those of Orphans Past. There was Quinn Reilly, too, a sixteen-year-old boy who was, evidently, a brilliant actor, but had gotten into some kind of trouble at Mimi's and didn't live there anymore. No one seemed willing to talk about exactly what he'd done, only that it was very distasteful and possibly sexual in nature, though not, in itself, overly serious.

"My head is just pounding," Ruth said, though it was actually her gut that was roiling. "I need to lie down for a little while before dinner. I thought I'd cook the ravioli." Knowing they'd have a long day today, they'd picked up some fresh pasta and marinara sauce at a Pavilions yesterday afternoon, and a loaf of crusty bread to go with it.

"That sounds good."

"Why don't you give Daddy a call? He should be home by now, and you know how much he likes hearing from you. He's lonely up there without us."

Bethany suddenly brightened. "Can I call Rianne?"

"Right after Daddy. Tell him I miss him," Ruth said, and for the first time in days, she actually did. It would have been lovely to send Bethy out on an exploratory walk with him while she dropped dead for a little while. Hugh always liked seeing new places. It was yet another irony of Ruth's being here that he was the intrepid one. How many times had Ruth joked, in the course of their marriage, that she'd be perfectly happy spending the rest of their days in the same little starter house they'd bought in Queen Anne when they were in their late twenties?

That's how far out of water she was down here. And yet she'd been driving, she'd been coping, without help from Hugh or anyone. She was proud of that. She'd often worried, in past years, about how she'd fare if Hugh were to die before her. Now she knew.

"Tell him I'll give him a call myself this evening," she instructed Bethy, lying back on her lumpy bed and closing her eyes. "And take the phone out into the courtyard, honey."

If only she could sleep for a little while, she'd rise again refreshed and ready for whatever astonishing thing might next come their way.

Chapter Four

IN FACT, WHAT CAME NEXT WAS A CHECK FOR $995, WHICH Ruth made payable to Mimi. The check was payment for Ruth's share of the cost of producing the industrial that would make Bethy, Hillary, and Reba all able to join the Screen Actors Guild. Laurel Buehl was already SAG because of all her commercials, but she and her mother, Angie, were helping with the industrial just to be nice. Angie and Laurel had evidently devoted hours to writing a script.

When Ruth first heard the term *industrial*, she'd pictured training films for factory workers, old black-and-white newsreel footage of Rosie the Riveter, that sort of thing, but Mimi had set her straight: in Hollywood parlance, an industrial was anything produced on film or video that was used to sell, train, or inform. It could be anything from an infomercial to a DVD training program on how to conduct business on eBay. Then there were commercials, which included network promotions and which everyone knew about, and PSAs, or public service announcements, which were really just commercials except that they paid squat and television stations ran them for free. "Movies," at least as Ruth had always thought of them, were classified as "shorts," "feature-length films," or "documentaries." Indies were a subset of all the above, made without the endorsement or marketing commitment of a movie studio like Disney or Paramount.

Mimi had made it very clear that the industrial they'd be making had to meet all the criteria of a legitimate production, which included hiring a couple of nonstudio child actors who would be selected by auditioning for Mimi. It would be directed by one of Mimi's young adult clients who had ambitions beyond acting.

And so Ruth and Bethany had spent the last several evenings prepping for *I Survived Middle School, and So Can You*. Bethy would be playing a smart, bookish, yet socially capable student named Rita. Her contribution to the film would be to describe in an inspiring way her ultimate success in Phys Ed after a rocky start, both athletically and fraternally. *I even made friends with the class bully, TaNiqua,* her monologue went. *She thought I'd be prejudiced against her because she's African American, so she made fun of me, but I told her I think everyone is just the same and we ended up laughing about how goofy we looked in our gym uniforms. We're really good friends now.*

The cast had assembled on a Saturday morning at Laurel and Angie's apartment, a two-bedroom at an upscale complex just blocks from Beverly Hills that bore no resemblance whatsoever to Ruth and Bethy's squalid little efficiency. In order to stay at a seemly remove from the filming, Mimi had sent Allison in her place. Allison was already a SAG member, so she was to keep an eye on things and help as production assistant. The director was an intense young man named Stafford Hahn, who traveled everywhere wearing a flash drive on a lanyard around his neck. As he'd explained to Ruth when they first arrived, it held his latest screenplay. "Keep an eye on me," he'd advised Ruth, "because in a year a lot of people are going to know my name."

Now Allison was bossing around the two "real" girls among the cast: a creamy-skinned blonde with dull blue eyes and an on-the-young-side redhead with dimples.

"You know, nobody wears their hair like that anymore,"

Allison was saying to the redhead, whose hair was wildly curly and held back by a bandana knotted at the top. "It's very eighties." The girl flushed and pulled off the bandana. Ruth saw Allison peer closer. "That's not a perm, is it?"

The girls had left their things in Laurel's bedroom, which Ruth noticed was expensively appointed with nicer furniture than anything Ruth owned. In the living room Laurel was helping the actors with their hair and makeup, dipping into a professional-looking cosmetic kit she said had gone with her to every pageant she'd ever entered. Ruth gathered there'd been a lot of them, which probably explained her poise and ready smile. But no, that wasn't fair; she was a sweet girl, both in her obvious devotion to her mother, on whom she doted, and in her gentle manner with the younger actors at the studio. Ruth watched her lead the devastated red-haired girl into her bedroom, gently brush out and French-braid her hair, and whisper in her ear something Ruth was sure was reassuring. The child smiled tremulously and rejoined the other actors in the living room.

"That was a sweet thing to do, honey," the redhead's mother told Laurel as she drifted by. "She's always been self-conscious."

"She shouldn't be," said Laurel. "She's beautiful, and it's a different kind of beauty than blondes or brunettes ever have. You tell her I said so."

"I will," the mom said gratefully. "She'll be so proud."

And then it was time to begin. Stafford had the camera and lights positioned, and the camera-and-sound guy—another actor who moonlighted on the side—had given a thumbs-up. The mothers and Laurel were relegated to the balcony and the shoot began. The top-of-the-line sliding glass doors blocked all the sound from within, so Ruth found herself completely cut off from watching Bethany at work, something she liked more than almost anything else.

The blond girl's mother was saying to Angie, "I think you did a really good job on this script, by the way. And your apartment is lovely." Ruth had seen this kind of earnest pandering before, had even been guilty of it herself on more than one occasion. You never knew when you might meet someone useful to your child's career, so it was always best to treat everyone as though they were important, at least until you knew better.

"Actually, Laurel wrote most of the script," Angie said. "She's always been a good writer."

"Well, you did a great job," the mom said to Laurel. "I really mean it." The redhead's mom nodded in agreement.

"How was your audition yesterday?" Ruth asked her. Laurel had gone to producers for a Nickelodeon sitcom. It was just a costar role but it could be a stepping stone to something larger, if she booked it. Everyone at the studio knew how badly Laurel wanted to break into theatrical work and leave commercials behind. Now, though, she just shook her head.

"I thought I did a good job, but we haven't heard anything, so I'm guessing I didn't book it. I think I was probably too old."

Ruth thought there was an air of sadness about the girl that wasn't normal in a teenager. During Ruth and Bethy's first week in LA, Laurel and Angie had invited them to lunch as a gesture of welcome. They'd lingered over their meal for hours, telling stories about the girls' respective acting experiences and the circuitous routes that had brought them to Hollywood. ("My husband thought we had lost our minds at first," Angie had said. "Oh!" Ruth had said. "Hugh, too!") To Ruth's lasting gratitude, Laurel had been very good with Bethy, very attentive despite the age difference between them. Ruth wasn't sure why they hadn't gotten together again except by happenstance in Mimi's greenroom, though it was true that Angie's perky Southern accent and impeccable grooming were somewhat daunting. And everybody was just so *busy*. But more than any of those things, Angie and Laurel tended to hold themselves apart, and it wasn't just Ruth's perception; other families had noted it, too. In Ruth's opinion, much as she valued her own excellent relationship with Bethy, there was such a thing as too much closeness.

The women were murmuring sympathetically. "I heard Hillary is auditioning for Chrissy in *Through the Window*," Angie was saying. *Through the Window*, Ruth had heard, was a suspense movie about a blind girl and her superdog, Theo. "I can't see it, myself—oh, no pun intended—but you never know what these casting directors are looking for."

The other moms nodded vigorously, and then the redhead's mother said, "By the way, for what it's worth, I found a dental practice that's running a tooth-whitening special, if anyone's looking. Fifty-nine bucks."

Nowhere in the world were teeth more brilliant than in LA. Ruth thought that if any of these women knew the enormous profit margin for whitening teeth they'd never have it done again. It was the come-on dentists used to attract new patients. That was true even in Seattle, though nothing like here, where there was a dental practice in every strip mall. But she kept her mouth shut for once, and the other women dutifully wrote down the name and location of the dental practice.

It was getting hot out on the balcony. Ruth could feel beads of sweat on her upper lip, and blotted them on her sleeve. She couldn't tell if the camera inside was rolling yet or not, but Allison was standing nearby, holding a clapboard to record the scene and take number. Ruth hadn't even known what the device was called until a week ago, when Hillary had told her.

"Please sit," Angie was urging the women when Ruth turned back. "I get the feeling we're going to be out here for a while. I'm sorry I don't have more chairs, but you can double up on the chaise longues."

Ruth obediently perched on the lower half of one of the teak chairs, sharing it with the redhead's mother. Angie flipped open a cooler the size of a child's coffin. Inside, prettily nested in ice, were diet sodas and wine coolers. Even though it was just noon, one of the women took a wine cooler. Ruth popped the top on a Diet Pepsi. She was drinking a lot of soda down here. Hugh would be disappointed. Soda and dental health didn't go together, he believed, even if it *was* sugar-free. Sure, it wasn't cavity-causing, but there was the enamel to think about, never mind the stains. She should have asked one of Hugh's hygienists to do a cleaning before they came down here. God only knew when she'd get the chance now.

The glass door slid open and the blond girl came out, clearly sulking. Her mother stood up and said with surprise, "All done already?"

"Just me," the girl said sullenly. "I mean, all I had was two lines. Everyone else got like five or six."

"But it was a good opportunity, honey," her mother said. "And it'll look great on your résumé." She picked up her outsize leather purse and smiled at them bravely. "Well, it was very nice to meet you all. And thank you for the information about the dentist. I think we'll have her teeth done this week."

Everyone murmured their good-byes. Inside, the kids were all standing around, clearly not filming. The woman and her daughter walked through them and to the door with a last wave. No one said good-bye to the blonde, which Ruth took to mean she'd been sullen the whole time. She'd probably figured out that the whole thing was a setup.

Angie stuck her head into the living room. "Do you have everything you need in here?"

Stafford didn't even look back. "Yeah. Close the door."

Angie closed the door, saying, "I guess they're about to start again. I hope nobody needed to use the little girls' room."

Soon, inside the living room, the children were all moving around again, gathering up their bags and totes. "Oh! Well, I guess that's it, then," Angie said. She slid the glass door open and caught Allison's attention. "Are you all done?"

"Yup," Allison said.

Bethy came over. "We can go," she told Ruth.

"So soon?"

"It was only a six-page script."

"Did it go well?"

"Hmmm?" Bethy's thoughts were elsewhere. "Mom, some of the kids want to go to Magic Mountain. Can I? It would be so cool."

"Magic Mountain?"

"It's that big amusement park out by Santa Clarita. Allison says it only takes like twenty-five minutes to get there."

"Oh? And who's driving?"

Bethy smiled impishly. "We were hoping you would."

Ruth knew when she was being set up. On her own, Bethy would never put Ruth on the spot like this. She sighed. "Who's going?"

"Allison and Hillary and Reba. They asked Laurel, too, but she said she didn't want to."

Ruth suspected that Allison had invited Bethy only so they could rope Ruth into driving, but even if that was true, Bethy hadn't had a day away from the studio and acting in more than three weeks. And it wasn't like Ruth had anything else to do except watch the balance in their bank account go down. She could call Hugh from the park just as easily as from their apartment, and at least she'd be out in the open instead of indoors, in the gloom.

"Okay," Ruth said. "But everyone needs to bring their own money and I think it would be a good idea if you all eat before we get there. Their food prices are probably through the roof, and you know how Daddy feels about that."

"Yes!" Bethy triumphantly pumped her fist in the air. "I'll tell them." Bethy crossed the room, whispered to Allison, and then came back to Ruth. "She wants to know if you can stop at Domino's so we can pick up a pizza. She says Mimi doesn't have anything at the house, plus we have to go right by it on the way to Mimi's to pick up a change of clothes for her."

Ruth felt a sudden wave of annoyance at Allison, but really, how could you fault the child for using whatever resources were available to her? Clearly, Mimi provided no guidance and very few services to her boarders. If Allison was cagey—and Ruth's capitulation was proof of that—she was only trying to make her way. She couldn't very well be faulted for wanting to eat, and she was trying to look after the other, younger girls. God forbid that Bethy ever had to fend for herself, but if she did, Ruth would hope that someone like Allison would step into the breach and make the day just a little bit easier for her, though not necessarily by buying her pizza. If she was a good person, Ruth would stop at Ralphs instead of Domino's and buy them all some fruit, whole-grain crackers, and low-fat cheeses. It's what she would have done at home.

She felt a sudden, blinding nostalgia for her old life as she watched Allison get some sort of signal from Bethy and flip open her phone. She evidently had Domino's in her speed-dial because a minute later Ruth could hear her ordering a pizza to go in an entirely adult and composed voice. That done, she

donned a pair of stylish sunglasses, put on lipstick, and began
loading her things—the clapboard, an enormous Super Big
Gulp cup from 7-Eleven, a small makeup case—into her omni-
present Coach satchel. Ruth thought the girl might never get to
be one, but she certainly *looked* like a movie star.

QUINN REILLY'S BED WAS ON THE FLOOR IN A CORNER OF
the living room like a dog's. Jasper and Baby-Sue's apartment,
where he'd been living for the past six months, was in the throb-
bing heart of West Hollywood, a couple blocks off Santa Monica on Norton near Havenhurst, in a spalling stucco apartment
building that had been cheaply built in the 1940s and hadn't im-
proved any with time. The place always smelled faintly of weed
and spaghetti sauce, which was the only thing Baby-Sue knew
how to cook. Mostly they ate cheap takeout, like everyone else
in LA who lived in un-air-conditioned apartments that were
too hot to cook in except for maybe December.

The day Quinn had moved in there'd been a pile of mouse
droppings in his corner. He'd cleaned it up, of course, but he
still imagined he could smell the sour, musky smell of rodent
feces every night as he fell asleep. It was a place to stay, though.
He could probably get a real bed instead of an air mattress at
Goodwill, but if he started moving in furniture, Baby-Sue
and Jasper might change their minds about him—they'd never
talked about how long he could live there, and it had already
been six months.

Baby-Sue was temping today at some law office, Jasper was at
an audition, and Quinn didn't feel like staying around the apartment by himself. It was dark, with hardly any furniture, and
when he was alone there he got the creeps sometimes, a squir-
rely feeling in his gut that something bad was about to happen,
though he couldn't say what. Baby-Sue said he was just being

superstitious, but he had had that same feeling the day his mom and Nelson, his prick of a stepfather, had told him he was being shipped out to LA when he was not quite thirteen. It wasn't the LA part he'd minded, and it certainly wasn't the acting, which he had been doing since he was nine and loved—and hell, some kids had to go to military schools, so there was that—no, it was the fact that they didn't just tell him he was going, they tried to *sell* it to him. "Just think, honey, you'll be surrounded by actors and celebrities, which I know is just going to be so exciting," his mother had said, "and you'll get to be in movies and on TV, and there'll be palm trees, which I think are so exotic. Doesn't that sound amazing?"

Well, it had, actually; but he wouldn't have said so on a million-dollar bet. He was being sent away from home. You could have sent him to a palace someplace and given him magic powers, and he still would've felt bad. You didn't send a kid away from home and then make it sound like he was going to paradise unless you not only wanted him to go, you wanted him to stay gone. That was his point. They didn't think he was smart enough to know what was going on, but he did.

Now it was one o'clock in the afternoon, he'd been awake for an hour, and he had this crappy, doomy feeling and he was hungry, so what was there to do but pull on the jeans that were least dirty and a T-shirt with a hole in the upper back—weird place to get a hole—and his purple Chuck Taylor high-tops, and head for Santa Monica Boulevard. It was hot but there was a breeze—he could feel it through the hole in his T-shirt—so he was okay with it. He headed west with the vague idea of getting something to eat. His feet, as he walked, looked flat and long and thin in his high-tops. He watched them walk past a gallery that specialized in gay portraiture, and then past a pet accessories store called Waggle & Dash that sold dog strollers lined in pink or blue satin, handmade Irish knit sweaters with a loop you put the dog's tail through so it stayed in place, Doggles, so your dog didn't get cataracts from overexposure to the sun, boots to protect its paws from scorching sand when you took it to the Huntington dog beach on a hot day, and poochy parkas that crazy LA people made their dogs wear when it dropped below sixty degrees. He'd never once seen a woman in the store, which was owned by a gay couple that clearly spent a fortune on hair care products.

Not that Quinn had anything against gay people. Hell, you *couldn't* have anything against them if you were going to live in West Hollywood, because West Hollywood was *theirs*; well, theirs and a bunch of people who'd come over from Russia— for the climate, he figured, because it must get pretty old living in Siberia or Chernobyl or wherever, where it snowed a zillion inches a year and you had to wear dorky fur hats and stuff to keep from getting frostbite every time you went out to feed the skinny ponies. He'd seen *Doctor Zhivago* about twenty-five times—that and *Fiddler on the Roof.*

Anyway, since moving to Baby-Sue and Jasper's apartment, Quinn had developed this great gay character—not over the top, because that was too easy, but a gay boy who spent most of his time alone watching other people have fun, people he wanted to be like but knew he couldn't; a character who, from the inside out, was beautiful and lost and sometimes brave. Quinn didn't think he'd want to be gay, though, except as his character. Regular people didn't really like gay people, no matter what they said. They looked at a gay person and all they could see were two of them doing it. He wouldn't want to know that everyone who looked at him was thinking about his penis.

He walked by a hair salon, Hazlitt & Company. Not much was going on in there. One of the stylists, a slight man wearing a brilliant white button-down shirt, was sitting in one of the salon chairs reading a back issue of *Vogue*. Just for the hell of it, Quinn went in.

"Hey," the stylist greeted him, getting up. He was one of the most beautiful men Quinn had ever seen. He had the delicate build and features of a faun. "Can I help you?"

Quinn shrugged, scratched his arm. "I was thinking of maybe getting my hair colored." He hadn't been, but what the hell.

"Really? Sit down and let's take a look." Quinn took his place in the chair. Beneath the mirror there were several head-shots of chisel-cheeked, square-jawed men, presumably but not necessarily there to show off their haircuts. They could have just been the stylist's boyfriends. In West Hollywood, you never knew.

Quinn sat back and the stylist ran his hands through Quinn's hair, which was long, almost to his shoulders, and hadn't been brushed or combed in a while. He'd washed it last night, though, and it was shiny.

"Yum," said the stylist. "So you were thinking, what, high-lights?"

Quinn tried to come up with something. "Maybe you could just, like, bleach it so it's pure white. Or white with red tips. That would be awesome."

The stylist made eye contact with him in the mirror. "You an actor?"

"Yeah."

"Then no can do. No *should* do. Unless you don't want to work."

"No, I want to work."

"Well, you won't, if we do something like that." Quinn liked that the stylist said *we*. "No producer's going to recolor your hair. They'll just find someone else." He ran his hands through

Quinn's hair again, contemplatively, and Quinn thought it felt better than maybe anything he'd ever felt before. It had been a long time since anyone had touched him. Baby-Sue used to hug him at first, but she didn't anymore, probably because she was sick of having him in the living room. Jasper wasn't the kind of person who went around touching people, and Mimi Roberts had been huggy before she'd kicked him out, but that was a long time ago. His mother hugged him sometimes, but it was mostly when he was leaving.

The stylist took a brush out of a drawer and began brushing Quinn's hair. That felt even better than his hands had. It felt so good Quinn was having trouble keeping his eyes open. The stylist said, "You know, you don't see good hair that much."

"So I have good hair?"

"And how."

Quinn yawned.

"I *know*," the stylist said, still brushing, gathering the hair up in a ponytail and then letting it fall. "Isn't it the best? My mom used to brush my hair when I got allergy attacks, which was pretty much all the time. Now I have this health insurance plan that has an allergy program where a nurse calls you a couple times a year and asks if you've eaten peanuts lately, or whatever—tomatoes or tomato products, in my case. The last time, when she asked me what I did when I had an attack, I said I looked for someone to brush my hair, and she thought I was screwing with her. I wasn't, though."

"I don't have allergies," Quinn said.

"Lucky you."

"Yeah." But it might not be so bad to have somebody call you up sometimes and ask how you were doing. He thought about asking the stylist for the name of his health insurance company, but the stylist had moved on.

"I could give you a cut, just to tidy things up." The stylist put down the brush and threaded his fingers through Quinn's hair and pulled it one way and then another way.

"I don't have any money," Quinn said.

"No?" The stylist's reflection was talking to Quinn's reflection in the mirror. "Well, come back with twenty-five bucks and we'll talk."

Quinn knew that no one cut hair for twenty-five dollars, not in West Hollywood and possibly not in the entire state of California. When he was living at Mimi's, Quinn used to go to a beauty school in Van Nuys where the students practiced on you, and even they charged thirty. "That's not what you charge, is it?"

The stylist smiled nicely at Quinn's reflection. "For you it is. I get to work with gorgeous hair, so it's a win-win."

"Okay."

"So, okay."

When Quinn stood up, the stylist put his hand very briefly on Quinn's back as if to steady him, even though Quinn wasn't wobbly. Quinn felt his eyelids get heavy again—what *was* that?—and then the stylist dropped his hand to the small of Quinn's back for a second, and Quinn walked to the front of the shop in a fog, trying to look as though people touched him all the time. When he got outside he closed the door carefully, so it wouldn't rattle or break a mirror or something. Even out on the sidewalk he could feel the stylist's eyes coming through the hole in his T-shirt. Maybe it should have been creepy, but it wasn't. What would it have felt like if the stylist had kissed him? He felt a thrill of revulsion in his gut, which was too bad. It would have been nice if they could spend some time together, maybe see a movie or something, but he was pretty sure you couldn't ask a gay man to spend time with you if you weren't gay, too, because that would seem like a come-on, and despite what just about every other person in LA thought, Quinn was pretty sure he wasn't gay, just lonely.

Suddenly recalling he was hungry, Quinn headed east, past a gay erotica shop and a Minute Man quick-print place and a men's clothing boutique and on up Santa Monica until he got to Los Burritos. No one was there except a homeless guy who halfheartedly extended an open palm toward Quinn. Quinn ignored him and ordered two burritos and a taco from a pretty little Latina behind the counter. She was tiny, not like a lot of the Hispanic girls. She probably didn't eat any of the food here. She probably lived with her family in a small, immaculate apartment with wrought-iron plant stands and a framed picture of the Virgin Mary and a mother who told her all the time how pretty and nice she was. She was probably loved just as much as her younger siblings and she probably knew without even asking that she could live there as long as she wanted. No one would turn her room into a hobby room for somebody's stupid fly-tying stuff.

He took his food to a table as far away from the homeless guy as he could get, so the guy couldn't watch him eat, and thought about the hair stylist. Thinking about how good his fingers felt massaging Quinn's head gave him goose bumps. They didn't make his balls take a little inward breath, though, the way they sometimes did when he saw girls bending over or running or something.

When he finished his food he watched his purple high-tops walk back down the street—*slap, slap, slap*—and east on Santa Monica again, on the opposite side of the street but toward the apartment. He passed a trendy tattoo studio and stopped to watch the action through the window. Two women were getting work done. One of them had the black outlines of a dragon on her upper arm that the tattoo artist was filling in with green and fuchsia ink. The tattoo started on her shoulder, so from the front it looked like the dragon was peeking around her arm. He liked that. The other woman was getting a tattoo on her lower back. If he ever got a tattoo, he'd get one that said, "Tattoo."

Watching the tattoo artists was surprisingly boring. They'd scribble on the person's arm and then wipe it off, scribble, wipe, scribble, wipe. The best part was their purple gloves. They'd look great on him with his purple high-tops. Maybe he should go in and see if they'd give him a pair. He watched for another few minutes, but then he lost interest and headed back to the apartment. Mimi had him in a showcase this afternoon at three. She was being pretty good about letting him do stuff at the studio any time he wanted, as long as he behaved himself and didn't do inappropriate things. He just couldn't live with her anymore. Mimi was pretty cool, even though she'd kicked him out. She'd tried to get his mom and dick of a stepfather, to bring him back home to Seattle after that. He'd heard her on the phone, saying, "—yes, but he's floundering and I think he needs to spend some time at home." It hadn't worked, though. His mom and Nelson were willing to send him a shit-pile of money as long as he stayed in LA. He could have taken a class every day if he'd wanted to. He could have told them he needed a thousand dollars a month and they'd probably give it to him. Hell, he could probably tell them he needed five hundred dollars a month to buy weed or Ecstasy and they'd have sent it, that's how much they didn't want him to ever come back home. They never even asked him about what had happened at Mimi's. He assumed Mimi had told them, though. He assumed pretty much everyone knew. That's why he wasn't in classes anymore with any kids younger than fifteen. Like he was some sort of sex freak. He didn't see what the big deal was.

Jasper was upstairs when Quinn got back. He was Pakistani, with a permanent five-o'clock shadow, dark brown eyes like a dog's, and an accent Quinn could mimic perfectly. He and Baby-Sue looked like a car wreck together—she was a big-boned redhead with rabbit teeth and an overbite—but they had a good time. They'd been living together for a year. Sometimes Quinn tried to imagine what their kids might look like. Then he usually gave up.

"Hey, bud," Jasper said when Quinn came in. He was sitting at a card table eating Chinese takeout from Win Sum Yum around the corner.

"Hey."

"Man, I aced my audition. I'm going to producers with this one, baby. Morty'll be happy." Morty was Jasper's agent.

"So that's good," Quinn said, even though he didn't really care. Jasper wasn't even SAG yet. All his gigs were nonunion and paid crap. The only reason he had an agent was because Mimi had begged a favor while she and Jasper were still on good terms, which now they were not. Quinn had seen him act once or twice in Mimi's showcases, and he was okay, but between the accent and the skin tone, he was doomed to play ethnic forever. At least that was one problem Quinn didn't have.

"So what have you been up to?" Jasper said, chewing vigorously. He had pink, pink fingernails. Some of the skin around them was very dark, darker than the rest of him, like the pigment had leaked out and pooled there. His palms were pink, too. Next to Jasper, Quinn looked like he was terminally ill, and Baby-Sue looked like she'd been boiled. She called her complexion peaches and cream, but Quinn just called it blotchy. "You been doing anything?"

"Nah."

"Yeah," Jasper said sympathetically.

"I'm in a showcase at three, though." It was two now. "You going over Laurel Canyon?"

"I could be. Sure. I need to reorder headshots. I'll go to ISGO. How long's the showcase?"

"I don't know. Depends on when I'm up." They both knew Mimi didn't make up her mind about that until right before the showcase, so you never knew where you were in the lineup.

"Well, at least I can drop you off. I'll probably be done before you, though."

Quinn shrugged. He hated that he always had to beg rides places. You could tell Baby-Sue and Jasper weren't parents. Parents fussed over you about stuff like whether you had a ride home. Even Nelson did that much. Quinn decided he would try to talk Nelson into buying him some beater car once he had his license. If he'd just do that, Quinn would be set. He wouldn't need Baby-Sue or Jasper or anyone.

Chapter Five

DILLARD BUEHL HAD MADE HIS FORTUNE SELLING BOILED peanuts at state fairs from Gatlinburg to New Orleans. By his own admission he was the purest form of cracker, a plain old South'n boy who was light on education and long on talk and hard work. He adored and worshipped his wife and little girl, so when Angie said she wanted to take Laurel to Hollywood to try her hand at fame, what could he do but pull together a little bank account, drive them out there in his brand-new Hummer, and settle them into a two-bedroom apartment? He couldn't be gone too long because he didn't trust his partner, Bobby, even if he was Dillard's brother, so he installed a GPS system for the snappy Hummer H3 Angie chose off the lot, put the Thomas Guide to LA in the driver's-side door pocket, kissed his little girl, and wished them well. He'd miss them like crazy, but he wanted them to be happy, and once Angie got her mind fixed on something, well, that was that. And his little peanut was beautiful and talented and had a voice as rich and sweet and smooth as caramel. She'd started singing at church when she was five, been competing in beauty pageants since she was seven, and people hearing her sing for the first time fell in love with her there and then, *that's* how good she was. But no church or pageant was big enough to hold her, not anymore.

And while Dillard might be a cracker, he was nobody's fool. He knew there were wives who went to Los Angeles and never came back except to make an appearance in divorce court. They got a taste of the glory life—movie stars and expensive clothes and shopping for jewelry on Rodeo Drive—and they grabbed hold of it and went for a never-ending ride. If that happened to his Angie it would kill him, just kill him, but he was wise enough to know that you couldn't get between a woman and her dream. The day you did that, you stopped being a husband and started being a jailer. Dillard was no dream-slayer and he was certainly no warden. He wanted his girls to be happy, and if he had the means to bring that about, why, he was duty-bound to do it. Money could be its own burden that way. It gave you choices when sometimes you were better off without any.

In any event, today was his last day in Los Angeles before he turned his Hummer around and pointed its nose toward home. It might be September, but there were still county fairs going on all over the American South, and Dillard needed to be there. He should have gone home yesterday, but Angie begged him to stay so he could see Laurel in a showcase. From what Dillard could make out, the showcase let Mimi Roberts's kids perform for a few talent agents and casting directors. Laurel already had an agent—they'd had a $175 lobster dinner to commemorate the occasion—but Mimi had said there'd be a casting director there today from Disney. Mimi had told Angie and Angie had told him that although she was on the old side, Laurel would be perfect for Disney because of her looks and her voice. She'd been a Little Miss Georgia runner-up two years in a row, too, so she was seasoned. Today could be her day, Angie said, and they'd both feel a lot calmer if Dillard could be there.

So here he was at the studio, his broad backside perched precariously on a tiny plastic folding chair, trying to shrink the big man he was into a smaller facsimile because the room was that small and that packed. Angie was fidgeting until he took her hand in his big paw and settled her. From the waiting room where they kept all the kids—greenroom, he was supposed to call it, though it was more like the color of old athletic socks—he could hear muffled laughter and chatter and nerves. And then it got quiet all of a sudden, and Mimi came in leading the two sequestered talent agents and one casting director to a place of honor in the very front of the room, where wooden TV trays had been set up to hold stacks of carefully ordered headshots and résumés and feedback forms. Mimi took her seat at the back of the room, lifted the first set from her pile, and announced the performer. Angie's hand tightened in his and the showcase began.

The first two children did TV commercials for kids' Crest and Pull-Ups, respectively. They couldn't act worth a damn, of course, but they were cute and perky in exactly the way Laurel had been at that age, and the casting director and agents wrote energetic notes on their feedback forms. Ten or twelve kids followed, doing scenes from actual movies and sitcoms. And then, by the painful pressure Angie's hand was suddenly exerting on his knuckles, he could tell that Laurel's turn must be next. The last trio of kids went back to the greenroom, a parent keeping watch out there said, "*Shhhhhhh,*" and Laurel emerged wearing a gossamer pink outfit that reminded Dillard of the inside of a seashell. Angie had bought it for her at Barneys yesterday. He knew because they'd brought him along for his opinion, which was sweet, given that his approval was guaranteed. She could have been wearing an old wrestler's uniform and he would have said it was beautiful. She had that much power to move him.

LAUREL STEPPED ONTO THE LITTLE PLATFORM THAT SERVED as a stage and brought a wooden stool into the middle. She moved slowly. She didn't want to start; at that moment she would have given almost anything not to have to start. She sent up a little prayer for help. Then she settled herself, hooked her heels over the bars of the stool, smoothed her skirt, and raised her eyes to Angie's in the second row of seats.

Then she began to talk. Her voice sounded fragile, almost ghostly, as though at any minute she might just *stop*; around the room people leaned forward in their chairs. She stared into Angie's eyes without blinking.

"The day my mother found out she was dying she asked me to go out and buy her these clear glass marbles. Dad and I hadn't even known she was ill."

She took a deep breath. In the audience she could see Angie mouthing the lines, as though she could will Laurel through the performance.

"I brought her the marbles and she counted ninety of them out and put them in this old cut-glass bowl. Apparently the doctor had given her three months."

Laurel could feel Angie breathing with her in perfect synchrony. Laurel gave a little sob, just one, like a cough.

"All day, every day, she would hold one of these marbles in her hand. She said it made the day longer. After the third or fourth day I saw one on the floor and started to pick it up but she said, 'Leave it.' She said she was learning to let go."

Laurel's chest heaved with the effort not to break down. Tears spilled over, though. Around the room people were gasping. Laurel's eyes were fixed on Angie's like a lifeline.

"I was in bed two weeks ago Wednesday toward dawn, when I heard this sound of falling marbles. Dad and I ran in there. The bedside table was turned over and she was gone. Dead. When the emergency medical people got there they found this."

Laurel opened her trembling hand to reveal one clear glass marble, which she held out toward the audience like prayer. *"The rest spilled when the table fell, but this one was still in her hand."*

She wept—she couldn't help it—but for just a beat or two. Then she forced herself to go on.

"*I keep it.*

"*I keep it in my hand all day.*

"*It makes the day longer.*"

Finally it was over. Laurel, stunned, just sat there. Everyone in the room was standing up; several people were fighting back tears, but not Angie. Angie was dry-eyed and resolute: *Eyes on the prize.*

Laurel wiped her nose with a tissue and fled the room. When Angie reached her in the parking lot, she was still trembling.

"Oh, God," she said, and her voice was still unsteady and nasal.

"That was brilliant," Angie said softly, massaging Laurel's shoulders. She was smaller than Laurel, so she had to reach up. "*You.* You were brilliant."

Laurel toed a bubble of tar into a crack in the asphalt. "How could you have *sat* there? How could you stand it?"

Angie smiled gently. "I could sit there and watch you act all day. You know that."

"It wasn't acting."

"It *was* acting," Angie said gently. "It was someone else's story, honey. You just delivered *someone else's story.* You can walk away from that."

"I didn't think I was going to get through it."

"But you did."

"I did, didn't I?" Laurel sought out Angie's eyes. Looking for truth and finding it there, she nodded and pulled a soggy wad of tissues out of her pocket, holding it out mutely and laughing. Angie smiled and pulled Laurel into a one-armed hug.

"So do you think they thought it was good?"

"They didn't think it was good, darlin', they thought it was *great.* You could see it. Daddy about popped with pride."

Laurel nodded, knowing who got the real credit: God. She had faith that He was guiding her. Her mother wanted her to be a star, and that would be wonderful, of course, but that wasn't what was driving her. What was driving her was the thought of Angie seeing her win major movie and TV awards like Emmys or Oscars; of Angie at her wedding, seeing her first grandchild. That's what she wanted. And if God would grant her that, she would do whatever it took for her to be the star she knew Angie so badly wanted her to be.

IN THE GREENROOM, BETHANY WAS WATCHING ALLISON delicately stroke on face powder with a badger brush and then refresh her lipstick. She had pulled her hair back from her face with a bright pink silk hair band that perfectly matched her pink capris and ballet flats. She wore a contrasting Juicy Couture T-shirt, and Bethany thought that either her breasts were growing quickly or she was wearing a Victoria's Secret gel bra. Either way, she looked gorgeous. When she was finished she took a long look at herself in the huge hand mirror Mimi kept in the greenroom so they wouldn't all crowd into the bathroom, which was tiny and had only two stalls, one of them for handicapped people even though no one had ever actually seen a handicapped person in there.

"Do you want to know why you didn't book it? Because I can tell you exactly why," Allison said to Bethany, handing the mirror to her. Bethy handed it straight on to Hillary, who was fumbling with her bangs and a curling iron. Bethy had been saying how disappointed she was that she hadn't gotten a callback for a costar role on a new, prime-time sitcom for which she'd been able to audition because of her brand-new status as a member of SAG. "You want to know why? You wanted it too much."

Bethy just looked at her.

"I'm serious. The thing is not to care," Allison said, impatiently taking the curling iron from Hillary and going to work on the girl's bangs. "They can smell it a mile away if you care too much. The more you want to book a role, the more you're not going to. If you go in there with the attitude that you don't give a crap, they'll be all over you. And even if you don't book it, they'll remember you." Expertly she curled Hillary's stick-straight hair. "You know Quinn? He auditioned one time to play this gay kid, which he's really good at because, you know, he *looks* kind of gay and everyone's always asking him if he *is*, which I don't think so. Anyway, he gives this awesome read, and on the way out the door he takes the casting director's hands"—and here she took Bethy's hands in hers—"and whispers, 'Have a really perfect day.'"

Bethany's mouth dropped open. "No way."

"Way." Allison fluffed Hillary's bangs with a brush and handed back the curling iron. "You don't know him because he's not around that much right now, but he used to live at Mimi's, too. He'll do *anything*."

"So did he book it?"

"No, but only because he didn't look old enough. They wanted someone to play eighteen, and he looks more like fifteen, even though he's really sixteen and a half. Oh, and listen to this. One time we were doing a showcase and somehow Mimi got an agent from CAA to be there—which never happens because they're one of *the* big-time agencies and they don't need to shop for clients—and Quinn was doing this scene where he plays a younger brother with a crush on his big sister's girlfriend. He's supposed to answer the door and she's there, right, and I don't remember the line anymore, but he's trying to get her attention. Leave them alone." She whacked Hillary's hand with a hairbrush so she'd stop fooling with her bangs. "Anyway, in the scene, he's just gotten out of the shower, so he's got a bathrobe on, but Quinn changes in the greenroom where Mimi can't see him and he comes out in nothing but a towel, this ratty old bath towel that he's holding together, and when he answers the door and sees the girl standing there, he *lets go of the towel*. I'm not kidding. I thought Mimi was going to pass out. She has high blood pressure, and seeing that towel drop—*hoo*. Do you remember that?" she asked Hillary.

"It was the best thing ever."

Bethy stared. "So was he naked?"

"Nah," Allison said. "He had on a pair of boxers. But you couldn't tell until the towel was off."

"Did the agent like him?"

Allison shrugged. "I don't remember. I know CAA didn't sign him, but the next day one of the casting directors who was there called him to go straight to producers for something. The guy was probably gay because, you know, tons of them are." Hillary was fidgeting with her bangs again, and Allison slapped her hand. "*Stop*. You're going to wreck them."

Bethany knew that some of the girls didn't like Allison just because of the way she looked, but she thought Allison was fun and funny and in a good mood a lot of the time, despite the fact that her mother gave her away to Mimi and she'd never even met her father. Hillary had told her that no one even knew who Allison's father *was*, not even her mom. Bethy couldn't imagine that. She couldn't even imagine having divorced parents, and just about everyone she knew had parents who were divorced except her. She knew Ruth and Hugh missed each other a ton, because sometimes Ruth got very quiet after hanging up the phone, like she was upset about something. When Bethy asked her, she just said she got homesick sometimes, but Bethy didn't think it was that simple. She knew they didn't agree about her being in LA. She knew Hugh thought it was a bad idea to have her put her education second by letting her be homeschooled like all the other studio kids. He thought she should still be back home at McClure Middle School, doing Seattle Children's Theatre classes and maybe auditioning for commercials or indie movies that were being cast—nonunion gigs where you hardly got paid anything and you couldn't ever book a TV show or a real movie, only stuff that someone was producing in their garage. She and Ruth had both told him it would be too late if they waited until after college, but he didn't believe it because he wasn't down here watching much younger kids book episodics and movies, even now leaving Bethy further and further behind.

"You're on deck, you two," said somebody's mom, checking off an item on her clipboard. Bethy closed her eyes for a minute, smoothed her ponytail, straightened out the kicky little skirt she and Ruth had found on the clearance rack at Forever 21, and ran her tongue over her teeth in case there was some last-minute lip gloss on them. She and Allison were doing a scene from an old episode of *That's So Raven*. She loved doing scenes with Allison, because, like Quinn, Allison would do absolutely anything, where Bethy still held back sometimes. "*Commit!*" Dee always hollered at her in class. "You've made your choice, so what are you waiting for?" Bethy took a deep breath and so did Allison, and then they burst into the showcase like gunslingers.

BEFORE JASPER HAD EVEN PULLED INTO THE STUDIO PARK-ing lot, Quinn could see kids swarming around outside. Little kids, mostly, seven years old, nine years old, mostly girls. Mimi always had a ton of girls. Thank God she didn't pair him up anymore, except with Cassie Foley, who was only eleven but

was a great, even a superb, actor. She had credits as long as
your arm already, mostly TV episodics. If *Grey's Anatomy* was
looking for a kid to play a terminally ill or molested character,
Cassie was on the short list. She'd had guest star roles on almost
every major dramatic episodic there was. She had a perfectly
heart-shaped face and a widow's peak and big blue eyes and she
smiled all the time and she meant it. She was a sweet kid, and
she liked Quinn, too. Not that many kids did. Hardly any kids
did. People thought you didn't know that kind of thing, but you
did. He did.

Now he spotted her on the far edge of the pack, wearing an
iPod and moving her lips. Getting in character and going over
her scene. She was a professional, and he liked her as a scene
partner because she was always prepared. They'd been on *ER*
together a year or so ago when she'd been running a fever of
102. Her mom had stood by with a puke bucket and when they
hadn't needed her on set she'd lain on a couch in her dressing
room and tried to keep tea and saltines down, and she'd *still*
delivered a performance that was great. After she was released
for the day they'd taken her to Cedars-Sinai, administered IV
fluids, and the next morning when he got to the *ER* soundstage
she was there and she was smiling. Now she saw him across the
parking lot and trotted over, her earbuds dangling around her
neck. "I was just running our scene," she said.

"I know—I could see you. You want to run it together?"

"Not unless you do."

"Nah." It was a scene they'd done a hundred times. He was
the big brother; she was the kid sister. He'd gotten her to run
away with him because his dad was beating them. He'd stashed
her in a park while he went off to try to find them something
to eat, and before he left her he kept telling her in this really
chipper way that they'd do great on their own, but you knew

he wasn't really sure he could do it. A lot of the scenes they all did were about fucked-up kids and families. He guessed writers didn't want to write about happy people. What would be the point? And there probably weren't that many happy people to begin with. Cassie was the only one he knew who seemed like she was really happy. Well, her and his kid brother, Rory.

It was hot out in the parking lot, and the younger kids were shrieking and running around and suddenly Quinn wasn't in the mood for it. He hadn't slept that well because the valve in his air mattress had broken and the mattress kept deflating; and since he was pretty bony, it hurt, so he kept having to reinflate it. He signaled to Cassie that he was going inside.

The little kids had finished and the studio greenroom was full of the latest crop of older kids and their stupid mothers. The mothers were standing around gossiping, taking up space and laughing a lot because they were nervous for their kids. Quinn had been doing Mimi's showcases for years, and he knew they were nothing like what Mimi described to the parents to get them to pay for their kids to participate. First of all, she bribed the casting directors and talent agents to come and give feed-back. Hardly anyone was ever discovered at showcases, though you might get an agent—one of the ones who would take just about anyone who breathed and then never pitched any of them, so you got only the auditions the whole world was in on. Show-cases made Mimi a wad, though. She was always in a good mood the day after. When he'd lived at her house, she'd always hummed while she was counting the money. Money made her happier than anything else did. Quinn sure didn't, even though he'd booked stuff more than just about anyone besides Cassie. She said she was still his manager, but when he turned eighteen he was going to fire her.

Allison Addison came up to him and said, "Hey, chicken-lickin'." Then she swung her hair around and over her shoulder. He couldn't stand that. She thought she was beautiful. So did everyone else. She thought it gave her power over people, and maybe it did, but it didn't give her any power over him. They'd lived together at Mimi's. He'd seen what she did to her arms late at night when the other kids were asleep.

Now, ignoring her, he walked across the greenroom to look at the order in which they'd run the scenes. There was one scene to go before his and Cassie's. That was good—he could leave after that. He didn't stick around for the feedback anymore. He didn't care about the feedback. All he cared about was whether he booked something or not.

The kids from the scene before theirs were just finishing up. He could hear polite clapping. The same kids had done the same scene a thousand times, and every time, the scene sucked. They couldn't act their way out of a paper bag, plus they were thirteen. He hoped Cassie wouldn't get all giggly and stupid like that when she turned thirteen. Maybe he'd talk to her about it sometime.

Some mother he'd never met before told him to go on in— like he needed to be told. Cassie was at his elbow, her face bright, her iPod and earbuds tucked away someplace. She smiled at him; he smiled back: *Ready?*

She nodded, tucking her small hand into his elbow. The door opened and the casting director, agents, and parents looked back expectantly. Mimi introduced them both and let the panel pull up their headshots, and then they were on. He could feel his character come over him like a fever. "*Come on,*" his character called back to Cassie's, because she had let go of his arm and stopped walking, not sure she wanted to follow him.

"*It's going to be fun,*" he said. "*It's going to be just fine. You'll see!*"

Chapter Six

AFTER THE SHOWCASE ENDED AND MIMI HAD ESCORTED the agents and casting director off the premises—mainly so parents wouldn't mob them, but also so Mimi could discreetly hand them envelopes with two crisp one-hundred-dollar bills inside—kids surrounded her, clamoring for their feedback forms while their parents stood back and waited anxiously for the stone tablets to be handed down from the mount. Let them wait. For forty-five minutes Mimi stayed locked in her office with Tina Marie, reading all the feedback forms filled out by the two agents and the casting director, Evelyn Flynn. Normally reading and collating took half that time, but Evelyn Flynn was a goddess in the casting world and Mimi had been trying to get her to one of her showcases for *years*. The TV episodics and pilots she cast were magic; she worked only with the best directors and producers in the industry. She'd come here today to shop, Mimi knew: some project she was casting must call for something unusual, or something she'd been casting for months hadn't burped up the right kid.

From what Mimi read, there was consensus that Laurel Buehl had been excessively overwrought in her scene from *Clear Glass Marbles*, but still, her performance had been authentic, definitely authentic. She might do well, Evelyn Flynn had noted, in daytime drama. Which, of course, she didn't cast. One of the agents had said, *Good commercial look*. They often said that when they meant, *Don't hold your breath*. Mimi went on.

Quinn, everyone agreed, had worked very sweetly with

Cassie Foley, whom he had not upstaged although the opportunity had certainly presented itself in the course of the scene. Only Evelyn Flynn was seeing him for the first time. *Certainly a young man to watch,* one of the talent agents had written on Quinn's feedback form. *Is he happy with his representation? If not, give me a call.*

Of Allison the other agent wrote, *Unless she turns horsey by seventeen, this girl is worth gold. I'm serious.* As though Mimi needed to be told. *Are her parents tall?* Evelyn Flynn had said only, *Good acting. Work on that.* And no one had had much to say about Bethany Rabinowitz, besides checking boxes that indicated she'd most likely be cast as a nerd, a sidekick, a brain. *Good diction,* one of the agents had noted. *Needs to bring more depth to the role. Experience will help.*

Once Mimi had distributed the papers, parents and children drifted away to look at them in private. They shared only rave reviews with other studio people, and hardly anyone got rave reviews because Mimi directed the panel to be tough or the kids would never learn. She watched the kids and parents flip through the pages with varying degrees of disappointment and letdown. In Mimi's experience there were rarely any surprises and even fewer discoveries, but it gave the kids something to work for and the parents handed over their $220 without a second thought.

Mimi had been running these showcases for years. In some of them, not a single actor stood out. Certainly one of the little-littles—the tiny children—might be picked up for representation by one of the agencies that had a big commercial department, but that would have happened with or without the showcase. All Mimi had to do was pick up the phone and make a call or two, send over a few headshots electronically—God bless the Internet—and the child was in. Placing the older kids was

tougher. Bethany Rabinowitz, for instance, had been a hard sell
to Big Talent. Mimi had had to court Holly Jensen with a box
of hand-dipped chocolates and a bottle of decent wine. Laurel
had taken considerable work, too. Her skin was what sold her,
initially, but her agent, Ruby Johnson, who was with one of the
medium-size agencies, had been pleasantly surprised when she
found that the girl could actually act, though Mimi had been
telling her so over and over.

Finally all the kids and parents had gone off to do whatever
kids and parents did on Saturdays. Mimi sent the Orphans off
with one of the studio moms to hang out at the Oakwood for
the afternoon. Then, finally, she locked the studio door and
kicked off her shoes—she'd been having trouble with swell-
ing lately, indicating a possible circulatory or water-retention
problem, neither of which she had time for—and turned with
some satisfaction to her computer screen. Tina Marie nipped at
an itch on her front leg, then curled up in her bed beneath the
desk, sighing heavily. Through hard experience, Mimi kept the
dog closed in her office during showcases rather than risk an accident on one of the panelist's handbags, which had been known
to happen when Tina Marie felt the studio's noise and activity
levels were excessive.

For Mimi, Saturday was a day to go through the past week's
breakdowns—the casting studios' calls for auditions. During the
week she went through them at warp speed—dozens, if not
scores, came out every day—but Saturday was the day to make
sure she'd gotten her clients matched up with every last audition
at which they'd make a reasonably strong showing. She could
introduce a new client to a casting director this way, even if she
knew there was no chance of a callback, never mind a booking.
It was dumbfounding how many kids most casting directors
could keep in their heads, and accurately, too. More than a few

times she'd had one call her to request a child she hadn't seen in a year, and she had the kid right, the part right, and always brought the child to at least one callback.

She paged through the calls: *House, The Suite Life, Ned's Declassified School Survival Guide, Ghost Whisperer, Unfabulous,* feature film, student film, student film, *The Closer, Entourage,* voice-over for a horror film (*must scream*), cartoon voice-over for the millionth *Land Before Time, The Mentalist, Heroes,* a CW pilot. The episodic season was in full swing. Mimi had just settled down to read the breakdown for the pilot—pilots always held the possibility of becoming shows that were picked up for years—when her phone rang. She looked at her caller ID and grabbed it on the second ring.

Fifteen minutes later she was in her car, headed for an exclusive little bistro on Ventura Boulevard.

EVELYN FLYNN WAS A GORGEOUSLY WRAPPED PACKAGE OF a woman. Her highlights had highlights; her sweaters were cashmere. She was what happened when money and ego met power. Feared by both child actors and parents alike, she had the perfectly honed instincts of a slave trader and could assess a kid in under ten seconds flat. Give her a child with talent—a Dakota Fanning, an Abigail Breslin—and she could peddle that flesh straight to the top with a network of contacts from agents and producers to network executives. She *made* people, and once you made people you could file your nails without a hint of conscience during the auditions of kids too green to cast until they'd toughened up on someone else's watch. She was not the bitch she was widely held to be; she just knew when to cut her losses. Though she prided herself on looking fifty-something, she was really sixty-something and had honed her craft in the trenches of early TV, when the technology consisted of baling

wire and electrical tape and the single essential quality in any
TV actor was his ability to withstand anything without losing
it live and on camera.

She clicked her nails on a glass of iced tea. Her hands were
her vanity, long and slim and younger-looking than the rest of
her. The tea had been garnished with a wedge of lime and a
sprig of fresh mint that Chef Paul grew in a window box just
for her. She regarded Mimi Roberts across the table, trying to
remember the woman's story: single, possibly lesbian, a veteran
of the industry; she'd been around for years and years, almost as
long as Evelyn herself.

"Talk to me about Quinn Reilly," Evelyn said.

The woman regarded her shrewdly for a minute or two.
"He's one of the most talented actors I've ever had," she said.
"Maybe *the* most talented. But he's difficult."

"Difficult how?"

"Unpredictable. Unless you keep him busy, he's disruptive."

"Can he be controlled?"

"Most of the time."

"ADHD?"

Mimi nodded. "His family gave him to me a few years ago,
and now they don't want him back."

Evelyn nodded. This happened sometimes.

"Why are you asking?" Mimi asked.

Evelyn stirred a packet of Splenda—she hadn't tasted real
sugar in decades—into a fresh glass of iced tea. When she finished she smiled and nodded to an actor at the next table who'd
been somebody to watch in the late eighties but had subse-
quently failed to deliver. Now he speared the last shrimp in his
lunch salad like it was his final meal. Mimi repeated, "Why?"

Evelyn nibbled a single spear of chilled asparagus. "I'm going
to be casting a pilot."

Mimi straightened in her chair.

"Disney's floating a treatment—it's still on the down low—about a wealthy LA family that has their own kid and three who are adopted—an Asian, a black, a Native American. Now they're expecting triplets. It's called *Bradford Place*."

"So what's the role?"

"The boy babysitter from the mansion next door."

"Is he gay?" Mimi asked.

"Not so far. Is Quinn gay?"

"He may have issues."

Evelyn just shrugged. "That shouldn't be a problem, as long as he keeps them off the set," Evelyn said. She'd seen this time after time after time with boys in their mid to late teens. Acting was a little too close to playing dress-up. They were teased mercilessly when they were young, and then they grew up and became Patrick Dempsey. Or T.R. Knight. A sweet revenge, whichever side of the street you were on.

"I'll send you the breakdown," Evelyn said. "The character's a regular, not a recurring. The producers are going to spend a wad on big names for the mom and dad, so they're looking for someone who's not going to cost a fortune."

"What's the timing?"

"It's a mid-season replacement, so soon. Officially, the breakdowns come out next Monday. Unofficially, I'm taking the kids to producers the day after tomorrow. I want him to read for me before then. If I like him and they like him, he'll go to network on Friday."

"No problem," said Mimi. "Sides?"

"They're already in your e-mail. I assume you can get them to him."

Mimi nodded.

"Good," Evelyn said, brushing her hands off. "Good, good, good."

She held up her credit card and their waiter came over instantly. For a woman with her reputation, Hollywood was a well-oiled machine. In just under four minutes she had taken care of the check, drained her iced tea, bid Mimi a pleasant good-bye, tipped the valet parking attendant, slid behind the wheel of her Mercedes, and set sail.

QUINN LOVED BEING ON STUDIO LOTS. YOU COULD SEE anyone and anything. He always went to the commissary after he auditioned on one of the lots, bought something cheap like a Coke, and sat for an hour just to see who walked in. He'd seen Colin Farrell, Vince Vaughn, Katherine Heigl. The last time, at the Warner Bros. lot in Burbank, he'd seen a woman in full evening wear—jewels, beaded dress, stole—with the hem of her gown chewed off and blood running down her legs from a shark attack or whatever. Probably a horror movie. She was walking with a guy wearing a tuxedo. No blood on him, though, so he must still be on the boat. Maybe he'd pushed her overboard. Maybe he was smuggling cocaine and she was a moll and squealed on him and now look. Bleeding makeup like crazy beneath the commissary table. He loved this shit.

Evelyn Flynn's casting office was on the Paramount lot. Today he was early, but not early enough to do the commissary first—he'd save that for after—so he just wandered around among the huge soundstages, peeking in when someone opened a door and dodging bicycles—the old, lumbering, funky kind with no gears and pedal breaks. There were bicycles all over the place. You picked one up, used it, then left it for someone else. You could cover a lot of ground on a bicycle in a hurry, which was important because the studio lots covered hundreds of acres and had twenty-five, thirty soundstages, plus all the outbuildings for the writers and casting directors and prop houses and costume shops and about a million other things, and cars were kept off the lot unless you were Steven Spielberg or Brad Pitt or someone. Otherwise you parked across Melrose Avenue and walked under a huge, fancy iron entry arch that made it look like you'd arrived at the gates to heaven. Which, as far as Quinn was concerned, you had.

At Mimi's explicit instruction, Quinn had dressed nicely and tried to look young and privileged, since the character he was auditioning for was sixteen and mega-rich. He wore his newest pair of jeans and a Ralph Lauren button-down shirt that he'd bought secondhand at *That's a Wrap!* for another audition and which he wouldn't be caught dead in, normally. He'd stuck the sides in his back pocket and looked them over again on his way to the casting office. He was off-book already; mostly he was reviewing them to keep his nerves in check. He still got nervous before almost any audition, which was why he had his little rituals: read the sides over one last time, even though he had a photographic memory; look skyward at the casting studio door, even though he didn't think he believed in God and certainly didn't pray; take a deep breath and do a shoulder shrug with his hand on the doorknob; and then he was in.

Evelyn Flynn's office was in a back corner of the lot, in a building that might have been a guest cottage once, in the days when the lots still had places for writers and visiting actors to live. The waiting room was dark and empty. He closed the door behind him, being careful to make sure it latched, and then stood there, trying to decide if he should call out and announce himself or just sit down and wait. Before he'd made a decision, an inner door opened, a pair of heels clicked in, and there was

Evelyn Flynn, standing before him with no smile and an out-
stretched hand, which he shook.

"I'm Quinn."

"I know. Come on back."

He'd been here at this casting office once or twice before,
but not in a long time. The waiting room was junky, which they
almost always were, because hundreds of people came through
every day—stained carpet, crappy folding chairs, a couple of
posters on the wall, a desk with a big phone console on it. The
back area was nice, though. Quinn could see that she'd tried to
make it feel a little homey—not like his home, but upscale, Pottery Barn homey. You could live in a room like this and never
leave, that's how nice it was.

The casting director walked behind a desk, grabbed a copy
of the sides, and then came around the desk again. A little video
camera was screwed onto a tripod in the corner, but she didn't
make any move toward it. "Okay. Let's run it once before we
put you on tape. Are you off-book?"

"Yeah."

She nodded. "Then let's go."

He was not unnerved by her lack of small talk. They never
talked. He sailed his headshot onto her desk and took a breath.
He was playing Will.

                    WILL
    Hey!

                JUSTIN ABERNETHY
    Will! Wow, are we ever glad you could come
    over! Listen, Cecilia's sciatica's bothering
    her again. I mean, when will these kids be
    born, right? So I'm going to take her out to
    lunch. Can you watch our guys?

                    WILL
Sure, no problem. I don't have to pick up
Stacy until five.
                    JUSTIN
You guys are still going strong, huh?
                    WILL
Yeah. It'll be eighteen months next Tuesday.
She keeps track.
                    JUSTIN
Well, good for you. But listen, here's a word
of advice from one who knows: don't have kids
until you're thirty-five.
                    WILL
No kidding. I mean, I love your kids, don't
get me wrong—
                    JUSTIN
Yeah, we know you do. Hey, did we tell you
Bruce is walking now? Yeah, last Wednesday
was the big day. Cecilia started crying. Her
hormones are totally screwed up.
                    WILL
Sweet.
                    JUSTIN
That Bruce.
                    WILL
Yeah. I bet his real mom was a beautiful
woman, like Pocahontas.
                    JUSTIN
Now, we don't talk about 'real moms' here,
because that would make Cecilia a fake mom,
right?

```
                    WILL
        Oh, jeez! I'm sorry.
                    JUSTIN
        That's okay. We just need you to be sensitive
        to that.
                    WILL
        Hey, sure, of course. Sure. Won't happen
        again.
                    JUSTIN
        Good man.
```

"Okay," Evelyn said. "That was the straight read. Now take it over the top. Pretend it's a sitcom."

They ran it again.

"Okay," said the casting director. "Now make it creepy."

"Creepy?"

"Yeah, like you're not sure whether you're going to cuddle the kids or feel them up."

Quinn flushed. He wondered if Mimi had told her anything about him. Still, he prepared himself and they ran it.

"Okay, now we're ready," she said. "I want to put you on tape playing it straight and then creepy. It's not a sitcom, so forget that one. I just wanted to see what you did with it."

"Okay."

She went to the camera and fiddled with a button or two, sighted him through the lens, and turned it on.

He slated, delivered his lines both ways, and she thanked him and turned off the camera. He took his ratty copy of the sides off her desk and was just turning to leave when she said, "You're good."

"Yeah," Quinn said. "I know."

Chapter Seven

HUGH ALAN RABINOWITZ LOVED THE PRACTICE OF DENtistry. The human tooth was one of Mother Nature's engineering marvels, infinitely variable in its colors, surfaces, and alignments, not to mention the mysteries that lay hidden beneath the gum line. A tooth, like a gem, was a paradox, at once strong and fragile, utilitarian and ornamental, perfectly designed yet containing, from the moment of its eruption, the makings of its own demise, whether it be from careless hygiene, vitamin deprivation, a misaligned bite, structural flaw, weakened enamel, or that enemy of everything dental, CornNuts. All your life you've exerted 150 pounds per square inch on all manner of food items—never mind the odd ballpoint pen—and your teeth have worked like a charm. Then, seemingly out of the blue, comes the fatal moment when you bite into something you shouldn't, and *bink!* The tooth falls away and the dentist becomes a demi-god. How many times had he been sent sentimental greeting cards thanking him for his technical prowess and delicate touch?

Many dentists are chatty, trying to keep their patients entertained or at least distracted until the Novocain takes hold. They prattle on about some achievement of a child's or spouse's, and the patient, out of good manners if not respect, is left struggling against cotton packing, dental instruments, and the suction device to form a decipherable comment. But Hugh had long since developed the habit of practicing dentistry quietly, even silently. Of the two of them, Ruth was the people person: warm, curious, and long-memoried when it came to children's names and natures, in-law troubles, spousal disappointments, and temperamental peccadilloes. He worked away in happy silence, scraping and drilling and shaping and packing and tamping his way to what was, in either half-hour or full-hour blocks, a tooth skillfully, even lovingly, restored.

In fact, over the twenty-two years of his marriage he had developed the habit of saying less and less about more and more, letting Ruth talk for them both. But Ruth was in Los Angeles with Bethany, hell-bent on making Bethy a star. As though, even if it were possible—which Hugh very much doubted— that ever worked out very well. He wasn't oblivious; he read the headlines about Lindsay Lohan and Britney Spears and that insipid blond girl, the Hilton heiress. Stardom, schmardom—it wasn't healthy.

But Ruthie didn't agree with him there. "It's up to the family to keep them grounded," she'd said. "Blame the family, not celebrity. Look at Natalie Portman, Jodie Foster, Meryl Streep. Regular people with solid families." For all he knew, she could have a point. Hugh didn't make a practice of studying movie stars the way Ruth did, though he subscribed to *People* magazine for the waiting room (after Ruth had finished reading them). All he knew was that Seattle Children's Theatre programs had been just fine for Bethany for years, and he saw no reason to change the scale or direction of her relationship with the dramatic arts just because some bottom-feeding talent manager wanted to sell them a bill of goods. And at least theater had its rich heritage. Hollywood successes came to a handful of greedy, manipulative, driven people whose main talent was knowing how to stand on the shoulders of sweet, ethical people like his Ruth to get themselves noticed. It was not a business to encourage a child to pursue. Already, from Ruth's stories, his belief that the industry was filled with unscrupulous sharks was proving true. Mimi was at the top of his list, though not Ruth's. Ruth thought Mimi walked on water. Hugh thought she was a toad-faced charlatan, gourd-shaped and squashy as aging fruit. How much money had they paid her—or someone else because of her—in the last six weeks for classes, coaching, headshots, wardrobe, and personal grooming? Never mind the travesty of Bethany's teeth—dear God, Invisaligns! You couldn't correct a bite with plastic, and Bethany happened to have a pronounced cross-bite that was guaranteed to give her TMJ problems later in life if it was incorrectly treated.

All of this was dangerous, possibly even ruinous, and not only financially. What did it do to a child to have the constant noise of rejection ringing in her ears? What did it do to her self-image to be hired or turned away based almost exclusively on her appearance? "We don't have anyone who looks like her on our roster," her agent had apparently told Ruth when she agreed to take Bethany on.

"Shouldn't it be about talent?" Hugh had said to Ruth over the phone, but Ruth wouldn't hear a word he had to say. She wanted what she wanted; and because there was very little that she wanted, she pursued whatever it might be with a single-mindedness that bordered on obsession. She'd wanted their little house in Queen Anne even though they couldn't afford it, and in support of their low-priced offer she'd harried the Realtor and the owner's Realtor with written pleas, statistics, even photographs of baby Bethany, then two, who had never had a yard to play in before. They'd gotten the house. When Ruth had her blood up about something, all you could do was step aside until the train had rocketed past, and then find a way to meet it at the end of the line.

So he ate the food he knew how to prepare and talked with

Ruth at least once a day, even if he had to leave a patient in the chair. Often, these conversations followed the lines of what he'd come to think of as Mimi Says. "Mimi says we need to get Bethy into a voice-over class." "Mimi says we need to buy Bethy audition clothes in corporate colors like red and blue for when she goes out for commercials for Safeway or Toyota." "Mimi says we need to smile, bend over, and take it in the financial ass." Not that Ruth had said that last one, of course—at least, not in so many words—but from where Hugh was standing it amounted to the same thing. He was up to *here* with Mimi Says. In the last six weeks Ruth and Bethany had spent more than six thousand dollars, though some of that, of course, was the refundable security deposit on the apartment that was, according to Ruth, an unredeemable piece of shit.

So Hugh worried. He worried all the time, though he'd probably never get credit for it. He worried about Ruth's nerves, Bethany's self-image, their overall health and well-being, the Toyota's solenoid going bad again. But what he worried about the most—and he'd only mentioned this once to Ruth—was the Big One. Every day he seemed to hear or see something in the news about California being way overdue for a major earthquake, and it scared the dickens out of him. The one in the Indian Ocean in 2004 had been a 9.3 and look what it had done to Indonesia. That *exact same thing* could happen in LA any day and anywhere, including under Ruthie's feet, and then what? But she hadn't wanted to listen to that, either, saying, "You drive a car every day, and that's more likely to kill you than any earthquake."

He'd said, "People in Pompeii scoffed, too, and look how *that* worked out," but he might just as well have been talking to air.

Last night she had called and told him, with great excitement,

"Bethy got a new monologue to perform at the next showcase. And it's harder than the last one. That means Mimi thinks she's ready for more advanced material. Isn't that exciting?"

"How much did it cost?"

There'd been a beat of stony silence and then Ruth had said in an injured tone, "Eleven ninety-nine at French's bookstore, but that was for a whole *book* of monologues, which she could be using for years."

"She's probably a shareholder."

"Who?"

"Mimi Roberts. She's probably a silent partner in that bookstore. Is there anything she tells you to do that *doesn't* involve money?"

Another beat.

"Honey?" said Hugh. There'd been more silence, and then Hugh had sighed and said, "Josh invited me to have dinner with him and Barbara Thursday night." Josh was an old friend from dental school. "He says I look like crap."

"I'm sure you look just fine, Hugh," Ruth said, and in her voice there was an edge of coolness he hadn't heard in years, not since they'd agreed it was best to talk about his mother as little as possible.

For the first time since the conversation had started he said something he actually meant. "I wish you'd come home."

"Well, but we're here now."

"I know you're there."

"Okay," Ruth said.

"I love you."

"I know you do, honey," Ruth had said contritely. "I'll call you tomorrow. I'm going to put Bethy on the line now."

He heard a minute or two of muffled conversation that, if he interpreted it right, was about Bethany's having to pick up the phone even if she *wasn't* in the mood to talk anymore, and then there she was on the other end of the line, using her false, sweet voice.

"Hi, Daddy."

"How are you, honey?" he said. "Mom says you're going gangbusters down there."

"I guess," she said in the distracted way that meant she had her Game Boy in play.

"Tell me about today. You feeling like a movie star yet? Your mom says you're kicking butt."

"I wish you'd come down here," she said, and just like that she was eight years old again and homesick at sleep-away camp. Now, as then, it probably meant she was overtired.

"Me, too, honey."

"So, when *are* you coming?"

"I don't know yet. Maybe next weekend. How would that be?"

"That'd be awesome, Daddy. I wish you could bring Ri-anne, too," she said, suddenly wistful. Ruth had told him she hadn't made friends at Mimi Roberts's Studio for the Swindled yet, though apparently there were lots of kids.

"Well, maybe we can work something out if you guys are still there for winter break," he said.

"What do you mean?"

Her voice was rising, never a good sign in his little girl. "What do you mean, what do I mean?"

"You said *if* we're still here. You're not going to make us come home? Because we *can't*—"

"No, honey," he soothed. "Of course I'm not going to make you come home." As though he could, even if he'd wanted to.

"Okay," she said, "because we really really can't come home, Daddy."

"No?"

"No," she said emphatically, and then she told him she loved him and he told her he loved her back, and she got off the phone and he got off the phone and was left to the deep, deep silence that happens when, by virtue of who's missing, a house is no longer a home.

THE NEXT MORNING, RUTH MOVED AROUND THE TINY kitchen at the Alameda Extended Stay Apartments, with its gummy shelves and scorched plastic cookware, making an omelet. She'd resolved that there would be no more calorie and cholesterol fests at Denny's. They were going to eat healthfully now, because if Ruth gained any more weight she'd have no choice, she'd have to move up another pants size, and the last thing they could afford to buy was new clothes. No, the money they spent down here went exclusively toward Bethany's career.

Bethany sipped at her glass of orange juice while Ruth plated the eggs, which they gamely choked down as the foundation for what looked like another busy day in Hollywood. Bethany had two auditions—a commercial audition over in Hollywood, and a theatrical one in West Hollywood—with a coaching session in between. Mimi had told Ruth emphatically to have Bethy looking bright and chipper. Neither of them was actually sure what this translated into, but they put Bethy in a cute little skirt and perky top and left the apartment without washing the dishes. With luck, this was the day housekeeping was scheduled to come by.

Their first stop was Kinko's on Pass Street, where they printed out MapQuest directions and Ruth ruminated over whether it would save money in the long run to look for a cheap printer at Costco, because this Kinko's business was not only getting expensive, it was also one more logistical complication in a day already chock-full of complexity. Back in the car they did their usual pilot-to-copilot routine, checking off their ready-list of headshot, résumé, sides, audition addresses and phone numbers, water bottles, PowerBars, lip balm, and maps. Troops went into battle less well-equipped.

In an act of God, the traffic was relatively light, and they found the casting studio at 200 La Brea without incident and ten minutes early. Parking, on the other hand, was a nightmare, with nothing available for three blocks in any direction. Ruth finally pulled into the Ralphs parking lot around the corner and Bethy told her they'd get towed—they were parked just two cars away from a sign claiming the lot exclusively for Ralphs grocery customers—and Ruth told Bethy they'd just buy a muffin or something after the audition, which made it all right.

The studio was one floor above a seedy old Petco and consisted of a huge central waiting room that smelled like feet, and onto which eight doors opened. These eight studios were assigned to eight different clients casting eight unrelated commercials. When Ruth and Bethany got upstairs they worked their way into a crowd of people wearing, variously, evening wear, beach attire, golf ensembles, Christmas-themed formal wear, and, most memorably, Halloween costumes. Ruth hugged her purse a little closer in her arms. On a large whiteboard they saw that their commercial audition was being conducted in Studio Six. Bethany filled out a size card, which listed her pants inseam, bust and waist measurements, and hat size. When she was done, a tall young man with spiky black hair and a number of lip rings approached them and took Bethany's headshot and résumé.

"Up against the wall," he told Bethany.

"What?"

He held up a Polaroid camera.

"Oh!" Bethany said, and put her back against the wall and smiled. The guy snapped a picture and stapled it to her size card.

"Who's your mother?" he said.

Bethany gestured toward Ruth.

The guy smiled. "No, girlfriend, your *audition* mother. Have we given you a mother yet?"

"Oh! No."

The casting assistant gestured to a woman easily five years younger and fifty pounds lighter than Ruth and stood her beside Bethany. "There. She's your mom. We'll take you two together. Okay?"

"Okay."

"Good girl." He winked at Bethany, for which Ruth was so grateful she felt momentarily teary. "Any little kindness," one of the other moms had said to her several days after they arrived here. "You'll see. Pretty soon you're going to be grateful for the tiniest little thing, like their remembering your kid's name for more than five seconds."

"Hi," said the faux mother, moving over on the gray carpeted benches in the bullpen.

"Hi," Bethany said. "You don't really look like my mom."

"I'm her mom," Ruth apologized. "So, you know."

"Oh," said the not-mom.

"Do you have children?" Ruth asked politely.

"God, no."

And that was that. A few minutes later the casting assistant called their names, and Bethany and her faux mom went into a studio and shut the door.

Ruth tried to get comfortable on the rocklike bench. On an opposite bench a woman was crocheting a circular garment with lurid orange yarn. "Ugly, I know," the woman said, seeing Ruth watching her. "I only do it so I don't eat."

"Eat?"

"I'm a serial snacker," she said. "Bad habit. My coach gave me this to do, instead." She held up the knitting.

"Coach?" Ruth thought the woman didn't look very athletic. Then she realized the woman must be referring to a life coach, someone who apparently helped you figure out what you wanted to be and how you were supposed to get there. Ruth had only recently heard of this. In her head she could hear Hugh say, *Funny—in the old days, that's what parents were for.*

"Yeah," the woman said. "I don't really know how to make anything, though, so I just make scarves, and then we give them to St. Vincent de Paul. I saw a street person wearing one of them once, just off Lankershim in North Hollywood. He had this huge shopping cart piled full of garbage and plastic bags and old clothes and stuff. And my scarf."

"Well, at least you know someone's using it."

"I guess. It was pretty nasty, to tell you the truth. I bet that man hadn't bathed in *weeks*."

"Well, it's probably hard when you're living on the street. I read an article once in the *New York Times* about how difficult it is to perform even the most basic hygiene—"

The woman gave Ruth a strange look and then rose as a curly-haired girl walked out of one of the studios and thrust her headshot at the woman snottily. "You gave me two. I looked pretty stupid. And you're always telling *me* not to waste them."

They walked away. Bethany was back just a minute or two later, with a lively step.

"It was pretty fun. We had to sing this song about frozen cookie dough." She sang a couple of bars. "*I love Chip-Chips, yes I do, from freezer to countertop in under two.*"

"Does that even make sense?" Ruth asked, but Bethany wasn't listening. She was soaring, making wings with her arms as they went down the stairs and out to the street.

"I bet I'm going to get a callback. I think he really liked me."

When they returned to the car and saw it hadn't been towed or ticketed, Ruth was tempted to just get in and drive away, but she had to set a moral example for Bethany, so they went into the supermarket, bought a *People* for Ruth and a *Teen People* for Bethy and two Snickers bars and a Diet Coke. From there, they drove to Greta Groban's apartment.

Greta Groban was Bethy's acting coach. She charged $75 for a half hour, $125 for a full hour, and either way Ruth suspected that Mimi received a kickback. How long the session lasted was up to Greta and Greta alone. She was German and she looked like Annie Lennox and her eyes were green and intense and possibly touched with madness and you didn't fuck with her. Mimi had told Ruth that; several of the studio moms had told her that; Greta herself had told her that. Ruth was scared to death of her. "You want your child to book?" she had barked at Ruth on their first meeting. "You bring her to me. And you *leave* her with me—no sitting in the room listening. You go away until I have Bethany call you on your cell phone. It could be fifteen minutes, it could be an hour and a half, and I can't tell you which because I won't know until we begin the work and once we begin the work we cannot be interrupted. Oh, and one thing: do not expect miracles. I cannot make your daughter book. If I could, I would charge more. That was a joke. What I can do is make her a stronger ac-tor. And the last thing is, my rates are not negotiable and I expect to be paid in cash, in full, at the end of the session. Period." It was like receiving ransom instructions from a convicted felon.

Greta's building, with its tony Beverly Hills zip code, was exactly two buildings on the right side of the city limits, in a building that Ruth imagined had seen better days—say, in the 1970s. Its tiny foyer had foil wallpaper with a big bubble pattern, and its canvas awning was worn through in a couple of spots. Ruth had gone upstairs with Bethy the first time, and the apartment was underfurnished, underaccessorized, and completely lacking in warmth or character. There was a leather couch, a huge flat-screen TV, a battered coffee table, a cheap and leaning floor lamp, and nothing else, not even a token vase. As Greta had explained it, the room was meant to be an empty vessel that would be filled with the energy of whoever performed there. Ruth found it depressing, but if it helped Bethany succeed at her audition, she was fine with it.

Once she'd made sure Bethy had the correct sides and had been safely admitted through the locked front door, Ruth slunk around the corner to a possibly illegal parking spot where she could hunker down, out of sight, until she was summoned. She felt like she was on a stakeout; if she could have located one of Greta's apartment windows and seen Bethy through it, she would have spent the entire session with a pair of high-powered binoculars in her hands. She loved to watch Bethy act. From the first time Bethy ever got onstage, she had come alive there. She outshined the other children, though she didn't know it; she became one of the unspoken favorites at the Seattle Children's Theatre, where she'd taken classes and performed in productions since she was seven. She'd already been to New York City to see, as Ruth had put it, the best of the best. Kristin Chenoweth and Idina Menzel and Joel Grey in *Wicked*. Taye Diggs in *Chicago*. They routinely went to the theater when the touring companies came through Seattle. They had CDs of nearly every major musical ever performed on Broadway.

Ruth's cell phone finally went off an hour and fifteen minutes later.

"I'm in the elevator," Bethany said. "God, Mom, she kept making me do the scene *over* and *over*, and I couldn't tell what she wanted me to do, and have you looked at your watch, because we're going to be *late*." Ruth could hear that Bethy was on the verge of either tears or hysterical laughter, which was pretty much the same thing.

"It's okay," Ruth said in what she hoped would pass for a calm and modulated tone while at the same time she started the car, threw it into gear, and gunned it away from the curb. Bethy came into view at a dead run and tried to get into the car while it was still moving, yanking repeatedly on the door handle, which released only when Ruth put the car in park, which allowed the door to suddenly fly open and hit Bethany on the shin with a crack Ruth could hear from inside.

"Ow," Bethy cried. "Owie owie. Go, Mom. *Go!*"

She slammed the door and buckled herself in and they ran a red light Ruth hadn't even *seen*, never mind stopped for. This was crazy; *they* were crazy, like a couple of bank robbers or bootleggers or Bonnie and Clyde. Bethy started giggling, Ruth did, too, and then there they were, pulled over to the curb and laughing themselves sick on Santa Monica Boulevard.

"She just gets me *going*, Mom," Bethy said when she could finally talk and they were on their way again. "She has this really intense *thing* she does when you don't do what she wants you to do because you can't *understand* what she wants you to do. She puts her hands on your shoulders and gets about one inch from your nose and says, *Focus, Bettany*—that's what she calls me, Bettany—*focus, for God's sake*. And I *am* focusing except now her nose is about the size of a rat and her breath is awful. Oh, and she said to tell you she charged a hundred and forty-five dollars this time because we ran long."

Ruth frowned. "Do you think she helped, though?"

"I don't know. I mean, she must have," Bethany said doubt-fully. "Mimi says a lot of her students are series regulars. She has this picture in her bathroom of her and some big-deal actor I never heard of. On the wall."

"Really? You used her bathroom?" Ruth asked. "So what else was in there?" Ruth loved visiting other people's bath-rooms.

"Well, she doesn't use toilet paper, I can tell you that," Beth-any said. "I had to use an old tissue I found in her wastebasket. There wasn't even a cardboard tube left. I bet she pees standing up. Maybe she's not even a woman. Maybe she's transsexual."

Ruth shuddered. She and Hugh set the highest possible stan-dard for bathroom hygiene. She tried not to let her horror show, but God only knew what had been on that tissue.

THERE WERE ONLY SIX OTHER GIRLS IN THE WAITING ROOM for the audition. They sat on opposing, heavy, old-fashioned wooden benches like you'd find in a train station. Bethany didn't recognize anyone, though she'd been hoping maybe Clara would be there. The girls and their mothers tried not to make eye contact with whoever was sitting opposite, and for a long time nobody came in or out, and the only noise was the rhyth-mic cracking of a tiny piece of gum that belonged to a rail-thin, bored-looking blond girl monitoring the sign-in clipboard and answering the telephone. Finally the other door in the room flew open, scaring them half to death because there'd been no sign whatsoever that anyone had even been in there, and a man Bethany assumed was the casting director appeared. He was balding, small, tiny-eyed, and had acne scarring on both cheeks. Bethany thought they probably hadn't had Accutane when he was her age. Maybe they hadn't even had antibiotics.

The casting director walked across the room to the skinny

blonde with the chewing gum and picked up the stack of head-shots.

"Let's see who we've got here," he said, leafing through. "Yeah, we'll start here. Tiffany? Tiffany, ah, Hanson?" He looked over the top of a pair of half glasses at one of the girls, looked at the headshot, looked back at the girl, and finally looked at a mousy woman sitting beside her. "Jesus. You the mom?"

The woman nodded.

"Look, get her new headshots, because you're wasting her time and mine. Okay? She's like four years too old. I'm not going to see her today. Sorry, kid."

The mother and daughter shuffled out of the room in silence and with their shoulders drooping. The casting director tossed her headshot back at the blonde and picked another from the pile.

"Anybody else not look like themselves?" he said. "No? Okay, Shana, Shana Stehnhope?"

A pretty little girl two seats away from Bethany hopped up, fluffing her hair, and followed him into his office. He closed the glass-windowed door behind them with a bang and a rattle.

One by one and without further incident the girls were ushered into his office. Bethany noticed that Ruth sat next to her with her hands tightly clenched in her lap and her eyes fixed on a square of old linoleum on the floor. She always got nervous before Bethy's auditions—more nervous than Bethy did, which seemed silly. Bethy had told her so, but she just said she couldn't help it. Because all that separated them was a door, you could hear each girl slate and deliver her lines, and Bethy thought most of them sounded pretty lame. No one was in the office for longer than about two minutes flat and no one said anything to anyone, not even her mother, until they were out in the hall.

The casting director said things in single-word sentences: *Go. Thanks. Okay. Next.*

Bethany was the last one to read. She didn't mind; Mimi had said you wanted to be either first or last, because those were the people the casting director stood the best chance of remembering, plus she was confident she'd be better than anyone. When he came out for her, he looked at her headshot, flipped it over to look at her résumé, flipped it back again, and said, "God."

Ruth's hands held each other more tightly in her lap. Bethany just sat up straighter, looking—she hoped—perky and worthy of fame.

"All right, honey, come on in," he said. A lot of people in Hollywood said *honey* and *sweetie*, and although it should have sounded friendly and reassuring, it never did. She followed him into his office, which was even messier than her room at home. There were stacks of headshots everywhere. He sat on a ratty sofa's one clear cushion, peered at her through the video camera mounted on a tripod to make sure she was in the frame, and gave her the go-ahead nod.

She looked straight into the camera and said, "Hi! My name is Bethany Rabinowitz, and I'm represented by Big Talent."

The casting director frowned at her headshot. "This says Bethany Ann Roosevelt."

Bethany clapped her hand over her mouth. "Oh, no. Can we start over?"

The casting director sighed and turned off the video camera. "Who came up with that name?"

"My manager. Mimi Roberts."

"Do you like it?"

Bethany started hearing a weird sort of roaring in her ears. She had no idea what she was supposed to say. "What?"

"Your name. Bethany Ann Roosevelt. Do you like it?"

"I guess. Not really."

"She didn't want you to sound Jewish, right?"

"No, I can be Jewish. I just can't be, you know, *Jewish*."

"She's a terrible manager. You might want to tell your mom that."

"She is?"

"She's a colossal pain in the ass."

Bethany sighed. "Yeah."

"All right. Go ahead and start over." He turned the video camera back on.

"My name is Bethany Ann Roosevelt, and I'm represented by Big Talent."

The casting director looked at a ratty copy of the script, and read the part of Heather, a bossy ninth grader. "*Who do you think you are, anyways?*"

Bethany as Lucy said, "*I'm Tina's sister and I don't think you should say things like that about her.*"

"*Yeah?*"

"*Yeah. She's nice to everyone and Stuart likes her better than you, so get over it.*"

The casting director turned off the camera. Bethany was confused. "But I had two more lines."

"That's okay, kid."

He stood up, walked across the room, and opened the door.

"Oh," said Bethany. "Well, thank you very much for giving me this opportunity." That was what Ruth had worked out with her to say at the end of every audition, no matter how abysmal a failure it might be.

"What? Yeah, sure. Thank you." He let her out, closing the door behind her. It was like being excused from Eden, except that even God would have at least said, "Have a nice day," or something. She could hear him on the phone before they'd even made it out of the suite.

By the time she and Ruth got to the top landing, she was crying. "He didn't even let me do it all. And that was the part Greta made me work on the hardest." She delivered the line, full of feeling, to the stairwell: "*I just think if someone liked someone else more than me, that I'd be nice about it and be happy for them. So you know what? I feel sorry for you.*"

Ruth put her arm around Bethany's shoulder wordlessly and led her downstairs and away.

EVERY NOW AND THEN, FOR REASONS THAT WERE UNCLEAR even to him, casting director Joel E. Sherman decided to give something away: a costar role to the kid who was *not* the sure bet; the decision to bring straight to producers a kid who'd never had a guest-star role before. These were things he didn't have to do; things he could even be criticized for doing, since they all involved an act of enormous faith that a child actor could deliver under the hellfire that was network television: *CSI, Grey's Anatomy, The Closer, Ghost Whisperer.* On prime-time dramatic sets, even more than most, no one—not the director, not the assistant director, not the PAs—had time to coach, pamper, or reassure. You'd been hired at big-boy prices to deliver big-boy goods; your scene came up and you delivered, period. It made no difference whether you had to cry or tremble with fear or contemplate your dead mother using only your eyes to convey your emotions. You had just minutes to dredge up what you needed, and you did it all by yourself. If you blew it, you could be replaced by the end of the first day.

Mystifying as these decisions were even to him, Joel had never had a kid replaced. Not once. Producers trusted him to weed out the crap and zero in on the diamond, and he did;

it was as simple as that. And this time, his gut told him to choose this wide-eyed kid, Bethany Rabinowitz—Bethany Ann Roosevelt, *such* a crock of shit—and plug her into next week's *California Dreamers* as the sweet and plucky kid sister of one of the teens around whom the episode turned. She'd delivered her lines well, and she'd kept her poise even when he cut her off. That was important. The kid sister had only two small scenes, but the working conditions were difficult, because the one thing that was always lacking on the *Dreamers* set was time. More than a handful of adult actors had been broken on the rack of its production schedule.

He picked up the phone, flipped through a stack of headshots until he found hers, and dialed the kid's pain-in-the-ass manager. Normally he would have called the kid's agent directly, but he couldn't help himself: he wanted to screw with her a little. "Yeah, Mimi Roberts," he said when someone finally picked up the phone on the fifth ring. Soon he heard her wheezing on the other end.

"Yeah. This is Joel E. Sherman, how you doin'? Listen, I want to bring one of your kids to producers. Yeah, Bethany Rabinowitz. New kid."

"You mean Bethany Ann Roosevelt?"

"Not if she's going to be on one of my shows."

"I'm sure we can work something out," Mimi cooed. He could hear that she was trying to sound blasé but was nearly pissing herself. There were very few agents or managers who weren't afraid of him. If he didn't like them, their kids didn't audition for him, period, and right now he was casting some of the hottest shows on prime time. Truth was, Bethany Rabinowitz had gotten into the initial audition pool only because whoever had photocopied and assembled her headshot and résumé had left a huge smudge over Mimi Roberts's logo and contact information, and he hadn't spotted it when he threw her headshot into the audition pile. *Roosevelt.* Please.

"All right, listen," he told the woman now. "Have her at my office at two o'clock tomorrow afternoon. Yeah. And make sure she's on time."

What he hadn't told her was that Bethany Rabinowitz was the *only* kid going to producers. They trusted him that much.

THE NEXT AFTERNOON AT EXACTLY TWO O'CLOCK, THE casting director introduced Bethany to the executive producer of *California Dreamers*, who had cost overruns on his mind and watched the kid's audition with a minimum of enthusiasm because it was just an under-five, for Christ's sake. Still, he maintained an absolute veto power over who set foot on his soundstage, right down to the one-liners. After she left he told Joel, "Yeah, yeah, set her up, she's fine. The mom's not going to be a nightmare, is she—you're willing to promise me she's not a nightmare? Because if she's going to be a nightmare—"

"Nah. Trust me, she'll be a mouse." He could promise this because he was going to give the mother explicit and personal instructions that if she so much as *spoke* to anyone, he'd never cast the kid in anything again for as long as he lived. Mothers couldn't stand him. He loved that. He picked up the phone and dialed Holly Jensen at Big Talent.

"Yeah, hey, Joel E. Sherman, how you doin'?" He liked Holly—young, good agent, big boobs, fun at a party.

"Joey?" she said. "Hey, how's my favorite casting director?"

The whole town turned on a wheel of bullshit.

"Just fine, baby, just fine. Listen, I want you to put one of your clients on avail for *California Dreamers*. They're on hiatus next week, so it's for the week after—Bethany Rabinowitz."

"Who?"

Joel sighed. "One of Mimi Roberts's kids, Bethany Ann Fucking Roosevelt. New kid."

"Oh, yeah. Really?"

He smiled at the phone. "Call me a nice guy."

"Sure, Joey. Everyone does."

"I must be slipping, then. I used to be a son of a bitch. Okay, but listen, here's the deal. We're going to credit her as Bethany Rabinowitz. You okay with that? Otherwise, there's no deal. Okay?"

"Okay."

HOLLY CALLED MIMI, AND MIMI CALLED RUTH, AND Ruth called Bethany to the phone and Bethany started crying and had to give the phone back to Ruth. "I don't know how we can ever thank you for everything you've done," Ruth told Mimi in a quavery voice. "You must be a miracle worker."

On her end of the line, Mimi just smiled.

October 2006

E*verybody wants to be special, it's just that in Hollywood it's not a dream, it's an industry. Delusion makes the world go round, but here it goes much faster and the spinning never stops. You can either hang on or you can let go. Or you can fall. A lot of people fall. Every day, all the time. Sometimes it happens in slow motion and sometimes it happens suddenly, but either way it's a hard landing. The kids are more resilient than the parents, at least most of the time. The parents are the ones who fall the hardest, and some of them never get up again.*

—VEE VELMAN

Chapter Eight

ON A BEAUTIFUL SUNNY TUESDAY IN OCTOBER, LAUREL Buehl reported to the PA on a commercial shoot for a Midwest fried chicken chain. Laurel hated fried chicken—some daughter of the South *she* was, Dillard was always teasing her—and she especially hated drumsticks. If you looked closely you could see that they were mostly tendons and blood vessels and cartilage. Even the thought made her a little sick. But she'd booked this commercial above hundreds and hundreds of other girls and she was going to do the best job she could.

The shoot was taking place inside an older production studio. Everything had been painted with shiny gray marine paint, including all the pipes and exposed wiring. A bank of monitors was set up at the far end of the space. The set itself was a kitchen, with a refrigerator, sink, range, cupboards, dishwasher, and microwave. The refrigerator had a couple of photographs stuck on it with magnets, like a real kitchen, and Laurel could see a takeout menu pinned up there, too—advertising the chicken chain, of course. She wondered who the kids were in the photos. Maybe they were the client's kids. Producers did little kiss-ass things like that on commercial shoots, she'd noticed. Someone from the ad agency that was making the commercial had said the budget to shoot it was $250,000, partly because it was a union gig. If it had been nonunion, she'd be paid peanuts, like she had been before she'd become a SAG member. Her nonunion commercials had paid $150. This commercial paid $2,000 up front, plus thousands in residuals every time the commercial was aired anywhere. The best of all was when you were in a commercial that was shown nationwide during prime time, like the McDonald's commercial she'd shot last week. Mimi had told Angie that they might be able to put away enough to pay for college with just that one commercial. Not that they were doing it for the money.

The PA, who Laurel identified by the headset and clipboard, was tall and skinny and had black hair, a lip ring, and sleeve tattoos. His T-shirt said THE MATRIX, so she figured he'd probably worked on the movie. She'd love to have a shirt or jacket with the name of a movie on it. It would mean she'd gotten theatrical work at last. Not that commercials were bad. When she checked in with him, he grasped her arm and said, "Thank God."

"Am I late? It's seven thirty. Wasn't that the call time?"

"For you, yeah," said the PA. "For your frickin' little brother it was seven. Do you see the little shit around here anywhere, because I sure don't, and the client's having a fucking *cow*. Come on over. I want you to sweet talk them, get their minds off the kid for a couple of minutes."

Laurel approached a young woman in jeans and very high stilettos, and an older man in a Hawaiian shirt that failed to conceal a considerable gut. He was from the chicken chain, and she worked for the ad agency making the commercial. Laurel recognized them both from her callback, and right now they looked furious. Laurel put on her best smile, and her best South'n voice, and said, "Hi! I want to thank y'all *so* much for letting me be in your commercial. And I love your chicken, by the way. We eat it any time we have family night, which is usually Thursday but if my daddy's working late, we make it Friday."

"How sweet," said the woman in the stilettos. Up close Laurel could see she had some hair loss on the crown of her head. She'd teased the hair around it a little and put a velvet headband on, but you could still see her scalp as plain as day. Laurel's nightmares included being bald by the time she was forty. Once you started paying attention, you saw women like that more often than you might think. There was a whole community of them out there using Rogaine in secret and considering spray-painting their scalps to make the thinness less noticeable. She'd seen commercials for that. Her hair was thin, but it was no-where near *that* thin.

Just as Laurel was trying to come up with something else to say—she was a pleaser, and she'd stay there doing her part as long as she possibly could or until the PA gave her the sign that she could be done—the kid playing her little brother showed up. His mother was just fit to be tied. "Oh, good lord—I'm *so* sorry," she said. "He's been up forever but he lost a shoe, and then he refused to leave without his Game Boy—"

"Yeah, well, at least you're here now," said the PA, taking the kid's elbow and pulling him a little roughly. "I need him in Hair and Makeup ASAP."

Laurel could see exactly why they'd cast him for the com-mercial. He was around nine or ten, and had freckles and huge ears and big front teeth. You could do really well in commer-cials if you had an extreme look; they didn't always want people who were conventionally good-looking. Laurel figured they'd cast her as the older sister because she was pretty, so she balanced things out. Plus the kid was the main person in the commercial. All Laurel was supposed to do was bite into a juicy drumstick and then high-five his piece of chicken with hers.

The smell of chicken was already coming from a catering truck. She hadn't even had breakfast yet. She started breath-ing through her mouth, a trick Angie had taught her when she was little because she'd always been odor-sensitive and used to throw up when she smelled things like bleach and garlic. Even so, her stomach rolled.

From across the set the PA signaled her to go to Hair and Makeup. She said, "Excuse me" to the ad agency woman and the client in the Hawaiian shirt and looked at Angie, who was sitting in a tall director's chair near the bank of monitors. She winked at Laurel and gave her a wan smile. Angie hated fried chicken almost as much as Laurel did.

"Okay, Brandon," the hair and makeup girl was saying. "I'm going to put some stuff in your hair, and then you can't touch it, okay? *Do not touch it.*"

The kid shrugged. "Whatever."

She put some hair product in her hands and then on his hair, which made it stand straight up all over. She stepped back a minute, pulled one piece into place, and said, "Nice."

The kid reached up and the girl slapped his hand away. "What did I just tell you? *Do not touch.*"

The hair and makeup girl did Laurel next, pulling her hair into a couple of low pigtails—Laurel hated low pigtails—and brushing on a little powder and eye shadow. "You did your makeup really well," she told Laurel. "I hardly have to do anything at all. And you have the most amazing skin. You probably hear that a lot, though." Laurel nodded; she did hear it a lot, but she didn't mind. "You know you're going to have to be really really careful, right?" the girl said. "How long have you been in LA?"

"Five months."

"Yeah, I figured you weren't from here. You're probably a skin cancer magnet."

"SPF 60, every day," Laurel said. "I've never even had a sunburn."

"Good girl." The hair and makeup girl fluffed her pigtails, pulled a few tendrils loose, stood back, and looked at Laurel with satisfaction. "Okay, you're done. Break a leg. Or I guess I should say, bite a leg." They both laughed, and then the hair and makeup girl said, "Next!" and a woman approached her who Laurel figured must be the commercial family's mom. Once she was ready, the director—a young guy wearing Tommy Bahama loafers and a linen shirt, like he'd just flown in from Cabo or someplace—had them all sit at the kitchen table.

"Okay, Mom, I want you to look your son right in the eye and say, 'You know, it *is* chicken-lickin' good!'" the director said. "Then you kids are going to do the high five and take big bites of chicken. Okay? There are spit buckets under the table, but don't spit anything out until I tell you it's okay, because otherwise you'll ruin the shot. You have to chew, too—not just hold it in your mouth. Okay?" Everyone nodded. "Okay!"

For the next hour, they high-fived and took bites of chicken, chewed enthusiastically, and then once the director said, "Cut" they got to spit it out. Laurel lost count after the fifteenth piece of chicken. She could see boxes and boxes of it out by the craft services table. She looked at Angie from time to time, who smiled and mouthed, "Stay strong!"

They let her go two hours later, when she started gagging uncontrollably at every mouthful. "Hey," the director said. "What was your name again—Laurel? You did good, girlfriend. You can sign her out," he told the PA. Then, turned away from the client and the ad agency woman, he whispered, "I'd have been tossing my cookies an hour ago."

Laurel smiled but, professional to the last, she just said, "I hope you got what you needed."

"What?" he said. "Oh. Sure, yeah. Thanks."

On the way home they stopped and bought a Coke to settle Laurel's stomach and a backup bottle of Pepto-Bismol, just in case.

IN WEST HOLLYWOOD, QUINN LACED UP HIS PURPLE
Chuck Taylor high-tops and took some pains to find a shirt
that might be clean. He waited for Baby-Sue and Jasper to leave
the apartment and then he headed out himself. The day was
warm—of course it was warm, it was LA—and there was a light
breeze blowing the trash around in the street. At the corner he
saw a used condom in the gutter. Someone had gotten lucky.
Where would you have sex on a street like this, though? In an
alley, maybe; or behind one of the spindly oaks embedded in
the sidewalk. But then you'd have to take off the condom, stuff
your slimy dick into your pants with one hand while you held
the loaded condom between two fingers of the other hand, and
carry it to the gutter. Who would bother with that? Maybe the
woman. Women did that kind of thing, putting stuff in the
right place even if it was trash and disgusting.

He stopped in front of Hazlitt & Company. The salon was
packed this morning, noisy with hair dryers and laughter.
Quinn's plan had been to come to the salon, see that the stylist
was busy, turn right around, and go back to the apartment. But
the stylist glanced at the door, saw Quinn, and waved him in.
He already had a client in his chair and Quinn intended to cut
and run, but his shoes took him inside, instead. The stylist said
something to the man whose hair he was cutting—an olive-
skinned, jet-haired, bright-toothed man who looked vaguely
familiar; Quinn could almost remember the skin-care ad—and
came over to Quinn, who was standing just inside the door like
he'd washed up there and stuck.

"Hey." The stylist put his hand on Quinn's shoulder. The
hand felt warm and light through Quinn's shirt. "I'm almost
done with this one, and then I've got a break. Stick around.
Read a magazine or something. I'll fit you in."

Quinn had never really meant to get a haircut, though he

did have money in his pocket because his mother had just sent him his thousand-dollar-a-month allowance. But the stylist had returned to his station before Quinn could tell him that he was only—what? Checking on the stylist? Lonely? Sadly, he did have time—no auditions today or classes, and of course there was never school—so he sat on a stiff leather chair and watched his shoes until his pulse slowed down. Then the client was paying for his haircut and blowing a kiss over his shoulder to the stylist, who was sweeping hair clippings efficiently into a dustpan. After dumping the dustpan he walked over and Quinn got up and followed him meekly, his heart beating like crazy. He sat down in the chair, and the stylist whisked a black nylon cape around him, fastening a snap at his throat—his fingers were light against Quinn's neck, like moth wings—and then he looked at Quinn in the mirror and said, "What are we doing?"

Quinn flushed.

The stylist smiled. "Cut? Color? I hope not color. We talked about that."

So he remembered. Quinn wasn't sure he would. "Cut, I guess."

The stylist wove his fingers through Quinn's hair just like the last time; and like the last time, Quinn went heavy in the chair. He'd remembered the way it had felt exactly. He had to fight to keep his eyes open.

"Let me guess," said the stylist's reflection to Quinn's reflection in the mirror. "Your father still has a full head of hair. No? He's *bald*?"

Quinn shrugged, looked away. He didn't know—his father hadn't been in touch in years and years.

"Oh." The stylist looked dismayed. "Hey, I'm sorry."

"It's okay."

"Okay." The stylist pulled Quinn's hair back. "So what are we thinking?"

I'm thinking I wish you'd brush my hair some more. But of course Quinn couldn't say that, so he just said, "I don't know. Something."

"Well," ventured the stylist, "you've got some natural blond highlights. Are you thinking, like, maybe a surfer dude sort of thing? You're, what, sixteen?"

"And a half," Quinn said. "Sixteen and a half."

"We could make you look wholesome and tousled." The stylist ruffled the top of Quinn's hair, making it go flying around in different directions.

"Nah."

"Too young?"

"Yeah."

"So something edgy?"

Quinn just looked at him, having no idea what that might translate into.

The stylist smiled. "Uneven places. Some of it very long, some of it very short, and none of it where you'd expect it to be. Let me show you." He went off and rummaged around in a pile of magazines, dog-eared a couple of pages, and brought them back to Quinn. "Here are a couple of looks," he said. He stood right behind Quinn. Quinn could actually feel him breathe. He concentrated on the pictures, chose one that didn't seem too radical—casting directors didn't like radical—and the stylist strapped on a black canvas apron full of scissors and combs. Then he walked Quinn over to a sink and washed Quinn's hair, and Quinn thought it might be even more wonderful than the hair brushing and the head massage. He felt drunk as the stylist walked him back to his chair.

"So how long have you been acting?"

"What?"

The stylist smiled. "How long have you been an actor?"

"Since I was six."

"Are you good?"

"Very good," Quinn said, and it wasn't bragging, it was just the truth.

"I'll bet," said the stylist, snipping away. "Have I seen you on anything?"

Normally Quinn hated that question, but it was okay now. He shrugged. "Maybe. *ER. Grey's Anatomy. Cold Case.* A couple of Disney sitcoms when I was younger. Like that."

"I'd better watch for you, so when you get famous I can say I cut your hair."

Quinn didn't say anything. He hated when people said that, because usually they were just patronizing you.

"You think I'm just saying that, but I'm not," said the stylist.

"Do you do many actors?" Quinn had meant cut their hair, not *do* them. He blushed, but the stylist just went on cutting.

"Sure. Everyone in LA's an actor, right?"

"Yeah."

"If you mean actors you've heard of, only a couple." He named them, and Quinn had heard of them. One had been a regular on an NBC sitcom that had been canceled after one season; another hosted a reality show.

"It's hard," Quinn said, and then he flushed again. "Breaking in, I mean."

The stylist nodded and snipped, stopping occasionally to weave his fingers through Quinn's hair and shake it.

"Do you act at all?" Quinn asked. It was a dumb question, but he couldn't think of anything else to say. It wasn't like you could say, *I hope you work in this hair salon forever so I can come here sometimes and have you put your hands in my hair,* even though that was what he was thinking.

"Me?" The stylist smiled at Quinn in the mirror. "No."

"Yeah," said Quinn.

The stylist put his scissors back in their holster, shook out Quinn's hair again, and examined it in the mirror. Quinn thought that was funny, that his head was *right there*, and the stylist still looked at it in the mirror. It was like directors watching scenes on the monitors when they were happening live right in front of them. "Okay?" the stylist said, cocking his head one way and then the other, examining Quinn's hair critically.

"Sure," said Quinn, because he didn't really give a shit what it looked like.

"Do you want me to blow you?"

"What?"

The stylist looked amused and, Quinn thought, just the slightest bit sly, mutely holding up and shaking a hair dryer he'd taken out of a drawer. Then he spent five minutes blowing Quinn's hair all over the place. By the time he was done, it looked like Quinn had been caught in a storm. The stylist took some paste out of a jar, rubbed it between his fingers, and then picked through Quinn's hair, singling out and positioning pieces over his eyes, examining his handiwork critically in the mirror. When he was done he handed Quinn a small mirror and turned his chair so Quinn could see the back of his head, though Quinn had no idea what he was supposed to do, so the stylist had to position the hand mirror and then point Quinn out to himself in the reflection. Quinn nodded, trying to look serious and appreciative.

"Marc Jacobs," said the stylist, satisfied. He holstered his comb. "You could be right up there on that billboard on Highland." One of the other stylists stopped walking by and looked Quinn over. "Absolutely," he said, before going on to the back of the salon. Quinn figured they probably tag-teamed each other like that all the time to make their clients feel like they

were something special when really they were just people sitting in a chair wearing a weird nylon cape and hoping a haircut
would change their lives. He'd never seen a haircut, on himself
or anybody, that did that.

He started to get out of the chair, figuring they were done,
but the stylist put a hand on his arm—*No, wait*—and brought
out a big, soft brush and whisked the back of Quinn's neck and
his face. It felt like a whisper would feel if a whisper had weight,
and Quinn must have closed his eyes because he felt rather than
saw the stylist's hands at his neck, gently unsnapping the nylon
cape and flicking it away like a matador. Quinn didn't want it
to be over. He wished they could just start again, the whole
thing, from the minute he'd walked in the door; but the stylist
was already sweeping Quinn's hair off the floor into a dustpan.
They were done.

"You can pay up front, okay?" the stylist said when Quinn
hesitated. "And when you're going to be on TV, let me know,
because I'd love to see you."

"Yeah," said Quinn uncertainly. "Okay." The stylist didn't
look like he meant *see you*, in a datelike way. He gave Quinn a
smile and went to the back of the salon to empty the dustpan.
Quinn paid for the full price of a haircut at the reception counter and stepped out of the salon into the stagnant Los Angeles
afternoon.

IN SEATTLE, THE AIR WAS SO CLEAN AND CLEAR SOME DAYS
it hurt.

When Quinn was twelve and a half and still living there, he'd
been outside messing around with his bicycle when he overheard through an open window his stepfather, Nelson, saying
to his mother, "Jesus, Mona, can't you do something?" Nelson
was a real estate developer. He built strip malls around Bothell,

as though that's what the world needed, another goddamn strip mall. Quinn's half brother, Rory, who'd grown into a chubby, happy, endlessly cheerful boy loved by everyone in his T-ball league, fit in with them way better than Quinn ever had.

"Not to put too fine a point on it, honey, but he's, you know, *light*," Nelson had said. "He's going to start bringing home boyfriends sooner or later, and what effect is that going to have on Rory? The kid's impressionable."

"He's not gay, Nelson."

"Oh, come on. What kind of kid wants to spend all day wearing costumes and reciting poetry?"

"It's Shakespeare."

"It's gay."

His mom had sighed, because what could she say? Quinn sang to himself; he tried out martial arts moves on the furniture; he had great difficulty staying in his chair all the way through a meal.

"I don't know what you want from me," she'd said. "What do you want? You want me to put an ad in the paper and say, *Kid needs new home?* You can't just get rid of him because he isn't working out."

"Yeah," Nelson said disconsolately.

Quinn had no friends; even the kids and parents at the Young Actors Are We neighborhood theater program tended to steer clear of him. The other kids acted for fun, but Quinn acted like he was running for his life. While it was widely acknowledged that he was immensely talented, it was also true that he had a certain unnerving intensity about him. Still, the hours he spent at the theater program had been the happiest he'd ever known. But no one had any good ideas for his parents or for him, not even the people who ran Young Actors Are We, so they went on the way they always had, knowing a train wreck lay ahead.

And then, like an act of God, his mother spotted an ad in the paper:

LA talent manager offering intensive two-day workshop on Acting for the Camera for young actors ages 11 to 18. Call for details.

So Quinn's mother had called and Mimi Roberts had answered and a month later Quinn was on his way south, alone, for a young actors' boot camp. He'd looked around the studio, with its wall of headshots and Post-its declaring success— *Kellogg's! Burger King!*—and knew that at last he was in a place that spoke his language. Even for LA he was still on the outer edge of the rim, but what had been liabilities of character in Seattle were suddenly greatly in demand: fearlessness; a willingness, even a need, to do or say anything; an unpredictability and courage in creating and endowing characters. He wasn't acting; he was in a never-ending delirium of *being.* And that made him believable. Believability was Hollywood's Holy Grail, the most sought-after quality in an actor, and despite all the classes and methods and exercises, you either had it or you didn't.

Quinn had it.

He had been in LA for less than two weeks when he booked his first commercial, and right after that he'd landed a costar role on *CSI.*

From zero to sixty in fourteen days.

"My husband can't even be around him anymore," Quinn's mother had admitted to Mimi on the first day of the workshop in Seattle. She didn't think he could hear them, but he could. She'd poured herself a cup of coffee from an air pot in the lobby of the Comfort Inn where Mimi always held her workshops, and over her scalding cup she'd looked Mimi right in the eye and said, "I love him—don't think that I don't love him. I just don't know what to *do* with him."

So Mimi had offered them a solution: send him to her and she'd put him to work. With his abilities, it was virtually a guarantee. That had been almost four years ago, before Mimi had Allison or any of her other current clients-in-residence, just a mopey fifteen-year-old girl who was already outgrowing the minimal talent she'd once shown, and a fourteen-year-old boy named Duncan, whom Mimi had re-christened Dunham— *Dunham*—in hopes that it would make him sound hip and well-heeled instead of like baked goods. Ten months after Quinn arrived, both of them were gone and Quinn was working like crazy: on commercials, in industrials, in the occasional theatrical costar role. He booked his first guest star eight months later, playing a hemophiliac on *ER*.

And it was odd—inexplicable, really—but on sets, as no place else, Quinn became calm. His blood slowed down in his veins; his thoughts came home like pigeons to roost. Ritalin was supposed to have that same effect, but it didn't. He didn't know why. Maybe he wasn't ADHD enough; maybe he was *too* ADHD, and his neural system overrode the stuff, kicked into high gear when the drug made it put up a fight. Who knew? Who cared? All Quinn knew was that acting was the one thing he knew how to do better than almost anyone. Every new script was like Christmas morning. He approached every role, every scene, with perfect serenity and confidence, even if the character and action were crazy. Acting allowed him to feel and to see through the eyes of someone who got it right, where Quinn on his own always seemed to get it wrong.

And the thing was, he was a good kid. He was polite. He was nice to Mimi's other clients, even the bratty ones. He did chores around the house without complaining, and when he bounced off the walls Mimi just told him to either dial it down or take out the old push mower and mow the lawn.

At first his family flew him back to Seattle for a weekend once every two months, plus Thanksgiving, Christmas, Easter, and some of the summer. Mimi hung on to him for the rest of the summer because it was feature film season and she got him cast in small indies. Small roles, unknown movies, but with directors who were on the To Watch list. And with every role he landed, his acting got a little bit better. Now he hardly ever went home. He didn't even have a room there anymore. Nelson had turned it into a home office and fly-tying hobby room, installing a futon where his old bed had been. They all pretended he was so extremely busy in LA that it was hard for him to find the time to come home more often. At least at Mimi's he was productive and safe. It wasn't the greatest arrangement in the world, but it worked. At least it had until he'd pinched that stupid kid's nipples. Right after that Mimi had made him move out, said she didn't feel it was a good idea anymore to have him around younger children until he'd sorted some things out.

What the *fuck* did that mean?

It had been improv!

IT HAD BEEN IMPROV! He'd screamed that at Mimi and then he'd started sobbing—he couldn't help it and couldn't stop—and she'd just looked at him with her doughy moon face and said softly, "I don't have any choice."

Which was bullshit. *Bullshit.*

He knew Mimi had talked with his mom about sending him home. He knew because he'd picked up the extension in the kitchen. He'd lifted the phone very, very quietly in time to hear his mother say, "I'm sorry, but it just wouldn't work out."

It. *It* meant him, Quinn. People said stuff like that about the pool man, about the gardener. They didn't say it about their own kid. Not that he'd have wanted to go back to Seattle. But he'd have liked to be given the choice; he'd have liked to have the *illusion*, at least, that his family loved him and treasured him and counted the days until his next visit home.

Yeah, right.

Chapter Nine

HUGH'S ALASKA AIRLINES FLIGHT A WEEK LATER WAS HALF an hour behind schedule, overbooked, and full of very large men, one of whom was sitting much too close to him, wheezing. The stewardess—*flight attendant*; he knew, he knew—was on the cabin mike giving some cheesy come-on about an Alaska Airlines MasterCard promotion, like *that* was going to make a difference in how he felt about being stuck out here on the tarmac. Their in-flight snack, he'd seen in the galley as they'd boarded, was a piddly-ass envelope of pretzels the size of plug nickels, as though the whole damned bag and all of its contents had been downsized along with the crappy economy.

Or maybe it was just him.

He'd done one extraction, two root canals, five routine examinations, and several fillings today, and he was in no mood to be jacked around by an industry that was, frankly, doing a piss-poor job of moving the country's human cargo around, and for way too much money. He'd let Ruth talk him into this flight into Burbank—the Bob Hope Airport, for Christ's sake; what was next, the Howdy Doody Freeway?—even though it meant he'd had to creep away from his practice an hour early like someone slipping out the back door on a bad date, clutching the carry-on he'd packed last night. He'd parked in the economy lot and ridden the shuttle and checked in at the kiosks where no one even talked to you if you weren't checking baggage, which who needed to for this two-day conjugal visit; and he'd taken off his shoes and emptied his pockets—now there was a metaphor—and removed his watch and metal-framed glasses, and handed over his boarding pass and driver's license and allowed himself to be wanded by two crappily paid TSA employees in fake law-enforcement polyester uniforms. He'd answered their questions about his flammables and gels and lotions while fighting the nearly overwhelming urge to scream to anyone within earshot that he was going against his will to visit the wife and daughter he loved as much as life itself and who had lost their minds in Hollywood, California.

Admittedly, he was a tad keyed up.

No small man himself, he struggled to keep his knee from resting against the fat knee of the fat man beside him—their hips having already melded beneath the armrest—when they were asked at last to fasten their seat belts and make sure their luggage was stowed in the overhead bins or underneath the seat in front of them and to turn off all cell phones and any other electronic devices that might interfere with the airplane's navigation because they'd been cleared for departure.

Once airborne, Hugh washed down his gnat-size pretzels with the canned tomato juice he seemed to drink only on airplanes, and thought about what he could say to Bethany that would be honest and supportive. That he loved her, she knew. That he wanted to see all of her dreams come true, she also knew. But this wasn't the way; this was madness. She wasn't even fully a *person* yet, let alone an adult, but she was making decisions—Ruth was letting her make decisions—that would affect her for the rest of her life. Never mind what she was missing academically; by being homeschooled she would also never star in her high school plays or know the teamsmanship of volleyball—not that Bethy was an athlete by any means, but she *could* be—and proms and pep rallies and gossip sessions in study hall and in the cafeteria. Before Mimi Roberts hove into view like Satan incarnate they'd planned on sending Bethy to the Bush School. They'd talked and talked and *talked* about the broad foundation a private school of its caliber could give her, a platform from which to spring into a good East Coast college— Amherst, Dartmouth, Tufts, Wesleyan. And after that she'd be able to choose anything.

"Sure," Ruth had remarked the other night, in an increasingly familiar and bitter refrain. "You're not down here. You don't see what I do. Kids are making career moves at four years old, jockeying for position by the time they can read. And it matters. You can be over the hill in this business at seven, washed up by the time you're in braces. That's the thing of it, Hugh; there's no time. She's already late."

How, he wanted to know, could a child be washed up at anything before she'd even conquered geometry? Weren't those hypertalented child performers just freaks who, a hundred years ago, would have been traveling the vaudeville circuit? You couldn't convince him this was healthy. No one could. He had eyes; he could see. In the endless stream of new headshots Ruth kept sending him—my God, the *money*—Bethy looked less and less like his daughter, and more and more like someone he'd never met and wouldn't necessarily like if he did. The smile was a bit too wide, the eyes a bit too disingenuous, the *lipstick*. And what about the hair? Goy hair, that's what they'd given her, and though he'd never say so out loud, it diminished her. She looked like she was trying to catch up to pert and chiseled blondes in a race she couldn't possibly win. And it wasn't that he wanted his child to be labeled a Jew. In truth he was somewhat ambivalent about being a Jew himself—certainly he was realistic enough to know that it wasn't always an asset. No, he just wanted her to be herself, exactly the way she'd always been, funny and unselfconscious, strong and upright, and if that included looking like the Jew that she was, so be it. That was her identity, as much a part of her as her fingerprints. If Anne Frank were alive today, would she spend five hundred dollars on hair-straightening so she could land a one-line part on some stupid TV sitcom? He thought not.

He loved his family. He longed for his family. He wanted what was best for them. Ruth thought he was being selfish when he said he wanted them home, and it was true that the way he was living now felt like punishment, but he would have endured it gladly if he'd thought it was important, or even healthy. But Ruthie didn't want to hear that. She had a powerful will and a death grip on denial. Right now Bethy could fall into a pit of vipers and Ruth would call it an opportunity to demonstrate her fear-management skills.

Hugh peeled his knee off the knee of his seatmate yet again and watched parched brown hills pass beneath the plane. Soon the head flight attendant told them they should secure their tray tables and return their seat backs to a fully upright and locked position; and if those on the right-hand side of the plane looked out the window they would see the world-famous Hollywood sign as they made their final descent into hell.

RUTH SPOTTED HUGH FIRST. HE CAME OUT OF THE TER-minal and into the outdoor baggage claim area in a thicket of businessmen and Paris Hilton look-alikes wearing shoes from which you could fall to your death. Hugh hadn't seen them yet—he seemed to be trying to extricate himself from a tangle of wheeled carry-ons—and Ruth was stunned by his appearance. He was visibly sweating and his hair was sticking up in the back and his skin tone was gray. Had he always looked like this, and she'd just gotten used to it? Her mind's-eye view of Bethany was always a year or so out of date. . . . Anyway the moment passed as Hugh caught sight of Bethany. His face lit up and he was, once more, just Hugh.

Bethany squealed, sprinted to him, and threw her arms around his neck. He dropped his carry-on, wrapped his arms around her, lifted her a few inches off the ground, closed his eyes, and breathed her in. "How's my sweetie-girl?"

"Daddy, we have so much to show you!"

With Bethy clinging to his right arm and his carry-on slung around behind him, Hugh put his left arm around Ruth and gave her a hug. They walked awkwardly, all three of them locked together that way, until Bethy caught her arm on the strap of Hugh's carry-on bag and he lost his balance and veered into Ruth and they came apart.

Once they were in the car, Hugh said he was starving, so Ruth and Bethany, in a spirit of hyperfestivity, agreed that they *had* to take him to Bob's Big Boy immediately, even before they off-loaded his suitcase at the apartment. Hugh had been here just once before, when Ruth and Bethy first moved into their little apartment. He'd stayed for only a day, and they hadn't spent any of it sightseeing, unless you counted the inside of Mimi Roberts's studio as a sight.

"Daddy," Bethany said from the backseat, "you're just going to love it here so much. We need to take him to the Disney building, Mom, so he can see the seven dwarfs holding up the roof, and there's an iron fence around it that has these *things*—"

"Finials," said Ruth.

"—that are shaped like Mickey Mouse ears. And there's this older Disney building, too—it's where they do animation—and part of it is shaped like a huge wizard's hat, blue with stars, right, Mom, like from *The Sorcerer's Apprentice*?"

"Right," said Ruth, and smiled at Hugh: *Do you see how much she loves it here?*

"Oh, and tomorrow we should take him to Poquito Mas—it's a restaurant near us and they have this sign, Daddy, that if you see someone famous you should respect their privacy because taking their picture is rude. Mom and I like to eat there sometimes. We haven't seen anyone famous, but we probably will soon."

Ruth made a turn onto Alameda. Below the overpass, evening traffic clogged the 134. Ruth indicated the mess down there with a slight inclination of her chin. Hugh looked down and shook his head. Bethy just kept on talking.

"And we really want you to see where I audition, Daddy, even though we probably won't be able to go in because if it's on a studio lot you have to have permission, and you can only get permission from your agent or manager, and Mimi said she'd get us on a list only if I was really auditioning for something, and you hardly ever do, on a Saturday."

Ruth could see in the rearview mirror that Bethany's coloring was high, her eyes sparkling. She looked at Hugh, looked in the mirror at Bethy, looked back at Hugh: *How can you think this isn't worth doing? Look at her!* She couldn't judge Hugh's frame of mind, though. He seemed subdued. She felt a pang of guilt: he'd been back there in Seattle, alone and in the damp, while she and Bethy had been down here in LA having the time of their lives. She said to Bethany, "Honey, let's give Daddy a minute or two of quiet, okay?"

"Okay." Bethany subsided momentarily. "Oh! But Daddy, guess who we saw at Starbucks the other day? You'll never guess." Then she paused to let him guess. He couldn't.

"Nicole Richie! She was right there in front of Mom. She looked just like herself, too—I mean, she wasn't all made up and stuff and she was just wearing these old jeans and carrying a huge purse like you could carry a whole computer in, except then this *dog* pops out, I think it was a teacup Yorkie, lots of people have them here—"

"*Breathe,*" said Ruth.

"—and anyway, she looked just like a real person, but it was definitely Nicole Richie. We saw Kyra Sedgwick pulling out of the parking lot one time at Ralphs, too. She was driving this regular old car. What was it, Mom?"

Ruth just raised her eyebrows in the rearview mirror. Bethany had recently started asking gratuitous questions just to sound grown-up. Ruth felt the faint but distinct call of a headache coming on.

"Whatever," Bethy said. "The thing is, you never know who you might see. I mean, you can be just standing in line at Sav-On or wherever, and *boom*, right behind you there's Will Smith. It's *so* exciting."

Bethany sat forward and said to Hugh, "How come you aren't saying anything? Are you tired?"

"I'm fine," Hugh said.

"You don't seem fine. You aren't saying anything. Neither of you is saying anything."

"I was listening, honey," Hugh said. "But you weren't leaving a whole lot of extra leg room in the conversation. So I was listening. I'm still listening."

Bethany chewed a nail. "You don't even really want us here, do you?"

"Did I say that? I didn't hear me say that."

"Well, you don't. I know you don't," said Bethany.

And then they were at Bob's, where the weekly Friday evening gathering of classic cars was well under way in the parking lot. Luckily the wait inside was brief and they were seated at one of Ruth and Bethany's favorite booths near the front of the restaurant, where they could watch people come in. Their waiter was the shy Hispanic man who never showed any sign of remembering them, except that Ruth was sure he did because she made a point of always making eye contact with him and saying "please" and "thank you," which she doubted most other people did. She had the absurd urge to introduce Hugh, so he'd know she wasn't some sad woman adrift in a sea of single, fat, middle-aged women.

While they ate their burgers—Bethy had *insisted* they all get burgers—Ruth and Hugh made small talk about what one of his dental hygienists had named her new baby and how the annual pumpkin pyramid in front of the Queen Anne Albertsons had been destroyed by a nighttime vandal, spreading orange gore from the Halloween massacre on streets and sidewalks for blocks around. Hugh said the Neighborhood Watch committee thought it had a credible lead, and the police said they hoped to arrest a suspect by Monday; and Ruth said, "Well, sure," and then Hugh turned to Bethy and asked whether hearing about home made her want to go back.

"No," she said flatly.

"Ah," said Hugh.

"Why?"

"I just thought it might."

"Well, it doesn't," Bethany said emphatically, and she made a production of sucking up the dregs of her milk shake, and then Ruth caught the eye of their gentle waiter and asked for the check. For some reason, as he set the slip down on the table in front of her, Ruth touched his hand and held it there for just a minute. He looked at her, alarmed, and she managed to smile as though all she'd meant was to say thank you when she didn't really know *why* she'd done it, hadn't planned to do it at all.

★

HUGH, STRUGGLING TO PULL HIS WALLET OUT OF HIS pants pocket, hadn't even seen the waiter put the bill on the table. Out of the blue he was recalling the phone conversation he'd had with his mother a couple of days earlier, when he'd mentioned that he would be coming down to LA for the weekend. The exact words he'd used were, "I'll be leaving for a couple of days. I have some things to talk over with Ruth."

"You're getting a divorce?"

"No, Mom."

"There's no shame in it."

"I *know* there's no shame in it."

"I read in the *Times* the other day that they even have an expression for it now. Starter marriage."

"We're not getting a divorce. It's not a starter marriage."

"She's in LA. You're here. And this is till death do you part?"

"You know why she's there, Mom. It's as much of a sacrifice for her as it is for me."

"So when are they coming back?"

When, indeed. Helene Rabinowitz let an eloquent moment of silence go by and said, "There's my point."

Hugh was increasingly aware of the flaw in their thinking: if Bethy did well—and Ruth was prepared to do whatever it took for her to do well—she wouldn't *be* coming home, potentially not for five years or even more, if she stayed in Hollywood the way most of the working kids did, and fit college around their work and audition schedules. Ruth would be coming home for holidays and the occasional vacation; and the more successful Bethy became—and he would admit that she could be successful if she got the right break—the fewer of these there would be. Hugh could just picture the increasingly strained conversations between them; the fewer and fewer shared moments to pore over, until the marriage didn't so much die as gutter out.

And yet, to leave his practice for one in Los Angeles would be financially suicidal. They needed every penny he was earning right now to stoke the ruinous bonfire that was Hollywood. Clothes that Ruth swore were necessary to clinch an audition. Haircuts and eyebrow-shaping and facial waxing that cost more every month than they would have spent in Seattle to coif the entire family. The never-ending classes and showcases and coaching upon which Mimi Roberts insisted. The higher car insurance and cost of automobile maintenance. The apartment. By his rough accounting, if the wholesale purchase of goods and services kept to its present level—and Hugh hadn't seen any sign that it would let up—they would be spending between twenty-five and thirty thousand dollars a year. In cash. Indefinitely.

When Hugh was in LA the last time, another studio father who sold boiled peanuts for a living had calmly told Hugh that he'd spent somewhere between eighty and a hundred thousand dollars so far to launch his daughter's acting career. At the time, Hugh had thought the man was a cracker and a blowhard, but now he could see that he had just been honest.

So Hugh had privately begun to peruse online listings for dental practices that were taking on new dentists. He could hire a young dentist to take over his own Seattle practice for a few months—six months, a year—and if he told his patients that it was strictly temporary, they'd stay with him, he was reasonably sure. He'd been treating some of them for twenty years now—*twenty years!*—and they were used to him. They'd wait. He wouldn't buy into the LA practice, of course, so he wouldn't make much money, but the Seattle practice would meet its expenses even with a 15 percent patient attrition rate, if he paid the fill-in dentist less than he had been paying himself, which he was sure he could get away with. The arrangement wouldn't work in the long run, but temporarily it would do. They'd never touch

Bethy's earnings to defray their expenses, of course, if there ever *were* any earnings, which Ruth kept assuring them there would be—*big* earnings, potentially. These they would put into Bethy's college fund. Still, he could see how not only less scrupulous but also more financially strapped parents than he and Ruth were could easily burn through a child's money. Just yesterday Ruth had told him on the phone about a boy Bethy's age who'd made a quarter of a million dollars in one year by making lots of commercials. The kid popped up on TV ads all the time; even Hugh recognized him now. Freckles, shaggy haircut, weak chin, lippy manner. Who knew homely could pay so well? Ruth had said the kid and his family lived in a condo just a block from the ocean in Santa Monica. One more year like this one, the mother had told Ruth, and they'd bring the whole family out from Tucson. Four kids and a husband and they'd all be able to live off the kid's wages, at least until the dad got his feet on the ground. On the other hand, Ruth had told Hugh some horror stories about families that had given up everything to come to Hollywood and their kids had never hit, or had given up the business, and they'd ended up bankrupt. *Bankrupt!* Putting that on a kid's shoulders was more than Hugh could imagine.

But for now all of this was strictly theoretical. For now he kept going to work and cleaning and drilling and filling and repairing and replacing the teeth for which he'd trained all those years, and it was satisfying work and for that he was grateful.

AFTER THEY'D FINISHED AT BOB'S AND RUTH HAD DRIVEN them by the Disney headquarters and animation studio ("Let Mom drive so you can see!" Bethy had insisted to Hugh), Ruth pulled into their designated parking space in the alley behind their dumpy building and helped Hugh get his carry-on out of the trunk.

"I'm okay," he said. "I can do it. I can do a lot of things by myself now."

"I know you can," Ruth said, mildly annoyed. "I just thought I'd help." She stalked ahead of him and Bethy, rattling their apartment key.

"This is the pool," Bethy said to Hugh as they skirted the swimming pool in the courtyard of their apartment building. "I mean, duh."

"I remember," Hugh said. "Do you swim much?"

"Not here," Bethany said. "Look at it—it's gross. I heard someone found a dead rat in it the other day."

Hugh just raised his eyebrows.

"*Please* let us move to the Oakwood, Daddy," she said. "Oh, please, please, pretty please? I mean, you wouldn't need to give me a single present for Hanukkah or Christmas or my next birthday or *anything*, if we could just get an apartment at the Oakwood."

Ruth looked back and saw Hugh inhale and, for just a moment, close his eyes. "Let's not talk about this right now, honey," Ruth said.

"You guys don't even care if I swim in a gross pool with a dead rat in it—"

"Bethany," Ruth warned.

"—even though I could get tetanus or rabies or dengue fev—"

Ruth wheeled around and snapped, "*Enough*. That's enough from you."

Bethany burst into tears and Ruth couldn't get the damned apartment door unlocked, and Hugh took the keys from her and got the door open just as Bethany shrieked, "*You don't even care about me.*" Hugh just sighed, and since there was nowhere to go inside the little apartment to get away from each other,

Ruth turned on the old TV and they had the lights out by eight forty-five.

BY THE NEXT MORNING BETHANY WAS CHEERFUL AGAIN— she wasn't a child who held grudges, God be praised—and Hugh looked more rested in spite of the lumpy mattress. They had him drive them over the hill to the Hollywood Farmers' Market, where he treated them to crepes and they caught a glimpse of someone who might have been Zach Braff. On their way back, they drove through Laurel Canyon so Bethy could show Hugh the two-million-dollar dream home that had slid down the hill in a mudslide and was now in pieces, pressed up against a chain-link fence with gang tags spray-painted all over it. "I saw this TV special about how all the hills around LA are unstable, and they had the owner on it and he was crying," Bethany said. "He said it took them two years to build it, and then it fell down the hill after they'd only been in it for, like, three months or something."

"Well, it's a terrible thing to lose a home," Hugh said.

Bethany said, "One of my friends here—her name is Allison—doesn't really have a home. Her mom moved in with her boyfriend and then they got married and they have this room that they call the guest room even when Allison is back there living in it. So she lives at Mimi's."

"Mimi Roberts boards kids?" Hugh said to Ruth, appalled.

"Sure," Bethany chirped from the backseat. "Their parents live in like Ohio or Arkansas or wherever. It's kind of all right, though, because they get lots of spending money and they can buy whatever they want at the 7-Eleven and stuff. Hillary—she lives with Mimi, too—bought six Snickers bars one day. We told her she shouldn't eat them because she'll get fat—well, that's what Allison said—but Hillary just said tough titties."

"Bethany," Ruth warned.

"What?"

"That's vulgar."

Bethany shrugged. "So anyways, she ate them all and then she threw up and now she says she's never eating another Snickers bar for the rest of her life, and I bet she won't."

"You don't even want to know what those things do to your teeth," Hugh said. "I could tell you some stories."

Bethany turned to look out the window. Hugh was always offering to tell them some stories. In his view, the dental landscape was a slippery slope that led straight to bridgework and periodontics. Now all he said was, "I'll show you the x-rays sometime."

"Yeah, yeah," Bethany said.

They agreed that Hugh would take Bethany to an acting class while Ruth stayed at the apartment and did laundry in the creepy laundry room. She refused to go there after dark, and their days were all packed, so she and Bethy were down to their last sets of underwear. Bethany's class was a special four-hour one with a guest teacher who was a former child star.

"Four hours—the kids are going to be in this class for *four hours*?" Hugh said when they told him.

"It's important, Daddy," Bethy assured him. "It's on audition skills and redirects and cold-reading and stuff."

"And those are things you can't learn on your own?"

"Not really."

"This is according to Mimi, I presume," he said to Ruth.

"It's very basic," Ruth said. "Every client has to take it. Bethy's lucky because there isn't a boot camp going on right now, so it's a small class."

"Boot camp?"

"It's an intensive program Mimi holds twice a year for kids

who are new to Hollywood. By the end of ten days, the kids hit the ground running."

"And is that a good thing?"

"What?"

"Hitting the ground."

Ruth just shot him a look.

ONCE THEY'D DROPPED RUTH AT THE APARTMENT BETH-any gave Hugh directions to the studio in what sounded to him like a new, grown-up voice. How had she learned this? In Seat-tle she didn't even know the names of the streets between their house and her best friend Rianne's, and she'd been traveling that route since preschool. Now her directions even included what lane he needed to be in.

At the studio, Hugh followed her into the greenroom, where a dozen or so children were milling around. Three girls were huddled on a sofa looking at something. They barely glanced up when Bethany came in.

"Guys! This is my dad. Daddy, this is Reba and Allison and Hillary."

The girls had already turned back to Allison's video iPod.

"Hi," Hugh said.

"What are you watching?" said Bethany.

"A commercial. It's Quinn. He's supposed to be a brain cell or something."

"A synapse," said Hillary. "He's a synapse. It's for Sparkz."

"Sparkz?"

"That new energy drink," Hillary said. "It's union, and it's national. He's making a wad."

"He should be," said Allison. "I mean, he looks gay in that suit."

Without a preamble of any kind, a small man with wild

white hair burst into the greenroom, took a stance, and yelled, "Are you ready to work those chops?"

The kids yelled as one, "We're ready!"

This apparition was apparently Smidge Robinson, a former child actor and now one of the most sought-after kids' acting teachers in the business, someone the girls were lucky to work with, Mimi had assured Ruth, for just $225 apiece. Hugh tried to identify the man's accent. It had a vague Southern twang, but actors put on and took off dialects like sweaters. Hugh thought with sour satisfaction that he'd probably come straight from the heart of Brooklyn.

Smidge swept the kids ahead of him into the classroom. Bethany had explained excitedly at the Farmers' Market that for the class's four hours, they got to say or do anything. The idea, apparently, was to get the kids to stop being themselves, so they could be other people. As she explained it, this was a guerilla acting class with no holds barred, and if they broke down and cried, they'd get one of Smidge's famous tin stars, which he would pin onto their clothing personally as a rite of passage. A lot of them hadn't cried yet, Bethy had said. She had, but only once. She said she thought about Zippers, their tuxedo cat, who had died a year before. She said some of the kids thought about grandparents and stuff, old people they knew who'd died, but since she didn't know anyone, she'd had to make do.

Now, in the sudden quiet, Hugh took a minute to scan the headshots of children and teens taped to the walls.

"The ones way up there aren't clients anymore," a girl's voice said from behind him. "Mimi gave them their starts, though."

Hugh turned. Which girl was this? She'd been one of the kids Bethy had introduced him to when they first came in. He found her headshot lower down on one of the walls: Allison

Addison. She was a dark brunette and strikingly, almost shock-ingly, beautiful.

"They have other managers now," the girl said offhandedly. "We're okay with it, though."

"We?"

"Mimi and me."

Was this girl Mimi's daughter? But he'd never heard any-thing about a daughter, and this girl, given her beauty, couldn't possibly have sprung from those loins. He sat on one end of the greenroom sofa. "Aren't you supposed to be in there?" He nod-ded toward the classroom.

"We're doing a game where one of us has to leave the room. They'll call me back in pretty soon." She circled the room languidly, tapping each photograph with her finger until she stopped directly in Hugh's line of sight with her back turned. Striking what he was sure was a pose, she lifted her shiny hair high off her neck and then released it so it spilled down her back, shimmering. Then she turned and plopped down on the couch beside him, crossing one long, thin leg over the other. "So you're a dentist," she said.

"I am."

"She talks about you a lot."

"Does she?"

The girl nodded. "Sometimes we get sick of it, but usually it's okay. I mean, you're her father, so." She caught up a hand-ful of hair and began searching for split ends. "I'm Allison," she said. "You've probably heard about me."

Had he? Conceivably. Ruth and Bethany talked about so many people he couldn't keep them straight.

"So I'm guessing you're not going to stay very long," she said.

"Probably not. Bethy's mom and I have to run some errands while—"

"No, I mean in *LA*. The fathers never do." She picked up his BlackBerry from the sofa cushion between them and pushed a few buttons.

"Well, some of us have jobs back home," Hugh said. "Does your father live here?"

"Nah." She let her knee brush his leg. She was sitting too close. Hugh pushed himself farther into the sofa arm, opening an inch or two of space between them. There was something unnerving about the girl; she gave off energy and heat.

She held his BlackBerry, stroking the screen with her thumb. "So do you like being a dentist?" Her knee was grazing his leg again. He had nowhere left to go.

He cleared his throat. "I do, yes."

"I wouldn't want to have someone's tongue touch me. I mean, they touch you with their tongues, right, when you're in there drilling or whatever?"

"Sometimes," he said.

"Gross."

"We wear rubber gloves."

"Yeah," she said, and tossed his BlackBerry onto the sofa.

The classroom door opened and Bethany poked her head into the greenroom and called to Allison, "Smidge says to come back."

Allison hopped up and trotted to the door. "Bye-bye, daddy-o," she said over her shoulder, and followed Bethany. Once the door had closed behind her, Hugh smoothed his hair and then his trouser legs, feeling vaguely uneasy. This girl, he was sure, was capable of causing trouble.

From another room he could hear a woman—Mimi, presumably—whining, "I *know* that, but he's funny-looking.

SEEING STARS

Funny-looking kids play character roles or they're in commercials. They don't play leads. I'm telling you right now that if he *really* looked like Zac Efron, things would be going a lot better. And you need to get him coached because the last time I saw him, he was still doing that thing with his mouth."

Hugh followed the voice and poked his head into Mimi's office.

"A hundred and twenty-five dollars," she was saying. "No, twenty-*five*. And she won't take a check, so make sure you have cash." Mimi looked at Hugh and gestured at the sprung, grimy armchair beside her desk. A malevolent-looking terrier in a dog bed stared at him from under Mimi's feet. Hugh vaguely remembered Bethany saying something about a dog that didn't like men. He sat down.

"And tell him he needs to be off-book *today*," Mimi was saying. "Tell him he's not fooling anyone."

She hung up the phone and sighed. "That's what happens when the parents are delusional," she said. "That child has the worst chin I've ever seen on anyone except maybe Chelsea Clinton. If they know what's good for him, they'll get him a chin implant. Of course, that still leaves the nose."

Hugh didn't know what to say.

"So," Mimi said, cutting her shrewd old eyes at him. "Is this about the money or the pressure?"

"What?"

"When parents come talk to me, especially new parents, it's usually either about the amount of pressure the kids are under or how much money they're having to spend. I'm guessing with you it's about the money."

Hugh bristled. "It's not about the money. Well, it *is* about the money, but it's not *primarily* about the money."

"Then you feel we're pushing Bethany too hard?"

"Well, I do think we need to keep in mind that she's only thirteen. It's all well and good to be talented and to want to be an actress, but she's also a kid. It's not normal to come down so hard on them. Not at that age."

Mimi smiled thinly. "If you want normal, you should take her back to Seattle." She shifted in her chair, resettling her substantial haunches. "You have to change your thinking. I don't run a day camp. This is an employment agency. That's the first thing."

Hugh just looked at her.

Mimi sighed. "New parents always get to this point, and I always tell them the same thing. There are two kinds of people. There are the ones who don't take this business seriously, and they usually don't stick around; and then there are the ones who buy into it one hundred and ten percent, and are willing to go to hell and back if that's what it takes to have a career in acting. I can't tell yet which one Bethany is—which worries me, frankly, because I'm not willing to work harder at this than she is—but your wife is definitely in the second category. Mothers like your wife will cheerfully kick other mothers in the head if they think it will improve their kid's chances. And I mean that as a good thing. There is no other way to make it. None."

Hugh felt a growing sense of vertigo. Could this woman possibly be saying about his gentle Ruthie what he thought he was hearing? Impassive, Mimi picked something out of her teeth with her fingernail and flicked it onto the floor. Hugh ran his palms down his thighs. "I must say that I also have concerns about how you're treating her religious affiliation."

Mimi looked amused. "What, you mean her being Jewish? I have nothing against that. A lot of my clients are Jewish, but their stage names aren't Bernstein or Lefkowitz or Shapiro. Their names are Burns and Lawford and Pearson. I will admit that

Roosevelt might be overkill, but I stand behind it. If you want her to scream Jewish—the name, the hair—she'll never work unless someone remakes *Fiddler on the Roof* or an Israeli SWAT team action movie, and *Fiddler*'s already been made and she's too young to be on a SWAT team, which means at best she'd play a bombing casualty with one line about how much she wants her mother to live, and that's it for the movie, which means there's an excellent chance she'll end up on the cutting room floor. Does that sound better to you? Because that's the way it works."

The woman had conviction, he'd have to give her that much. "I'm just saying I don't want her to be ashamed of her heritage, like it's something to hide. We've worked very hard to make her proud of what and where she comes from."

"Look, you're in charge of her heritage. I'm in charge of finding her work, and I won't find her work if she's too Jewish—which I worry about, frankly, since we're calling her Rabinowitz again—and if I *can't* find her work you should know that I'll drop her as a client and so will her agent."

Hugh could hear his pulse in his ears. Mimi's e-mail had continued to ding continuously as though signaling incoming mortar rounds. She swiveled, checked the screen, typed something, and sent it off before she turned back. "Do we have a problem? Because if we do, tell me now. I like your daughter's look and she's got potential, but I don't need her. There are a hundred more out there just like her."

"No, she's here now," he said.

"Then let me be clear. I didn't invent the entertainment industry, I'm just telling you the rules. And rule number one is do whatever you can to find your clients as broad a niche as possible and then fill it. Rule number two is be realistic about the kind of work you'll get. I can get her commercials. I can probably get her costar roles."

"Costar?"

"Parts with maybe three or four lines. And she won't even book those until we've seasoned her. So I'm submitting her for everything and pitching her for student films. They won't pay, but they'll give her respectable credits, so that's where we start."

Hugh looked at her. "Do you have children of your own?"

"No."

"Really?"

"Really."

And with that, there was nothing left to say.

IN THE DANK LITTLE LAUNDRY ROOM AT THE APARTMENT complex, Ruth stuffed their whites and darks together into the single working washing machine, which she'd been grateful to find empty. Screw it—if the whites got a little dingier, they were pretty dingy anyway, and most of what was dingy was underwear and unless they were in sudden need of an ambulance, who would see it? She just couldn't be expected to work miracles down here. She couldn't. She was on the edge of exhaustion and if her marriage was a bond, its rating would have just been lowered from an A ranking to a low B. She could just hear Hugh's mother Helene's voice in her head: *What, you can't keep up with the laundry now? Is it really that hard living down there, that you can't wash some panties in the sink? This is how infections happen. You get some kind of bacteria growing and next thing you know you're peeing in a cup.* Could that possibly be true? It sounded true. Ruth turned the water temperature dial to hot/hot. It couldn't hurt to be careful.

Ruth had been over it and over it in her head: on the one hand, a mother's obligations included helping her child achieve or even exceed her goals. Everyone said how talented Bethany was, and they'd been saying so for years. Ruth took this to mean that Bethy had what it took to go all the way to stardom, be it on Broadway or in Hollywood, if—and granted, this was a huge if—she had the focus and opportunity to prove it. But since you never knew when the big break, that single key moment, might come around, you had no choice but to be ever ready and make sure your child was, too, which meant that sometimes your child was working twice as hard as the kids around her. It meant treating every audition like the most important one of her life, treating every new casting director like the one person to whom Bethy had to prove that she had not only raw talent, but the stamina and nerve to deliver on set. Which was, as it turned out, much tougher than Ruth had originally imagined. When you watched TV or a movie, it always looked like the actors were alone, had been caught by chance in the eye of a single, lightly manned camera. But now she knew the truth, that there were dozens, even scores, of grips and gaffers and sound guys and script supervisors and people whose only job was to remember that the girl at the counter in the diner had had a barrette on the right side of her part and that the older ac-tor playing the has-been detective had had a bottle of schnapps that was not quite half full in the scene filmed two days ago. All these people watched, and all their livelihoods depended in a very real way on whether Bethany or any other actor did her job well—which was to say flawlessly—because if they weren't delivering that level of excellence, other actors every bit as good and just as hungry were standing right behind her in line.

And that was what Hugh didn't understand. He still lived in a world of school plays and pageants where whether your child was likable and earnest was every bit as important as whether she could act; where turning out a child with a strong self-image was more important than her actual talent. In LA the state of your ego meant bupkes, and good enough got you a ticket straight back to Seattle. Ruth had known what was what from the first week they'd been here. The problem was getting Hugh or anyone else from the normal world to know it, too. And if they *didn't* know it, it made Ruth look like Gypsy Rose Lee's mother. The Ghosts of Stage Moms Past dogged her constantly. It was impossible to tune out the background whine of the devil's question: Who was driving whom, the mother or the child? Ruth had heard of Munchausen syndrome by proxy, a grotesque mental illness in which mothers made their children sick so that they, the mothers, got attention. Could there be such a thing as an actress by proxy?

But Ruth could take only so much self-incrimination. She fled the laundry room for the courtyard, sat in one of the sagging pool chairs, dug up her cell phone, and called Vee.

"Hugh's here."

"Here where?" said Vee. "Are you at the apartment?"

"I am. Hugh's at the studio."

"Is Bethany there?"

"No, she's at the studio, too."

"Then why are you whispering?"

"Was I whispering?"

"You were."

"I don't know," Ruth said, sighing. "Probably because I feel like a fink."

"Really?" She could hear Vee perk up. "There's a word I haven't heard in a long time."

"The poor man is here for the weekend and I sent him to deal with Mimi alone."

"That wasn't nice," Vee agreed.

"I can't imagine what he'll say to her. He thinks we're down here reinforcing the wrong values."

"Really? Is he Mormon?"

"With a name like Rabinowitz? Why would you think Mormon?"

"I don't know. He could have converted. I thought Mormons talked a lot about the right values for girls. Though I think that's because Mormon girls don't automatically get into heaven like the men do. Save a soul and you're in. No soul-saving, no entrée. It's a pretty savage religion, when you think about it."

"Well, he's not a Mormon. We're not."

"Huh," said Vee. Ruth could hear her sucking deeply on a cigarette and exhaling straight into the mouthpiece. "Too bad, though. We could have had some fun."

"Right now it's hard to imagine ever having fun again. Do you know what I think about now, when I think about fun? I think about taking a Vicodin. Hugh has some left over from muscle spasms in his back."

"Yum," said Vee.

"Really?"

"Hey, don't knock drugs," Vee said. "I only survived the last year of my first marriage because I was stoned out of my mind on Percocet. I told the doctor I had sciatica from being pregnant with Buster. I bet I still have a couple in an old shoebox somewhere."

"Well, I think it's sad."

"Yeah." Vee subsided. "So how long is he staying?"

"Till Monday morning."

"Bethy handling it okay? Sometimes when the disapproving parent shows up the kids take it like a punch in the face. You know it's happened when they suddenly try to make plans with anyone who'll let them come for a sleepover."

"And how do you know this?"

"Honey, I've seen couples like you destroyed in one long

weekend. Two days together they can handle, but three and thar she blows."

"I think you should be saying something to comfort me."

"Get out of the business."

"That's not comforting."

"Isn't it? I guess it only works on people who are pretty far gone," said Vee. "There was an acting kid in Buster's tai chi class who decided to quit and go home, except he was testing for a black belt so it meant they had to stay in Burbank for an extra three days. To this day I'm sure if his mother had had a scalpel or even a reasonably stiff piece of paper she'd have slit her own wrists right there in the dojo or whatever by the time those extra days were up."

"Really? So what happened to them?"

"They went back to Minnesota and no one's ever heard from them again. She's probably putting up a tuna hot dish and her kid—what was his name, Larry, only they insisted everyone call him Lawrence—is smoking pot all day in some provincial little high school where the state fair is the biggest deal of the year. Maybe he's raising hogs." Ruth could hear Vee draw on her cigarette, reflecting. "Hey, you just don't know," she said, though Ruth hadn't said anything to challenge her. "Maybe 4H is everything it's supposed to be. Maybe winning blue ribbons for your swine is the ultimate thrill. Maybe our kids would be a lot better off if they were up to their ankles in manure and slopping out the barn, only nobody told us."

Ruth shuddered. "God forbid."

"Okay, but am I taking your mind off your troubles?"

"Yes."

"Well then. Tonight when you crawl into bed, count swine."

"Okay," said Ruth.

"Love ya, babe," said Vee.

RUTH WAS CARRYING CLEAN LAUNDRY BACK TO THE APART-
ment when Hugh got back. She handed him the basket and dug
out her keys to let them in. It seemed silly to have locked the
door when she was only crossing the courtyard, but there had
been several thefts recently. "So how was it?"

"I don't know," Hugh said.

"What do you mean, you don't know? Were the kids there?
Was the teacher? Sometimes they don't show up on time, which
I think is very inconsiderate, given what we're paying them,
because the classes always *end* right on time."

"No, the teacher was there. Midge something. Strange guy."

"Smidge. He was very famous when he was younger."

"I've never heard of him."

"That's because you didn't watch TV. I used to see him all
the time." Ruth's parents had been much more relaxed than
Hugh's. As a result, Hugh could name a million book titles
and authors, and Ruth could hum the jingles for nearly every
household product marketed in the ten years or so before she'd
gone off to college.

"So how does she seem to you?" Ruth tried to make the
question sound offhand.

"Mimi?"

"Bethy."

"Oh. Bubbly, I guess," Hugh said. "A little manic."

"She's glad you're here. She wants you to be as enthusiastic
as she is."

"I'm enthusiastic," Hugh protested.

Ruth took her time, shook out a pair of Bethy's jeans, and
then folded a T-shirt that had a picture of a playing-card joker
on the front with little bells stitched to its hat. To keep it from
being distracting during auditions they'd had to carefully bend

every bell to remove the ball-bearing that made it tinkle. "The thing is, it's different down here. She wants you to see that for yourself, because she figures once you do, you'll be as nuts about it as she is."

"Is she nuts?"

"Yes. She is. You should see her on the days she has auditions. We run her lines and she has to choose exactly the right clothes and she does MapQuest because you know me and directions—"

"She does seem to have that part down," Hugh allowed.

"And by the time we get there she's right in character and she stays that way even when we have to wait an hour, which happens more often than you'd think it would. Not like a dental office."

"But she's getting turned down."

"All the time," Ruth agreed.

"And you think that's a good idea? Doesn't that bother her? She's thirteen. She's a teenager, and everyone knows that even the most even-natured kids auger in."

"So you want to take away her one gift, the thing that makes her special? You know what she'd be if you did that? She'd be the kid who's bullied because she's a good, nice girl whose socials skills, let's face it, are developing a little bit late. It's like *Lord of the Flies* out there, honey. Is that what you want for her?"

"Of course it's not what I want for her, but I think you're being a little simplistic—"

"Oh no, I'm not," said Ruth darkly. "Believe me, I'm not. She's a good girl with talent that can bring the world to her doorstep."

"And is that what she wants—to have the world at her doorstep? Or is that what *you* want?"

Ruth shook out a pair of her pants with a report like a gunshot. "You think I'm doing this for *me*?"

"I'm just saying."

"Well, let me tell you something," Ruth said. "I'm giving up *everything* to make this possible for her. I sleep in a terrible bed in a crappy little apartment with bugs"—that wasn't actually true, but her blood was up—"and crime and a pool like a petri dish, and you think this is what *I* want?"

"Yes. I don't know. Yes, I think this is what you want. I think you want her to stand out from everyone else."

"This is what *she* wants. Just watch her!"

"Maybe she thinks she wants this only because you're so gaga about it. Maybe she thinks she wants it only because she hasn't tried anything else," Hugh said evenly. "If she could try being in a courtroom maybe she'd want to be a lawyer. Maybe she'd want to be a doctor."

"She doesn't want to be a doctor," Ruth said.

"I'm just *saying*."

"I know what you're saying. What *I'm* saying is, we're giving her the opportunity of a lifetime but you don't want to spend the money."

"It's not about the money," Hugh cried. "Why is everybody saying I don't want to spend money? Have I ever said I don't want to spend money? I haven't."

"No," Ruth conceded.

"So let's stop talking about the goddamn money. What I don't want is to have my family living down here when I'm up there. For the record."

"So it's about you."

"It's *not* about me. But as a matter of fact, I don't like the idea that this might last for years. I miss you. That's the main thing. Slap me for it, but I'm a family man. I miss you and I miss Bethy."

Ruth softened and deflated. "I know you do."

WHEN THEY GOT TO THE STUDIO, BETHANY WAS WAITING in the greenroom with a couple of other girls. Her face was flushed, and it looked as though she'd been crying. Reba and Hillary had their arms around her and were whispering something to her protectively.

"She's pretty upset," Hillary said importantly when she saw Ruth.

She and Reba stood back so Ruth could get to her. "Why?"

Across the room Allison was folding a sweater elaborately and putting it into the giant Coach tote she carried with her everywhere, as though she might at any minute be transported to the wilderness for, say, years. "Allison?" Ruth said.

"It was *improv*. You're not supposed to take it personally."

"Take what personally?"

"She called me a loser," Bethany said miserably. "She called me a loser and a baby."

Ruth bridled. "Why would you say those things?"

"It was a *scene*!" Allison shrieked, and her voice quavered slightly. "Okay? Jeez! You're supposed to keep it separate. Haven't you ever done improv before?"

"As a matter of fact, she's taken several classes," Ruth said. "She knows what improv is."

"Smidge made them scene partners," Hillary explained officiously, "and then he told them they were best friends who were jealous of each other because one of them won some stupid award in a math class, as though *that's* ever going to happen."

"Yeah," Allison spit out, "and she was the one who won the

award, of course, because she's so smart and she knows a lot of big words, and because Daddy's a dentist and she has you guys just wrapped around her little fingers like she's perfect."

"She isn't perfect," Ruth said. "But weren't you supposed to be characters and not yourselves?"

"Yes," Bethany said, wiping her nose on the back of her hand and then wiping the back of her hand on her jeans.

"Whatever," Allison said. She pulled a tube of lipstick and a little mirror out of her bag and applied the lipstick with a show of bravado, except that Ruth noticed her hands were shaking.

"Sometimes we forget to draw the line," said Smidge Robinson, who had emerged from the classroom unnoticed. The knot of girls parted and he put his arm around Bethy's shoulder, touched his head to her head. "We need to toughen up, right? We talked about that in there, about how actors are tough, tough people, even though we're marshmallows inside. And that's what lets us do anything our character needs us to do, even if it's ugly, because it's our *character* doing it, not us. Right? So we're going to work really hard on that, aren't we?"

Bethy nodded and took a deep breath. Smidge gave her shoulders a squeeze and released her. "Kids," he said ruefully to Ruth and Hugh. "They're at a tough age. They're not even going to be civilized until they're twenty."

Bethy walked a couple of steps to where Allison was sitting on the sofa filing her nails impassively. Bethy sat right down next to her, so her shoulder touched Allison's, and Ruth saw Allison stiffen almost imperceptibly. She thought, not for the first time, that there was a certain feral quality about the girl. *They have this room that they call the guest room even when Allison is back there living in it,* Bethany had said. *So she lives at Mimi's.*

Bethy was saying, "I'll do better the next time. I'm really sorry."

Allison took a tissue from her Coach bag and held it under her eye. Ruth was startled to realize that she was fighting to not cry. Smidge was gone. Except for Reba and Hillary, the other children had trailed out, leaving only Bethany and the Orphans, who had nowhere else to go until Mimi was ready to leave. From what Ruth had observed, that was likely to be hours from now. "Hey," she said impulsively. "Who wants a burger?"

"We do!" said fat Reba and little Hillary in a chorus.

"I do!" shouted Bethy.

"Honey?" Ruth asked Allison, who still seemed subdued.

"Okay," said Allison.

"All right, then. Go tell Mimi and get your stuff and we'll meet you at the car," Ruth said.

Hugh just looked at her and shook his head. "What have you done?" he said.

"In what sense?"

And he spread his arms wide, taking in the girls and the room and conceivably the city itself and then he walked out the door.

November–December 2006

The thing about Hollywood is, it's no different from heroin or gambling or crack cocaine, except in Hollywood the high is adrenaline. Every day's a crap shoot, a spinning wheel of possibility. Actors get up every morning hungry to score. And sometimes—sometimes—they do. Not often, but enough to feed the craving, to keep them crawling out of bed aching for the big break, the moments they'll look back to when they're asked when exactly their lives changed forever.

And at any given moment there are ten thousand stunned and hopeful actors driving down the LA freeways, and every one of them is believing exactly the same thing: that the big break is coming just as surely as sunrise.

—VEE VELMAN

Chapter Ten

ANGIE AND LAUREL BUEHL SAT SIDE BY SIDE ON UNYIELD-
ing plastic chairs in the Urgent Care on Olive, holding hands at
six thirty in the morning. It wasn't Angie who'd brought them
there—thank God, it wasn't Angie—but Laurel. The girl had
been awake since two A.M., with a rising fever and back pain.
She'd been peeing every ten or fifteen minutes until, by four
forty-five, she told Angie it felt less like she was urinating than
like she was passing acid. At six o'clock she was no longer able
to pass urine at all, and now she was sitting beside Angie in the
Urgent Care with her legs squeezed tight together, making a
low moaning noise and rocking.

A nurse came out finally—*finally!*—and called Laurel into
the clinic. Laurel reached out her hand to Angie. She had dark
wells under her eyes, which were filling with tears. They were
not from pain, Angie knew, though Laurel was clearly in ag-
ony; they were for the producers' session she would now almost
certainly miss, for a role in a feature film. Angie took a deep,
strengthening breath and followed the nurse and Laurel into an
examination room.

The nurse wrapped a blood pressure cuff around Laurel's
arm, inflated it, then released it, scribbled a number, raised her
eyebrows, inflated the cuff again, and took another reading.

"Whoa," she said to Angie.

"She's in pain," Angie said.

"I'll say," said the nurse. "I'm going to have the doctor come
right in, okay? Can you lie back, sweetie?"

"I don't think so," Laurel said. "I can't pee, either, and I really really have to."

"Hold on," said the nurse. "Just hold on, okay?"

Once the nurse was gone, clicking the door ever so quietly behind her, Laurel started moaning. Angie cleared her throat, went to Laurel's side, grasped her hand firmly, and said, "Breathe." There had been nights when Laurel had said that to her, and it had helped. "*Breathe.*"

Laurel drew her knees up to her chest. Angie could hear her teeth grind together. The examining room door opened and a male doctor came in with the nurse, went straight to Laurel—peeling a stethoscope from around his neck as he walked—and said, "Well, well. What do we have, here?"

"Oh," Laurel sobbed, "I *hurt.*"

"I'm sure you do, darlin'," said the doctor. Angie found herself thinking, bizarrely, that he'd been perfectly cast. Gray hair whitening at the temples, chiseled features, gray eyes. Not blocky like Dillard, but more like a man who'd made fitness a lifelong religion. *So* LA.

"Let's roll you over," he told Laurel. "I need to get a gander at those kidneys."

The nurse and the doctor rolled Laurel onto her side and the doctor pressed gently. "Ow, ow, ow."

"Sorry, sweetie," the doctor said.

They rolled Laurel onto her back. Her face had no color, Angie noticed; none whatsoever. The doctor palpated her abdomen. "We'll do some blood work," he said, "but it's not going to tell us anything we don't already know."

Angie raised her eyebrows: *So?*

"Big-time urinary tract infection," the doctor said. "And it's backed up into her kidneys. When did she start showing symptoms?"

"Two, two fifteen," Angie said.

"We don't usually see these come on so fast."

"It's probably been brewing for a day, at least, and she never said anything. She has a high pain threshold," Angie said.

"I'll say," said the doctor.

"Let's call ahead," he said to the nurse. "Let them know she's coming."

"What do you mean?" Angie asked. "Call ahead where?"

"I'm sending her up to St. John's Hospital. She needs to be catheterized, and she needs IV antibiotics. This is pretty far along."

Laurel gave a little shriek. "No! No no no! I'm going to producers today. At ten o'clock."

"Not today, you're not," said the doctor.

"Yes! Yes, today! I have to! It's a *Spielberg* film! Just give me something. You can give me something and then I'll be fine."

Angie stepped over to the exam table, brushing past the doctor to stand by Laurel's shoulder. "Stop it," she said firmly.

"*Ohhhh.*"

"Stop."

Laurel brought it down to a whimper.

"Better," said Angie.

"I have snot in my ear," said Laurel.

"I know, honey," Angie said gently. "Now, you listen to me. We're going to the hospital and they're going to pump you full of painkillers and antibiotics and a drug called Pyridium that will make you pee in Technicolor—which I know because I've been on it—and you're going to feel much much better."

"*When?*"

Angie looked at the doctor, who shrugged and held up one, then two fingers: *Tomorrow or the next day.* "If we start right now," he said.

"Soon," said Angie.

The doctor headed for the examining room door. "All right, I'm going to go let them know to expect her."

Angie went out with him and said very softly and very firmly, "Tell them to knock her out the minute they get her."

"I beg your pardon?"

"I know my daughter. They're going to have to knock her out if they're going to keep her, because otherwise she'll go to that callback even if it means crawling up Barham Boulevard on her knees in a hospital gown."

The doctor shook his head.

"I know," said Angie. "But do it anyway."

An hour later Laurel was ensconced in a hospital room and wobbly-headed from a merciful morphine infusion. Angie listened quite calmly to the soft, mewing sound Laurel was now making; a nearly happy and certainly musical sound, which made Angie wonder, and not for the first time, if she should get Laurel enrolled in voice lessons again, as well as an intensive voice-over workshop. She should ask Mimi. She'd heard from more than one mom in an audition waiting room that voice work paid very well.

"Mom," Laurel said, yawning hugely. "I'm so sleepy."

"Good," Angie said.

"Am I better? Because I might feel better." She flipped the bed sheet aside and looked at a catheter draped over her leg into a collecting bag hanging beside the bed. Angie could see, though Laurel could not, that the urine was a dark rust color. Blood.

"Yes, you're better," Angie told her.

"Really?"

"No, but you will be in just a couple more hours. In the meantime they've given you some morphine."

"What if I'm not better, though?"

"I've already asked Mimi to reschedule. If they liked you enough, they will. And if they didn't, you wouldn't have booked it anyway."

"I wasn't really thinking of that."

"No?" Angie smoothed Laurel's damp hair off her forehead.

"What if it isn't just an infection?"

"Why wouldn't it be?"

She and Laurel locked eyes briefly, and then Laurel looked away.

"Cancer?" Angie said. "Do you mean what if it's cancer?"

"Yes," Laurel whispered.

"Oh, honey." Angie pressed Laurel's hand hard, hard enough for her platinum wedding ring to bite into her finger. "*I'm* the one with cancer. *I* am, not you."

"But what if—"

"*Not* what if. Cancer is not contagious. All you have is an infection that women get all the time—*all the time*. And it doesn't mean a thing, except you'll feel like God stomped all over you for a couple days, and from now on you'll be more careful about cleaning yourself after you poop."

"Really?" The relief in Laurel's eyes was heartbreaking.

"Really."

Laurel closed her eyes and said dreamily, "That's good."

TWO HOURS LATER ANGIE SAT IN AN UNCOMFORTABLE vinyl visitor's chair beside Laurel's hospital bed, holding her hand lightly and watching her sleep. Laurel had finally, thoroughly conked out an hour ago. Angie traced the faint blue veins on the back of her daughter's hand, admired the young, pale, flawless skin, the delicate, pearly color of a body at one with itself. Ever since Angie's first round of chemo last summer, her own hands had become terribly dry, with rough and splitting cuticles and nails that chipped like mica. It was as though, to slake itself, the cancer had appropriated everything, all of her.

That was Angie and Laurel's secret: Angie Buehl was dying. *Slowly*, mind you, slowly. But she was dying. She had chronic myelogenous leukemia, a usually but not always slow-burning form of leukemia that would eventually do her in, though no one could say when. They didn't talk about it much, because really, what was there to say? You could devote your remaining time to the business of dying, or you could say screw it and not give it the satisfaction of besting you until the very end—or that's how Angie chose to look at it, anyway, so Laurel looked at it that way, too.

As an act of love and knowing he'd be devastated by the news, they had decided back in Georgia not to tell Dillard, not yet, anyway. When Laurel went with her to chemo they'd told Dillard they were going on trips out of town so Laurel could take a modeling class in Atlanta; thankfully, Angie's hair loss hadn't been total and Angie had simply told Dillard it was female trouble, something to do with a hormone imbalance. Sweet man, he'd believed her. Over the interminable drip of the IVs they'd agreed that if they were going to launch Laurel's career in TV and movies while Angie was still alive and able to help, they had to start *now*. So when the chemo was over they'd told Dillard that Laurel had been invited to Hollywood to take part in a talent competition for young actors and, if she won, she'd be given a manager and invited to stay. Dillard hadn't questioned it, as Angie had known he wouldn't. He was like that: a good, busy, simple man who worked hard, believed what he was told, loved with ferocity, and made a surprisingly good and satisfying living standing over a vat of boiling peanuts all day, talking to men and women just like him.

Laurel shifted her legs restlessly under the light hospital blanket and moaned. Angie checked the pee bag. The urine was clearer, though brilliantly hued from the Pyridium. She smiled; Laurel would get a kick out of seeing the colors of sunrise in her toilet bowl. Despite her starlet exterior, she was a plain-Jane girl. She talked comfortably about bodily functions, farted freely if it was just her and Angie (*Well, goodness!* she'd say. *Excuse me!*), and liked to hold babies whenever anyone would let her.

And so they'd come to Hollywood with a steely resolve. Had this kidney infection been even somewhat less fast-moving, Angie knew for a fact that they'd have made the producers' session this morning. Time was their enemy; all they had were now and very soon. Angie knew it was going to be hard—unspeakably hard—for Laurel to be without her. Angie's own mother had died of an aneurism when she was just twelve, and her life had been like nuclear winter until she'd met Dillard when she was eighteen. Plus she and Laurel had always been unusually close. Laurel had been a compliant, happy baby, given to shrieks of delight and a tendency to giggle in her sleep. She'd loved beauty pageants and sparkles and sequins and little boots and high kicks. A natural, the pageant directors and judges all said; a child to watch. She knew people made fun of pageant girls and their mothers, but in Angie's opinion that was just small-minded. Look at Laurel's poise; look at her drive and focus. She was one of the girls who was going to make it: Angie knew that without a doubt. And she'd have earned every mile she gained as surely as if she'd walked there over hot coals.

Once they'd arrived in Hollywood, they'd called Dillard to say that Laurel had won the competition, she'd *won*! Then they'd applied themselves with singular purpose to the busi-ness of establishing Laurel as an A-list actor. They studied every set of sides together, going over and over them until they both admitted dreaming about them in their sleep. But the point was, Laurel was always exquisitely well-prepared, and this, they believed, was critical, especially in light of Mimi's mantra, to which they fully subscribed: *Luck is being prepared when the opportunity arises*. "Lord," Laurel had prayed aloud more than once in Angie's presence, "let me be the living proof."

Now, though, Angie knew something that Laurel did not: after only the briefest reprieve, the cancer was on the move again. Bruises were massing on her arms and legs like storm clouds; sometimes at night she could actually *feel* the cancer cells at work, boring like worms through her bone marrow. She'd have to go back on chemo soon; she had already set up an appointment with an oncologist at UCLA. She intended to lie about it, telling Laurel she was just going in for some routine psychological counseling. In the meantime she was careful to wear long-sleeved shirts and long pants, and to change privately. If Laurel suspected anything she wasn't letting on, and that was fine with Angie. The girl was under enough pressure.

Mimi Roberts had initially resisted taking Laurel on as a client because of the girl's age and regional specificity, but she was prepared to milk her now. Just in the last month she'd booked a national commercial for JCPenney, and another for the California Avocado Commission. She also had a callback later in the week for a costar role on *Desperate Housewives*, which could very well be the breakthrough into theatrical work that they were all waiting for.

Laurel Buehl was so hot she was on fire, and Mimi knew it.

Chapter Eleven

THE CW's *CALIFORNIA DREAMERS,* STILL IN ITS FIRST SEA-
son, was about groups of privileged teens in Malibu and under-
privileged teens in Long Beach. The Malibu kids were snotty
and the Long Beach kids were earnest and the early reviews
had been mixed. Bethy's episode was only the fifth one, and
Joel Sherman had warned Holly Jensen, who'd warned Mimi,
who'd warned Ruth, who'd mentioned to Bethy in a very up-
beat way that they had to be very, very professional and reliable
and pay extremely close attention at all times.

"How am I going to know what's professional?" Bethy had
asked Ruth, worried. "I've never been a professional before."

Ruth allowed that she was right, so in lieu of more specific
instructions she should behave the way she did at Nana's house,
which meant being hypervigilant, listening instead of talking,
and leaving no messes behind. It was a code of behavior Ruth
herself still followed when it came to visiting Hugh's mother,
and it had worked very well over the years, even though it was
exhausting.

After a relatively sleepless night, Ruth pulled up to the guard
shack outside Occidental's Soundstage 5 in North Hollywood at
six o'clock sharp on Monday morning. Given Ruth's poor track
record, she and Bethy had made a dry run yesterday to make
sure they knew how to get there. From outside, the soundstage
looked exactly like an industrial warehouse—plain brown with
just one door and no windows. Six or seven propane barbecues
were lined up outside, and a green tent was set up beyond that.

Was it Ruth's imagination, or did the security guard in the guard shack look at them with respect when she gave him Bethy's name and it matched one on his checklist? "It's her first job," Ruth couldn't resist telling him. "We're so proud."

"Hey, congratulations," the guard said, bending down and looking in at Bethany. He was Hispanic, young and handsome. He handed Ruth a square of green paper. "You need to put this pass on your windshield and only park here. Okay? Don't go around back." He gestured to a row of spaces, all but one of which was already taken. How early did these people start work? "You can go right on in, ladies." And to Bethy, "You tell me when the episode's going to run and I'll watch for you."

"Okay!" Bethany said, thrilled; and for all Ruth knew, he meant it.

Ruth swung into the last parking space and Bethany hopped out. "Mom, I'm *floating*. I'm serious. I'm not even touching the ground. I'm going to be acting on a TV show. Can you believe it?"

Like Bethany, Ruth was thrilled beyond words. She clutched a day planner, manila folder, sweater, water bottle, *USA Today*, the ubiquitous *Seabiscuit*, her cell phone, and cell phone charger. "We're not going to the moon, Mom," Bethy had said, watching Ruth pack, but Ruth felt the need to prepare for any eventuality, like her cell phone losing its charge around all the equipment that was bound to be in there. Actually, the fact was that she was nervous. It wasn't that she doubted Bethy's abilities; it was herself she was worried about. She was sure there were matters of protocol, things you were allowed to do and not allowed to do, and she only hoped someone would tell her what they were, so she didn't do something wrong and blow the opportunity for Bethy. Mimi had told them very clearly that even once you'd booked a role, you could be released for the simplest things.

They entered a big area furnished with eight or nine picnic tables, at which were sitting a handful of sleepy kids and parents sipping coffee from Styrofoam cups. Ruth was trying to figure out whether she was supposed to be sitting there, too, when she spotted a sturdy-looking young woman carrying a clipboard and wearing a headset, T-shirt, jeans, and running shoes. Her hair was pulled back in a messy ponytail and she had no makeup on and Ruth thought she hadn't seen anyone so sensibly dressed since they'd left Seattle. The young woman approached them and said, "Lucy?"

"Bethany," Ruth said. "Bethany Rabinowitz."

The young woman frowned at her clipboard. "Okay, but what character is she? Is she Lucy?"

"Oh!" Ruth said, embarrassed. "Yes. I'm sorry."

"No prob." She made a note and then started walking. Ruth and Bethany hurried to keep up with her. "I'm Emily," she said over her shoulder. "If you need anything, you find me, okay? Don't go to anyone else. I'm going to put you in your dressing room, and Wardrobe should be back there in a couple of minutes. Why don't you look this stuff over while you wait?" She handed Ruth a run sheet of the day's scenes and which actors were in them, and a copy of the script printed on blue paper.

"We already have one of these," Ruth said, handing the script back. It had been delivered to their apartment by a courier yesterday afternoon.

"Is yours yellow?"

Ruth looked at Bethany, who pulled it out of her messenger bag and held it aloft. It was yellow.

"Okay," said Emily, "but the newest draft is blue. The writers made a couple of changes last night, so throw yours away and check your lines in this one, in case anything's different." She looked at her clipboard. "So, it looks like she'll be working today, tomorrow, and Thursday, and she's on hold for Friday, so don't make any plans. And I still need your Coogan information."

Ruth pulled out the manila folder and handed it to Emily, who opened it and flipped through.

"Okay, she needs to take the work permit to the classroom with her when she gets done with the first scene. But I'll take the Coogan stuff."

Ruth and Bethany trotted past a props depot holding two floor lamps, a janitor's mop and bucket, a bicycle, a U.S. Postal Service street-corner mailbox, some garden trellises, and a store mannequin. Then they broke through into the interior of the soundstage, sweeping past a living room set and an office set; past several mobile cameras and a bunch of men wearing tool belts from which dangled rolls of electrician's tape; and along a plywood wall that ended in midair and was punctuated by six or seven doors. Emily finally stopped at one on which had been taped a paper sign neatly labeled LUCY and HUNGRY GIRL. Hungry Girl, Ruth had noticed, not only had no name but just one line. Bethy had four lines and a name. Ruth was thrilled anew. Emily opened the door and showed them into a small, ceiling-less cubicle furnished with a cheap vinyl couch, a wooden cube, and two hard chairs. They took the couch.

"Okay, now don't go anywhere," Emily told them. "Wardrobe needs to see her, because she's in the first scene. Don't go find them; they'll come to you. Copy that," she said into her headset. "Lucy's here, so let Wardrobe know, okay? Five minutes." This last was to Ruth. "They'll be here in five minutes, and then we'll want her in Hair and Makeup. Wardrobe will tell you where to go. 'Kay?" And then she darted out before Ruth could say anything, closing the door behind her.

Ruth wished Emily had left the door open so they could watch whatever was going on out there, but she didn't want to make a mistake, so she and Bethy sat on the hard couch side by side with their hands in their laps and their feet flat on the floor. "Look at the script," Ruth whispered, "and make sure your lines are the same."

They flipped through the pages, but nothing looked any different, either in Bethany's lines or anyone else's, at least as far as Ruth could see. Then they looked at the other paperwork in the pile Emily had thrust at them. One was a form saying Bethany's earnings could be used to pay her AFTRA initiation fee; another was a contract saying she would be paid seven hundred dollars for her work this week.

"Mimi didn't tell us anything about AFTRA," Ruth whispered. "I have no idea what we're supposed to do. I'll have to call her."

Another harried-looking young woman knocked on their door and came in. She had black hair with purple tips and a tattoo on the back of her hand that looked like a Japanese character, though she wasn't Japanese. Ruth had read once that a lot of jewelry and T-shirts—and tattoos, probably—with Asian characters were supposed to say things like *Happiness* or *Joy* or *Prosperity*, when really they were just nonsense or, worse, swear words.

"Lucy?"

Bethany hopped up.

"I'm Candy from Wardrobe. We've got this"—she held out a skirt and matching T-shirt—"and these"—a pair of black boots and tights—"and this." She handed Ruth two plastic Ziploc bags holding earrings and a necklace. "I need you to try these on right away and let me know if we have any problems, okay?"

"Okay," Bethy said. She was so excited she stripped off her clothes without even remembering that she didn't let Ruth see her anymore, not even in her underwear. Ruth tried to look without looking. Bethy's breast buds were growing, and there was a hint of curve to her waist and hips that hadn't been there even four months ago, which was the last time Ruth had seen her in a swimsuit. Bethany pulled on the skirt and T-shirt. They were heavily spangled and the shirt said, LOOK AT ME, I'M HOT in pink glitter on the front.

"Mom, did you remember the camera?" Bethy said. "Because you've got to take a picture of me so I can show Rianne. She's not going to believe this."

"Let's wait till you're through with Hair and Makeup," Ruth suggested, thinking how experienced they already sounded.

A minute later, Emily poked her head into the room again. "How's that stuff working for you? Good, I'll let Candy know she can come check, and here comes Hair." She darted out, and this time a young man came in wearing an elaborate apron full of brushes and wands and compacts and pots of every imaginable thing.

"You look great, honey," he said to Bethany. "I'm Elliot, by the way." Over his shoulder he said to Ruth, "Don't you wish you still had skin like this?"

"I'd just take the hips."

"I hear you, sister," The young man looked Bethy over closely. "You know, I think all we'll do is pull your hair up and give you a little powder and lip gloss." He stood back for a minute, considering. "Maybe not even lip gloss. Are you already wearing anything? *No*—that's your natural color? Oh my God." He flipped Bethany's hair around and tucked a little here and bound a little there and in no time flat she had two ponytails stacked vertically and twisted into little buns. "Perfect," he said.

"Let's take a little of that shine away and you're set." He plucked a big soft brush from his apron, twirled it expertly in a pot of loose power, dusted Bethy's face, and stood back to regard her. "There. You're *radiant*."

"This is her first time," Ruth confided.

"For real?" He put his arm around Bethy's shoulders and gave her a little squeeze. "Well, welcome to the funhouse, girl-friend. You, too," he said to Ruth. "Craft services is just across the way if you want coffee or a bagel or anything, by the way. In case they didn't tell you."

"I'm allowed?" Ruth asked. "Or is it just for Bethy?"

"Of *course* you're allowed, honey. You're not a prisoner here, despite what you might have heard." He laughed. "*We* are, but you're not." He leaned into her and stage-whispered, "And whatever you've heard about Peter, he's ten times worse. You didn't hear that from me, but gird thy loins, honey. You, too," he told Bethany. "Bye, girls."

THE FIRST SCENE OF THE FIRST DAY'S SHOOT—ONE OF the two scenes Bethany was in—took place in the Malibu beach house living room set. Bethy trotted brightly after Emily. When they got to the living room set, which she and Ruth had passed on their way in, it was filled with cameras and actors and ladders and gear of all kinds. Nearby, a clutch of men and women were huddled around a bank of television monitors. Emily put a hand on Bethy's back, pushing her gently toward an extremely tall man wearing a baseball cap. "Peter, here's Lucy," she said. To Bethany she said, "Lucy, this is Peter Tillinghast. He's the director."

"Yeah," said the man without looking away from the monitors. "Okay."

Emily took off, talking into her headset. Bethy stood where

she was, unsure of what she should do. "Hey, kid," said a man she recognized as Stuart, one of the Malibu teens. In real life he looked about thirty, but she guessed you could get away with that on television. "You're my girlfriend's little sister, right?"

Bethy was confused, and then realized he was referring to her character. "Oh! Yup, I'm Lucy."

"*Stop talking*," said the director.

Crestfallen, Bethany looked at her feet. The Stuart actor nudged her gently in the ribs with his elbow, and when she looked up he gave her a wink and a rueful smile and mouthed, "Sorry."

She mouthed back, "That's okay."

She was sure she hadn't made a sound, but the director snapped, "What did I just tell you?"

"Hey, look, I'm sorry," the Stuart actor said. "My bad."

"Yeah, okay. Lucy? Over there," the director said, gesturing vaguely. "No, *there*. Behind the sofa. You're going to be watching Stuart and Tina."

Bethy went, and so did Stuart. There was no actress, though.

"Where the fuck's Tina?" said the director.

"In Makeup," said Emily, who'd materialized out of thin air.

"Well, get her."

"I'm going," called Emily, already gone.

"Honey, do your lines for me," Peter Tillinghast said.

"Me?" Bethany asked.

"Aren't you Lucy?"

"Yes, sir."

"So go."

"*I think you're a bad person with a bad attitude,*" Bethy said.

"Yeah, but you're not just confused, you're ticked off. I mean, this is your sister they're fu— screwing with."

"*I think you're a bad person with a bad attitude,*" Bethy said again, but angrier.

"Yeah, okay. Do we have Tina yet?"

An actress hurried up with tissue paper from Hair and Makeup still flapping around her shoulders. "God. Sorry."

"Yeah, whatever," the director said. "All right, let's run this, people!" A flock of grips and sound guys and lighting techs and wardrobe people with pins in their mouths scattered like starlings, and the actors started to run the scene. The Tina actress strode in the door and went to the Stuart actor's side and Bethany got goose bumps of amazement that she was here at all, and then Peter yelled, "*No!*" before they ever got to her line, and they took it again from the top.

RUTH HAD STAYED IN THE TINY CUBICLE ON THE AWFUL, rocklike couch for three full hours—she'd always been an eager, obedient person in the face of authority—but she couldn't stand it anymore. She'd seen Bethy for only five minutes, tops, when Emily ran her to the dressing room for her work permit and school things, and then away again, bound for the classroom. "Mom, it was so fun," Bethy had blurted, but the rest would have to wait. What Ruth had expected to be one of the best days of her life was turning out to be an incarceration. When she couldn't take it for one more minute, she peeked out the dressing room door. No one was in sight, and she could only distantly hear activity, so she crept out and headed for the smell of coffee. She wound up in a small room stocked not only with coffee but black, green, and herbal teas; juices; energy drinks; healthy snacks; unhealthy snacks; and lots and lots of sugar. A Hispanic woman was consolidating bagels on a tray.

"*Hola,*" Ruth said, because she'd always felt it was polite to greet a member of another culture in their own language.

"Hey," the woman said, with no accent whatsoever. "Are you hungry? No one's eating this morning."

"To tell you the truth, I don't even know," Ruth admitted, eyeing a tray of chocolate old-fashioneds longingly. "My daughter's working here, and we were too excited to eat breakfast because it's her first time on set ever. I probably shouldn't, though." She sucked in her stomach.

"Oh, go ahead." The woman put a chocolate old-fashioned doughnut on a paper plate and handed it to her. Then she picked up an apple and gave that to Ruth, too. "See? The apple cancels out the doughnut. It's a law of dietary physics."

Ruth laughed.

"Anyway, it always works for me and my daughter." The woman, who Ruth couldn't help but notice was a little bit pudgy, dragged a wet dishtowel around the counter beneath the platters of cut fruit and granola and cold French toast, then swabbed the bottom of the syrup pitcher.

"How old is she?" Ruth asked.

"Twenty-four."

"Oh, a big girl. Mine's only thirteen. I can't imagine what it's going to be like when she's grown up and out of the house."

"I wouldn't know. Mine's grown, but she's not out of the house. You must not be from here. No one can afford their own place in LA until they're thirty-five and in a two-income marriage. Says me, anyway."

"No, we're from Seattle," Ruth said.

"Then I guess things must cost a lot less in Seattle."

"I wouldn't have thought so until we came down here. It's like there's a hole in the bottom of my wallet."

"You here because of her?"

Ruth nodded, biting into the doughnut and closing her eyes

briefly. "Yum. Yes—this is her dream. We've been here for only a month and a half."

"Husband?"

"He's still in Seattle. It's hard."

The woman shook her head. "I wish my husband was in Seattle. Well, ex-husband. He's only in Van Nuys. Once I was stuck on the 101 and he was in the car next to me for an hour and a half. What are the odds of that?"

"I miss mine," Ruth said, but even as she said it, she knew it was more complicated than that. She *did* miss Hugh, missed sharing the responsibility of the big decisions, and right now everything seemed like a big decision. On the other hand, if he were really here with her, they'd be disagreeing about everything. "I guess I should go," Ruth said reluctantly. "I'm Ruth, by the way."

The woman smiled at her and held out her hand, then changed her mind at the last minute and gave Ruth a warm, one-armed hug. "Renata," she said. "I'll be here all week. Come see me sometimes."

Ruth could feel mortifying tears building behind her eyes. She cleared her throat. "Thanks for talking to me."

"Hey, no problem," said Renata. "I'm probably the only one who will. Me and Emily."

Ruth had learned enough already to know that she was probably right.

Instead of returning to the dressing room, Ruth walked back out to the area with picnic tables, now empty—the background players must have been dismissed already—and dialed Hugh. His office manager, Margaret, said he was with a patient doing a particularly nasty root canal and did she want her to interrupt him, and she said no, she'd try again later.

That took three and a half minutes.

For the first time in her life, she knew what it felt like to be invisible. If someone were to walk by her right now, they wouldn't even know she was there. Certainly they wouldn't care. She was in the belly of the beast, a parasite in the gut of Hollywood: she was the Mom. She had no other name. "Where's the Mom, for God's sake?" she'd heard one of the set teachers say to another one when they were at the Rialto. "Jesus Christ! It's not our job to track them down." Clearly, it was the Mom's duty to anticipate and to serve. Household domestics were treated with greater respect.

Suddenly she thought of Vee Velman. Ruth could ask her stupid questions and not feel embarrassed, and it would be a relief to talk with someone who knew the ropes. Before she could think better of it, she found Vee in her cell phone's contact list. Vee answered on the third ring.

"Am I interrupting?" Ruth asked.

"Nah. I'm sitting outside Buster's school waiting to take him to the orthodontist for the first time. I'm thinking of just handing them all my charge cards up front and getting it over with. How are you? How's Bethy?"

"We're good, I think," Ruth said. "We're on the set of *California Dreamers*. It's been a whirlwind."

"Hey, that's great! I've heard the director's a dick, though."

"I don't know. I haven't met him."

"Yeah, and you won't. He hates parents. Well, I mean, everyone hates parents, but he *really* hates 'em. He doesn't like kids much, either. Why they let him get his hands on this program is completely beyond me. But completely. So do you guys have a trailer or a dressing room? Clara had a friend who was on episode two, and they put her in a trailer all the way out behind the soundstage. No air-conditioning, nada. She complained to the set teacher, who complained to the AD—"

"AD?"

"—assistant director, who complained to the PA, poor thing, and the upshot was, they ended up in a little closet behind craft services. At least they were in the building, though."

"No, we have a room—well, a cubicle. We're supposed to share it, I think, but so far no one else has come in. It's just me."

Vee snorted. "Poor you. I'd rather be at the gynecologist than on set."

Ruth heard a loud buzzer go off. She held the phone away from her ear. "Did you hear that? I keep hearing this loud buzzer."

"It means the cameras are rolling. And let me tell you, some directors will have you hunted down and shot if you so much as *cough* when the cameras are rolling. I kid you not. If you haven't turned your cell phone ringer off, do it right now, because if you get a cell phone call while they're taping and they can hear it, which they always can—I swear to God, it's *unnatural*—you'll be out of there so fast you won't know what hit you."

Ruth felt herself pale. "I never even thought about that. Hold on." She took the phone away from her ear and quickly switched it to vibrate.

"So what's she playing?"

"Lucy, who's someone named Tina's younger sister."

"Ah, yes, the Little Sister. Bratty or heroic?"

"Heroic, I think. Plucky."

"Yeah," Vee said. "Clara always likes the bratty parts better, but then she's a redhead. Thank God Buster's a brunet, because if he'd been a redhead, too, I'd have been calling Family Services *myself* and asking them to come take me into custody. He's ADHD, and let me tell you, *there's* a nightmare."

Ruth made a sympathetic noise.

"That which does not kill me . . ." Vee intoned.

"You do seem very strong."

"Nah, I just scare 'em with talk. Their mistake is, so far they believe me. The minute they catch on, I'm a dead man."

Ruth sat down at one of the waiting area's picnic tables. "Do you know an acting coach named Greta Groban?"

"Uh-uh. Is she good?"

"Mimi seems to think so. She's peculiar, though. I'm respectful when we talk about her because I'm trying to set an example for Bethy, but in my heart I'm sure she's a fascist. Is that bad?"

"Nah. Whoops, here comes Buster. Listen, has anyone mentioned the lunch line to you yet?"

"The lunch line?"

"Obviously not. Here's how it works. Actors and directors eat first, then Production, then Hair and Makeup and Wardrobe, and *then* parents. Depending on how good craft services is, you could end up licking the bottoms of the steam trays. Probably not, though—there's usually enough food."

"I had no idea," Ruth said. "Thank you for mentioning it."

"No prob. Look, just say, '*Yez, boss,*' and shuck and jive a lot, and you won't get into any trouble. When in doubt, always remember: the PA's the most important person on the set, bar none. Do whatever you can to please her."

"I keep hearing that."

"Yeah, because it's true." Ruth heard a scuffling noise and then Vee said, "Okay, hon, I better go. The fruit of my loins has returned. Call me later and let me know how it went."

Ruth returned to her plywood cell.

WHEN BETHANY WAS FIVE HELENE RABINOWITZ, WHO was a hoarder, gave her a dress-up kit called *Make Me Beautiful* that she'd been saving since the 1950s. It was in pristine condition, the size of a steamer trunk, and filled with dozens of chiffon scarves, slippery satin sheaths, and petticoats as stiff as ballet tutus, as well as felt cloches, picture hats, and a tiny wool pancake topped with three artificial cherries and held in place with an elastic chin strap. A swing-out tray held enough makeup to last Bethany's entire life—possibly several lives—and below that she found a second tray holding different-colored, high-heeled plastic mules that *smick-smack*ed as she walked.

Bethany had been in ecstasy, though she'd heard Ruth hiss to Hugh, "Is she crazy?" when she saw what was in the trunk. "What kinds of values are these to teach to a girl? What about a scientist's lab coat maybe, or a hard hat?"

"It's just dress-up," Hugh had said. "It's just make-believe. If she wants to become a princess, who are we to stop her?" Apparently Ruth hadn't come up with a good argument, because the trunk was still in place in Bethy's room, though she used it as a table now. She'd always loved wearing costumes. Drape a simple scarf around her shoulders like a shawl and she was an old woman from Romania. Add a hat and she became a beautiful woman on her way to a ball. She clicked around the house in the mules—which were really only a little too big if she stuffed the toes with tissue—until she'd worn a scratch pattern in the kitchen floor and Ruth had relegated them to the closet in the guest bedroom. She still looked in on them sometimes, even though she'd outgrown them a long time ago.

Bethy knew Ruth worried about the day when she realized she wasn't beautiful, but she'd always known that. She knew she wasn't even pretty. She had something else, though, even if she didn't have a name for it. She could be all kinds of characters— kid sister and villainous bully, screechy hysteric and classroom brain—and with each one, she not only was different, she actu-

ally *looked* different. After lunch when he was prepping Bethy
for her second scene (though she didn't have lines in that one),
Elliot confirmed it when he told her she had a face like a perfect
canvas.

"Honey, what you've got is better than beauty. You're an
Egyptian Spanish Jewish Gypsy Girl."

"But *you're* beautiful," Bethy pointed out, because he was: he
had the darkest brown eyes and the squarest jaw and the most
perfect nose she'd ever seen.

He sighed, twirling his brush in a pot of powder. "Looks
fade, honey, and trust me, once they do, they never come back.
In twenty years—less, if I stop moisturizing—I'll look exactly
like Joel Grey, and let me tell you, that's not a good thing. What
you've got is going to last."

"I don't know," Bethy said.

"Close 'em," said Elliot. Obediently she closed her eyes and
he smoothed her hair back and powdered her face, running the
soft badger brush over her eyelids as lightly as a kiss.

"I mean, I'd like to be beautiful like you and my friend Alli-
son, but maybe this is better," she said. "Look at Hilary Swank.
She's not beautiful but she's an awesome actor. You saw *Million
Dollar Baby*, right? Plus she's from Seattle, too."

"Lips," he said, and she opened her mouth and stretched her
lips so he could stroke on lip gloss. "There. Now you're perfect."

"Thank you."

"My pleasure, honey."

Emily popped her head in. "Lucy? They're ready for you."

Elliot whisked the nylon cape from around her shoulders
with a flourish. "You go, girlfriend. Strut your stuff."

WHEN THE SHOW WRAPPED FOR THE DAY, BETHY AND
Ruth went to Bob's for dinner, of course. Unlike Ruth, who

said she was wiped out, Bethany was exhausted but flying. "And the thing is," she was explaining to Ruth about Peter, having been on a nonstop talking jag since they'd left the set an hour ago, "he might be a jerk and everything—I mean, he *is* a jerk, he yells at everybody and he's really mean to Emily—but when we finally taped the scene in the living room with Stuart and Tina, they were really, really good. And maybe they wouldn't have been as good if he hadn't been mean to them. Like, maybe they wouldn't have tried so hard."

The Hispanic waiter slid their check under Ruth's plate. Noisily, Bethy sucked up the very last dregs of her shake through her straw. "And there's this guy named Hal—I think he said his real name is Halbert, isn't that *weird*?—and he'd keep track of where we were in the script, and time everything, and also keep track of props and stuff so there's continuity, because you wouldn't want there to be a clock in one take and then have it gone in another one. You see that, though. He was telling me about some of the scenes where people have screwed up, how an actress would have a purse and then it'd be gone. What?"

"Eat," said Ruth, tapping her fingernail on Bethy's plate. Half her hamburger was left.

"I can't," Bethy said. "I'm done."

Ruth pressed her lips together. Ruth hated when Bethy wasted food, but Bethy didn't think it should count on a day that was this important. While Ruth was at the front counter paying the bill, Bethy went outside, dug up her cell phone, found Allison in her contact list, and called her.

"Allisolicious," Allison answered. "May I take your order?"

Bethany burst out laughing. "You're funny."

"Is this Rachel calling?" Rachel was the name of Bethy's character in their showcase scene.

"It was," Bethy said, "but now it's Lucy."

"Lucy Goosey. How are you, Goosey?"

"I'm fine," Bethy said, but she was annoyed—there was an unfamiliar edge to Allison's voice. "I just got back from the *California Dreamers* set."

"I know," Allison said. "Mimi's pissed."

"Why?"

"I don't know, she just is. She thought I should have gotten the part and not you."

"But you didn't even audition," Bethany said.

"She got me in at the last minute."

"Oh."

"You know she's changing your name back to Rabinowitz, by the way."

"I know."

"So no more Roosevelt. Now you're just plain Rabino-witz."

"I don't see why it mattered in the first place," Bethany said.

"Because it's Jewish."

"So?"

"People don't like Jewish people."

"I don't think that's true," said Bethy.

"Oh, it's true."

"Huh," said Bethy, because she couldn't think of anything else to say.

"Okay," Allison said. "So I'll see you, Lucy Goosey."

And just like that, she hung up.

Chapter Twelve

Winter in Seattle was as dank as a sewer, but it wasn't just that. No, it was time to confront the truth head-on: Hugh Rabinowitz felt like hell. He had been feeling like hell for weeks, and conceivably for much longer than that. And it wasn't that he was a hypochondriac, either—that was Ruth's province. He didn't have the imagination for it, plus he had such a high pain threshold that you usually had to hit him over the head with a symptom before he paid any attention to it. When he was a kid his appendix had ruptured before he'd even admitted that his stomach hurt. So whatever this was, he knew it was real: a persistent, transcendent fatigue coupled with a vague sense of dread, of not-rightness. He knew what Ruth would say: depression. But if it was depression—and he prided himself on being very open-minded about mental health issues, for a man of his generation—why was he so damned thirsty all the time? He should be turning into a camel, that's how much he was drinking, but it didn't matter. What the hell?

So he put in a call to Manny Kalman, who'd been his internist for about a thousand years, and Manny said, "Get in here, guy, and let's talk." So Hugh got in there and they talked, and then they did some lab work, and now Hugh was going back to get the results. It made him nervous that Manny had had his office manager, Sonja, schedule the appointment. Usually Manny just talked to him over the phone and then called in a prescription for some anti-inflammatory or antibiotic, and that would be it for another year or until his annual checkup rolled around.

So at two o'clock on a drizzly Tuesday afternoon he pulled into the last spot in the practice's parking lot and trudged into the waiting room with the sound of doom ringing in his ears. He might not be a hypochondriac, but he did have an active imagination, and he couldn't imagine that Manny had called him in because he had good news.

Mercifully, the office was empty of patients. Sonja was on the phone behind a sliding glass window, absently clicking impeccably manicured nails on her pharmaceutical endorsement desk blotter as she talked. She was beautifully groomed, unlike Margaret, who managed Hugh's office with the efficiency of a drill sergeant but who wasn't, let's face it, much to behold. When Sonja saw him she slid the glass door open and said, "How's tricks, sweetie?" She was always calling people sweetie. Hugh thought that was nice.

"I don't know. I guess that'll depend on Manny." Hugh handed her his debit card for the copay.

She looked at her telephone console. "Well, let's get you back there, then. I'll process this"—she waggled the card—"while you're in with the doctor."

She walked him down the hall in what looked to Hugh like extremely expensive leather shoes that had probably been fabricated on distant, sophisticated shores. Ruthie would have admired them. The heavier she got, the more she appreciated shoes—shoes and purses, which, he'd noted from his patients, seemed to be a large woman's place of escape. Not that Ruth spent money or even dressed that way—she lacked the confidence. She once told Hugh she'd had a dream in which she'd been dressed by a TV show specializing in updating people's images, only when she was all done and came out tremulously to join her assembled friends and family, Hugh's mother had said, *Oh, please.* Poor Ruthie.

Sonja showed Hugh into Manny's office—as though he didn't know the way after all these years—and closed the door behind him.

The room was richly furnished with thick carpet and wall-to-wall mahogany. Hugh really needed to spiff up his own office suite one of these days—like there was even a fat chance as long as Ruth was in LA. No money, no one to line up the contractor or supervise the remodel. God knows *he* wasn't qualified.

"Hey, man!" Manny said disingenuously, as though the fact that Hugh was coming in had slipped his mind. Hugh knew because he did the same thing himself from time to time, when a patient—usually a phobic one—needed bolstering with a particularly hale-fellow-well-met declaration. He reached across his desk and gave Hugh a handshake that could bend steel. A manila folder sat in front of him in the exact center of the otherwise unobstructed desk. Manny had always been on the anal-retentive side, but in Hugh's opinion that was as good a quality in a doctor as it was in a dentist, and more than once he'd said as much.

"Well?" Hugh said.

All doctor now, Manny frowned as he opened the folder, looked at a sheet of lab results, and then turned it around so Hugh could see. "Diabetes," he said.

Hugh stared at the numbers, as though he had any idea what they meant. The ringing in his ears got louder. "What?"

"You've got diabetes, my friend."

"But we're a heart family."

"You're also an overweight family."

Hugh sagged in his chair.

"Look," Manny said, folding his hands over his immaculate

desk blotter. "It isn't cancer, it isn't neurological, and if you take it seriously, it isn't fatal. And if you lose seventy-five pounds you might be able to kick it. Think of this as a wake-up call. Make it a family project. It wouldn't hurt Ruth to take off a few pounds."

Hugh rubbed his face.

"Okay," Manny said, gliding away from his desk on the silent wheels of his expensive chair. "Go home and call Ruth. Bring her onboard. Get her to come in with you the next time and I'll have Sonja give you some literature to take home with you today. Start reading. Knowledge is your best ally. And I'm going to call in a couple of prescriptions that I want you to start taking right away, so we can get you back on track." He described each medication, and Hugh did his best to look like he was listening, but all he was hearing was the pounding of his mortal heart. "The good news is, you're going to be feeling better as long as you work at this thing," Manny was saying when he next tuned in. "Just remember: you're the one in control."

Easy for Manny to be glib, Hugh thought sourly. He didn't have diabetes. He'd probably never carried an extra pound in his life, and neither had his elegant wife, Lenore.

"All right, so let's bring you back early next week and see how we're doing," Manny said. "You're going to have questions by then."

He walked Hugh back to the reception area, where Hugh got a bag full of pamphlets from Sonja. Then Hugh went to Rite Aid to fill his prescriptions and buy a whole basketful of para-phernalia, and drove home in a daze. You thought you knew your future—how you might look, where you might vacation, how you might feel about retirement. And then this. It turned out that you didn't know a thing.

He called Ruth from the driveway.

"But there isn't a single diabetic in the family," she argued, once he'd told her the news. "Heart, yes, but—"

"I said the same thing, but evidently the numbers were clear. This is real."

Ruth was silent.

"Hello?" said Hugh.

"I'm here. So what do you have to do?"

"I don't really know yet. Learn to control it. I have some things to read." Hugh started fumbling among the pamphlets Manny had given him and some that he'd picked up himself at Rite Aid along with his medicine. *You and Diabetes. How to Live with Diabetes. So You've Been Diagnosed with Diabetes: Now What?* Indeed.

"Manny thinks it might be a good idea to have you come home, for us to go and meet with him together," he said. "This isn't a summer cold."

Ruth didn't say a word.

"Ruthie," he said quietly. "Please don't make me ask."

Ruth sighed. "I know, honey. It's just that—" There was an awkward silence. He was appalled to find his eyes tearing up.

"No, nothing. Of course I'll come home," she said.

"That's my girl," Hugh said bitterly.

ALTHOUGH SHE KNEW SHE SHOULDN'T BE, RUTH WAS FURIOUS. Hugh was fat and he'd been fat for a long time, which he should have pretty much known he would be, at his age, given the shape his mother was in; and now he had diabetes. She was fat, too, of course, but she was working on that, plus if you got right down to it, she wasn't *as* fat, to begin with. And she had no intention of *staying* fat, whereas Hugh didn't care. So now she was supposed to, what, leave Bethy here with Mimi? There were auditions lined up through the whole next week. But she was a wife, and wives stood by their husbands, especially when they were sick and scared like Hugh. She would have to go home and deal with this, and maybe it would be all right after all if she just left Bethy here for a week or so with money for decent food—lots of fruits and vegetables, easy on the carbs—and instructed her specifically to beware of the deleterious effects of sticking to the Orphans too blindly. Once Hugh had come to terms with his health and learned how to eat right and test himself and shoot up his insulin or whatever else diabetics had to do—after all, people were coping with diabetes every day; it wasn't like it was life-threatening, more of an annoyance; manageable was the thing; it was *manageable*—she'd come back down and they'd pick up right where they'd left off, except maybe Hugh would finally spring for a studio apartment at the Oakwood. That would give Bethy something to focus on while she was at Mimi's and dining, no doubt and despite Ruth's warnings, on Funyuns.

Hugh would probably give Ruth a hard time about not bringing Bethy back with her to Seattle, but you never knew when that one audition might come that would turn out to be Bethy's big break. A guest-star role on *CSI: Miami*; a recurring character on *Unfabulous* or *Ned's Declassified School Survival Guide*. So Ruth would call Mimi and work it out, and she'd call Hugh and tell him to book her a flight, and she'd pack up the apartment—there was no use paying for it while she and Bethy were both away—and fly out the following morning.

She told Bethy that Daddy needed her to handle a few things around the house (why scare her and then leave; the truth could wait) but that she'd be back within a week, and in the meantime how would she feel about staying with Mimi and Allison? Evidently she and Allison had patched up whatever little tiff they'd had, because, to Ruth's relief, Bethy was not only willing, but enthusiastic.

So Ruth picked up the phone and called the studio and when Mimi answered she asked whether she could come by and talk for a minute. Mimi said yes, which didn't necessarily mean she'd be there when Ruth arrived, a hard truth Ruth had learned over the past weeks. The woman was very casual about other people's time. She hustled Bethy into the car and drove directly to the studio. Mimi's battered little car was in its usual spot by the Dumpster.

Allison was in the classroom pretending to do schoolwork when they came in. Bethany, who'd had the presence of mind to bring along some schoolwork herself, pulled a TV tray out of the rack, set it up beside Allison, and unfolded a chair. Ruth knocked on the doorjamb of Mimi's office, went in, and sat down beside her desk. Mimi's computer screen was filled with e-mail messages, which she continued to answer while Ruth sat and waited. Beneath Mimi's feet Tina Marie roused herself briefly to give Ruth an annoyed look before turning around several times and dropping back heavily into her basket.

Five minutes later, Ruth was still sitting and waiting. She could feel a hot flush cresting near her ears. She cleared her throat.

"Just another minute," Mimi said.

Ruth waited another minute.

"All right," said Mimi, finally looking at her with exactly the same expression Tina Marie had shown her.

"I need to ask a favor," Ruth said. Her voice came out froggy with nerves. She cleared her throat and started over. "I need to ask a favor."

"Oh?"

"Hugh needs me at home for a few days, and I don't want to take Bethy with me. She has those auditions, and I don't think she should miss them. Do you?"

"She's always going to have auditions."

"Still. I think she has a certain amount of momentum. What I was wondering was, could she stay with you for a few days?"

Mimi looked at her shrewdly. "I didn't think you approved of that. I charge seven hundred dollars per week."

Ruth barely kept herself from gasping. Still, she wasn't going to put a price tag on Bethany's career.

"And you'll also want to leave her a couple of hundred dollars in cash for food," Mimi said.

Ruth sighed. "All right. I'm going to try to fly out first thing in the morning, so I think it would be the easiest thing if I drop her at your house tonight. I'll take her home and she'll pack and I'll give her dinner and then I'll bring her by."

Mimi nodded vaguely, her eyes having returned to her computer screen. Ruth sighed again and left the office, finding Bethy in the greenroom with Allison.

"I'm going back to pack," Ruth told her. "I can pack for you if you want to just stay here, or you can come back with me."

"No, I'll stay here. Allison is going to order a pizza."

"Ha cha cha," said Allison.

ALLISON WAS USED TO PEOPLE CONSTANTLY COMING AND going from Mimi's house, but that didn't mean she liked it. Right now it was just Mimi and her, because Hillary and Reba had each gone home for a week, but there had been times during boot camps when she'd had eight girls sleeping in her room, and more were on the sun porch and in the living room on futons, and the only way you could get into the bathroom was by pretending you had diarrhea. The best times were when it was just the two of them, and Mimi let Allison give her a manicure even though Mimi had fingers as fat as sausages and liked colors that were completely out of fashion, like frosted pink. Those were the cozy times, the times when Allison was able to talk her into leaving the studio by seven and taking her to El Pollo Gordo for dinner.

Partly what she hated about sharing her room (which was furnished with two bunk beds that Mimi had let Allison choose from Ikea, plus Allison's own twin bed with matching dust ruffle, comforter, and sheets) was that she liked her things to be just so: the Coach tote, the arsenal of MAC cosmetics, the clothes she kept arranged by item type—skirt, skirt, skirt, blouse, blouse, jacket—in her closet and bureau drawers and bathroom vanity drawer. Kids were always moving stuff or using it, so she'd started a color-coded system where she tied yarn around her dresser drawer pulls and cosmetics cases and clothes hangers and shampoo and conditioner bottles. Red yarn meant *Hands off*; yellow yarn meant it belonged to Mimi (there were very few yellow-tagged items because most of Mimi's things were in Mimi's room, which no one was allowed to enter *ever*, not even Allison, under pain of being dropped from her roster); and green yarn meant, *This stuff is crap so everyone can use it*. Mostly her system was respected, especially since she'd told Reba and Hillary she'd stop advising them on their wardrobe choices if they so much as laid a finger on her things.

Allison wasn't exactly thrilled about having Bethany staying with them. Bethany was *so* naïve. She'd never owned anything from Juicy or had her own makeup or French-braided her hair or *anything*. But while she was moisturizing her face with a new Clinique lotion sample she'd picked up at the Beverly Center last week, it occurred to Allison that she could try some products out on her, which would be good practice in case Allison had to go into cosmetology and become a famous Hollywood makeup artist, which was her backup plan if she wasn't a famous actor by the time she was twenty-one. She sat down at her desk and pulled a piece of bright pink construction paper and some felt-tip markers from the drawer and very, very carefully and decoratively made a sign for their door that said ALLISON AND BETHANY, in that order.

RUTH FOUND HUGH WAITING FOR HER IN THE AIRPORT THE next morning. Over the years they'd flown in and out of Sea-Tac so many times that it felt like an extension of home.

Hugh was standing at the baggage carousel, wearing his dental smock under his coat, so he must have gone in to do an early filling or two. She felt herself soften. He was a good man, a responsible man, and an excellent provider. She thought of Angie Buehl and her husband, Dillard, and gave thanks. She knew it was wrong to be such a snob, but there it was.

On the ride into town Hugh caught her up on his meeting with Manny. It had thrown him for a complete loop, he said; he'd always been so healthy that he took it for granted. Normally, Ruth was the one: endometriosis, a faulty thyroid, vicious summer allergies, gout—and, of course, there had been the fertility problem. But now that she was here, he said, he was sure he'd come to grips, even though his mortality was staring him right in the face. And as he told her about diabetes, she could see why. She'd had no idea. There could be organ complications as well as unhealing ulcers, limb amputations, nerve death, heart disease, blindness, and stroke—dear God.

Hugh turned into their driveway, and Ruth eased a little. She loved their little craftsman bungalow. Some people moved in and out of houses as casually as they changed sweaters, but Ruth was a nester. Over the years she'd invested great care in acquiring and displaying her household things: a hand-blown witch's ball in the garden, bird feeders in the shapes of Victorian houses, tastefully framed photos of Bethy at all ages; seasonal and holiday knickknacks that she felt warmed up a house, especially when there were children. One whole wall of the garage was lined with color-coded tubs for the various times of year. She stood in the middle of the living room now, drinking in the peach-colored walls and warm lighting. As Hugh brought her suitcase in from the car, she actually felt her heartbeat slow down. Coming home to Seattle was like stepping through a wormhole into a parallel universe, a place where Hollywood was just a figure of speech; where the foliage was lush, the air smelled sweet, and even the bad traffic was a *better* bad.

Hugh came up behind her and put his arms around her. "Good to be home?"

Ruth nodded.

"I told Mom we'd stop by later," Hugh said. "I want to tell her in person."

Ruth went into the kitchen to take inventory. Hugh had printed out several of Bethy's latest headshots and attached them to the refrigerator door with magnets. Ruth thought she looked pretty up there, with her straightened hair cut in a bob and the slightest hint of lipstick and blush. Older. Is this what she'd look like when she was eighteen? Ruth had been right there in the photographer's studio, helping Bethy in and out of different outfits and hairstyles and makeup, but in the photos it all looked spontaneous and effortless. You'd never know they'd been in a semi-abandoned building in downtown Los Angeles, where the photographer's vast loft studio had been furnished with a boomerang-shaped thrift-shop coffee table and a couch held up by three wobbly legs and a brick. The shoot had lasted for two hours, and Ruth had been limp by the end, but not Bethy. Bethy had been in her element. "I bet this is what it feels like to be a movie star," she'd whispered to Ruth as they changed her outfit behind a flimsy rice-paper screen. "I could just keep doing this. Maybe I could model, too, while I'm down here?" Ruth had made what she hoped was a neutral, let's-wait-and-see noise, hoping Bethy would forget all about it. She didn't want to pop the child's bubble, but she was realistic enough to know that while Bethy could be made to look very appealing and fresh-faced, she didn't have the bones for beauty. At the end of the photo shoot, when the child floated out of the building on wings, saying, "I can't wait to see the pictures," Ruth had merely said, "Oh, me, too," and left it at that.

She opened the refrigerator and the cupboards and could see almost immediately that the household needed virtually everything—the refrigerator, in mute accusation, held only a half dozen eggs, some orange juice, and a couple of takeout containers from Wing Fong. The pantry was picked clean. There wasn't much more than a box of saltines, several cans of soup, and some tomato paste. Poor Hugh. Maybe he didn't have diabetes at all. Maybe he was simply suffering from malnutrition.

Ruth heard him on the phone in the third bedroom, which they used as a den. She went down there and poked her head in, whispering that she was going to the store. Hugh lifted his hand in acknowledgment. "No, let's schedule it Wednesday. The day after tomorrow," he was saying, which meant he was on the phone with Margaret. Even in the middle of a health crisis— was this a crisis?—he was a conscientious man.

Outside, the air was cold and weepy. Seattle in the late fall was Ruth's favorite time of year, when you could hole up and make soup and bake and finally feel all right about the fact that you weren't climbing a mountain or at least taking a hike along one of the area's hundreds of trails. Not that she'd ever been the hiking type. She was more of the sitting-on-a-bench-watching-other-people-exert-themselves type.

She drove to their neighborhood Albertsons, at which she'd been shopping for groceries for eighteen years. There were still traces of pumpkin gore in the gutters and on lesser-used side streets. People had probably just figured what the hell, it was organic—it would decompose eventually and replenish the earth. Ruth thought affectionately that if someone had vandalized a display of Styrofoam takeout containers, the mess would have been cleaned up in an hour flat. Seattle was the home of militant recyclers, rabid reusers, and loathers of all things plastic.

Ruth pulled into a parking space, disconcerted that everything felt at once deeply familiar, yet strange. She hadn't noticed before how many people drove SUVs and pickups, had piercings and tattoos, wore strange leg-wear and everyday shoes that could be worn to cross a wilderness. No one in Hollywood would be caught dead in any of it. Ruth felt somehow more urbane, though she was wearing the same Seattle-wear herself that she wore, to her shame, in LA. Her eye was being trained, was the thing. She might not be a sophisticate herself—who had the money?—but she could tell the difference.

"Ruth Rabinowitz!" sang a woman's voice. Ruth turned with dread. Speeding toward her was Bonnie Rowan, a perky, spandex-clad woman with the build of a boy and the leathery face of an elf. She always seemed to be coming from or going to an exercise class, athletic outing, or racing event. Over the years Ruth had been subjected to countless travelogues: sailing off of Greece, rock climbing in Utah, trekking in the Himalayas.

"Bonnie!" she nevertheless warbled back, matching the woman note for note. She hated that duplicitous side of herself, but it seemed to be the expected thing between women who had seen each other at school and neighborhood functions for years yet had absolutely nothing else in common.

"Where have you been keeping yourself?" Bonnie cried—as

though they'd ever gotten together for so much as a cup of coffee. "It's been forever! We heard you left town."

"Bethy and I are down in LA," Ruth said casually, loving the
sound of what was coming next. "She's acting professionally."

"No kidding?"

"No kidding."

"Well, we've missed seeing you," Bonnie said. A cell phone
went off in the pocket of her Gore-Tex anorak, the ring tone
set to the theme song from *Rocky*. She flipped the phone open
with one hand, waggled her fingers good-bye to Ruth with the
other, and set off down the aisle. Ruth watched her walk away.
Who dressed in spandex to go shopping? She probably did it
just to make dumpy people like Ruth feel bad about themselves.
Ruth wouldn't wear spandex to the Apocalypse.

For the umpteenth time she took out her own cell phone,
double-checked that the ring volume was turned to high in case
Bethy needed her, sped through the aisles, and hurried home.
When she got there, Hugh said that his mother was expecting
them. He'd called her, he said, and she had an hour before she
was supposed to be at the Stroum Jewish Community Center for her monthly current events discussion group, which she
hadn't missed even once since 2002.

Helene Rabinowitz was a tough little bird. She had small,
bright, judgmental eyes; coarse, wiry gray hair; a short, thick
build; and a combative stance. And this was not merely, or even
primarily, a reflection of her old age: Helene had looked exactly
the same since the day she had first met Ruth twenty-three years
ago and summarily judged her unworthy of Hugh. Apparently
Ruth was what Helene termed a *fluffnik*—a person without serious intent. Evidently an artist, especially a ceramic artist, was a
fluffnik of the first order. *You want someone who plays with clay all*

day, you should make friends with a preschooler, Hugh said she'd told him. *Find someone serious, a lawyer, a medical school student.*

Still, Ruth had to give Helene her due: she had raised Hugh alone, a feat about which Ruth was newly respectful after single-parenting Bethany in LA. Hugh's father, God rest his soul, had been killed in a freak collision with a bakery truck in 1963. "Well," Helene often said, "at least he went surrounded by the things he loved," these things evidently including rolls, Danishes, butter horns, and rugelach still warm from the oven. From his photographs Ruth could see that Jacob Rabinowitz had been a big man. Hugh had obviously gotten that from him. From Helene he'd inherited the tendency toward jowls and a shape like an apple.

When they arrived at her condominium complex that noon, Helene must have been watching for them because her door swung open before they'd even gotten to the top of the stairs. The buildings were sided with weathered gray clapboard and trimmed in crisp white. Each of the residents had a panic button in every room in the event of something dire.

"So," she greeted Ruth with a quick, hard cuff on the fore-arm as Ruth stepped past her in the foyer, "if it isn't the prodigal daughter-in-law." Helene often delivered short bursts of pain, though Hugh dismissed this when Ruth pointed it out: a pat on the cheek felt more like a slap, a pinch on the arm turned purple by morning. And she continued to hang the disclaimer daughter-*in-law* around Ruth's neck like an albatross years after her friends' in-laws had dropped the qualifier.

"Bubbala." Helene gave Hugh a strong hug, then held him out at arm's length for a good look.

"Hi, Mom."

"Nu? You look terrible. Look at your color, it's like putty, and is that sweat? Why are you sweating? It's like Siberia outside."

"Look, why don't we go sit down?" Hugh said.

The three of them moved into Helene's living room, which was a masterpiece of rigidly enforced order: the sofa's feet sat on protective disks; contrasting throw pillows were arrayed with mathematical precision. Ruth estimated there hadn't been a speck of dust on the coffee and end tables since Hugh was in high school. Reverently framed family photographs occupied every free surface, mostly of Bethy and Hugh. Two included Ruth.

Hugh sat in his usual place, a soft, deep club chair that had evidently been Jacob's, and which Hugh had inherited upon his father's death. Helene laid her palm tenderly on his cheek. "Are you hungry? I've got some nice babka. What about cake and a fresh cup of coffee?"

"Coffee would be nice, Mom."

"No cake? It's from Goldberg's."

"Just coffee."

"You?" Helene said to Ruth.

"No, thank you, Mom. Can I help?"

Helene waved her hand dismissively, already halfway to the kitchen. Ruth sighed. Hugh glanced at her and made a downward motion with his hand: *Let it go. This is going to be bad enough.* It was with just such hand signals that they had navigated the minefields of twenty-three years of holidays, birthdays, school plays, and Easter—which, unaccountably, Helene loved best of all the holidays, both Judaic and Christian, probably because it meant that Bethy would come and hunt for the plastic eggs Helene liberally filled from her massive coin jar.

Helene returned from the kitchen with cups of coffee, setting them in front of Hugh and Ruth.

"Look, Mom, there's something we want to tell you," Hugh said. "Some news. It turns out I'm diabetic. I just found out."

Helene discounted this with a wave. "We're a heart family."

"Even so. We have an appointment to go over everything with Manny Kalman. But the good news is, it's manageable."

"Of course it's manageable." Helene sat down in the chair beside Hugh's and stirred a spoonful of sugar into his coffee. "Herb Rosen had it forever, and he lived to eighty-five. Then again, he'd never been much of an eater. His wife was a terrible cook. Always too much salt." Helene took a sip of coffee.

Hugh sighed and pushed his cup away. Ruth crossed the room and switched her black coffee for his sweet cup. Helene pretended not to notice. "Yes, and that's exactly what we'll concentrate on—how to manage it," Hugh said.

"And for this you left my granddaughter alone in that terrible place?" Helene asked Ruth.

"It's not a cold, Mom," Hugh said. "Diabetes is a potentially life-threatening disease."

"He's rattled," Ruth said. "It came as such a shock."

Helene fixed her small, bright eyes on Ruth. "I don't know why. You know what he's been living on since you left him? He's been living on macaroni and cheese—the kind that comes in a box and gives you a heart attack."

"I didn't leave him," said Ruth.

"I eat other things," said Hugh.

"What? That spaghetti you fix, with the sauce that you don't drain the grease off of? That's good for you?"

"Eggs," Hugh said. "I scramble eggs."

"Well, you could eat an apple."

"I've eaten an apple."

Ruth thought she might scream.

"Anyway, that's not the point," said Hugh.

"I didn't leave him," said Ruth.

"I'll make you some soup," Helene said. "When she leaves again, I'll make you some chicken soup with spaetzle. You like that." She held up her hand imperiously. "White meat only. Who couldn't lose a pound or two?"

"All right, Mom," Hugh said.

"So you tell that to Manny Kalman. Tell him from now on, your mother who loves you will feed you."

THE CREEPY THING ABOUT HIS LIFE NOW WAS THAT HUGH was navigating a grotesque and never-ending obstacle course. Test himself too infrequently or fail to keep his numbers in the acceptable range and he would find himself bucketing down the road toward maiming, organ failure, and death. Keep it under control—*if* he could keep it under control, which Manny had told him could be extremely challenging—and he got to stick around. What kind of purgatory was that?

Not that he had any intention of revealing these musings to Ruth. After they'd left Helene's condo they'd gone to see Manny together and had had nearly an hour's orientation about Hugh's new diet and exercise regimen, as well as a practicum for Hugh on how to test himself with a meter and what to make of the results. The finger-stick hurt, the meter was unnerving, and its results were tyrannical: bad numbers, bad man.

Ruth insisted on buying an expensive digital bathroom scale at the Sharper Image, and then loaded the cupboards with entire product lines of sugar-free foods, all of which tasted like crap. She was worried about him, he knew, but she was also fretting about Bethany down in LA. He was horrified that Ruth had left her down there with Mimi Roberts, but on the ride home from the airport she'd made it very clear that the decision was not up for discussion. "I'm not going to talk about it," she'd said.

"Bethy has some important auditions coming up, and she needs to be there for them. So leave it and let's deal with this." *This*, of course, being his diabetes, which, she implied, he had obviously brought upon himself.

He missed his wife. This woman was no one he knew, and certainly no one he would have married if he'd met her today for the first time.

Chapter Thirteen

As soon as Hugh and Ruth had gone to bed, the phone rang. Ruth, who never slept well when Bethany was out of the house, sat up and grabbed the receiver before the second ring.

"Mom?" Bethy's voice was high and shrill.

"What's the matter, honey?" She could hear Bethy breathing shallowly. "Bethy? What's the matter? Honey, slow yourself down—you're going to hyperventilate."

"We just heard like a really loud bang out by the garage and we're scared," Bethy said. In the background, Ruth could hear Allison say, "I think it's moving! I think it's coming around the front!"

Bethany gave a little shriek. "We're really really scared. We think there might be a burglar or something, or an Armenian. Allison says that sometimes Armenians sneak around and look in your window to decide if they're going to rob you or something."

"Where's Mimi?" Ruth said, peering at the clock on her nightstand. "Isn't Mimi there? It's almost ten thirty."

"We don't know where she is." Ruth could hear Allison saying something, but she couldn't make out the words. Bethy began to moan, and Ruth could hear her teeth chattering. The child had never had a level head when it came to a crisis.

"Honey, let me talk to Allison. Okay? Bethy? Put Allison on the phone."

Ruth could hear Bethy saying, "No, she wants to talk to *you*."

"Hello?" Allison said casually.

"What on earth is going on there? What do you mean it might be an Armenian?"

"We heard a noise," Allison said. "This, like, *thump*. It was right outside the front door."

"And?"

"Well, I mean, *I'm* okay, but Bethy's kind of freaking out."

"Do you know where Mimi is?"

"Work, probably. She went back after she dropped us off."

"Have you tried calling her?"

"Nah," Allison said. "She left her cell phone here, and she never answers the office phone at night. She says that's why she stays late in the first place."

"But, honey, she's got young girls home alone."

"Yeah. We could always call 911, though."

"But you haven't? Why haven't you?"

"It's not really that big of a deal." Allison was beginning to sound annoyed.

"Are you hearing anything now?"

Ruth could hear Allison put her hand over the receiver and say, "Are we hearing anything? I mean, I'm just hearing your mom."

Bethy said something Ruth couldn't make out and then Allison got back on and said, "We don't hear anything." Then she could hear Allison put her hand over the receiver again and say, "But what if they're just waiting out there for us to get off the phone?"

Ruth heard Bethany give another little shriek. She sounded far away.

"Allison?"

"Yeah?"

"Stop trying to scare Bethany. I mean it. Stop it right now. Was there ever anything in the bushes?"

"Sure. It was something big, like a man, maybe, or a bear. I think it's gone now, though."

Ruth gritted her teeth. "Can you swear to me that there's nothing there?"

"Yeah," Allison said, clearly bored with the conversation.

"All right. Put Bethy back on, please."

Bethany got back on the line. "Are you calmer?" Ruth said. "Show me how you're breathing." Bethy inhaled and exhaled several times into the receiver. "Good," Ruth said.

"I'm still kind of scared, though."

"Listen to me. You're both fine. Allison is just trying to scare you. I want both of you in bed and with the lights out as soon as you hang up the phone. And I mean immediately. That goes for Allison, too. Have Mimi call me in the morning."

"You sure there isn't anything to be afraid of?"

"Well, you can be afraid of Allison, but otherwise, no, nothing."

"Do you think we should wait up for Mimi?"

"No," said Ruth. "I don't. Make sure all the doors and windows are locked, and then go to bed."

"Okay, Mom. I love you," Bethany said in her little girl, bedtime voice. "Do you want to say good night to Allison, too? Here."

Ruth could hear the phone being handed off, and then Allison said, in a crisp, womanly, maddening voice, "Hello?" As though she didn't know who was on the other end of the line.

"If you ever do that again, and I mean *ever*, there will be hell to pay. Am I clear?"

"Okay. Well, good night. We love you," Allison said in a singsongy imitation of Bethy.

Ruth suspected that the girl was mocking her. She hung up thinking that she should never, ever have left Bethy down there with those people. What on earth had she been thinking? And now there was nothing she could do but try to hurry Hugh through his crisis and get back to LA as quickly as she possibly could.

Hugh rolled toward her and said sleepily—he could sleep through a tornado—"What was that about?"

"Nothing. It's all right," Ruth said. "Go back to sleep."

BY THE THIRD DAY, BETHANY LOVED ABSOLUTELY EVERY-thing about Allison. For one thing, she had flawless skin, whereas Bethany had begun having outbreaks, and in noticeable places. She scrubbed and scrubbed, using a variety of exfoliating products that Allison didn't want anymore, but it was going to take more than that, at least from what Allison had told her when they were talking in bed last night: it was going to take Accutane, and she couldn't get that without a prescription, which she couldn't get until Ruth took her to a dermatologist, which couldn't happen until Ruth got back, which just frustrated Bethy to *death*. How was she supposed to book anything if she had pimples? You could slather on foundation and concealer—both of which she'd now learned to apply, under Allison's close supervision—but you really couldn't fool anyone. "They can still tell you have zits," Allison had said. "They're just zits you've covered up. If the person who books a role comes down to either you or me, they're going to choose me, especially if it's a movie role, because in movies they do insanely tight shots that are your face like six feet high on the screen. They don't want people sitting in the theater going, *Look at that gross zit!*"

And of course she was right. Allison had already gotten Reba and Hillary started using Proactiv, which was just one step down from Accutane, and neither of them even had breasts yet. Bethany didn't exactly have breasts, either—at least not like

Allison's, which Bethany had caught a glimpse of when Allison left the bathroom door open a little bit while she was taking her shower—but at least they'd *started*. She bet she'd get her period any minute. Allison had told her a ton of things it turned out she needed to know, to be ready: why you should always carry a tampon (because otherwise you could stand up at some random time and leave a big sticky pool of blood behind without even knowing it, and how gross was *that*); what brand of tampon was best (one with an applicator, because otherwise you just had to shove the thing way up inside you with your own finger, which Allison said she was pretty sure God never ever intended you to do), and what cramps felt like and what to do about them (ibuprofen, immediately). She'd also begun instructing Bethany about what hair styles and accessories made you look the oldest, what it felt like to smoke a cigarette, why you should always carry Purell hand sanitizer and Tic Tacs, and what an erection was (though Bethy was pretty sure Allison was making that one up). It turned out there was a whole world that Bethy hadn't known was out there, but which she now understood was very important if you were going to be liked and admired, never mind if you were going to book anything.

But the thing Bethany really loved about Allison was that she was a woman of the world. She'd kissed boys, been drunk, had her own debit card, had had a makeover at the MAC counter at Macy's (which Bethany was going to put on her list of musts when Ruth got back), and traveled alone between Los Angeles and Houston as fearlessly and casually as Bethy took a school bus.

They'd shared lots of other secrets, too, since Bethy had been at Mimi's. ("You can't tell any of it to Reba or Hillary when they get back, because they're just little kids," Allison had told her firmly, a fact that Bethy knew would make Hillary just crazy if she ever found out.) One of them was that sometimes Allison cut herself with a box cutter. She even let Bethy watch her once. She put the blade against the blue-white skin on the underside of her upper arm and pressed, and as Bethy stared in horrified fascination, a line of blood had bloomed, as delicate as a cobweb. Allison had just laughed and said it didn't hurt. She'd turned her arm over so Bethy could get a better look at the delicate cross-hatching of scabs and scars. Sometimes, Allison told her, she'd sit there and work on it for hours. Bethy said she thought it was awful, but Allison said there were tribes in Africa that did exactly the same thing to their faces, and no one thought a thing about it. Look at Seal. It was no different than tattoos. Bethy thought there was plenty of difference, but she kept it to herself. Instead she said, "But why?"

Allison had just shrugged. "Sometimes I get, I don't know, jumpy. Like I'm waiting for something bad to happen. So I cut, and it calms me down."

The earliest they turned their light out was one in the morning, and Mimi didn't even care. Her rule was, you could get up whenever you wanted, and if there were two of you or more and Mimi had already gone to work, you could call a taxi and take a cab to the studio whenever you were ready, as long as you had the money. Allison not only paid, but she also tipped the driver, which Bethy didn't even know you were supposed to do, never mind how much it should be, because she'd really been in a cab only a few times in New York City, and Hugh had paid; and Allison's voice, when she was talking to the driver, was cool and impersonal, like she'd had someone driving her around all her life. In her mind, Bethy already saw Allison as a movie star, she was that worldly.

She'd have to tell all of this to Rianne when she saw her, which who knew when that would be, especially because Bethy didn't miss her as much as she used to. She figured Rianne would still be all about finding neat decals to put on her notebooks and other tween stuff, and Bethy was way beyond that now. She talked to producers and casting directors like it was no big deal, and a few of them were starting to remember her.

Yesterday, both Bethy and Allison had auditioned for an independent film with a well-known director of family films who, of course, Bethy had never heard of because, she now realized, she used to be clueless, just *clueless*, about things like that. Allison was having her spend at least half an hour every day on IMDbPro.com to cram on who produced, directed, and starred in what movies, and then she drilled Bethy until she got it right. Allison knew it all by heart, of course, but she told Bethy that she shouldn't feel bad because she'd been in LA for *years*, so naturally she knew a ton of stuff Bethy didn't, and maybe wouldn't, ever.

This afternoon they both had an audition for Carlyle, one of the leads in *After*, a to-die-for feature-length film being directed by Gus Van Sant. Allison said Gus Van Sant was one of the greatest movie directors of all time, and he liked to use nonactors, or barely actors, even for some of his movies' major roles. So now, on the morning of Bethy's fifth day at Mimi's house, they were taking turns running the lines in the kitchen. They were sitting on opposing countertops in the kitchen, each with a copy of the sides in one hand and a mug of steaming coffee (Allison) and hot chocolate (Bethy) in the other. They'd agreed that Bethy would read first, and then they'd switch.

"I bet Quinn's going out for the brother. He'd be really good," Allison said, taking dainty sips of coffee. Bethy had watched her put three soup spoons full of Splenda in the cup— "Never use real sugar," she'd told Bethy, "*ever*"—so it was probably palatable. Allison had made a face when Bethy said she wanted hot chocolate—"Really? I didn't think anyone drank that anymore, except for maybe Reba"—but on this Bethy had stuck to her guns.

"Go," Allison said now, so Bethy did.

                    BUDDY
I'm not buyin' it.
                    CARLYLE
What do you mean, you're not buying it? It's the truth!
                    BUDDY
Yeah? So where's your wand?
                    CARLYLE
            (with infinite weariness)
Buddy. That's only in Harry Potter. Harry Potter is a book.
                    BUDDY
So show me something. If you were a real witch you'd be making something happen!
                    CARLYLE
                (sweetly)
I am. I'm making us argue.
                    BUDDY
Oh, for God's sake.
                    CARLYLE
So, okay. Do you remember before, when Nana left her dentures in a glass and the next morning they were blue?

Allison said, "I think the brother's kind of a douche. I mean, he sure whines a lot."

"I think it would be awful to have your mom die."

"I guess."

"You don't think so?"

"Well, I mean, it would be hard and everything, because where would you keep all your stuff? Plus you'd probably have to go live in an orphanage, at least until you could get emancipated."

"What's that?"

Allison dipped her finger in her coffee and idly colored in one of the countertop tiles. "It means you divorce your family. It means you have money and stuff so you can be on your own even if you're not eighteen yet. I think Quinn should get emancipated. I mean, he never even goes home anymore except for Christmas and Easter. When he goes back they totally ignore him and stuff. Jasper thinks Quinn should just tell his family to take a flying—"

"Who's Jasper?"

"—fuck. What? He used to work at the studio sometimes. I haven't seen him in a while, though, so maybe Mimi fired him. He wasn't booking anyway. I heard he wasn't even getting callbacks anymore. Plus he's like twenty-five and he isn't even SAG yet."

"I haven't booked anything in a while," Bethany said apprehensively.

"Mimi would never fire me," Allison said.

"Do you think she'd fire me?"

"Nah. Not yet. I don't think she likes your mom very much, though."

"Why?"

"I don't know. But when they talk on the phone Mimi rolls her eyes sometimes and stuff."

"I don't think that's very nice."

"Whatever. So do you think Quinn is cute?"

"He's *sixteen*," Bethany said.

"He's almost seventeen," Allison acknowledged, dipping her finger in her coffee again and licking it. "That's what I mean."

"That's old."

Allison smiled.

"I mean, I think he's pretty cute for an *old* person," Bethany ventured.

"Everyone says he's gay. He pinched this kid's nipples once, but what does that prove?"

"He did?"

Allison just shrugged, slapping her dangling flip-flops against the soles of her feet with her toes. "Anyway, Quinn doesn't come around here anymore. I miss him. He'd be really good as this character, though. As Buddy."

"Yeah," said Bethany.

Then it was Allison's turn to read, and she did, and they both agreed that hers was the best.

THE NEXT MORNING, MIMI DROVE THE GIRLS TO THE Universal Studios back lot, pulling up to a ghetto of modular trailers that were used as overflow casting studios. Mimi stayed in the car, talking on her cell phone, while Allison led the way to the right trailer and then inside. A tough-faced redhead with a chain of skulls tattoo running all the way up her arm had them sign in, deposit their headshots and résumés on a sloppy pile, and take two of the plastic folding chairs ringing the small room. The floors were so flimsy the girls bounced when they walked. Bethy had a sudden vision of them trampolining right out the window, as though they were wearing those shoes with springs on the bottoms that she'd been asking for since she was six years old. She smiled. Sometimes she just cracked herself up. She thought about telling Allison, but decided not to. Allison would probably just think she was being juvenile. She was always saying that about Hillary and Reba. "You're just so young," she'd tell them—or, worse, "I remember when I was your age," like it had been a thousand years ago instead of just two.

Bethy waited for Allison to pick a chair and then took the one beside her. She'd found that if she fell back until she was six or eight inches from Allison's right shoulder, she could follow her without *seeming* to follow her.

There were already four other girls waiting, and then two more arrived. The mean-looking casting assistant told the women who were with them that they'd have to wait outside because there was room for only the girls auditioning. When one of the mothers started to protest, the assistant snapped, "*Out!*" and the woman pressed her daughter's shoulder, whispered, "You'll do fine, just remember—" and lifted the corners of her mouth to make a smile, then turned around and left. Allison rolled her eyes at Bethany.

Through the thin, hollow door between them and the audition room they could hear a girl saying, "*That's only in* Harry Potter. Harry Potter *is a book.*"

Allison leaned into Bethany and whispered loudly, "So she sucks."

Bethy nodded vigorously, because she did. On the other hand, Bethy wondered how *she* would sound when it was her turn. What if she wasn't any better?

"*So, okay. Do you remember before, when Nana left her dentures in a glass and the next morning they were blue?*"

"Are you nervous?" Allison whispered.

"No," said Bethany, because she hadn't been until Allison asked. "Why—are you?"

"I never get nervous."

"Shhhh," hissed one of the girls, the one whose mother had

told her to smile. Allison made an ugly face at her, at the same time elbowing Bethy conspiratorially in the ribs. Normally Bethy was very respectful of other people, but she didn't want to seem like a Goody Two-shoes, so she smirked at the girl, too, and then felt bad about it when the girl turned bright pink and hunched down in her seat. She'd probably only been trying to concentrate, to stay in character. Bethy would hate for someone to do to her what they had just done to the girl, but she couldn't think of any way to take it back except maybe to wink if she could catch the girl's eye—*we didn't mean it; you're one of us*—which she couldn't because all of a sudden the girl seemed to be crying. Surely they hadn't done anything bad enough to make her cry? Bethy snuck a look at Allison to see if she was watching the girl, too, but Allison was diving deep into her Coach tote, rummaging around for a nail file. Bethy had noticed that she put a lot of time into her nails. She had pretty hands with long, tapering fingers, so that was probably why. Bethy's hands were blocky and utilitarian, and she hated them. "These are good, honest hands," her grandmother had been telling her from the time she was little, taking them in her own hands and turning them over and back, over and back, as though there were some secret message printed there. "These are hands that God loves."

The girl on the other side of the room seemed to be trying to pull herself together. She sat up straight, cleared her throat, and surreptitiously wiped her nose on her sleeve. Bethy willed her to look up, but the girl didn't. Allison brushed the fingernail dust off her hands, then buffed her nails on her pants.

The three girls ahead of them on the sign-in sheet each went in and read and came out without redirects or anything besides a perfunctory thank-you. They came out with emptied faces, grabbed their things off the chairs, and slammed the trailer door closed behind them. Every time they did, the windows rattled and the mean casting assistant flinched. Bethy thought she might get mean, too, if she had a door slamming right in front of her twenty or thirty times a day. She'd try to remember to close it gently when they left.

Since Bethany had signed in first, she was called into the audition room ahead of Allison. She hadn't been able to see inside before, but when she went in she saw that the casting director was Joel E. Sherman. She broke into a smile. "Hi, Mr. Sherman! I didn't know we were going to be auditioning for you."

He motioned for her to shut the door. "Yeah, well, I'm just filling in." He walked behind a video camera the size of a deck of playing cards, found her in the viewfinder, picked up a mangled copy of the sides, and said, "Okay, go."

He was all business, which was confusing. Didn't he recognize her? She thought about saying, "It's me, Lucy!" but that would probably just make things more confusing, so she took a deep breath and slated, using Rabinowitz for her last name. She was always Rabinowitz now. Mimi had even had them print a whole new stack of headshots with Rabinowitz on them instead of Roosevelt. Bethy thought he'd appreciate that, since he was the reason, but he didn't react except to look up at her and say, "Go."

"What do you mean, you're not buying it?"

Just outside the door, Bethy knew, Allison was sitting there listening.

"All right, stop," Joel said before they'd even gotten to the second page of the sides, turning off the camera. "Stop, stop. You just dropped two lines."

"What?"

"Have you even read the sides?"

"Yes."

"Then show me."

"I'm sorry, Mr. Sherman."

The casting director just shook his head. "C'mon, kid. Start over."

"Oh, thank you."

He fussed with the camera. "I don't usually allow do-overs," he said, "so get it right."

But she was too rattled.

He switched off the camera, walked around her, and opened the door. "Next time you audition for a lead, honey, at least be off-book."

Bethy flushed a deep crimson. She could feel the tips of her ears getting hot, and there was a telltale roaring in her ears that meant she was this close to crying.

"Go on," he said, making a shooing motion toward the door with his hands. "Go. *Go!*"

She went. Allison was on her feet, fluffing her hair. Her lip gloss was fresh, her hair shiny, her clothes in perfect order. She sailed right past Bethany and into the audition room as though she didn't even see her.

Stunned, Bethy just sat there listening to Allison's audition. From what she could hear, which was everything, Allison did a beautiful job. The casting director gave her several redirects and then thanked her. When she came out she hitched her Coach bag over her shoulder, gave her hips a little twitch, and danced out the trailer door pushing Bethany ahead of her and singing, "I'm-get-ting-a-call-back."

"How do you know?"

"I always know."

And then she slammed the door.

MIMI HAD KEPT THE CAR IDLING AND THE AIR-CONDITIONING turned on. To hell with global warming: she was old, fat, and hot, and as far as she was concerned, that trumped every polar bear on the planet.

Allison skipped out to the car and hopped into the front seat beside Mimi. Bethany Rabinowitz trudged after her, looking like she was about to cry. As the girls described it once they'd buckled in and Mimi had driven into the blessed, blessed shade of Riverside, she'd choked during the audition, which was a shame, because Joel E. Sherman was a rainmaker. Allison had had her shot three years ago and had gotten a couple of costar roles out of it. Not that Bethany Rabinowitz had a snowball's chance in hell of landing a lead role, but still, she'd be lucky now to land even a two-line part.

Allison put her earbuds in and began rapping along to some song on her iPod. Mimi pondered for about the millionth time enrolling the girl in a hip-hop class at Millennium. Look what *High School Musical* had done for Ashley Tisdale. Allison's voice was just as good, possibly better. But getting the mother to pay was the trick. The woman had gotten stingy in the last six months, which was ironic given that she was now a rich oilman's wife. She'd shelled out money left and right when she'd been poorer, so the new husband must have put on the brakes. Allison had said he was a cheapskate. Maybe Mimi would have to just bite the bullet and pay for the lessons herself. She'd be paid back and more when—*when*, not if—Allison hit. Of that Mimi was sure.

"Can we stop and get something to eat?" Allison said, plucking out her earbuds. "I'm starving. Hey, Carlyle. Aren't you starving?"

In the rearview mirror Mimi saw Bethany shrug miserably.

"I'll do the McDonald's drive-through, but that's all," Mimi pronounced. "We've already been gone for two hours." Mimi hated to be away from the studio, especially to cart kids back and forth to auditions, but all the pliable parents were out of town. She'd have e-mails up the wazoo by now.

"Not Mickey D's, we've done that tons of times this week," Allison moaned. "Come on, Mimi, take us someplace decent. *Please?*"

Mimi checked on Bethany again in the backseat and thought it looked like the girl was rallying at the prospect of food. "All right. We'll do Thai." Thai food was quick and cheap, and there was a little place in a strip mall just four or five blocks from the studio.

"Yay," Allison crowed. "Hey, Carlyle, aren't you glad?"

Bethany shrugged.

"Come on, cheer up!" Allison said. "Stop being a whiny baby or we're going to have to slap you around."

"I'm not a whiny baby," Bethany said, trying to hang on to her petulance but starting to smile in spite of herself. The girl had an excellent nature, Mimi had to give her that.

THE MINUTE THEY GOT BACK TO THE STUDIO BETHY CALLED Ruth and told her about the disastrous audition. Then she directed her to an Internet link so she could read the sides.

"Now?" Ruth said.

"Yes, please."

Ruth was quiet for a few minutes and then she said, "What is this for again?"

"A feature film. It's called *After*."

"I take it it's not a comedy," Ruth said dryly.

"Mom."

Ruth sighed. "Honey, Carlyle is one of the leads."

"I know," Bethy wailed, and started crying.

"Why are you crying?"

"Because I screwed up and now Allison's going to get a call-back and I'm not."

"You don't know that."

"Yes, I do."

"Well, that's going to happen sometimes."

"But I don't want her to get it! If I can't get it, I don't want her to get it, either. But shouldn't I want her to? She's my best friend."

"Honey, Allison is *not* your best friend," Ruth said.

Bethy bristled. "She *is*, Mom. She's the only one who understands about acting and stuff. I mean besides you. So shouldn't I want her to get it?"

Ruth hesitated for a minute and then said, "Honey, is it possible that she might have made you screw up the audition? Deliberately, I mean? Did she try to make you nervous or distracted or anything?"

Bethy frowned. "I don't know. No. She's my friend. She wouldn't do that."

"No?"

"No," Bethy said firmly, but it made her think, and she didn't want to think. What she wanted was to take it all back—making the girl in the waiting room cry, the flubbed lines, and the cold look on the casting director's face—and start again, except that she'd have Ruth drive her instead of Mimi, and Allison wouldn't be in the car and then sitting right beside her in the waiting room, criticizing the other girls. It would be just her and Ruth and she'd be in character, in that special place in her head where she didn't *pretend* to be the character, she *was* the character. She'd be Carlyle talking to her brother and trying to make him feel better about something awful that she didn't even really understand except that she loved him and he was in pain. That's what she wanted to show Joel Sherman; that's what she had to offer him, if only he'd give her one more chance.

She stopped crying, and Ruth told her she loved her, and

Bethany told her she loved her back, and then they got off the phone and Bethany found a piece of notebook paper and her best ballpoint pen, and she wrote a letter to Joel E. Sherman:

> Dear Mr. Sherman,
> I know I did a bad job at the audition for Carlyle today, and that you may never ever let me audition for you again, but I want you to know that I can be Carlyle. I don't mean I can act like her. I mean I can be her. I know her really well. I just want you to know how I feel, and how I feel is that I can do this part better than anyone else, period. If you'd just give me another chance to audition, I promise I won't let you down again.
>
> Sincerely yours,
> Bethany Rabinowitz

When she was done she found a Mimi Roberts Talent Management envelope, put her headshot and the letter into the envelope, wrote *Joel E. Sherman* on the front, and pretended to go to the restroom so she could drop the envelope into the courier box outside the studio unseen. When she got back inside she asked Allison if she needed any help with her vocabulary assignment, because Allison wasn't very good at vocabulary, and, surprisingly, Allison said yes. They cuddled up on the green-room sofa and did homework until nine o'clock, when Mimi was finally ready to drive them home.

IN HOLLYWOOD THAT EVENING, AFTER THE LAST KID HAD read, Joel E. Sherman sorted through his stack of headshots. What a fucking day. Kids who were unprepared, kids who were too prepared, kids who were too old or too young or too thick or too green or just too wrong. He was only pinch-hitting today for another casting director, Sharon Shue, an old fossil like him who was out on her ass with the flu, but this was going to be a good project. He wished he'd gotten in on it. He knew Van Sant—hell, everyone knew Gus Van Sant, he was that great: a good man who genuinely loved working with kids, and who had both excellent artistic judgment and an uncanny sense for what made a movie sell in Altoona. Joel would have to read the script again, but if he still liked it he might play a little game of poker, see if he could get himself attached. He'd done it before; he was a good player, though he prided himself on being a straight shooter when he could afford to be, which unfortunately wasn't all that much of the time. You tasted the water, you chose the Kool-Aid.

He flipped through the headshots in his *Yes* pile. He liked to make a gut decision as the kids left the room, then go back and cull later. Carlyle was one of the movie's two lead roles, so there'd be multiple callbacks, though probably no recruiting beyond LA. From what he'd heard, the timeline was too short for that. He'd heard that the executive producer—who, despite a reputation as a real hard-ass, had always been a pussycat to Joel—wanted to be in production within two months. Despite that, Sharon had told Joel that Gus Van Sant was willing to consider unknown actors for the leads, if the fit was just right. An unknown was usually someone who wasn't from here, or was a recent immigrant. Look at Ellen Page. She was from goddamn Halifax. And she was brilliant. And how about the poor kid in *Bad Santa*? He was a Canuck, too, and he was gold at the box office. You never knew. Sometimes the LA kids were *too* Hollywood, too polished.

He kept about half of the headshots that had started out in his *Yes* pile, maybe six, and dumped the rest on top of the *No*s. One of the keepers was the kid Mimi Roberts pushed at him every time he talked to her, which was as seldom as possible. Allison Somebody; cocky kid, but there'd been something compelling about her today, something dangerous. You saw that in some of the great actors—Russell Crowe, Ralph Fiennes. He rooted through until he'd found her headshot: Allison Addison. Jesus. Mimi Roberts must be the master of stupid names. Of course, if you had a name like Mimi yourself, you were entitled to a certain amount of payback, especially if you were ugly, which Mimi Roberts most definitely was. That reminded him: Bethany Rabinowitz, her other client, had been a fucking mess today. He pawed through the *No*s until he found her headshot. He'd looked forward to seeing her again, but Jesus, what a disappointment. It happened all the time, though. Half these kids were held together with Ritalin and Red Bull. But he'd gotten good feedback about her from Peter Tillinghast, and if she could hold her own on a set with that dick, she had to have something going for her. He moved her headshot to the *Yes* pile. What the hell—he'd let Sharon take a look at her. The kid was way too green to hold down a movie, but there might be some bit part for her.

He yawned as he tapped both piles into order. In the old days he could have put in another twelve or fifteen hours, and often had—hell, he'd gone without sleep for days on end when a movie or TV show came down to crunch time. A little blow, a little coffee, and he was good for another twenty-four hours. But at sixty-two, he was weary. The Business did that to you. It was like playing an endless game of chess. Sooner or later, you were going to make a stupid move—cast the wrong person, take on the wrong project, piss off the wrong producer. He sensed that he was approaching his use-by date, but he wasn't ready yet. It wasn't the money; he had plenty of money. What he wanted was to leave behind a legacy in the form of the next Dakota

Fanning or Freddie Highmore. He wanted to find an actor who would have a long and brilliant career, during which he or she would tell James Lipton and Billy Bush and every other interviewer from every little burg and hamlet that Joel E. Sherman had given him or her that first break. If Joel could have that, he would retire a happy man.

He rubber-banded the two piles of headshots together. He'd have a courier deliver them to Sharon's office in Century City overnight. Then he checked his cell for voice- and e-mail messages. There were the usual million from agents and managers, wanting feedback, pitching kids, generally busting his chops. He didn't plan on returning a single one of them. Fuck 'em. Instead, en route to his car, he speed-dialed Sharon to fill her in on the day.

What happened next was nothing short of a gift from God.

Sharon Shue had not had the flu at all. She had had appendicitis. She had undergone emergency surgery at Cedars-Sinai at two o'clock that afternoon, but not before the appendix had burst. At her age, the recovery could take weeks. It was an incredible piece of luck.

One quick phone call, and *After* was his.

Chapter Fourteen

IF QUINN COULD HAVE ANYTHING OTHER THAN A CAR for his upcoming seventeenth birthday, he might just choose a washer/dryer. At least he felt that way on laundry days, when he'd worn everything he owned—and there wasn't that much— at least twice, and even he could detect a faint odor. He hated the Laundromat. Launderland on Santa Monica Boulevard was a long march with a duffle bag full of clothes and his el cheapo but machine-washable sleeping bag. He always swore he'd get up early the next time just to go and get it over with in relative solitude, but every time he slept in anyway.

As he approached the Laundromat he could see that the place was hopping. Men and women, but mostly men, were wheeling steel laundry carts back and forth between washers, dryers, and the folding tables. A lot of them seemed to know one another. It was probably a laundry club. He'd run into them before— groups of gay men who did their laundry at the same time and turned the whole thing into a social event. On one of the big folding tables someone had laid out a tablecloth and a spread of bagels and Danishes and cut fruit and croissants and condiments and coffee. Quinn heard his stomach rumble. He hadn't eaten since yesterday, and then all he'd had was cereal, because it and a quart of about-to-turn milk were the only things in the apartment that belonged to him and Baby-Sue had been on a bitching jag about Jasper and Quinn eating all her food.

Quinn humped his duffle over to the single available washer, dumped in as much as he could, tamped it down, then dumped in the rest. He'd probably wind up with packed nuggets of laundry soap again when it was over, but he had only so many quarters, and the change-making machine was still broken. ESTA MÁQUINA ESTÁ ROTA. The sign surprised him, not because it was there, but because he didn't think there were that many Latinos in West Hollywood. There was the girl at Los Burritos, though. Maybe it was just that the Anglo population was so out there—41 percent were gay, bi, or lesbian—that you didn't notice the Hispanics.

He turned his box of laundry detergent upside down and saw there wasn't even enough left in the box to clump up. He'd just turn the water up to the hottest setting and hope that if the soap didn't get the stuff clean—and with that little, it couldn't possibly—the hot water would sterilize the dirt that was left.

"That machine walks when it's on the spin cycle."

Quinn turned around and saw the hair stylist from Hazlitt & Company watching him with a smile. "It gets out of balance, so keep an eye on it."

"Yeah," Quinn said. "Okay."

The stylist was wearing jeans and an incandescently white T-shirt, and his hair was perfectly mussed. "You look like a lost soul," he told Quinn. "Are you okay?"

"Yeah. Sure."

"Do you live near here?"

"On Norton." Quinn pointed over his shoulder. "Near Havenhurst."

"Family?"

"No."

"Really? You seem a little young to be on your own."

"I'm not that young," Quinn said.

The stylist smiled. "I meant that in a good way."

"Oh." Quinn didn't know what else to say. It was one thing to see the stylist in the salon. Out here, in the world, it felt weird, part good and part bad. Good because he seemed like a nice guy and Quinn was more or less on the outs with Baby-Sue and Jasper—he seemed to be getting on their nerves, though he had no idea why—and it was Saturday, so there'd be no auditions or classes until Monday and he was lonely. Bad because he kept thinking of how the stylist's hands had felt, moving through his hair, rubbing his head, and he didn't think he should be remembering those things in front of the washers and dryers at Launderland.

A black man in a canary yellow button-down shirt with the sleeves turned back called to the stylist, "Hey, Quatro! Paulie wants to know what you did last night. He says you never showed up."

The stylist smiled a little apologetic smile at Quinn and shook his head. "Yeah, yeah," he called back, but he was still looking at Quinn.

"Quatro?" Quinn said. "That's your name?"

"Yeah," said the stylist. "Technically it's John Robertson the Fourth. So, Quatro." He shrugged.

"Awesome."

The men in the laundry club were elbowing one another. "Leave that child alone and come get a mimosa!" someone said, and the others laughed.

Quinn bridled.

The stylist said, "Don't listen to them. Look, are you hungry at all?"

"No," Quinn lied.

"Okay. If you change your mind, though, come on over. There's plenty of food."

Quinn nodded. The stylist went back to the group at the

folding table. A few of the men elbowed him, but he shook it off. "He's a kid. Leave it alone," Quinn could hear him snap.

Quinn wanted him to come back and talk, but the stylist had been absorbed by the group at the folding-table buffet, so Quinn pulled a batch of papers from his back pocket. It was the sides for a scene he was auditioning for on Monday. He jumped up to sit on the washing machine. You weren't supposed to sit on the machines, but screw it; the machine was walking, just the way the stylist had warned.

He straightened out the pages. First he read the breakdown Mimi had given him at the showcase.

Friday, November 2, 2006, 6:30 P.M. Pacific
AFTER
Miramax Films
UNION
Producer
Writer-Director: Gus Van Sant
Casting Director: Sharon Shue
Shoot/Start Date: TBD
Location: Portland, OR / LA
8899 Beverly Blvd.
LOS ANGELES, CA 90048
SUBMIT ELECTRONICALLY
SUBMISSIONS BY 11 P.M. FRI Nov. 9
SEEKING:
[BUDDY DONNER]
Lead / MALE / 15 / Caucasian
A tall, skinny kid with anger issues. He is, by turns, defiant, sullen, fiercely protective of his little sister, and almost always on the brink of rage. Actor must have an extremely wide spoken and nonspoken emotional range.

STORY LINE: Buddy Donner and his 13-year-old sister
Carlyle are living with their mother's younger brother Wayne,
who is almost never home. Their mother has just died.
Buddy, Carlyle, and Wayne are doing as well as possible,
considering that they're in almost unsustainable pain.
When a run-down motel goes up for sale, Buddy and Carlyle
decide to buy it with their mother's life insurance money.
With Wayne to help, they find themselves surrounded by
eccentric long-term guests with whom they slowly forge
relationships and begin a new life.

Quinn knew—every actor knew—that Gus Van Sant was
one of *the* most respected directors in the movie industry. Almost as important, to Quinn, was the fact that he was known
for working with unknown actors, sometimes even pulling kids
off the street and casting them. Mimi had told Quinn that Van
Sant wasn't auditioning for *After* anywhere outside LA. The
production schedule was tight, and word on the street was that
he would open the call beyond Hollywood only as a last resort.
The part of Buddy—one of the leads—had just been released,
and Mimi wanted Quinn to be ready, even though he didn't
have an audition scheduled yet. Quinn knew as well as anyone
what a break this role could be. He frowned and turned to the
sides.

BUDDY and CARLYLE are sitting in the living
room.
                    BUDDY
  I'm not buyin' it.
                    CARLYLE
  What do you mean, you're not buying it? It's
  the truth!

                    BUDDY
Yeah? So where's your wand?
                    CARLYLE
               (with infinite weariness)
Buddy. That's only in Harry Potter. Harry
Potter is a book.
                    BUDDY
So show me something. If you were a real
witch you'd be making something happen!
                    CARLYLE
                   (sweetly)
I am. I'm making us argue.

Raucous laughter broke out across the Laundromat. Quinn told himself he wouldn't look over—he didn't want the stylist to think he was paying attention to anything going on over there—but at the last minute he couldn't stop himself. He was hungry and his ass was getting sore from sitting on the hard metal of the washing machine, which had just finished its final spin cycle. He couldn't concentrate anyway, so he folded the pages, hopped off the washing machine, and stuck the sides back in his pocket. The laundry club was done, apparently: food was being wrapped and put back into coolers and sacks, and everyone had neatly folded baskets and hampers and duffel bags full of freshly clean clothes. Quinn saw Quatro bending over a wicker basket, tucking in a stack of blue towels. So he'd be leaving now, too. Quinn told himself it didn't matter, that they didn't even know each other except in a professional way.

Anyway, he'd need a haircut in a month. A month was nothing.

★

ACROSS TOWN AT 200 LA BREA, LAUREL BUEHL WAS CON-
fiding to the camera as though to a close girlfriend why she
wouldn't be able to play in the final and most important water polo game of the season: her "friend" was visiting, and she
didn't feel she could rely on her tampons.

Then she and three other girls who were auditioning for
the same commercial were asked to tell one another, on camera, about their greatest personal hygiene fears: leakage, bloat-
ing, cramping, or moodiness. They were to talk about these
problems as though they were monsters in the room, and the
girls were defending themselves against them as if their lives depended on it. *Over the top, girls,* said the dweeby casting director.
Waaay over the top, now. Good. Excellent. Thank you.

Angie was waiting for Laurel outside in the bull-pen waiting
room, sitting on the gray carpeted benches. Across from her a
young woman held a baby on her lap and bounced her, trying
to keep her quiet while they waited for the baby's big sister,
who was evidently auditioning for a soup commercial. The baby
was fidgety—it was three o'clock in the afternoon, which Angie well remembered as Laurel's worst time of day when she'd
been tiny—and Angie watched the mom fishing, with growing
desperation, object after object out of a string bag inside her
enormous tote: a set of plastic keys, her set of real keys, a pen
flashlight, a travel-pack of tissues, a set of plastic teething rings
that made a nice clattering sound, a binky; and one after another, the baby threw the objects down in growing agitation.

"Will she let me hold her, do you think?" Angie asked the
mom. "You look like you could use a break."

The woman looked at Angie with tears welling up in her
eyes. "God, would you mind? She's got a double ear infection,
we got about two hours of sleep last night, she hasn't napped at
all, and I'm at my wit's end."

Angie took the baby gently under the arms and lifted her onto her lap. The baby was astonished into silence. "Boo!" Angie said softly. "Who's a pretty girl? Who's a beautiful girl?"

The baby blew a spit bubble, farted into her diaper. Angie laughed.

The mom stood up, wiped her eyes, did a side bend or two as though she were warming up for a marathon. "I've *told* my husband this is too much," she said, "but Lily—that's this one's big sister—had a second callback, and it's a national commercial, which could help us get her a better agent, so here we are."

"How old is Lily?"

"Three."

"Oh, a *big* girl," Angie said, smiling. The baby began to fidget in Angie's arms. Angie turned her around, holding her under her armpits, and murmured, "See? Mama's right there. Is that better? Yes, that's better."

"You're great with her."

"She's just being good because she's startled," Angie said. "Her diaper feels pretty heavy. Do you have a clean one? We can change her right here, if you do."

"Oh, God, you're wonderful," the woman said. "I'll change her, but if you can watch her so she doesn't wriggle off the bench—"

"Oh, sure," said Angie, gently laying the baby down on her back. "Let's just get these snaps undone. You are *such* a good girl!"

By the time the baby was changed and back in her clothes, a small girl came dawdling out of the casting room. "All done, pumpkin?" said the mom. The little girl was one of the most beautiful children Angie had ever seen, of mixed race, with truly green eyes, a cleft chin, and wild curls dancing around her face. No wonder she was here.

"See?" said the woman to the baby. "Here's Big Sister. Okay? What did they say, honey?"

The little girl looked at her solemnly and popped her thumb into her mouth.

"Did the man say anything to you?"

The girl shook her head.

"Oh. Okay," said the mom, clearly disappointed. "I know you did a wonderful job, though. Okay? We have a juice box and snack in the car. Then you can watch a DVD on the way home."

Angie helped the young woman gather up the dirty diaper, the extra clothes she'd dumped out of the diaper bag, the scattered keys, both real and plastic, and the other objects the baby had discarded.

"You've been a godsend," the woman said. "This is just so, so hard. I've told my husband if it's so easy, why doesn't *he* try it one day, but he just laughs, like I'm kidding. I'm not kidding, though."

"No," Angie said. "No, I can see that."

"Well, thank you. And tell your daughter good luck."

"I will." Angie watched them disappear down the stairs and wondered if she'd ever had the stamina to do what that young woman was doing. She was so tired all the time now—she spent more and more of her energy fighting, or at least masking, a crushing fatigue. She remembered being that age, though. You came up with the energy when you had to. Not that Laurel had ever been hard to take care of. They'd wanted another child or even two more, but God hadn't seen fit. And that was all right, too. Laurel was everything Angie could have ever wanted in a child, and more. People said you shouldn't look upon your children as friends, but Angie didn't see what was wrong with that. Laurel and she were even closer than most friends. They had never kept anything hidden, and Angie wouldn't have wanted it any other way. Dillard loved them—Dillard adored them—but he wasn't much for girl talk, as he'd put it to her on their honeymoon. Laurel was the one Angie told things to. Until now. Now she was determined to keep her sickness to herself for as long as possible. That was her work. Laurel had her own work to do, and Angie didn't want anything to get in the way of that, even though she missed her quiet strength and unfailing support.

Laurel came up, breaking Angie's train of thought. "Done?" Angie said.

"Done."

"Scale of one to ten?" This was their system—to rate auditions on a scale of one to ten, with ten being an absolute certainty of booking the commercial, one being no chance at all.

"Eight," said Laurel. "Eight and a half."

"Oh, good."

"You okay?" Laurel said, peering at her.

Angie turned away. It was getting harder and harder to mask her deterioration. "Of course."

Chapter Fifteen

MOST OF MIMI'S OUT-OF-TOWN CLIENTS WENT HOME FOR Thanksgiving, but there were always some who got trapped in LA because last-minute auditions or callbacks trumped any holiday. Mimi had a long-standing tradition of rounding up the strays and newly relocated clients and hosting a Thanksgiving potluck dinner. This year both Hillary and Reba had flown home, but Allison had landed a last-minute callback on the following Monday morning for a guest-star role on *House*, and she convinced her mother to let her stay. Dillard, Angie, and Laurel Buehl, as well as Hugh, Bethany, and Ruth Rabinowitz, would also be there. Even Quinn Reilly would be coming; like Allison, he'd been stranded in LA by a last-minute callback. Though he was less than enthusiastic, he was still enough of a child to need a holiday observance someplace, and Mimi's was the only port, Baby-Sue and Jasper apparently having been invited to a gathering that had not included him.

The one thing Mimi could cook, for reasons that were inexplicable even to her, was a tender, juicy, golden Thanksgiving turkey. Allison was making homemade cranberry sauce, so the two of them were out of bed and in the kitchen at the ungodly hour of seven o'clock Thanksgiving morning. They worked side by side, taking up, between them, every available bit of grimy counter space. Tina Marie lurked underfoot, snapping at scraps of dressing that fell like manna from above, while Allison sang an impromptu Thanksgiving carol to the tune of "Deck the Halls": *Stuff the bird with mounds of stuffing, fa la la la la la la la la la. / Tis the season to be hungry, fa la la la la la la la la.* If she minded missing Thanksgiving with her mother and stepfather, Mimi thought, she certainly didn't let on.

Mimi shoved stuffing into the back-end cavity of the turkey, a twenty-pounder she'd been thawing since Monday. Allison seized the bird for a minute to murmur into its neck cavity, "You're going to be yummy, aren't you, because you like us and you chose our table from all the tables in all the houses in LA." Then she turned back to the stove and transferred her cranberry sauce into a turkey-shaped copper mold Mimi had picked up at a swap meet however many years ago. Already assembled and in the refrigerator were a green bean casserole; a small pumpkin pie (as an emergency backup—the Buehls had signed up to bring two others as well as a cherry pie); and cornbread muffins Allison had baked last night in a fit of holiday zeal.

"Don't you just love Thanksgiving?" she asked Mimi now, across the countertop. "I didn't use to, but now I do."

"Does your mom cook?"

Allison just gave her a look. "We always went to the Holiday Inn. This year she said they're going to this fancy hotel downtown for like a twenty-course meal or something. They're not even having turkey, they're having goose. Who'd want to eat a goose?"

"Lots of people like goose," Mimi said, dipping up a handful of Crisco to rub on the turkey. In the old days her mother had used lard, but she'd never been able to bring herself to try it.

"Well, I'd rather eat a pheasant than a goose. At least I've never seen a pheasant." Allison ran the back of her wooden spoon over the glossy surface of her cranberry sauce, making it perfectly smooth and evenly distributed in the mold. Then she leaned down and kissed it, leaving the faintest lip print in the sauce. "Don't tell anyone I did that," she told Mimi.

AT NOON THEIR GUESTS BEGAN TO ARRIVE. RUTH, HUGH, and Bethany came first, and Allison gave each of them an impulsive hug. She wore a filmy skirt, tiny sweater, and high-heeled pumps. Mimi herself wore a sweatshirt and baggy pants, plus a pair of Dearfoam slippers that Allison had given her last Christmas. The Rabinowitzes held a middle ground in Dockers and button-down collared shirt (Hugh); knit pants and a Thanksgiving-themed sweater (Ruth); and jeans and a tight-fitting T-shirt (Bethany), which showed she was finally beginning to develop breasts. The three of them hovered around the kitchen—Ruth had made a fruit salad and a yam casserole with marshmallows—until the casserole had been stowed in the refrigerator and Mimi shooed them all into the living room. The girls headed for Allison's bedroom, where Hugh saw Allison kicking off her high heels in favor of a pair of pale pink rubber flip-flops. Hugh and Ruth sat side by side. Ruth said to Hugh in a stage whisper, "They've cleaned."

Tina Marie hopped up beside them, kissed Ruth repeatedly on the lips, and then heaved herself, with a deep sigh, against the sofa's throw pillows. Ruth brushed dog hair from her holiday sweater as the Buehls arrived, bearing the promised pies and an assortment of microbrew beers, Dillard apparently not being much of a wine man. Under his arm he carried a photo album as hefty as a family Bible, which he brought straight into the living room and laid lovingly on the altar of the coffee table in front of Hugh and Ruth. While Laurel and Angie were dealing with the pies in the kitchen, Dillard hitched up a ladder-back chair and opened the photo album to the very beginning, adjusting its position so Hugh and Ruth could see better.

"You must be very proud," said Hugh, dutifully examining the first two pages and gathering that Ruth intended to stay mum.

Dillard blew his nose on a red bandana and shoved it back in his pocket. "Yes, sir, I'm real proud of my girls. Best couple of women the South has ever produced, if you ask me, but then I guess you could call me partial." Page after page revealed pictures of Laurel and Angie at pageants all over the South: little Laurel in spangly boots and a patriotic stars-and-stripes ensemble; Angie in a makeshift dressing room, curling Laurel's hair with a curling iron and laughingly waving Dillard and his camera away; a preteen Laurel holding a microphone with the ease of Sinatra during the talent portion of some long-ago extravaganza; Angie and Laurel in matching mother-daughter outfits, which Dillard explained they'd worn at the one pageant in which Angie had also participated, taking second place. There were no photographs that included either Dillard—who was, presumably, the photographer—or other children, except incidentally in the background.

"She's lovely," said Hugh, because she was; and tragic, too, he thought, because whose only friend was her mother? He had read about pageant moms—close kin to stage moms, evidently—who made their daughters' lives a living hell of never-ending pressure and competition, but he didn't see any signs of that here. Both Laurel and Angie looked relaxed and exuberant, and it was clear where Laurel's looks had come from, though Hugh thought Angie was now thin to the point of gauntness. A late-life eating disorder? He gathered that was a growing problem. Whatever the current trouble was, in almost every photograph they seemed completely at one with their surroundings, so perhaps theirs was a perfect harmony, a pageantry world yin and yang.

On and on Dillard went, turning pages patiently, allowing Hugh and Ruth enough time to examine each photograph in minute detail. Beside him, Hugh could feel Ruth stiffen, but he put his hand over hers on the sofa cushion between them

in a petition for patience. From his limited experience Hugh
had found Southern men of a certain educational and economic
background to be crass, but Dillard was endearing, even sweet,
in the seeming simplicity of his adoration.

IN THE KITCHEN, LAUREL HELPED ANGIE SET OUT CHEESE
and crackers that she recognized as leftovers from Mimi's
last showcase, at the same time watching Dillard torment the
Rabinowitzes with what she and Angie had simply dubbed The
Book. Laurel was mortified, but she couldn't bring herself to
fault him for it. He loved them truly, nakedly, and uncondition-
ally. As long as they were in it, his was a perfect world. In her
experience you couldn't say that about other fathers, many of
whom didn't even show up at their daughters' pageants. There
had been some summers when Dillard had driven all night to
be there for just a few hours before driving back to wherever
his boiled peanut booth was set up, not trusting Laurel's uncle Bobby for longer than a day because he was, though well-
intentioned—and this from Dillard's own mouth—an idiot.

Laurel couldn't imagine how he would handle Angie's cancer, if a time came when they'd have to tell him. She still believed that the cancer would go away, though. She planned to
prove herself and Angie worthy by working just as hard as she
possibly could. He was a good and loving God—hadn't her
church made a point of teaching her that in Sunday school,
year after year after year?—so although Angie had been visibly
weakening lately, she had explained to Laurel that it wasn't the
cancer at all, but an uncommon but nevertheless recognized
bounce-back reaction to all the chemo and radiation; and Laurel
chose to believe her.

QUINN ARRIVED JUST SHY OF ONE O'CLOCK—HALF AN HOUR
before Mimi's estimated turkey time—sullen and bearing two
packages of dinner rolls he'd picked up at the dollar store. He
set them on the kitchen counter without a word. It was the first
time he'd been back in the house since Mimi had kicked him
out six months ago. Tina Marie, the one creature here who
seemed happy to see him, danced around his feet, piddling. He
picked her up and tucked her under his arm like a football. He'd
always been a sucker for the little dog, even though she was
pretty awful most of the time.

"Thank you," Mimi said over her shoulder about the rolls as
she basted the bird in the oven. "How did you get here?"

"Jasper," said Quinn. Jasper and Baby-Sue had gone out of
their way to drop him off before going on to some party at
a comedy club in North Hollywood. Baby-Sue had been all
dolled up in a gauze skirt and strapless top that would have
looked great on lots of women, none of them Baby-Sue. They
said he could call them and they'd give him a ride back if they
could, but he'd brought enough money for cab fare because
by the time he was going to be ready, he knew, they'd be totally
wasted.

He looked around the kitchen, at the familiar takeout
menus curling and wilting on the refrigerator door; at the dingy
dish towels hanging on the oven; at the dying plants on the
grimy windowsill over the sink; at the permanently darkened
floor vinyl where Tina Marie liked to sleep whenever the temperature rose above eighty, which was to say more than half
the year. There wasn't a single trace of him anywhere, and it
suddenly, violently pissed him off. He'd *lived* here. For three-
plus years, this had been home. And then, all of a sudden and
without due process, it wasn't anymore. Now he slept on the floor
in a corner like a dog and was widely considered to be either

gay or a pervert. For a minute, for a fraction of a minute, he was so angry his vision changed, made everything around him float and spin.

"Pass me that can of Crisco, would you, Quinn?" said Mimi over her shoulder, her face flushed from the heat of the oven. "It looks like I missed a spot."

Quinn found the can of Crisco and handed it to her. She scooped up a gob in her fingers and let it melt on the turkey.

"Hey!" said Allison, coming back into the kitchen and seeing him. "'S up, dog?"

Quinn shook his head. "That sounds pretty stupid."

The girl assumed the stance of a gangsta. "Who you be callin' stupid, dog?"

"If you did that in East LA you'd be dead in less than a minute."

"So you *do* care."

Quinn shook his head.

"Come on, homie," she wheedled. "Come play solitaire with me."

"You can't play solitaire with more than one person. It's *solitaire*."

"Yes, you can," Allison said. "You each use a separate deck, but you share the aces."

One of the new girls at the studio was coming across the kitchen toward them, looking nervous. Kids were scared of him now. This stupid girl with the face of a sheep—what was her name, Brittany, Bessie, something—was watching him like she expected him to expose himself or something. At least Cassie Foley and her mom seemed completely fine with him. Cassie was worth a thousand Allisons and Belindas or whatever the fuck the other girl's name was.

"I wondered if maybe you guys would want to play Pictionary?" the girl said now. "My family plays that sometimes. We brought it with us."

Quinn just shrugged. He didn't want to play that or any other game. Kids played games. He wasn't a kid. He'd stopped being a kid the night Mimi threw him out.

Fuck them. *Fuck* them.

MIMI CALLED, WITH UNCHARACTERISTIC GAIETY, "It's turkey time!" and hoisted the bird to the kitchen counter. Allison slid a trivet under the roasting pan while the others helped lay out the food on the dining room table, spruce in a snowy linen tablecloth Mimi had whisked out of a box in a distant closet. Hugh uncorked two bottles of wine, one red and one white, and put out an assortment of the beers that Dillard had brought. Allison and Bethany folded paper napkins to look like flowers, Laurel and Angie made giblet gravy, and then, at last, it was time to eat.

At Mimi's request, Dillard carved the bird using an antique carving knife Mimi said she'd found at a swap meet. The group was about to disperse and begin eating when, somewhat apologetically, Angie asked if anyone would mind if Laurel said a quick grace, which of course no one did, though Ruth thought Hugh looked a touch uncomfortable.

"Oh, Lord," Laurel said with a devoutly bowed head and faint smile, as though, Ruth thought, she were addressing an old friend, "we thank You for bringing us together today with our new friends and family over a really lovely dinner—especially the turkey—and all the other wonderful dishes. We feel that we have been truly blessed. Amen."

"Amen," Dillard and Angie and Ruth said, Ruth being of the belief that one should encourage spiritual expression, and that it didn't kill you to be a part of it, either. Out of the corner of her eye she thought she saw Hugh winking at Bethany, but no one else seemed to notice, so she kept mum and exclaimed, instead, over the abundance of food and the excellent look of the turkey. The grown-ups, with heaping plates, took seats around the living room, letting the four "young people"—Allison, Bethany, Laurel, and Quinn—sit at a butcher-block table that Mimi and Allison had humped in from the kitchen.

Ruth watched the tense set of Quinn's shoulders and his sullen expression. She'd heard stories from Bethy and Allison about some of the boy's antics, but she took most of them with a grain of salt. He was obviously a gifted actor, and with that degree of talent often came eccentricity. Laurel exclaimed over the excellent dinner rolls that Quinn had brought; Allison ran over to Mimi and threw her arms around Mimi's neck, thanking her extravagantly for the delicious turkey. Still, the atmosphere at the table was clearly strained. Quinn ate silently and with his mouth not quite closed. At one point Ruth caught Bethany's eye and Bethy returned a brave smile. Ruth hoped Bethy didn't develop indigestion; she tended to be sensitive when she was around people who were out of sorts with one another.

For Bethany's sake, Ruth and Hugh had been trying very hard since Hugh's arrival yesterday evening to convey a festive mood, despite the fierce argument they'd had over his coming to LA at the last minute instead of Bethy and Ruth coming home the way they'd planned. On Tuesday evening, Mimi had called to tell Ruth that Bethy had a callback for a costar role on *That's So Raven* the next afternoon, one hour after their flight was scheduled to leave. Mimi thought Bethy might have a good shot at booking it, and though it was a small part, landing a Disney role could lead to other, more sizable things, so Ruth had called Hugh and told him she'd made a reservation for him on a flight down because they couldn't come home after all.

He had objected strenuously, but Ruth had simply said that this year wasn't like other years and required flexibility from everyone, and Hugh had said, I know that, and Ruth said, Then let's do our best to enjoy the holiday, and that Mimi had invited them to dinner, to which Hugh had said, My God, is there anything that woman does *not* have her hand in? and Ruth said she thought it was nice that they'd been invited instead of being left to shift for themselves, and Hugh had said bitterly that they wouldn't *be* shifting for themselves except for Mimi, and Ruth had sighed deeply and said, This is getting us nowhere; and on that they agreed.

Through Hugh's intervention, Helene was invited to spend the holiday with several widowed friends from Hadassah, but she complained bitterly to Hugh that she'd never thought she'd be left to spend a major holiday with leftover women. Ruth had made a point of telling Hugh over the phone that Helene was welcome to come with him, but he said she said she didn't feel welcome. If they'd really wanted her there, she said, they'd have asked her in time to get a plane ticket at a decent price.

Now, perched on a chair with one wobbly leg, Dillard asked Hugh about his dental practice and then Angie and Ruth had a lively discussion about which casting studios were their favorites, and Mimi weighed in with her own opinion, and in no time at all Ruth realized, to her relief, that dinner was done.

WHEN THE GROUP BROKE UP LATE THAT AFTERNOON, Dillard offered Quinn a ride home, Angie having told him that Jasper and Baby-Sue's apartment wasn't all that far from theirs at the Grove. The boy seemed reluctant at first, but Angie and Laurel chimed in, and it was a rare person of the male persuasion who could resist those two, at least in Dillard's experience. So, armed with the leftover beer and a sizable package of turkey and stuffing, they all climbed into Dillard's Hummer and set sail for Laurel Canyon.

"I thought that was real nice," Dillard said affably to no one in particular. "If you can't be at home, why, I'd say that was second best. Where's your family, son?"

"Seattle."

"Never been there," Dillard said. "I've heard it's mighty wet, though. Georgia's got the heat, of course, but it's got blue skies most of the time, and that balances things out, in my book."

Quinn made no comment. When Dillard looked in the rearview mirror, the boy was looking out the window with an unreadable expression. "Your folks come down here often? I bet they're real proud of you."

"Nah. Not that often."

"No? Well, that's a shame. I'm driving us all back to Atlanta next week, auditions or no auditions. A family's got to make time for itself. These girls used to do a pageant a month, but we always said December was off-limits and put up a big ol' tree in the living room—we've got fifteen-foot ceilings we had built especially—and Angie and Laurel decorate the whole house, top to bottom. Too bad we're so far away, because it's something to behold."

"Oh, Daddy," said Laurel.

Dillard just grinned. "I know, baby girl, I embarrass you."

"Yes, you do," said Laurel, but she was smiling.

"Well, anyhow," Dillard went on, "I think it was a nice Thanksgiving. You going to call your folks, son, and wish them a happy holiday? I imagine they're not feeling right, having Thanksgiving without you."

"Yeah, I guess I'll give them a call," said Quinn.

ONCE THE BUEHLS HAD DROPPED QUINN OFF THEY DROVE in silence until Dillard pulled into their space in the parking garage. Then, in the most casual way, Angie said to Dillard, "You know, I'm sleepy from all that food. I haven't eaten that big a meal in I don't know how long. I think I'll lie down for a little while and take a nap."

In the front seat, oblivious, Dillard took Angie's hand in his big paw, raised it to his lips, and kissed it. Laurel stiffened. The only time she'd ever known Angie to nap, *ever*, was a year ago, when she'd been so sick Laurel had thought that she was dying.

Chapter Sixteen

THE WEEKS BETWEEN THANKSGIVING AND CHRISTMAS were, in Ruth's opinion, the most tedious, if not the most downright deadly, of their entire stay in LA. First Holly Jensen, Bethy's agent, left town for a two-week cruise around the Aegean Sea; then Donovan Meyer canceled his last class before the holiday and announced to Mimi that he was going to Aspen. Even Mimi seemed bored. So though it cost them a few hundred extra dollars to change their tickets, by December 4—the first day of Hanukkah—Ruth and Bethy were guilt-free and on their way home.

It was Bethy's first trip back since they had moved to LA in September. She ran through the house, exclaiming over everything—the living room furniture, the posters on the walls of her room, the ordinary fixtures in her bathroom—as though she'd been gone for years.

It felt exactly the opposite to Ruth. Though her quick trip home several weeks ago had clearly felt like a visit, an abnormality, now that they were *both* here it was as though a portal had been opened to an alternate life in which they'd never left, except that the cupboards were once again bare. She and Bethany made a run to Costco the day after they got home, stocking up on items in quantities that had defeated Hugh when he contemplated buying them. When they'd gotten home and had unloaded the car, Ruth began putting together a pot roast. Bethy hoisted herself onto the kitchen counter and watched Ruth cut up vegetables. She stole a carrot and munched on it, ruminating. "I miss home."

Ruth looked at her.

"I know, but it doesn't feel the same. I mean, it looks like home, but it doesn't feel like home anymore. Nothing *happens* here."

"Things happen," Ruth said. "Rianne got a job." Rianne was helping out in her aunt's pottery shop, wrapping holiday gifts.

"You know what I mean."

Ruth nodded. She knew what Bethy meant.

"She has a boyfriend, by the way," Bethy said, punching the plastic tip of her shoelace in and out of the ventilation holes in her sneaker.

"She does?"

"Some boy named Winslow Levy. He's new here. I guess he just moved from Bladenham."

"Winslow," Ruth said. "Like Winslow Homer the painter?"

Bethany shrugged. "I guess. Weird name."

"No weirder than Allison Addison or Bethany Roosevelt."

Bethy smiled. "Yeah."

Ruth handed her a carrot and a carrot peeler. Bethany started shaving carrot peelings into the sink from her seat on the counter. "She thinks he's cute. She has pictures of him on her phone."

"Is he cute?"

"I don't know. He's okay. But most of the time she talks about stuff that's happened in school, and I don't know what she's talking about."

"That's natural. You've been away."

"I know. It just makes me feel bad."

"Like an outsider," Ruth guessed.

"Yeah."

Ruth traded Bethy the peeled carrots for four unpeeled potatoes. "Yukon Golds," she said.

"What?"

"The potatoes. They're Yukon Golds."

"Oh." Bethany stared at the potatoes.

"Peel," Ruth said.

Bethany began to add potato peelings to the pile of carrot shavings in the sink. "Don't you miss it?"

"What, LA?"

Bethy nodded.

"Honey, we've been home for only a day and a half," said Ruth. "And anyway, when I'm there I miss Daddy. They both have their pitfalls."

"I miss him, too."

"Not half as much as he misses us."

But Bethy was thinking about something else. "I was wondering if maybe I could ask Allison up. Like, for a week. She's in Houston, but she says she doesn't want to stay there." She lowered her voice to a stage whisper, even though there was no one home besides her and Ruth. "I think she's cutting herself again."

She had told Ruth about the box cutter and Allison's arms. Ruth had been horrified. "Why do you think that?"

"I just do. Her stepdad doesn't like her very much. I mean, he isn't very nice to her and stuff. Plus she says her mom doesn't stick up for her when he's mad at her."

Ruth smiled a little. "Second marriages are never simple."

But Bethy didn't care about that. "So can I ask her? I know she'd really really want to come."

"Was this her idea?"

"No," Bethy said firmly—too firmly. Which meant it probably was.

"We'll see."

"That means no."

"It doesn't mean no, it means I want a minute to think about it."

"Okay." Bethy looked at the wall clock. "There. That was a minute."

Ruth sighed. "All right. But only for a week. She'll want to be home by Christmas, anyway."

Bethy said, "How long do you think we'll be here?"

"I don't know," said Ruth. "Until just after New Year's, probably. It's partly up to Daddy."

Bethy nodded gravely. "You mean because of his having diabetes."

"That," Ruth acknowledged. "But he also likes to have us here, so we won't leave until we really have to. He gets lonely."

"I wish he'd move to LA."

"I know, honey, but he'd have to give up his practice here and find one down there, and God knows he'd have some competition." It was a running joke of theirs that there was a dentist on every street corner in Studio City, and all of them were running specials on tooth whitening.

"Yeah," said Bethy. She put the last peeled potato on Ruth's cutting board. "So I can ask her?"

Ruth sighed. "Yes. Go ahead and ask her. One week."

"Yay!" Bethany jumped off the counter and skipped off to the den.

"*One week!*" Ruth shouted down the hall.

★

THEY MET ALLISON AT SEA-TAC AIRPORT THE FOLLOWING Friday. The girl stood out even in the midst of the mass of travelers surrounding the baggage carousel. Tall and willowy, she wore a pair of oversize sunglasses and carried over her shoulder a new buckled, riveted, belted, cinched, glazed leather tote that had probably cost as much as Ruth's monthly food allowance. With the sunglasses on, she could have been anywhere from eighteen to thirty-five; men sized her up as they walked by, and more than one woman looked back at her as she passed. By contrast, Bethy looked like the young girl she was as she raced across the baggage claim area squealing.

The girls hugged extravagantly; Allison twirled Bethy around. "I've missed you so much!" Ruth heard Bethany say.

"I know!" Allison put her sunglasses on top of her head and looked around. "So this is Seattle?"

"Well, it's Sea-Tac," Bethany said. "Where we live is about forty-five minutes from here."

"I can't wait!"

Ruth remembered Mimi telling her once that although Allison looked like a sophisticate, the only place outside of Texas she'd ever been was LA.

At the carousel the girls had spotted Allison's suitcase—big enough to hold a body, but with wheels, thank God—and hefted it off the carousel. Ruth thought of the steamer trunks that movie stars and celebrities had once traveled with. God knew what Allison had packed, to take up so much room. Ruth had visions of a microwave, small TV, and other light appliances.

"We're ready, Mom," Bethy panted. She and Allison towed the suitcase between them. "She brought only this one bag."

Ruth gave Allison a hug. "Welcome to Seattle, honey."

"We're going to have the best time," Bethy said.

"Oh, I know," Allison said; and then, to Ruth, with heart-breaking simplicity, "Thank you so much for inviting me."

When they got home, Ruth watched her move from room to room, taking it all in: the oak bookcases and built-in china cabinet and cheerful barnyard watercolors on the living room walls; Ruth's ceramic pieces on the coffee table and fireplace mantel; the deep window seat at the end of the dining room; the braided rugs and warm fir floors throughout the house. There was a troubling wistfulness about the girl—exactly what you might expect, Ruth thought, from an orphan. Or from a girl who had too many houses and too few homes.

ACCORDING TO FAMILY TRADITION, FRIDAY WAS SPAGHETTI night in the Rabinowitz household. Ruth made her from-scratch marinara sauce with sausage and meatballs, plus garlic bread and a salad, and the girls made up an extravagant dessert using a graham-cracker crust, chocolate pudding, half a melted Hershey's bar, a half cup of crushed peanuts, a touch of Kahlúa (Ruth's contribution), and lots and lots of Cool Whip. Poor Hugh would have to settle for a sugar-free pudding cup.

On a whim Ruth said, "Girls, let's use the silver tonight, how about that? Honey, go into the pantry and bring out Nana's flatware."

Bethy and Allison retrieved a heavy oak box lined in flannel. "Whoa," said Allison when Ruth opened it up. "This is all silver?"

"Sterling," Ruth said, pausing to look. "It's pretty, isn't it? We hardly ever use it, though, because it tarnishes too fast. In my mother's day, people had more time for that kind of thing, polishing silver."

Allison turned the pieces over and back, examining them minutely. "Well, I'd use it all the time."

"Would you?" Ruth smiled. "You two can set the table, please. Bethy, use the cloth napkins."

"We never use cloth napkins," said Allison.

Ruth wasn't clear on whether she was referring to her mother's house or Mimi's, so she just said, "Sometimes it's nice. Especially when there's company."

"Oh, I know," said Allison quickly.

The conversation around the dinner table was lively. Ruth believed in honoring her guests with the conversational spotlight, so she asked Allison about her house in Houston.

"It's huge," the girl said, wiping her mouth neatly with her napkin and tucking it back in her lap. "It's probably like two of your houses. He'd just finished building it when he and my mom met. There's a home theater, which is cool, and a swimming pool that has this bubble you can put over it in winter, except that the water's still freezing. Plus he has a workout room. With weights and stuff."

"It sounds lovely," Ruth said.

"I guess," Allison said indifferently. She turned to Hugh. "May I have the bread, please?"

It surprised Ruth that the girl had such excellent manners. Whatever the particulars were of her home life, someone had either raised her right or she was a very quick study. Bethy had told her once that Allison's mother had been a stripper before she married her current husband. Ruth never got a straight answer about whether or not the mother had ever been married to Allison's father, who, anyway, seemed to be long out of the picture. And the mother had probably been a stripper because she couldn't make enough money doing anything else. Ruth had heard of girls— women—putting themselves through college that way. Just because you were a stripper didn't mean you were a bad or immoral person. Ruth thought it was important to remember that.

"You have very nice manners," Hugh was saying as he passed Allison the bread basket. "Our Bethy could get a few tips."

"Thank you. Mimi sent me to this etiquette school last year, where they teach you which side the fork goes on and which is your bread plate and stuff like that. How to say *please* and *thank you*."

"Well, whoever it was did a good job," Hugh said. "Your mother must be very proud of you."

Allison smiled at him enigmatically and wound up a fork-load of spaghetti using her spoon as a backstop. "She doesn't understand why I don't work more. She thinks actors just work all the time, like it's no big deal to book things. She says Mimi isn't trying hard enough to sell me."

"Do you think so?" Hugh asked her. "One thing I'd have to say is the woman seems to have excellent sales skills."

"I know—she's really good," Allison agreed. "She's one of the best managers in LA. She's been written up in a bunch of magazines and stuff."

"Oh?" said Hugh. "I wasn't aware of that."

"You should hear her on the phone, Daddy," Bethy chimed in. "She isn't even that polite. She just calls the casting directors up and tells them who she wants to audition for stuff, and they usually say okay."

"Usually," said Allison.

"Usually," agreed Bethy.

"Well, you girls are in a hard line of work, that's for sure," Hugh said.

Allison shrugged. "We like it, though. Don't we?"

"A lot," said Bethy.

"Well, sure," said Ruth.

★

WHILE SHE DID THE DINNER DISHES, RUTH WATCHED Allison and Bethany playing something on their twin Game Boys, curled side by side on the living room sofa. They had their arms linked; now and then, a forehead quickly touched a forehead. Once, Allison planted a loud, smacky kiss right on the top of Bethany's head, the way Ruth sometimes did, and Bethany smiled, shy and radiant that this beautiful creature had chosen her.

"It's really nice here," Ruth overheard Allison tell Bethy.

"It's fine. I mean, it's not fancy or anything, like your house."

"I meant your parents. Your mom seems pretty stressed down in LA, but she's different here. And I like your dad."

"Yeah?" said Bethy.

"Yeah," said Allison, and Ruth could tell by the tone of her voice that she really meant it.

WHEN HUGH OFFERED TO MAKE THE GIRLS PANCAKES ON Sunday morning—despite the fact that he couldn't eat them himself, because what was the point of pancakes without syrup, and sugar-free syrups just weren't the same—Allison offered to help.

"Well," Hugh said. "I've never had a helper before. It's pretty much a one-man job."

"I could make bacon," the girl offered. "Do you have any? I always make it at Mimi's."

The truth was, he wasn't all that eager to be alone with the girl. He couldn't shake the memory of her backing him into the sofa corner in Mimi's greenroom. Still, she was only a little older than Bethany, and she was trying to be useful, which he applauded. So after consulting with Ruth, he dug a package of turkey bacon out of the refrigerator and handed it to Allison. "It's nasty stuff, though, I warn you," he told her.

"I've never heard of turkey bacon."

"Someone's bad idea," Hugh said. "But it's good for us, so we eat it. There are days when I miss fat more than I miss sugar. Here's a lesson for you: keep an eye on your weight. Not that I imagine you'll have any problems."

Allison opened the package of turkey bacon and rummaged around in the cupboards until she found a pan. "Nah, I could eat like ten Twinkies and a whole pizza and I'd still be skinny. We're both thin, me and my mom."

"Lucky you."

"Mimi's fat, though."

"I saw that."

"I'm trying to get her to go on a diet, but she sneaks stuff. Like she'll wait until she thinks we're asleep and then she'll bake a whole batch of Pillsbury crescent rolls and eat them all herself. She's got high blood pressure, too. If it's quiet you can hear her breathing and stuff. Wheezing."

"That's not good," said Hugh.

"I *know*." Allison turned the bacon strips with a fork.

Hugh ladled batter onto his skillet. Impulsively he said, "Do you really like this acting stuff? The whole Hollywood bit?"

"Of course."

"So do you think you'll be a big star one day?"

"I have to be."

"Why?"

"I just do."

"That's a lot of pressure to put on yourself," Hugh said, surprised. Allison looked back at him strangely. "No?"

She shrugged.

"Tell me about Bethany. Is she good?"

"She's pretty good. She could be better, though."

"Really?"

"Yup. She just needs more practice. You can tell she still gets nervous and stuff."

"Okay." Hugh stacked finished pancakes on top of a plate with a paper towel on it, and put the plate in the oven so they'd stay warm. Then he spooned out more batter.

"Do you *really* like being a dentist?" Allison asked.

"I do. Very much."

"Yeah, well, you guys have a high suicide rate, though. Dentists."

"We do?"

Allison nodded. "I read that once in a magazine."

"Huh." Hugh flipped four pancakes, two at a time. "Well, I can't speak for all dentists, of course, but the ones I know seem pretty well adjusted."

"Yeah, but still." Allison sniffed at the bacon. "So this smells okay. I mean, not like real bacon, but it smells pretty good."

"What did you say your father does?" Hugh asked.

"I don't have a father," Allison said matter-of-factly.

"Oh. That's tough," said Hugh, and meant it.

Allison shrugged. "Yeah. I have a stepfather."

"Do you?"

"His name is Chet. He owns oil rigs or oil wells or barrels or something. My mom likes him for his money, but he's not that nice to her. He makes her ask permission before she uses his stuff. Like the last time I was home he yelled at her for borrowing this junky old sweater of his that he probably wouldn't even be caught dead in. She said it was just a stupid sweater, and he called her the C-word, and then he didn't talk to us for like five days."

"Ow," said Hugh.

"I told her we should've kept our apartment just in case, but she said it was too expensive. Which it wasn't, because it was a dive."

"Oh?" Hugh was at a loss.

"But I'm not around that much anymore, anyway," Allison said bluntly. "He pays for me to stay with Mimi."

"So I gather. Don't you miss home?"

"Nah. It's not like here."

"*Here* here?"

"You know—this." She spread her arms wide. "You're like the perfect family."

He looked to see if she was mocking him, but if she was, she wasn't showing it.

"Anyway," she said, tapping the bacon strips with her fork, "These are done."

"Okay," said Hugh.

It went like that all week: to Ruth's lasting surprise, Allison was a perfect houseguest, blending in, picking up after herself, tidy to a fault—no child should be that dialed into her own care and maintenance—and offering to do dishes and other household chores that Ruth could get Bethy to do only by hitting her over the head with them. Who'd have thought the girl would be a *good* influence? As a reward, Ruth took them to the top of the Space Needle and for a ferry ride so Allison could see killer whales, and then for lunch in Friday Harbor. Another afternoon she dropped the girls at Bellevue Square, the Seattle area's most upscale mall, where they wanted to go even though it had exactly the same stores as the Beverly Center in Hollywood. Bethany bought a flippy little skirt that Ruth thought was a tad too short, and Allison bought a silk scarf that Ruth thought no fourteen-year-old should have wanted. As it turned out, she didn't: she presented it to Ruth as a gift that evening at dinner.

"Oh, honey," Ruth said in dismay. "You shouldn't spend your money on me."

Allison looked crushed. "I thought you'd like it. It's for Ha-nukkah." The holiday had begun several days ago, and each evening they'd been lighting candles in Ruth's favorite pewter menorah and the girls had each received small gifts: plush slipper-socks with pictures of dogs on them that vaguely resembled Tina Marie; gift certificates for a new Game Boy game apiece; packs of lip gloss in different flavors like bubble gum and cotton candy; matching, hand-carved dreidels made of horn.

Now Bethy told Ruth loyally, "It's from Gucci, and it took her forever to pick it out."

Hugh shot Ruth a look across the table: *For God's sake, keep it.*

"It might be the most beautiful scarf I've ever seen," Ruth told her sincerely, because it was true, and wrapped the silk around her throat.

Allison beamed and said, "I know some other ways you can tie it, too."

Ruth didn't doubt that for a minute.

To Hugh she presented a calfskin wallet, and then, when they all got up to clear the table, she approached Ruth shyly and gave her a long, tight hug, and then gave Hugh a chaste kiss on the cheek. In their bedroom that night, Ruth and Hugh agreed that the girl's transformation was nothing short of astonish-ing.

BUT BY THE END OF THE WEEK, THE GIRLS HAD FINALLY begun to wear on each other, so when a neighbor called to see if Bethy could babysit for the afternoon, Ruth suggested that she say yes. Allison stayed behind at the house and helped Ruth unload the dishwasher.

"I think you two have done very well together," Ruth said. "A week's a long time."

"Yeah," Allison sighed. "Plus she's younger than me."

"You've been a good role model for her," said Ruth, because, surprisingly, it was true. "That's the thing about being an only child. There's nobody to learn from."

"I'm an only child," Allison pointed out.

"Well, you seem to have a natural sense of the world."

Allison nodded. "I read a lot of magazines."

Ruth ran her dish towel around the lip of a casserole to dry it before putting it away in the sideboard. "Do you think you're pretty?"

If Allison thought this was a strange question—as strange a question as Ruth herself thought it was; it had just popped out—she didn't show it. She just said, matter-of-factly, "I think I'm beautiful. *Hillary's* pretty."

"I'd think it would be hard to be beautiful," Ruth said, wiping down the sink.

"Sometimes," said Allison. "People want stuff from you."

"Such as?"

"I don't know. They want you to like them and pay attention to them. It's like if they can't be beautiful, too, they can borrow some of it by being around you."

"I guess I can see that."

"Mostly I don't mind, though. I'm used to it."

RUTH HAD AGREED THAT THEY COULD USE THE SILVER FOR the rest of Allison's visit. Allison loved knowing they were eating off precious metal, plus the silver made every meal a festive occasion, even breakfast, when, except for the morning they had pancakes, she and Bethany usually ate cereal and bananas by themselves because they got up so late. Allison always sat in the chair that looked out the bay window into the tiny backyard— the garden, Ruth called it, even though in Allison's opinion it wasn't much of a garden, more like a patch of grass the size of Mimi's dining room table with big, spindly rhododendrons all around it, plus a few rosebushes and some kind of shrub that Allison didn't recognize but Ruth said was gorgeous when it flowered in the summer. Whatever you called it, the garden was pretty even now, when it was dripping wet. Lots of birds came to use the birdbath and eat seeds from a feeder shaped like a mansion. You never saw little birds like these in LA, or maybe there was just too much else going on for you to pick them out. Allison thought it might be nice to be a bird living here, where all you had to worry about was whether the people remembered to put out enough seeds. From what Allison could see, Ruth always put out plenty—or now Allison did, since Ruth had given her permission. These were fat little birds; you could tell they'd always been well fed. The birds around their house in Houston—well, Chet's house—didn't look fat and content the way these birds did. They looked skinny and anxious, like they couldn't count on things. Her mother had never put out a bird feeder in her life.

If she were Bethany, she'd never leave this place, not even for LA. Why would you? You got to eat off nice dishes that all matched; you got good night kisses, and several times a day someone asked you if you needed anything, and if you said yes (which Allison rarely did), that person usually got whatever you needed: a warmer sweater, a fresh diet soda, a hug. When someone called your name here, it was often followed by a term of endearment: honey or sweetie. People called you names like that in LA, too, but they didn't convey love, just prompts. "Go over there, honey, and read that line again," or "Thank you, sweetheart, you can go."

Maybe Allison wasn't being fair, though. Her mother used to call her baby sometimes. "Baby, I'm going to go out for a little while. Make sure you keep the door locked." Now Chet-the-douche called her mom baby and no one called Allison anything at all.

She had told Mimi that, and Mimi had just shrugged and said, "Well, you're here now, so." Mimi wasn't much for terms of endearment, but she cared about Allison, which Allison knew, so it was okay.

Now, for the first time during her visit, Allison had the house to herself. Bethany was next door babysitting, Hugh was off drilling teeth, and Ruth had run out to the grocery store. Allison walked from room to room, running her hands over things: the backs of the living room chairs and sofa, the top of the TV, the simple dressers in Ruth and Hugh's room. She lay down on the bed, on her back, looked at the ceiling, and thought, "This is what they see when they go to bed at night," and it sounded safe and serene. At Chet's house, bedrooms were places where you closed your eyes and tried not to hear things like the headboard knocking rhythmically against your wall or your mom shouting, "You goddamn son-of-a-bitch bastard." The odd thing was, Allison could never make out what Chet said back. Maybe he didn't say anything at all. Sometimes Allison thought she'd rather hear *something*, even if it was loud or violent, than emptiness into which she couldn't follow them. She'd even tiptoed from her room down the hall to their closed door once and tried to see through the space between the hinges, but she must have made a noise because Chet, pissed off, had yelled her name, and she'd gone back to the guest room.

She opened a jar of moisturizer on Ruth's bureau and sniffed. It smelled like Ruth. She liked that smell, though it wasn't sexy in any way, just clean and comfortable. She put some on her finger and worked it into her hands, then sniffed. It still smelled good, but it didn't smell like Ruth anymore, just like Allison.

She opened some of the bureau drawers. Most of the clothes were ugly, boring women's clothes, like big white panties and bras that must have been a D or even a double-D cup. Allison was never going to need a D cup; her boobs were on the small side, and so were her mother's; and since she'd had her period for a couple of years already, they probably weren't going to grow much more. Her mother had looked at them once and said, "Good thing you weren't planning on making a living as a stripper, honey, because you don't have the tits for it. Nice legs, but no tits."

Someone like Ruth would never say *tits*.

In the bathroom, Allison looked for a razor, but found only an electric shaver. She'd been thinking about cutting again. She liked it here a lot, but she'd be leaving pretty soon, and cutting always made her feel much calmer. It had started in Texas a year ago, when Chet had yelled at her mother for spending too much money on Allison's clothes. They hadn't even spent that much, and what they had spent had been at Target: some socks, a new pair of jeans, a jacket. All of it had cost less than a hundred dollars, but Chet had freaked out anyway, making a huge deal out of examining each item on the receipt before getting right into Allison's mom's face and saying, "You don't spend my fucking money on her without asking me." He hadn't cared at all that Allison had been right there in the room.

Later that day, when her mom had left to go drinking with her best friend, Shelley, Allison had gone swimming topless, though she couldn't say why, except that it had something to do with Chet's being such a prick, and her wanting to get back at him somehow.

So from the side of the pool's shallow end—the end closest to him—she'd reached back and untied the strings holding up her wet bikini top, which came away with a faint sucking sound. She'd balled up the top and slapped it onto the concrete apron of the pool, right near his feet. He'd been pretending to read the Sunday paper, but she knew full well that what he was really doing was watching her as she swam a few slow laps. He watched her all the time, with those hooded eyes and slack mouth. So she pulled herself out of the pool and walked right past him, *slowly*, into the cabana—that's what he called it, only it was more like a converted garage with cheap, thin carpeting— and he followed her. He came up behind her and without saying a word he put his hands on her breasts—not gently, not at *all* gently—and yanked her backward. She'd felt his hard-on against her. He'd forced her against him with one arm while he yanked his pants down with the other, and then he spun her around. She had just enough time to see his erection—a horrible, red, veiny thing—before he locked his mouth over hers in a kiss that burned like acid. Then he hooked her behind the knee with his foot and she folded up like she was hinged, dropping onto the carpet. He was on the floor, too, right on top of her, and he shoved his cock at her over and over—and it hurt, it hurt a *lot*—until he broke through and drove all the way up inside her, right up to the hilt of him like a knife. She would swear she heard her hymen tear, though it probably wasn't possible. She could feel the cheap indoor-outdoor carpet scraping away skin on her lower back as he drove into her over and over; and then he must have come, because he stopped and slackened abruptly on top of her, suddenly so heavy she couldn't breathe. She started pushing at his shoulders so he'd get off her, get *off*. He rolled away but reached out to stroke her cheek, except she slapped the hand away. Then he got up and she got up, too; and he pulled his clothes into place but she just *stood* there, thinking that she didn't want to put her bathing suit back on because it would be cold and wet and it would sting the rug burn on her back. When he finished with his clothes and brought his face toward hers she thought he was going to kiss her again, but instead he brushed her cheek with his cheek lightly, lingeringly, which gave her goose bumps, and whispered, "If you ever tell a living soul, I will know and I will kill you."

After he went outside she looked at her back in a mirror and found on her lower back an abrasion the size of a fist, weeping clear liquid. She left her wet bathing suit where it was on the cabana floor, walked into the house stark naked, and went straight to her bathroom, where she filled her Waterpik—she'd always had excellent dental hygiene—with water too hot to touch. She brought the thing into the shower with her and inserted the Waterpik nozzle into her vagina as far as it would go. She hadn't been able to feel the heat until it was dripping down her legs like blood.

She'd stayed in the shower until the hot water ran out, and when it did she sat naked on the bathroom's fluffy pink, little-girl rug, sucking on her knee until, by accident, her eyes lit on the disposable razor she used in the shower to shave her legs and underarms. She crawled over and picked it up. There were ten perfectly round bruises on her arms, five on each from Chet's fingers. She held the double blade so it connected two of the bruises and pressed the razor home. Two thin lines of blood welled up like tears.

She was on a plane back to LA two days later, with five one-hundred-dollar bills zipped into a new Coach bag that had been left on top of her suitcase. Inside there was a note, written in script like barbed wire, that said, "Remember." Every month after that she got another five hundred dollars in cash in the mail. She made a point of spending every last penny. Once she gave a fifty-dollar bill to the homeless man who lived in a freeway cloverleaf and panhandled near Mimi's studio, but usually

she spent it on whatever. The day after she got back, she bought
a box cutter at Kmart and cut four intersecting lines into her left
arm: tic tac toe. You win.

Allison wandered out of Ruth's bedroom and into Bethany's. The girl had a ton of stuff. Books, books, books, paintings
on the walls instead of posters, a nice TV, and all these Starbucks teddy bears in different outfits. Bethany had told her she
had every Starbucks bear that was ever sold in Seattle, and that
meant about six a year since she was eight. She had so many, she
said, that a lot of them were in plastic totes in the garage. Allison
picked up one that was dressed in bunny pajamas, bunny slippers, and a hood with bunny ears. It must have been an Easter
bear. She kissed it on the lips, put its stubby arms around her
neck, then put it back on Bethany's bed and wandered out to
the kitchen. The kitchen was her favorite room, with nice windows, cheerful yellow walls with white trim, and a generally
homey feel. From there she drifted into the dining room and
over to the sideboard that held the oak box full of silverware.
The inside of the box was lined with thick, metallic-smelling,
plum-colored flannel, which, according to Ruth, kept the silver from tarnishing. Allison picked up a serving spoon, looked
at her reflection in the bowl, and stuck out her tongue. When
she heard Ruth's car crunching in the driveway she slipped the
spoon into her pocket, closed up the box, and met Ruth at the
door to see if she needed any help with the groceries.

It was always hard on Mimi when Allison was away,
though she'd never tell Allison that. During the two weeks
the girl had been in Seattle and then Houston for Christmas,
the house had echoed; even Tina Marie had been abnormally
clingy. Not that Mimi was at the house much, but still, you
had to sleep some time, and the greenroom couch at the studio

was too soft and too lumpy, though if she'd been twenty years younger, she probably wouldn't have cared. Now it just made her sciatica kick up, so she worked through the evening, buttoned the place up, and drove home at the DUI hour, when all the drunks, drug users, and belligerents came out. This she knew from experience. In the past she had had too much to drink herself on more than a few occasions after a client blew a network mix-and-match, underperformed for the role of a lifetime, or choked on what should have been a cakewalk of a guest-star audition for a casting director who was a fan. That's when the bottle of wine came out of the beat-to-shit credenza she had picked up, like many of her other furnishings, at a swap meet in Tarzana, along with the juice glass with the picture of Tweety Bird on it that had been given to her by one of her little six-year-olds however many years ago. The first glass of cheap chianti was always bitter, but the wine mellowed over the next three or four glasses until she could drink it like fruit juice.

MIMI PICKED ALLISON UP AT LAX. SHE'D BEEN CIRCLING the airport for an hour, she said, with Tina Marie barking in the backseat every time a plane flew over. She gave Allison a quick hug after Allison hoisted her suitcase into the trunk and hopped into the front seat.

"So?" Mimi said. "Did you have a good time in Seattle?"

Allison nodded. "They have a cute house. Small, you know, but cozy. They don't have expensive furniture and stuff, though, which is weird since he's a dentist and he probably makes a ton of money. But it was the kind of house where you could eat in the living room and put your feet up. We went bowling, and we shopped, and it was Hanukkah, so we lit candles and played with these little tops and stuff. Oh, and we saw a couple of movies, except at the end we were the only ones clapping. I guess people don't clap at the movies unless you're in LA. Hugh—he said I should call him that, not Dr. Rabinowitz—was in a really good mood the whole time. You could tell because he made us waffles and pancakes. He's probably really lonely when they're gone."

"And Houston?"

Allison shrugged and looked out the window. "They gave me a pair of diamond studs and some Jean Paul Gaultier perfume." She stuck out her wrist so Mimi could smell it. "Mostly they were never around, though. They had all these Christmas parties to go to, but Chet made me stay home because I'm underage. Like that counts if you're at a party in someone's *house*. I guess the bubble over the pool broke, so no swimming. They had this Wii thing, so I played that."

Mimi nodded. "Did you download the sides?"

Allison patted the side of her Coach tote. "I printed them this morning so I could work on them on the plane. Oh, and guess who was in first class? Jessica Alba. She was with some guy, I can't remember his name, but you could tell he wanted everyone to see him with her. He'd make eye contact with everyone he could as they went by. I didn't look at him, just because he wanted me to so much." She fished a compact out of her bag. "She's pretty."

"Who?"

Allison rolled her eyes. "Jessica *Alba*. Her skin's not that great, though." She pulled down the car visor and opened the compact so she could powder her nose. "She had a zit right here." She touched a place on her chin. "You could tell she'd tried to cover it up, but you could see it anyway." She put the compact away and settled the tote on the floor by her feet. "So what's new at the house?"

Mimi shrugged. "It's been pretty quiet. Tina Marie ate a

shoe, we found a mouse in the kitchen. Little things. Nothing interesting."

"Whose?"

"What?"

"Whose *shoe*?" Allison turned and shook her finger at the little dog in the backseat. "If it was mine, I'll be *so mad*." Tina Marie straightened her narrow shoulders and looked out the car window dismissively. She was riding in the doggie booster seat that Allison and Mimi had bought for her after reading an article on dog auto safety, and she clearly considered it an assault on her dignity.

Mimi answered for her. "Not yours. Reba's or Hillary's, and it was only a Croc flip-flop. I've told those girls how many times that anything chewy is fair game."

"Oh, whew. Did anyone book anything?"

"Perry booked an Alpha-Bits commercial." Perry was one of Mimi's few African American clients, a four-year-old with a smile like an angel. "He's booking everything right now."

"Sure, because he's cute," Allison said. "Nobody else?"

"No."

"Good."

When they got home Allison climbed out of the car, freed a haughty Tina Marie from the loathsome booster seat, and wrestled her suitcase out of the trunk. Mimi took her tote. Allison was glad to be home; she danced into the front hall and turned to Mimi, her eyes twinkling. "So did you miss me?"

"Of course I missed you," Mimi said.

"Oh, good. Me too," said Allison, looking around the house and hugging herself. "Let's order out—Chinese. Please? Can we? My treat."

"It's just us," Mimi said. "Hillary and Reba won't get back until the day after tomorrow."

"Then bring it on, dog," said Allison in her gangsta voice. She pulled a takeout menu from a drawer in the kitchen, tucked the phone receiver between her shoulder and her ear, and ordered without even asking Mimi what she wanted, because Mimi always wanted the same thing: double happiness chicken and potstickers. For herself Allison ordered lo mein with pea pods and shrimp, and an order of pork fried rice to share.

"Did you TiVo *Ghost Whisperer*?" Allison asked Mimi while they were waiting for the delivery. It was one of their favorite shows, and neither one of them thought Jennifer Love Hewitt was fat; she just had big boobs, which Allison, for one, envied. The guides at the Universal Studios theme park said you could see her Rollerblading around the lot at lunch sometimes, and that she always waved at the trams full of tourists. "Did you remember?"

Mimi had remembered.

When the food finally arrived they paused the TV while Allison paid. She tipped the delivery guy eight dollars because he was cute and he always blushed when she answered the door. The first time he ever delivered to them he included a headshot of himself and a résumé with the food order. A lot of delivery people did that. You never knew whose house you were going to; the worst that could happen was it got thrown away, but that wouldn't matter if you made even one decent contact.

They watched the rest of their show while they ate. Mimi pointed out that she used to manage one of the guest stars, a good-looking guy in his twenties with a nice smile. "He always overacted," she said. "It used to just drive me crazy. Someone must have finally gotten through to him, though. That or he's just finally growing up."

"Hey!" Allison said, suddenly leaning forward and pointing

at the TV. "Look, that's right off Lankershim. Remember when we got stuck in traffic because they had that whole detour set up, and we thought it was for *CSI*? I bet it was this."

When the show was over they put all the trash together and Allison stashed away the extra soy sauce and an extra pair of chopsticks, which she used to put her hair up sometimes when she washed her face. Mimi said she was going to take a bath, so Allison dragged her suitcase back to her room and unpacked. She hadn't worn a lot of what she'd brought, so it was all still neatly folded.

And underneath it all, carefully nested in one of her socks, was a single silver spoon.

January 2007

In Hollywood, the sheer number of celebrities makes you a celebrity, too, if only by proxy. You spend, because they do: on clothes you won't wear, on handbags and hair extensions and waxing and toning and being, in general, ready—for your moment, your ascension, your destiny. And it's not the destiny you already know, because that one can't possibly be all you were meant for; no, it's your other destiny, the one for which you've been preparing for years, the one where you wave to the crowds and shop on Rodeo Drive even for your socks and cigarettes; the destiny where your car windows are tinted to lend you some privacy you won't really want until the thrill of recognition wears off and you no longer walk down a street watching for people to catch sight of you, elbow the next person over, and whisper your name. Cell phone pictures of you fly through the air like angels, and you graciously stop to sign your name on cocktail napkins and T-shirts; for this, you carry a Sharpie with you at all times. You are prepared because you've practiced; you have perfected your public smile and gracious, musical, lilting laugh as you protest, over and over, "I'm no different than you, you know," when the thing you love the very most is that you are. You pull your fame around you like a cloak that you wear to restaurants like Nobu, where you lunch now with your celebrity friends because your old friends couldn't possibly understand anymore what it's like to be you.

—VEE VELMAN

Chapter Seventeen

TWO OR THREE TIMES NOW, QUINN HAD DREAMED ABOUT hands. Disembodied hands that stroked him lovingly—his arms, his legs, his back, his head. Especially his head. He didn't think they were Quatro's hands, but he couldn't tell for sure, since he didn't really know what the stylist's hands looked like, only the way they'd felt. This stroking wasn't sexual; it was almost parental, or at least what he imagined parental hands felt like, since in reality his mom had a tendency to slap rather than stroke. In his dreams he was unconcerned with how long the hands would stay because he just seemed to know that they'd be there as long as he wanted them to be, maybe forever.

He hadn't been back to the hair salon or the Laundromat in a couple of weeks. Though he passed the salon every day, he didn't look in—he struggled not to look in—but just went by at a normal walking pace, which he figured was slow enough for Quatro to spot him, if he was looking, and come to the door before Quinn reached the end of the block. He hadn't come out, so Quinn assumed he either wasn't looking or didn't care or both. Fuck him.

And anyway, he was busy. Last week he had gone to a mix-and-match and then on to network for *Bradford Place*, the babysitter pilot. Then Mimi had gotten a call from Evelyn Flynn with the news that the network had decided they wanted the babysitter to be a girl: too many sponsors had thought there was something creepy about a seventeen-year-old boy who chose to spend his time looking after little kids. Quinn was bummed and Mimi was bummed, too. Though the show was a total piece of crap, Mimi had negotiated a deal that would have paid him twenty thousand dollars a week for a twenty-two-week season—and, much more important, it would have launched him, been his ticket at last to the party that was episodic TV.

But Evelyn Flynn had given him something even as she was taking something else away, because in the same phone call to Mimi, the casting director had offered to coach Quinn on the lead role of Buddy in *After*, the feature film that Bethany and Allison had auditioned for before Thanksgiving. It was highly irregular for a casting director to act as a coach, and even more so when she wasn't even casting the project.

When Quinn called her, as she'd asked him to do, she told him to print out a full script for the feature film, read it through, put it away, think about it, read it again, and then come see her on the Paramount lot this coming Saturday. Evelyn Flynn was old and a little scary, but she was also a goddess, at least in Hollywood. He didn't know why she was taking an interest in him, but he also didn't care. Whatever her reason, Buddy was a lead in a Gus Van Sant film, and Quinn would kill, literally *kill*, to get it.

So he'd gone over and over the script and was now walking onto the Paramount Studios lot with the script in hand. Being here on a weekend felt different from being on the lot during the week. Many of the soundstages were still working, but the suits—the accountants, the executives, the salespeople—were all at home in Toluca Lake or the West Hollywood Hills or wherever, pretending to have a home life. It was peaceful, almost like being in school on the weekends, at least from what he remembered—he hadn't been in a real school since he'd come to LA.

"Well," Evelyn Flynn said when he came into the darkened

outer office. "It's Quinn, is it?" She said it like she hadn't been expecting him, but how could that be? He'd called ahead and left a message. He might be sloppy with the rest of his life, but he was very careful when it came to talking to people who could make a difference in his career.

"Is this okay?" he said.

"It's what I told you to do, isn't it?" She walked behind him to close and lock the door, saying, "It's Saturday. I don't normally see anyone on Saturdays, ever. I also don't answer my phone or my e-mails. You let your guard down and this business will eat you alive."

She didn't volunteer the reason she was breaking her own protocol for Quinn, and he wasn't about to ask. He didn't want to jinx anything.

She led him into her office, but instead of sitting behind the desk, she sat on the couch, patting the other seat cushion to indicate he should sit beside her. He sat.

"Now tell me about Buddy," she said.

"What do you want to know?"

"Everything."

"Couldn't I just show you?" He wasn't big on developing a whole character biography, giving a character a favorite color and a horoscope sign and crap like that, the way some of his acting teachers had wanted him to. He usually just got that stuff intuitively as he went along.

She narrowed her eyes at him for a minute and then said, "Fair enough." She stood up and retrieved a copy of the screenplay from her desk blotter. "We'll do the audition scene—at least, it's what Carlyle auditioned with, so I'm guessing Joel Sherman will have you do the same one." She picked up her script. "Page ten."

He knew exactly which one it was, even before he got there.

It was where Buddy and Carlyle are talking about the candy machine at the hospital. He'd read it so many times he was already off-book.

"Do you want me to start?" she asked him. *She* asked *him*. How weird was that? He nodded.

They ran the scene.

                    BUDDY
I'm not buyin' it.

                    CARLYLE
What do you mean, you're not buying it? It's the truth!

                    BUDDY
Yeah? So where's your wand?

                    CARLYLE
             (with infinite weariness)
Buddy. That's only in Harry Potter. Harry Potter is a book.

                    BUDDY
So show me something. If you were a real witch you'd be making something happen!

                    CARLYLE
                  (sweetly)
I am. I'm making us argue.

                    BUDDY
Oh, for God's sake.

                    CARLYLE
So, okay. Do you remember before, when Nana left her dentures in a glass and the next morning they were blue?

                    BUDDY

Yeah.

                    CARLYLE

That was me.

                    BUDDY

That was food coloring!

                    CARLYLE

Then why didn't it wear off for six days?

BUDDY laughs.

                    CARLYLE (cont'd)

You know, we should really be nicer to her,
now that she's living here and everything.

                    BUDDY

Aw, c'mon on. We're nice to her.

                         (a beat)

A witch, huh? So can witches go back and fix
stuff that's already happened?

                    CARLYLE

Like what?

                    BUDDY

You know. Mom.

                    CARLYLE

No one can keep someone from dying, Buddy.
Only God.

                    BUDDY

Yeah, well, to hell with God.

                         (a long beat)

Do you think she knew I wasn't there? When
she, you know—

                    CARLYLE

I don't know. No, I don't think so.

BUDDY
(bitterly)

I do. I think the last thing she ever
thought about me was that I was down the
hall beating the shit out of a candy machine.
When all those Mars bars and M&Ms and crap
came flying out it was like I won the goddamn
jackpot, honest to God. By the time it
stopped, you couldn't even see my shoes. I
looked like a fucking Easter basket.

CARLYLE

Everyone understood.

BUDDY

Not her. If she had, she'd have waited five
more minutes. Five stinkin' minutes and I
would've been back. I would've been there.
Why didn't she wait for me?

CARLYLE

I think maybe she just couldn't anymore. You
know how when you've been hanging off the
monkey bars for a long time your arms get
so tired and suddenly you weigh a hundred
thousand pounds and you just have to let go?
I think that's what happened to her.

BUDDY

She fell off the monkey bars.

CARLYLE

Yeah.

BUDDY

And that's supposed to make me feel better?
(visibly pulling himself together)
Some magician you are.

                CARLYLE

Witch. And I never said I could make you feel
better.

                BUDDY

So how come you are a witch, anyway?

                CARLYLE

I don't know. Maybe it's because I'm not
strong enough to break a candy machine.

                BUDDY

Nah, you're strong. You're like her. You
remind me of her.

                CARLYLE

I do?

                BUDDY

Yeah.

             (a beat)

Except she would've used yellow.

CARLYLE just looks at him, not getting it.

   On the dentures. Then everyone would have
   thought Nana had liver failure. She drinks,
   you know—she drinks a lot. I've seen her.

                CARLYLE

That's orange juice.

                BUDDY

That's vodka.

                CARLYLE

She misses Mom too, you know. Sometimes she
cries at night.

                BUDDY

He's heard her, too.

   Yeah.

            (a long beat)

```
        Think you can make it all go away? Make
        it just seem like she's at the store for a
        minute or something, like she's coming back?
CARLYLE just looks at him. They both know she
can't. Suddenly he's pleading.
        But hey, you could try, right? I mean, you
        could try. You could just try! You don't know.
CARLYLE comes around behind him and puts her
hands gently over his eyes. The hands are small
and inadequate, but they're what she has to
work with. BUDDY leans into them.
                    CARLYLE
                 (very softly)
        Abracadabra!
```

"Bull's-eye," the casting director said softly.

Quinn wiped his eyes and then his nose on his sleeve.

"Now we'll do it again," she said.

"What?"

"Now we'll do it again. And after that, we'll do it again."

"I don't think I can."

"You're going to have to. If you're going to carry a feature film on your back, honey, you're going to have to be rock solid even on the tenth take."

Quinn took in a deep breath, and then he did the scene again, and after that, again.

And so she began to teach him. Not like Dee and all those teachers Mimi kept making them work with. She taught him like a director would. They worked on holding back; on building; on breaking and cresting and digging for gold in an empty mine and bringing up just a little bit more. Once or twice she screamed, "God, no. *No, no, no.* You had it right and now you're fucking it up."

And of course he *had* had it right and then fucked it up, he just didn't know *how*. So she taught him that, too.

Two hours later, abruptly, she said, "Enough."

"What?"

"That's all—that's enough. We're done."

"I don't want to be done."

"A mature actor knows when to say done, but you're not a mature actor, so I'm saying it for you. We're done."

"For how long?"

"For now."

"Can I come back? When can I come back?"

She regarded him through the same cool eyes that had freaked him out every time he'd seen her, except now he understood that through them, she *saw* him. How many people actually see you? Not many, at least not in Quinn's experience.

"I don't know," she said.

"We've done only four pages!"

"That's all you need. That's the scene you'll audition with."

"But there's so much more." He could hear his voice rising, but he couldn't stop it. "What if they change the scene? What if they choose some random scene and say do that? I won't know how."

"Oh, you'll know how."

"*I won't!* I thought I knew this scene when I got here, and look how much of it was crap!"

She took a cigarette out of a pack in her desk drawer, lit it, and narrowed her eyes at him through the smoke. "All right. Be here next Tuesday at six."

His heart began to race. Mimi had said if he missed Dee's class one more time, she'd drop him as a client. "I have a class."

"Skip it."

"If I do, Mimi says she'll drop me."

She smiled out of her old eyes and said softly, "Fuck Mimi Roberts."

That night, as he lay on his air mattress in the corner of Baby-Sue's apartment, trying not to hear Baby-Sue and Jasper screwing in the other room, he thought of the ground rules Evelyn Flynn had laid out for him: he would dump Mimi as a manager and Evelyn would act as Quinn's manager instead, at least for now. In return, she owned him: he would work whenever, however, and at whatever she told him to.

"I gather you can be difficult," she said.

"Sometimes."

"Well, not with me. I don't have time, and neither do you—they'll be starting to audition for Buddy in the next few weeks, and you're not ready. You act up just once and you're done."

He nodded.

"Whatever personal life you do or do not have gets checked at the door. Period. You are not my son. I am not your mother. I don't love you, so I won't be cutting you slack. That needs to be crystal clear."

"I get it."

She also told him flatly that she would not call in favors for him. Whatever he booked, he did on his own, though with the help of her coaching. She'd told him she knew Gus Van Sant, and that she thought he'd give Quinn a fair shake, if Quinn made it that far in auditions; but even so, he was a long shot at best, and he'd have to put everything he had on the table if he was even going to stand a chance.

Quinn was okay with that. He wanted this part more than anything he'd ever wanted before. The role was dark, which suited him; it was a lead, which meant he'd never have to bottom-feed again on guest-star roles that came months apart; and he'd get to work with Gus Van Sant. *Gus Van Sant!*

So he called the studio the next morning, before there was any chance Mimi would be at work, and left a message on her phone, saying that he knew she'd drop him because he wouldn't be at class, so he was going to find a new manager. She'd be relieved about that. *He* was relieved about that. He would have been relieved even if he didn't have Evelyn Flynn. Mimi was for babies, for little kids, and Quinn was no longer a little kid. Mimi forgot about that all the time, which pissed him off. A lot of things she'd done pissed him off, now that he thought about it—now that he could afford to think about it. She always told him what to wear to auditions and showcases, which was so much crap—he knew how to dress himself. She made him call her after every audition to report in, even if it was for piddly stuff like commercials, which he didn't give a shit about because he had plenty of money from his monthly allowance, and if it strapped Nelson, so much the better. The asshole had kept his distance the whole week Quinn was home for Christmas, and when he was forced to be in the same room with Quinn he said stuff like, "This isn't Hollywood. We *work* for a living up here." Nelson could just go fuck himself. His mom could, too. The only person in his family who really gave a shit was Rory. The kid was cute and nice and he loved Quinn completely and without reservation. His Christmas present to Quinn had been a framed picture of himself with their dog, Schuyler, and near the bottom he'd written the date and then his own first and last name and the name of the dog, as though Quinn might not remember who they were. His mom and Nelson had given him a new sleeping bag and a camping cot so he didn't have to sleep on the floor anymore. Big fucking deal.

He felt too restless to sit around the apartment after he talked to Mimi's voice mail, so he pulled on his purple high-tops and turned right at the foot of the stairs, toward Hazlitt & Company. He'd thought it would be nice to see Quatro for a minute, but things turned out to be busy at the salon. Quatro looked harried, and all the clients looked bitchy, and there wasn't a woman in the place. But just as Quinn was about to move on, Quatro caught sight of him, said something to his client, and came up to the front of the salon.

"Hey, you," he said. "I've only got a second, but I was thinking I might go to the beach after work. Want to come with me?" Like he'd had Quinn on his mind all along. Quinn knew better, but still, it was nice to pretend. There weren't that many people who wanted to hang out with him, except for scene partners during showcases and acting classes. He was trying to figure out whether this was a pity invitation when Quatro misread his hesitation and said, smiling, "I won't drug you and carry you off or anything."

"What? No. I mean, sure, I'd like to," Quinn said. "Go to the beach, I mean."

"Okay. So get back here at four fifteen, and I should be done by then. We can figure out the rest on the way."

Quinn felt a little thrill in his gut and shoved his hands deep in his pockets so he wouldn't give away how amazing it was that someone wanted to make plans with him. Four o'clock was only an hour and a half from now. Maybe he'd go back to Los Burritos and see if the Hispanic girl was working today. Maybe he'd try to order something in Spanish.

Back out on the street, he stood for a minute and breathed. He was suddenly glad he lived in West Hollywood. When Jasper and Baby-Sue kicked him out, which he bet would be within the next month or so, he hoped he'd be able to find a room to rent someplace over here. He could probably find something. He wasn't thrilled with the idea of living with someone he didn't even know, or with a gay person, but he figured there wouldn't be much of an alternative.

Like Hazlitt & Company, Los Burritos was busy, even though it was two thirty in the afternoon. The Hispanic girl, along with two women, was behind the counter when Quinn got there. He got into her line, even though it was the longest one, and when he got to the front, he smiled at her. She smiled back, but he couldn't tell if she recognized him or not. She was wearing a pair of earrings shaped like chili peppers. He liked that: you couldn't wear something like that unless you had a sense of humor. He bet she had a really nice laugh. Maybe he could say something funny and find out. He wasn't really a funny person, though, at least not in a way that made other people laugh. He was good at shocking them, but no one usually got his jokes.

"*Hola,*" he said. "*Cómo estás?*"

Her eyes lit up. "*Muy bien—y tú? Hablas español?*"

"No, that's the only thing I know how to say. But I'm thinking about learning."

She smiled. "*No es difícil,*" she said. "What would you like?"

For a fraction of a second, Quinn thought she meant the question in a general way, and he was going to say, "Everything," but then he realized she was just trying to take his order. She punched it up on her register and then it was time for him to move on. He'd have liked to stay and see if he could make her laugh, but he didn't want her to get in trouble, plus he'd run out of things to say, so he just said thank you and paid her and found a table where he could watch her as he ate. She was very, very small, not much bigger than Cassie Foley, and she had a tiny gold cross around her neck, so she must be religious. Was there a saint who watched over small Latinas with crappy food-service jobs who still knew how to smile and mean it? Jasper had told him once that there was a patron saint of waiters—Saint Notburga. Weird name. Quinn liked the idea that there was someone—something—out there watching over her. Maybe he'd ask her about it the next time he stood in her line. Maybe he'd look for a necklace that had a chili pepper charm or something. One that would match her earrings. He could look for one while he waited for Quatro. At least it would give him something to do.

Energized, he finished his food, threw out his trash, and left. He'd like to have seen the little Latina girl smile one last time, but she was busy when he looked over. That was okay. He'd bring her his present and then she'd smile at him.

He could wait.

"SO IS IT TOO TOURISTY IF WE GO TO VENICE BEACH?" Quatro asked him across the roof of the car when Quinn came back to the salon at four fifteen. "Sometimes you're just in the mood to see weird, and block for block, Venice Beach has more weird than anyplace I know." Quatro unlocked his car—a metallic blue BMW convertible, a pretty thing—and climbed behind the wheel. Mimi's car was a moving trash heap, full of girlie shit and fast-food wrappers, but the BMW was pristine. There was a small trash bag in the back, but it didn't look like there'd ever been any trash in it. The leather smelled new and supple.

"I've never been there," Quinn said, getting into the car carefully so he didn't hit or scuff anything. "I mean, I've heard about it, but, you know."

"You're kidding."

"No."

"Well, for God's sake, then, let's go there! Where else haven't you been?"

Quinn shrugged. "I don't know. Places that you need a car to get to."

"You don't have a car?"

Quinn wondered how old Quatro thought he was. He tried to think of something cool to say, and then he decided to hell with it and just told the truth. "I don't have a driver's license. It's hard to find someone to take you to the DMV. My manager took me once, over in Glendale, but I flunked the test."

"Hey, there's no shame in flunking. I know a guy who flunked three times before he got it right. He had test anxiety. Did you study the book?"

"Sure," Quinn lied.

"Well, just look it over again right before you go in."

"Yeah. I could take the bus over there, too, I guess."

"Tell me you've been to the Santa Monica Pier, at least."

"Yeah. I audition over there a lot, so."

"Whew."

"Yeah, it's okay."

Quatro adjusted his seat. "Buckle up, son, because we are out of here."

TRAFFIC SUCKED ON THE 405, OF COURSE, BECAUSE IT always sucked. But Quatro seemed to take it in stride. On the way out of town they'd stopped at a Ralphs and Quatro bought them bottled water, tortilla chips, and small tubs of salsa, guacamole, and sour cream. Then, from beneath his seat, he pulled three snowy white cloth napkins, which he laid over Quinn's lap, his lap, and around the stick shift between them. By the time they were even with the Getty Museum, they were crunching away and Quatro was telling Quinn about his high school in Lincoln, Nebraska. "Drama Club, that was my godsend," he was saying.

"I didn't think you acted," Quinn said, surprised.

"I *didn't* act. I was the costumer. And hair and makeup, of course. I was good, too. I mean, I was *good* good. My mom had been teaching me everything she knew from the time I was five and discovered her makeup. My dad would leave in the morning and out would come the jars and wands and lotions, and I was in heaven. *Heaven.* My mother was surprisingly accepting, for a native Nebraskan."

"That's good," Quinn said, because he couldn't think of anything better to say. And it *was* good. His own experience was that his generation was not only as homophobic as any other, but more outspoken about it, too. Gay, not gay—suddenly it was on everybody's tongue, everybody's business. He'd been a target for gay-bashing since before he could remember. He didn't know why, except that he'd been a small kid, and spindly, and of course he hadn't been able to sit still for five minutes on end so he was everybody's nuisance, teachers included. If they didn't have another name for you—and most of the kids still didn't know about ADHD then, even though it wasn't that long ago—they called you gay. One day he'd gotten a note at their house that said, *You're a queer faggot and you're ugly, too. Suck my dick.* Nelson had bawled him out, like it had been Quinn's fault that someone had sent him hate mail. ("Well, you must have done something to provoke it, bud, because that kind of trash doesn't just appear on its own.")

When he told Quatro that story, the stylist just shook his head. "You know," he said, "if everyone got great parents, there'd probably be no wars. I'm serious. We spend a lifetime getting over the damage they do when we're kids. Some of us get more than our share."

"I've never told anyone that story," Quinn said, looking out the window.

"Let me guess. You feel like you made it happen some-how."

Quinn nodded.

"It's not true, though."

Quinn just shrugged and kept looking out the window. Some people liked to talk about themselves constantly, but he wasn't one of them. You talked too much and you simply gave out ammunition for people to dislike you more. He loaded up a tortilla chip and very, very carefully brought it to his mouth, holding his hand under it the whole time to catch any drips. The car made him nervous, it was so perfect.

Quatro made him nervous, he was so perfect.

Quinn wanted to tell him about the little Latina at Los Bur-ritos, about how she smiled at him; wanted to ask him if he thought they might be able to find a chili pepper necklace in Venice Beach, since his search while he was killing time had been a bust. But he wasn't sure if Quatro would want to hear about a girl since he was gay, so instead Quinn just watched the world of Southern California go by out the window. In the cars around them, everybody was talking on their cell phones except for one man who was reading a script.

"There's this woman," he said to Quatro.

"Uh-oh."

"What? No, nothing like that—she's old." Quinn blushed furiously. "She's this casting director named Evelyn Flynn." Then he told Quatro about *After*, and how Evelyn was his new manager on top of coaching him for Buddy, and about how the movie was being directed by Gus Van Sant, who Quatro had heard of, of course, because everybody had.

"Man," he said when Quinn was finished. "That's some big fucking deal, huh?"

"Yeah."

"When's the audition?"

"I don't know yet. Pretty soon, though."

"Well, once you know, let *me* know, so you can come in and we'll tidy you up."

Quinn said thank you because he didn't want to make Quatro feel bad, but in his mind he saw Buddy as being shaggy and messy, kind of like Quinn himself; especially since no one really cared about him now that his mom had died—at least no one besides Carlyle and their grandmother and Uncle Wayne

"So how come you have a new manager? What happened to the old one?"

Quinn shrugged. "She kicked me out," he said, though strictly speaking that wasn't the reason. Strictly speaking, though, it was *part* of the reason. He might not have dumped Mimi, not even for Evelyn Flynn, if she hadn't kicked him out of her house first. Probably he would still have fired her, though. Evelyn Flynn was like Hollywood royalty. Mimi was more like one of the peasants plucking chickens in the market square.

"What, she dropped you as a client, you mean?" Quinn was saying.

"No. I mean she kicked me out of the house. I used to live with her and a couple of other kids, but she made me find someplace else. She thinks I'm a pervert."

"Why?" Quatro raised an eyebrow.

And before he even realized what he was doing, Quinn was telling Quatro the whole story. About how Dee had been teaching his class in Mimi's living room, which was what he always used to do until the thing with Quinn. Dee had had them doing an improv exercise where they were each given a slip of paper that described a character, paired up with someone by drawing names from a box, and then went off to some part of the house to work out a scene. Quinn drew a kid named Lonny. He was only twelve years old so he didn't even belong in the class, but whatever. He'd been Mimi's client for only a few months by then, and he lived at the Oakwood with his mom. He was pale and whiny and he looked like Macaulay Culkin.

Quinn's room at Mimi's—or, more accurately, his *area*—had been the landing at the top of the stairs, between two attic dormers. He had a mattress and a box spring and a blanket chest for a bureau and a lamp. And it was all right with him. No one came up there because it was hotter than hell most of the time, but not so bad when you were lying down in front of a fan. He could read up there or jerk off or pick his nose, whatever—no one ever came up to disturb him. He'd been living up there since he was thirteen. So when they were told to find a spot to work in, it was only natural to go up to Quinn's landing.

The slip of paper Quinn had drawn said, *You don't like animals or small children, you want to join the army when you grow up, you like the taste of beer, and you tend to be a bully.* Quinn never read what Lonny's paper said, but by his behavior his character was a loser, a whiner, and a brain. One of you was supposed to create a situation by defining a setting and a problem. Quinn came up with a bowling alley and a missing wallet.

So they'd begun sparring, with Quinn's character goading Lonny's character about having stolen the wallet even though Quinn's character had actually been the thief. "What's the matter, you little creep, you can't even admit you took something that wasn't yours? What are you going to do with the money, anyways, buy yourself a dress and some Tampax?"

It had been a great role, but the stupid kid had started crying, which only egged Quinn's character on, until he reached over and pinched the kid's nipples. Hard. Quinn's *character* had done that, not Quinn, but the kid had screamed and everyone had come running and Mimi had sent Quinn out into the backyard until she and fucking Dee had gotten the thing figured out. Then they brought Quinn back in, except that the kid wouldn't look at him, which pissed him off, and then Mimi had sent him out of the house again while she talked to the kid's parents. Now it had been immortalized in studio lore, and no one, not *one fucking person*, had heard him when he said, over and over, "It was *improv!*" All Mimi had said was, "The problem with you is, you just don't know when you've stepped over the line."

"Fuckin' *A*," Quatro said. "Man. You got kicked out for *pinching a kid's nipples?*"

Quinn nodded miserably. Every time he thought about it, it made him feel just as bad as it had that first day.

"And that was how long ago?" Quatro asked.

"Eight months. I don't know. Yeah—like, eight months."

"So, what, do you live with this new manager now?"

"Nope. With a couple of actors, this Pakistani and a red-head."

"Men?"

"One man, one woman."

"Huh."

"They're getting sick of me, though, so I'll probably have to move again pretty soon."

When they were on the outskirts of Venice Beach, Quatro asked Quinn to pack everything back up and put it back in the shopping bags so nothing spilled. Quinn was extra careful, wiping the sides of the tubs in case one of them had dripped. Then they were in Venice Beach, scouting for a parking spot, which they found surprisingly quickly on the street in front of an old shack of a place just a couple of blocks from the beach. Even though you'd have to knock the house down and start over, the place was still probably worth a million dollars.

Quatro snugged the car into the curb, locked everything

that could be locked, and led them to the boardwalk and the beach, saying, "You look like a man who needs his name carved on a grain of rice."

The boardwalk was concrete instead of wood, which had always been the way Quinn had pictured it. People were moving in every direction and wearing every imaginable thing: sarongs, tiny Speedos, thongs, nylon workout wear, tank tops, wife-beater shirts, flowing hippie skirts and baggy cotton pajama pants, and tourist T-shirts that said things like VENICE BEACH LIFEGUARD: MADE YOU LOOK. Every couple of steps there were sidewalk vendors selling everything from paintings to the Lord's Prayer etched on a seashell. Bongs, glass pipes, roach clips, psychedelic black lights, clothing, cheap leather goods from Mexico—you could find it all.

Quatro had abruptly dodged ahead and pulled out his wallet. A wizened little old person—could be a man, could be a woman—was working on something with a jeweler's loupe and then Quatro paid and pressed something into Quinn's hand: a glass vial with a grain of rice inside.

"Two *N*s, right?"

Quinn nodded, feeling strangely moved. He didn't get many presents except at the predictable times and from the predictable people, which was really more like the fulfillment of an obligation than the expression of a spontaneous and heartfelt sentiment. He thanked Quatro more than he probably should have—he probably came across as needy—but he couldn't help it. "Is there something you want here?" he asked Quatro, pretty sure that he should reciprocate.

"Your company. That's all."

"Oh."

"Hey, c'mon, man, I see the living statue!" Quatro put his hand on Quinn's back and walked him ahead quickly. Quinn's back burned where Quatro's hand rested. "There. Is this guy too good for words?" Through the crowd Quinn saw a man who was silver from head to foot—or, more accurately, from hat to shoes. His skin, right down to his eyelids and the palms of his hands, was also painted silver. It made Quinn feel strangely breathless, seeing someone all encased in metal that way, even if it was just paint. He'd heard you could die—suffocate—if all your skin was covered like that, because it couldn't breathe or something. Hadn't that actress in *Goldfinger* died? The human statue probably wasn't silver under his clothes, but what if his clothes couldn't breathe, either, with the silver paint all over them? He didn't look like he was suffocating, though. He was standing perfectly still, frozen in a position that looked agonizing. One leg was up and bent and he held one hand over his eyes like a visor, as though he had his foot propped up on something and was straining to look out beyond the horizon. In reality it was hazy and you couldn't even *see* the horizon, but the effect was still impressive. They watched for five minutes and the human statue didn't so much as blink. Quinn wondered how much more you'd be able to see in the course of a lifetime if you never had to blink. A single blink wasn't much, but if you strung them all together, it would probably add up to a couple of years. He decided not to ask Quatro about the suffocation business, because it would make him sound stupid. Obviously the guy wasn't keeling over or anything, so it must be okay.

"Oh, wait, come on. Man, you've just *got* to see this!" Quatro hurried ahead to a clearing in the crowd. Quinn could see five or six people lined up shoulder to shoulder, bent over with their hands on their knees. A black guy with dreadlocks stuffed under a baggy knit cap was giving his spiel to the crowd. "Okay, I'm going to need your energy, your positive thoughts, right? So think, all of you, about how I'm going to clear these people by a mile, no problem, piece of cake. Think now! *Think!*" And he took a running start and leaped, actually *leaped*, over all those people with room to spare.

The crowd clapped and the guy looked around for someone to add to the lineup. He caught Quinn's eye and said, "You! I need you to help this time. Come over here, mon, that's right." And before Quinn could protest, the guy had positioned him at one end of the line and bent him over. Then he backed way off and started energizing the crowd again and took a running jump. Quinn could feel the air rushing across his back as the man cleared him. He wondered what it would feel like to be airborne like that, powerful enough to leap great distances. It would be sort of like flying, Quinn guessed. Or would it feel like barely avoiding a fall?

The leaper added two more people after Quinn and cleared all of them, too. Then he bowed to the crowd, took off his knitted hat, and passed it around so people could drop money in. Quinn just passed it on, but Quatro put in a couple dollars, which made Quinn feel cheap. He fished in his pocket to add something after all, but Quatro put his hand on Quinn's arm and said, "That was for both of us."

As they went down the boardwalk Quinn matched Quatro stride for stride even though Quatro was smaller. It was like there was some magic field connecting them. Quatro seemed at ease in his body in a way that Quinn had never been. Maybe that would happen once he stopped growing and filled out. He felt tall and lanky and awkward, like Abraham Lincoln probably felt around all those olden-day, smaller people. Quatro had probably been a great-looking teenager, with good skin and great hair and clothes.

Quatro dug an elbow gently into Quinn's side. "You hungry?"

He was, so Quatro steered them down a side street where

there were booths filled with cheap, tooled leather goods from Mexico and a pizza concession. "Pizza, beach—they just go together," he told Quinn.

Quatro paid for both of them, and they carried their food and drinks to the far side of the boardwalk and sat on some grass under a palm tree. Three Chihuahuas went by in a pink stroller, pushed by someone vaguely familiar-looking, a young brunette who reminded him of Allison Addison and was probably one of the zillions of character actors in LA who worked just enough to feel the breath of fame pass them by.

"You having a good time?" Quatro asked him.

Quinn nodded.

"Good. I thought you might need that."

"A good time?"

"Well, someone *showing* you a good time. Not that I mean that in a cheesy way. You seem like the kind of person who spends an awful lot of time alone."

Quinn shrugged. It sounded bad, the way Quatro said it, like he was defective. "I'm okay."

"I know you're *okay*. But that's not the same as happy."

"Yeah." Quinn watched a muscle-bound young black man go by on inline skates. He moved like the skates were part of his body, so smooth and relaxed, weaving in and out of the crowd like a wave moving through water. "What about you?"

"Am I happy? By and large."

Quinn nodded as though he understood, but he didn't really know how to talk like this.

"I have great friends and I work in an excellent salon," Quatro was saying. "I'm not in love with anybody right now, so that could be better, but I'm in no hurry. I was in my last relationship for four years, and I'm still kind of tender. Calling it quits was his idea, not mine." He paused, looked at Quinn beside him in the grass. "Is this okay with you?"

"Is what okay?"

"Me talking about this."

Quinn swirled the melting ice around in his drink. "Sure."

Quatro nodded, watching a couple of bodybuilders walk by all oiled up. "I'm glad you came with me."

Quinn watched his toes squirm under the canvas of his purple Chuck Taylors.

"Hey, buddy," Quatro said, bumping Quinn's arm with his arm.

Quinn poked an ant, watched it climb up the toe of his sneaker.

"I know you're not gay," Quatro said. "That's not what this is about."

Quinn let out a long breath he must have been holding without being aware of it. He looked up and found Quatro grinning at him. "When I asked if you wanted to come down here with me, did you think it was like a date?"

"I don't know. Maybe."

"And you said yes anyway. That was brave. A lot of guys your age act like gay is contagious."

Quinn looked at the ocean. He could see a big tanker way out toward the horizon. "No, I wanted to come."

Quatro watched Quinn for a minute or two. "Be honest: are you afraid I'll put you up for adoption now that we know I know you're straight?"

Quinn tried to smile, but that was exactly what he was afraid of. Why would someone like Quatro, a successful person with lots of friends, choose to hang out with him if it wasn't for the possibility of sex?

"Gay people have straight friends, too, you know," Quatro said. "We do it all the time." .

"So that's good."

Quatro smiled broadly. "Yep. Looks like you're stuck with me."

Quinn wiped some sweat off his upper lip with his sleeve. It wasn't that hot, but he was dripping. He hoped they were done talking. When you brought things out into the light, sometimes they just faded away and you were left with nothing. He didn't want to risk that. So instead, he said, "Do you think there's like a jewelry store here?"

"Jewelry?"

"There's this present I want to find for someone. A necklace that's a chili pepper."

"You mean like a charm?"

"Yeah, like that."

"We can sure look."

They stuffed their trash in a bin and headed back along the boardwalk. A pod of teenage girls rode by on beach-cruiser bicycles, and right after they passed Quinn they all laughed. Reflexively Quinn assumed they were laughing at him, even though he knew that was unlikely. Mimi had told him once, after he'd overreacted to teasing at the studio, "You've got to stop assuming that everything's about you. It isn't. Most of the time no one's thinking about you at all." Later, thinking about it, Quinn hadn't been sure which was worse.

A good ten minutes' walk farther down the boardwalk (food stand, tattoo parlor, bad art, bad art, leather, glass bongs, tie-dye, henna tattoos, elephant ears, falafel, sweatshirts, T-shirts, and hats), they found a table with a bunch of jewelry laid out. Quatro started at one end of the table, and Quinn at the other. At almost the exact same moment they both spotted a pretty little silver and enamel chili pepper, bright red or green, take your pick. Quinn tried to remember her earrings. Red? He was pretty sure they were red. The charm cost eighteen bucks, which was more than he had on him. He pretended it wasn't quite what he was looking for, but Quatro just said, "Put down what you've got, and I'll make up the rest. You can owe me," and Quinn accepted the offer. The vendor, a beat-to-shit-looking woman with the hair of an eighteen-year-old and a fifty-year-old face, wrapped the charm in a piece of well-worn tissue paper and handed it to Quinn.

"Meth," said Quatro once they were away from the table.

"What?"

"Meth. She's a meth user. She's probably younger than I am."

Quinn didn't know much about meth, except that it scared the crap out of him, and he said so.

"Good," said Quatro. "Keep it that way. Weed's okay, 'shrooms are even okay, Ecstasy's definitely okay, but that's where you've got to draw the line. You already know that, though, right?"

"Yeah." He'd tried Ecstasy at the apartment a couple of times with Jasper and Baby-Sue and a bunch of their friends. He'd liked it a lot. It had calmed him down. He didn't really have the budget for drugs, though. He'd rather spend his money on acting classes or coaching. Or a chili pepper charm for the little Latina at Los Burritos.

He liked the fact that Quatro was counseling him about what to do and not do. He didn't get that very much. In Seattle they didn't know enough about him to say anything, and down here no one cared. That wasn't exactly true: Mimi used to care. Now Evelyn did. But they cared only in a way that was mutually, professionally beneficial, so their telling him what to do was as much for their own sakes as it was for Quinn's—sometimes more. Quatro had no ulterior motive. Quinn wished he'd tell him some other stuff that would be good for him, but Quatro only paused for a minute and asked Quinn if he'd mind walking back to the car along the beach.

"Sure. I mean, no. No, I don't mind."

They walked carefully between two beach volleyball courts. One court had a coed game going on, and the other had an all-guys game. Quinn watched the girls and Quatro watched the guys. The guys were all wearing long, baggy shorts, but the girls were wearing bikinis, which Quinn thought was impractical. If he were a girl he'd be worrying all the time about his boobs popping out or something. You reach up, nail a shot, spill a boob, and the whole thing's ruined. Then again, these were pretty athletic women and they looked like their boobs were pure muscle, so they probably *couldn't* spill; plus their tops covered a pretty big area and were tight, so maybe it never happened.

"They're good," Quatro said.

"Yeah. I don't have that kind of coordination," said Quinn. "I could never even play soccer, and frickin' *everyone* in Seattle plays soccer."

WHEN THEY REACHED THE WATERLINE THEY TOOK OFF their shoes and started wading back. Quinn found himself telling Quatro all about his Seattle life, before Mimi, even before acting, right up until his moving to LA—stuff he'd never told anyone.

"So you're saying they gave you away?" Quatro said. "To your *talent manager?*"

"Kind of like that. I mean, it's okay, because it's not like I had a bunch of friends back there, plus I wanted to be an actor. I *am* an actor. And I couldn't be, back there. I mean, the only things going on in Seattle are musical theater, nonunion, or rinky-dink. The only good thing back there is my kid brother. He's pretty great."

"Still," said Quatro, shaking his head.

"Yeah," said Quinn. Then they were back where they'd started, two blocks from the car. Quinn was reluctant to leave the water, so he stopped and just stood there, looking out at the horizon. What if your vision traveled like light, so by looking out toward Japan now, you would actually *see* Japan in a few minutes, transmitted back to you? It was too bad it didn't work that way. He thought about explaining his theory to Quatro, but it was too complicated, plus that sort of thing was why people thought he was weird. So instead he looked down at the water rushing away beneath his feet, and although he knew he was standing still, it looked like he was hurtling backward at impossible speeds. He staggered a little. Quatro steadied him with a hand beneath his elbow. "I've got you," he said, and then it was time to go home. And all the way back he could feel Quatro's steadying hand under his arm, and the little red chili pepper beating in his pocket like a heart.

Chapter Eighteen

MIMI DELETED QUINN'S PHONE MESSAGE: HE WAS JUST ONE more client who'd cut and run, another betrayal in a never-ending succession. It was a sad truth that the good clients left her much sooner than the bad ones, who seemed to stay on forever, dragging on Mimi's time and energy. Quinn was one of the most promising actors she'd had in years, maybe ever. He was difficult, granted, but most of the good ones were. And they were worth the hardship. Just one client could easily pull down twenty-five or thirty thousand a week as a TV series regular, which, at her 15 percent commission, would bring her forty-five hundred dollars a week, or ninety-nine thousand for a standard twenty-two-episode season. And this was *entry level*. An actor could easily bring home two or three times that much, and substantially more if the show stayed on the air for four or five years. And if that actor was the star of the program, Mimi would be looking at retirement; and even in retirement she'd continue to collect her commission. She'd been waiting for this kind of score for her entire professional life, and if Quinn and not Allison had been the One—and it was certainly possible—the whole thing, the vicarious fame, the money, the mention at the Emmys or the Oscars, was lost.

She didn't deserve that.

She never should have let him live with her to begin with. She'd known how volatile he was, and how few social skills he possessed. Not that he was dangerous, because he wasn't. He was just extraordinarily immature. Sixteen going on fourteen,

or younger. He'd gotten carried away and acted inappropriately, and even though the episode was over as quickly as it had
started, she couldn't let him stay until he reconciled his issues.
Her standards might be lax in some ways, but not when it came
to sexual misconduct. If her other parents caught wind of what
he'd done, there could be charges brought against her, and she
couldn't afford that and neither could Quinn, not at his age. So
she'd banished him as much for his own good as for hers, and
now he was dumping her for Evelyn Flynn, who, God knows,
didn't need either the money or the recognition.

And that was a bitter, bitter pill.

But Mimi wasn't a woman to dwell on things she couldn't
change, so she gave herself five minutes to wallow and then
picked herself up and reminded herself that she still had Laurel
Buehl, who was on fire, commercially speaking. That might
very well be where she stayed, though Angie had had a small
hissy fit the day before, during which she demanded that Mimi
get Laurel more theatrical auditions or they'd walk. Angie
didn't want to hear that some people never made the jump from
commercial to theatrical; there were lots of reasons why, but the
upshot was, they made commercials and then they were done.
Done, but with a lot of money in their pockets. Laurel could
act, Mimi wasn't denying that—her *Marbles* monologue, for instance, was raw and uncontrolled, but hinted at a talent much
deeper than even Mimi would have guessed. For the most part,
though—at least for now—Laurel's looks were stronger than
her acting chops. There was also the problem of her Georgia
accent, which was so heavy that she sounded like a cracker half
the time. Angie needed to get her to a dialect coach, but Angie
didn't think her accent was strong enough to warrant one and
there was only so much Mimi could take on.

And then, of course, there was Allison, who, Mimi worried,

was already heading into the Bermuda Triangle of the midteen years. She hadn't booked anything in months now, wasn't even getting many callbacks, and she was looking older every day. It would be another two years before the child could procure her legal-eighteen status, and anyway she was such a poor student that she'd probably flunk the proficiency exam even when she was finally eligible at sixteen. As an alternative, there was a school in Hollywood—and Mimi used the term *school* loosely—that would, for six hundred dollars, administer exams in all the major scholastic areas and award the student who passed them a high school diploma that same day. If the student failed any of the exams—and they always did—the school would coach her until she passed. One way or another, every student who had the money was guaranteed a same-day diploma even if it meant being coached well into the night. It was a scam, of course, but so far the California State Board of Education hadn't challenged the validity of the diplomas. The fact that some of the children were nearly illiterate didn't seem to trouble anyone, especially Hollywood's producers. Mimi had recommended the school to Quinn's parents, who'd sent him over; he'd procured the diploma and from that day on had been booking something almost every month.

The immediate challenge for Mimi was going to be keeping Allison motivated and moving forward. Allison knew what was what; Mimi had had a long talk with her recently about what she would likely find in the next few years, professionally speaking. As a hedge, Mimi had enrolled the girl in several intensive voice-over workshops, because Allison had excellent diction and vocal expression. These jobs could also be very lucrative, and of course it didn't matter if you were two or a hundred and two, as long as your voice sounded like a four-year-old's or whatever other age you were auditioning for. Allison was a poor reader but a quick memorizer, so as long as she could get the sides ahead of time and work with Mimi, she'd be eminently em-ployable, which was as important emotionally as professionally. Mimi had noticed a growing tendency for Allison, like Quinn, to act out. Though her triggers were different, she was as hun-gry for attention as he was. And that, as Mimi well knew, could lead to trouble.

"Do you believe in immaculate love?" Ruth asked Vee Velman. They were sitting in a booth at Paty's, and Clara and Bethany were sitting at one just behind them.

"You mean like Joseph and Mary?" Vee said. "I didn't think you people bought into that."

"That was immaculate sex. I mean immaculate love—per-fect love. The kind where the man is handsome and sensitive and loves you without wavering from when you're young and beautiful and nothing sags, right up until he can see your scalp through your hair and you're squashy."

"Isn't that why people get dogs?"

"What?"

"I'm serious," Vee said. "Are you okay?"

"It's hard being back. I talked to Hugh while Bethy was at an audition, and he was really struggling. He makes it sound like we've abandoned him."

"That's because he's a Hollywood widow."

"What's a Hollywood widow?"

"It's like a soccer dad. You know, the guy who comes home from work and Mom and the kids are always someplace else, like at soccer practice or an away game, and he has to fend for himself."

"I'm only doing what's good for Bethy. Isn't that what I'm supposed to do? Isn't that part of being a parent?"

"It is what it is," Vee said philosophically. "For every acting kid there's a mom, and for every acting kid's mom there's a Hollywood widow waiting for dinner. And the saddest ones are the ones waiting in another state."

"Widower," Ruth said.

"What?"

"A Hollywood wido*wer.*"

"Widow, widower—you know what I mean."

Ruth knew what she meant. "So does that mean we're wrong to bring our children here?"

"Depends on why you're doing it. Most people do it because they want their kid on the cover of *People.* If they tell you they don't, they're lying."

"Do you think that's what's going to happen to Clara or Buster?"

"No, because ultimately neither of them gives a shit."

"Hugh thinks I'm delusional."

"Could be," Vee allowed. "But that doesn't make it wrong. If they're going to stand a chance, we have to have *absolute faith* that these kids can be stars. And they have to believe it, too."

"But they're *not* going to be stars—at least they're probably not. Hugh keeps telling me that over and over, and of course he's right."

"Honey, the day you start thinking that way, you might as well go home."

Ruth's cell phone rang, and it was Mimi. Ruth dug out a pen and started writing. By the time she finished the call, her hands were shaking. She breathed in deeply, closed her eyes, and took a fortifying gulp of her strawberry shake. "Well."

Vee raised her eyebrows.

"I have no idea what this might mean," Ruth said, trying to

be calm, "but Evelyn Flynn has asked to see Bethy tomorrow afternoon. It's for a pilot. She'll be going straight to producers."

"Which pilot?"

Ruth consulted her napkin. "It's called *Bradford Place*. Something about babysitters. We've never even seen a breakdown for it. Does that sound at all familiar to you?"

"Nope," said Vee, frowning. She called over her shoulder, "Clara! Have you heard about a pilot that has to do with babysitters?"

"Nope," said Clara.

"Me neither," said Bethany.

"Well, you're going straight to producers for it," Ruth said. "That was Mimi. I guess they changed the breakdown from a boy to a girl at the last minute, so they're scrambling. They want to see you." Ruth's heart was pounding so hard that her ears were roaring. This could be how Bethy's career would begin. "She said you have to get coached for it *now*. Greta's booked, so she's already set you up to work with Donovan."

"Donovan Meyer?" Vee said.

Ruth nodded. "She's taking a class with him. The kids seem to like him."

"You know he's a terrible actor, right?" Vee said.

Ruth turned her palms up: *What are you going to do?*

"Dee's cool," Bethy called across the booths.

"I heard he was a jerk," Clara said through a mouthful of cheeseburger, "but the kid who told me was pretty much of a jerk, too, so, you know." She sucked up the last of her shake.

"Whoa," said Ruth to Vee, eyes wide. "*Whoa!*"

"Don't get ahead of it," Vee said, pinching up a half dozen fries. "This happens all the time and it doesn't usually mean a thing." She frowned thoughtfully. "Evelyn Flynn, though. She doesn't waste time, so she must have her reasons."

"Could it be something big?"

"Sure."

"Bethy," Ruth called to the other booth. "Finish up, honey, because we've got to get going. Donovan's going to meet you at the studio in an hour, and we have to go by the apartment first and download the sides."

"But I just got my burger!"

"I know," Ruth said. "So eat fast. We have Pepto-Bismol in the car."

"IT ONLY HAS, LIKE, SIX LINES," BETHANY SAID ON THE way to the studio, flipping quickly through pages that were still warm from their new printer at the apartment. "Do you think there might be more and they didn't give it to us?"

"I don't know, honey." Ruth tried to concentrate on driving. She'd nearly hit a man crossing the street just outside their parking lot. She really had to pull herself together. "Read the breakdown again."

Bethany flipped through the pages, extracted one, and read, "'*ASHLEIGH, 13: A sweet, motherly girl who lives next door to the Abernethys. Although her parents are rich and well-connected, she babysits for pocket money and wants to be a preschool teacher one day.*' That's it."

"Is that enough to go on?"

"Sure, Mom. You don't need them to spell everything out. You make up the character yourself."

"Well, I'd be lost," Ruth said admiringly, "but that's why you're the actor and I'm not."

Ruth turned into the studio parking lot. Bethany jumped out with her Mimi Roberts Talent Management tote full of sides and headshots and God knew what other detritus. Ruth had been trying to get her to clean it out for days. She reminded

herself that the chaos of a busy life was better than the tidiness
of an empty one. For that matter, if housekeeping wasn't taking
care of their crappy apartment once a week, God only knew
what kind of wildlife it would support.

"Are you coming in?" Bethany called back to her through
the open door.

"Probably, but I'm going to stay out here for a few minutes,
maybe take a little walk. You go on ahead."

"Okay. Wish me luck!"

Ruth smiled. "Luck."

And Bethy was gone, a girl at one with her dream. Ruth
rolled down all the windows and dug her cell phone out of her
purse.

"You'll never guess," she said when Hugh got on the line.

"You're coming home?"

Ruth tightened her jaw, felt the slightest twinge in a cracked
back molar Hugh had been saying would give way one day. She
unclenched her teeth. "Bethy's going to producers for a pilot.
And honey, she didn't even have to read for it! I mean, she will
now, but she didn't have to go through the first read at all. And
the woman who called her in is *the* number-one casting director
in Hollywood." Ruth was pretty sure that Mimi had said this; if
she hadn't specifically said number one, she'd certainly implied
it. "Isn't that amazing?"

"I don't know. Is it amazing?"

"It's amazing," Ruth said. "Trust me."

"Well, that's wonderful, then. What's the part?"

"She's a neighbor kid who babysits. They say this never happens to kids who've never even really worked before. Well,
I mean, she's worked, of course, but she hasn't really *worked*
worked. Extensively. I wish you could see her, honey. She's over
the moon."

"You're not letting her hopes get too high, are you?"

"No, I think she's realistic," Ruth said, but she felt a little seizure in her gut. *Was* she letting Bethy's hopes get too high, not to mention her own? She changed the subject. "Anyway, how are you?"

"Good. Busy. Lonely. You know."

"I know," Ruth said. "I do know."

"Well," said Hugh. The line went silent for a minute. "You don't sound like yourself, Ruthie."

"No?"

"No. You're breathing a lot."

"What do you mean?"

"I don't know. You're just, you know, *breathing*. Breathless."

"So I shouldn't breathe now?"

Hugh sighed heavily. "Never mind. I know you're excited."

"Because this could launch her career, Hugh. Of course I'm excited."

"Here's something I've been thinking about: if a kid gets famous, she had the most wonderful, most supportive, most self-sacrificing parents in the world, but if the kid dies on the vine, you're looking at a schmuck who thought his kid was better than everyone else's, and the kid grows up having been a failure. And you have no idea which outcome will be the right one."

"She *is* better than anyone else," Ruth whispered. "Well, than almost anyone. I know it, Hugh. And it's not just wishful thinking. Why can't you see that?"

Ruth heard him turn away from the receiver and say, "Okay, I'll be right there." Then he came back to her and said, "Margaret says they're ready. So, okay, tell Bethy to break a leg or whatever—break a bank. Tell her to call me tonight."

"All right, honey, I will."

"Okay."

"I love you," she said, but he'd already hung up. If she sat in the car alone she'd start thinking, and absolutely nothing good could come of that, so she locked the car and went inside.

In the studio classroom Donovan was sitting in a chair collating the pages that Bethy had just photocopied for him. "So go ahead, talk to me," he said to her. He was always telling his students to talk to him.

"Well, her name is Ashleigh and she's my age and she's a nice person who likes little kids and stuff. She probably has a couple of dogs, not those little purse-dogs, but a couple of schnauzers, maybe. A male and a female. Willy and Maude. And she's the one who walks them when the staff is gone for the day." She paused, looking at Donovan, who looked back at her with his fingertips together in a steeple. "Do I like having staff? It seems like that would be so weird."

"I don't know. Do you?"

Bethy frowned thoughtfully. "Well, having them around makes me feel sorry for them in some ways, because I don't think they're paid very much and their own children are alone every day in a crummy part of LA where no one can afford a nice house like mine and good clothes and stuff. But, hey, I know! I give them *my* clothes when I outgrow them or get tired of them. And maybe I even make my mom buy me stuff I don't need, just so I can give it away. Is that okay?"

"You own this character," Donovan said. "You say what's okay. So keep going. Why do you like your neighbors? They have an awful lot of kids."

"Yes, because they've adopted poor children who had nothing to eat."

"Is that why?"

"What do you mean?" Bethany said.

"Well, did the, ah"—he searched his script for a minute—"Abernethys adopt them because the children needed them to, or did they adopt them because they have great big egos and more money than God and they know it'll make people think they're wonderful?"

Bethany frowned, considering this. "No, they adopted them because they needed it. *And* people think they're wonderful. Aren't I supposed to like them?"

"You tell me. You like their kids."

"I think I like them, too, because I'm a good person."

"So, okay," Donovan said. "Let's run it. Are you off-book?"

Bethy had a photographic memory, so memorizing her lines was never any problem for her. "Well, I have only like six lines. I mean, I'll be off-book once we run it a couple of times, but we just downloaded it right before we came over."

"Go," said Donovan.

                    ASHLEIGH
Hi, Mr. Abernethy!
                JUSTIN ABERNETHY
Hey, wow, are we ever glad you could come
over! Listen, Cecilia's sciatica's bothering
her again. I mean, when will these kids be
born, right? So I'm going to take her out to
lunch. Can you watch the kids?
                    ASHLEIGH
Sure, no problem. You know I love to play
with them. Maybe we can do finger paints.
                    JUSTIN
Just ask Consuelo to help you set things up.
She put the paints somewhere, probably in the
nursery. And don't let the baby eat anything.

> ASHLEIGH
>
> That Bruce. Isn't he just the cutest thing? I
> bet his real mom was a beautiful woman, like
> Pocahontas.
>
> JUSTIN
>
> Now, we don't talk about real moms here, because
> that would make Cecilia a fake mom, right?
>
> ASHLEIGH
>
> Oh! I'm so sorry. I just meant—
>
> JUSTIN
>
> That's okay. We just need you to be sensitive
> to that, because the kids love you and they
> trust you. And so do we.

Donovan lowered his script. "Jesus Christ."

Bethy looked up, crestfallen.

Donovan said, "Look, it's okay—it's not your fault that the writer's an incompetent moron. Let's take it again, and this time I want you to be really in the moment, because that time your acting was showing."

"But if the writing's bad—"

"Oh, it's bad," Donovan said, "believe me. But that's no excuse for *you* to be. You should be able to move people by reading a Tide commercial, right?"

He said that at every single class. "Right." Bethy shook the tension out of her head and shoulders the way he'd taught them to, tapped her pages back into order, and took it again from the top. "*Hi, Mr. Abernethy!*"

"Hey," Donovan intoned. "Wow."

WHILE SHE WAITED IN THE STUDIO GREENROOM, RUTH stared sightlessly at the unread pages of *Seabiscuit*. She figured she was averaging a reading speed of about a sentence every ten minutes. Could she be developing late-life attention deficit disorder? *Was* there even such a thing?

Mimi came into the greenroom and put a sticky note on Laurel Buehl's headshot. The note said, *McDonald's!*

"That's wonderful," Ruth said; and, because it was a commercial, she meant it. She had more trouble feigning delight when another child booked a theatrical part. That, as far as Ruth was concerned, was Bethany's province. Ugly but true.

"It's the second national commercial she's booked this week," Mimi said. "Yesterday was Target. And she's got callbacks on one more. The girl's amazing." She listened for a minute to Bethany and Donovan. "You realize this is a long shot," she said to Ruth.

"I know," Ruth said, and then, miffed, "You know, you're very negative."

Mimi sighed. "Because new parents have false hopes, and then when things don't work out, they blame me for it."

"I don't think our hopes are false," Ruth said. "I think we're very realistic about how talented Bethy—"

Angie and Laurel Buehl walked into the suite. Mimi used them for cover and slipped away. Ruth sighed and then said brightly, "Hey, you two! Congratulations! I just heard the good news."

"About McDonald's?" Angie said. "I know, isn't it wonderful? We haven't even had a chance to tell Dillard yet. And it's national."

Laurel sat down in the chair farthest away from Ruth, pulled a copy of *Vogue* out of her Mimi Roberts tote bag, tucked her feet up beneath her, and opened her magazine. For all her successes, she seemed subdued. Ruth thought there was an air of premature aging about her, which was odd, because Ruth thought of pageanteers—was there such a word?—as bubbly and extroverted. Was that too simplistic? Though Laurel and Angie were unfailingly friendly, they'd stopped short of forming friendships. And for the most part, the studio community left them alone. Even Bethy and Allison respected the barriers the Buehls seemed to have built around themselves. Bethy had explained it to Ruth this way: "They seem like they don't want to be disturbed or something. Like friends would just be getting in the way."

But if Laurel hit the big time all that would change in a heartbeat, Ruth knew. If Laurel became a star, they'd have so many friends they'd have to fight them off with a stick.

On any given afternoon if you were dropped onto Sunset Boulevard from far away—outer space, say, or North Dakota—you might expect to find a floral essence in the air, because it's warm enough and sunny enough and there's a breeze and palm trees and the occasional bougainvillea; but you'd be wrong. All you can smell is car exhaust and dirt and fast food.

There's a famous diner in North Hollywood that's been there forever, but it doesn't look authentic, just ordinary and tired, like an old waitress counting her tips out back by the Dumpster. The walls are scaly with tier after tier of framed headshots, mainly of women who look like gun molls or Bette Davis. "To Bugsy from BooBoo, XOXO." "To my one and only—I love ya, doll." Cornball stuff that looks fake, even though it isn't.

They say that America has movie stars because it doesn't have royalty. But there are no stars anymore, not like the old days when it didn't matter how many highballs you drank as long as you were beautiful. Now we pick them up and discard them as casually as garbage; we clamor to know every little thing and then, once we do, we blame them for it. We wouldn't miss them on Oscar night, but as we watch them—and it's like shooting fish in a barrel out there on the red carpet—what we're thinking is, they're older or uglier or fatter or shorter than we'd thought they'd be, not godlike at all; and we abandon them, because there's always, always, someone better.

—VEE VELMAN

Chapter Nineteen

IN THE SPACE OF ONE WEEK, THE PACE OF THEATRICAL auditions accelerated wildly. Some of the Mimi Roberts studio kids—though not Bethany—were going out every day. Pilot season had arrived.

"I don't see why everyone comes from all over the country for this," Ruth said petulantly to Vee on her cell phone one afternoon. She was walking briskly around and around Greta Groban's shabby block while Bethy was being coached. She'd resolved to lose fifteen pounds by Easter, like *that* was going to happen. But still. "Yesterday I saw two cars from Rhode Island. Two. In the same hour. There are only, what, fifteen hundred cars in the whole state, and two of them were here." She could feel little beads of sweat crawling through her hair. Once more around and she was done, or she'd have to find deodorant and a shower. And she and Bethy had an audition and an acting class to get through after this. "I know some of the kids are going nuts, but Bethy's had only two auditions since we got back, and one was the one for *Bradford Place*. Straight to producers and then nothing—we haven't heard a single word, so she obviously didn't book it. I keep asking Mimi to get feedback from the casting director, but of course she hasn't done it, and I don't know how many more times I can nag her about it."

"We heard they canceled it."

"Canceled what?"

"*Bradford Place*. Clara heard it was scrapped. Whoever played the female lead got a better offer so she backed out, and then one of the producers backed out, and the network just said screw it."

"You're kidding," said Ruth.

"Happens all the time, babe," Vee said cheerfully.

"So do you think the whole pilot season thing is just a collective delusion?"

Vee snorted into the phone. "For kids without credits, of course it is. No one is going to cast a kid with no experience as a potential series regular in a pilot for huge bucks. But the kids with credits have a chance. It's not like they're likely to *book* anything, but they have that glimmer of hope—at least the parents do—so they show up just like lemmings running to the cliffs or the sea or whatever that expression is."

"Yeah," Ruth sighed. "Has Clara been going out much?"

"Are you kidding? I keep telling you, honey—Clara's a redhead. She's even more of a niche actor than Bethany is. The last thing she went out for wasn't even a pilot, it was a feature film. She was the weird kid in a middle school class. She booked it, worked for three days, and then *hasta luego*."

"But doesn't she mind that? Don't you?"

"Why?"

"I don't know. Isn't it like getting a sip of water when you're dying of thirst?"

"Well, sure. That's what makes Hollywood go round. You always want more. More, more, more."

"Well, it seems cruel."

Even over the phone, Ruth could hear Vee shrug. "It is what it is."

"I hate that saying," said Ruth peevishly. "You know what other one I hate? 'Just sit down and shut up.' "

"It does seem apt, though," Vee agreed. "You know what your problem is? You want to be in control. No one's in control down here—*no one*. You'd be much better off if you'd give up and stop fighting it."

"I know," Ruth moaned. "But I *can't*."

"Why don't you go see a psychic? Maybe it would help if you knew the future."

"A psychic."

"You can scoff, but I have a great one."

"You've been to see a psychic?" Ruth said.

"Babe, this is LA. Everybody has. There are more psychics in LA than any other city in the world."

"There are?"

"I don't know—I made that up. It's possible, though. Do you have a pen?"

"I will when I get to the car. Talk to me about something else, and I'll tell you when I get there."

"How's Hugh?"

"He says he feels like a pincushion, pricking his fingers all the time. I think he's resigning himself to the whole thing, though. My mother-in-law has read every diabetes pamphlet and magazine article there is. She sends me these diabetes-friendly recipes—like I'm there to cook, which of course is her point. She keeps hinting that if we get divorced it's okay with her. I don't know how people do this. I mean, I'm not there, but I'm not really *here*, either. No matter where I am, I feel like I'm supposed to be in the other place. Am I whining?"

"Sure. But people who live in two places live in neither. I got that in a fortune cookie one time."

"You did not."

"I could have."

"God, finally!" Ruth had arrived at the car. She unlocked and opened the two curbside doors for some ventilation, then fished a pen and an old MapQuest printout out of the glove compartment. When she'd parked she'd been in the shade, but the sun had moved. She thought about sitting down on the grass strip between the curb and the sidewalk because it looked cooler, and then she remembered all the dogs that lived in the neighborhood and peed there, and changed her mind, sitting on the burning passenger seat with her legs out. "Okay, I've got a pen."

"Her name is Elva." Vee rattled off a phone number.

"Elva? You're sure this isn't a joke?"

"No, I'm dead serious. Now tell me you're going to call her."

"I'm going to call her," Ruth said; and it was possible that she would, that's how conflicted she felt about everything—Hugh, Hollywood, the wisdom of being here in the first place, of doing any of the crazy things they'd been doing. And that wasn't even including the whole school charade. Ruth had found Bethy a math tutor for seventy-five dollars an hour and sent her to him twice a week with limited success, which was to say the child would graduate from high school mathematically illiterate if she continued the way she was going. Ruth unstuck one leg from the car seat ruminatively, and then the other one. "Do you really think this is good for our kids?"

"Psychics?"

"Acting," said Ruth, and then, "No, not acting. Rejection."

"Sure. If they have the right expectations, it toughens 'em. You could hit Clara with a baseball bat and she wouldn't even flinch. Figuratively speaking."

"And that's good?"

"Sure. She's going to make her own way in the world, fuck what everyone else thinks."

"But did she ever really want the fame, the recognition, the whole star thing?"

"Maybe not as much as you and Bethy, but remember, she was raised on this stuff. She didn't just drop into it after years of actor worship. We always knew it was a crock of shit. It's more lethal when you don't find out until you're older."

"You make it sound like chicken pox."

"Don't you get shingles if you're older when you get it? I remember a neighbor of ours once had shingles. It's supposed to be very painful. I don't even know what that means, though. I always picture these scaly patches, but isn't that actually psoriasis?"

"I have no idea," said Ruth.

"Yeah, well," Vee said. "It took your mind off rejection for a minute, though, didn't it?"

Then Ruth's call-waiting went off and it was time to go.

"Remember," Vee called down the line in closing. "They're stronger than we are by a mile!"

MIMI HAD AGREED TO ANGIE BUEHL'S ULTIMATUM TO push harder theatrically because otherwise she'd lose Laurel as a client and Laurel was worth a ton of money. And she had tried, she really had, she just hadn't had much luck. Nevertheless, Angie was standing in Mimi's cluttered office with her hands on her hips, saying, "You need to get Laurel in on *After*." Laurel hovered anxiously just behind Angie's right shoulder. "Everyone else is auditioning, so why isn't she?"

Mimi sighed. She had already, and at almost the last possible second, gotten the girl an audition for the re-released babysitter part in *Bradford Place*. Not that there'd been any chance of her booking it, even if it hadn't been canceled. A reliable, precancellation rumor had had it that the part had belonged to another girl, a Hollywood insider, all along; the casting director had just been window-shopping so that the producer would feel he was earning his exorbitantly high fee. It happened all the time.

Mimi turned from her computer with a lecture on her

tongue about the wisdom of choosing your battles. Then she took a closer look at Angie. The woman, normally so bright and well turned out, looked like hell. It had been several weeks since Mimi had seen her. Had something happened? It had to have, for her to look like that. So Mimi toned down what she'd been about to say, but the bottom line was still the same: there was no way that Laurel would be considered for the part of Carlyle.

"For one thing, the breakdown's for thirteen, and there is no way that Laurel can play thirteen. Right now I doubt she can even play fifteen." You could almost watch the child's breasts grow. Dillard's family must have a large helping of boobs in his genetic pie, because Angie was as flat as a board. And, Mimi couldn't help noticing, incredibly, even alarmingly, thin. Something was going on there. It wasn't unheard of here for a woman in her late thirties or early forties to develop an eating disorder.

"The character could be older," Angie was saying. "There's nothing about her that's specifically thirteen. I think it has a wider age range. She could just as easily be older than Buddy instead of younger, and it wouldn't make any difference."

"Except to the director," Mimi said drily.

"Try," said Angie.

"Please?" said Laurel.

Mimi sighed. She could either make the phone call and piss off Joel E. Sherman—who, let's face it, wasn't one of Mimi's fans to begin with—or she could lie, not make the call, and risk having Angie call Joel herself, which would not only call Mimi's bluff but also be certain death for Laurel forever. Angie Buehl was exactly the kind of mother who crashed auditions in the honest but fatal belief that if the casting director caught even one glimpse of her child, he would book her on the spot.

"Look," Mimi said. "There's another part, for a sixteen-year-old neighbor who has a crush on Buddy. I can get her in on that. They haven't even started casting it yet."

"It's not the lead, though," Angie pointed out.

"Which is why she's got at least a shot at it. I know you don't want to believe me, but no director anywhere ever is going to cast a kid who has never done anything but commercials as the lead in a feature film."

"But she has years of pageant experience," Angie cried. "I don't know why you never count that."

"And if they were looking for someone to wear a swimsuit, she'd be in like Flynn," Mimi said. "*After* is set in Portland, Oregon, in the dead of winter."

Laurel pulled on Angie's arm. Angie gently shook her off. "Just wait a minute!" Then, to Mimi, "Get her in. If they won't see her for Carlyle, then get her in for the other girl. I know there's a place for her in this movie. I think you should be able to see that, too."

OUTSIDE, IN THE STUDIO PARKING LOT, ANGIE SAID TO Laurel, "Because you're good enough, that's why."

"But if Mimi doesn't think I can—"

"Mimi isn't God, honey. And we don't have time for negativity. I'm not saying you'll book the part, I'm just saying let's get you in there so they can at least *see* you. If you don't audition for this man, he'll never be able to consider you for other roles. I'm right about this, honey."

"Maybe," said Laurel. "All right."

ALLISON THOUGHT THE EARLY EVENING WAS THE MOST depressing time of day. Mimi wasn't home yet and Hillary and Reba were cranky and hopped up on junk food and energy drinks. When Quinn still lived with them, they'd played Game

Boy together or fooled around with Tina Marie. Now Allison devoted the time to personal grooming. Her dark leg hair was fast-growing and inclined to be stubbly—she'd been shaving her legs since she was twelve—so she'd picked up a bottle of Nair hair depilatory the last time Mimi had taken her to a drugstore, and now seemed like a good time to try it. When her phone rang she was in the bathroom, standing on one leg with the other propped up on the vanity, her left leg and most of her right one slathered in stinky cream. She answered without looking to see who was calling.

On the other end of the line she heard a long, thin wail and knew immediately it was her mother, Denise. "Honey, Chet's dumping me."

Allison narrowed her eyes warily. "What do you mean?"

Denise snuffled. "He's kicking me out of the house. He said this weekend he's bringing Eddie and Virgil and Julio over and they're going to load up my stuff and take it to some apartment the bastard's rented for me."

"Good," said Allison, lowering her finished right leg and holding the phone with her chin and shoulder so she could put the cap on the bottle. "He's a douche. Make sure he's paid like a year's rent in advance." Allison could hear ice cubes clinking in a glass. From the slightly off-kilter sound of her, Denise had probably been drinking since noon. "Manhattan?"

"Just a little one, honey. You can understand that."

And Allison could, because whenever Denise's men dumped her—and a lot of them had dumped her—Denise mixed up a pitcher of Manhattans along with the morning coffee. "Well, I say good riddance. He's a fucking *douche*." Allison wiped her hands on a length of toilet paper and sat down on about one inch of the closed toilet so she wouldn't mess up the Nair.

"How can you say that to me? He's my husband!"

"Yeah, for like fifteen months or something. I mean, I was surprised he even married you. You lived with him for, what, a couple of years? It wasn't like you weren't going to have sex with him or something unless he married you."

"I don't know how you can be so hateful," Denise said. "He's everything to me."

Allison squinted, looked into the middle distance. "Who sings that?"

"What?"

"Isn't that a song? 'You're Everything to Me'? Do you think somebody sang it on *Idol*?"

"I cannot *believe* you're so hard-hearted," Denise snapped. "You're no help."

"You don't *need* help. You get people to dump you all by yourself," Allison pointed out. "Plus I'm like a thousand miles away."

"Yeah, and about that," Denise said.

"About what?"

"Being a thousand miles away. You need to come home. A mother needs her daughter at a time like this."

Allison snapped to. "What?"

"I need you at home."

"I can't hear you." Allison flapped her fingers between her lips and the phone as she talked, to make the transmission sound weird. "I think this connection is breaking up."

"Other girls would fly to their mothers' sides," Denise huffed.

"Get Shelley. You guys can drink and stuff and then you'll feel better."

"She's out of town. She has this fabulous new boyfriend. *Her* daughter would come, I'll tell you that."

"Then ask her. I've got to go."

"Why? Go where?"

"To class," Allison lied.

"Well, we'll talk about this later."

But they wouldn't, not if Allison could help it. The minute she hung up, she programmed her cell phone with a special ring tone for Denise. That way, she'd know not to answer it. Then she recorded a message that said her voice mail wasn't working and the caller would just have to call back later, so her mom couldn't leave a message and then accuse her of not returning the call. The strategy would keep Denise at bay until Allison could figure out what to do. The one thing she was certain of was that she wouldn't go back to live in Houston. Allison and Mimi might shout and scream at each other and have their fallings-out, but Allison loved Mimi deeply and genuinely, and she was pretty sure that Mimi loved her back. Nevertheless, she was also pretty sure that Mimi would deport her to Houston anyway, if that's what Denise told her to do. Denise had legal custody, after all. And Mimi had tried to send Quinn home, which would have worked if his family had wanted him. Allison had listened in on the conversation from the living room phone.

"Yes, he's extremely talented," Mimi had told them, "but it's not always about talent. I'm just his manager. I'm not the one who needs to get to the bottom of whatever issues he's having. You are." Quinn's mother had just said, in this very smooth, very professional voice, "Thank you for filling us in, but we really do think the best place for him is down there." And Mimi, who was never at a loss for something to say, had simply hung up the phone, come out into the kitchen where Allison was nonchalantly pretending to read a Thai takeout menu, and said, "That boy deserves better." That's how Quinn had ended up staying in LA with Jasper or whatever his name was and nasty Baby-Sue.

And Allison knew that, if given half a chance, Denise would

book her on the first flight out of LAX, and she would be mix-
ing drinks for Denise by morning. So Allison would have to
keep Mimi and Denise as far apart as she could, and for as long
as she could, until she could put a more permanent solution in
place. So in addition to armoring her own phone and voice-
mail message, she sent her mother a text message, immediately
followed by an e-mail, informing her that Mimi's phone number and e-mail addresses had just been changed because of a
stalker—of course, no one in their right mind would stalk Mimi,
but it was the best story Allison could come up with on short
notice—and, at least for now, any and all new contact information was being kept strictly confidential. In the meantime, the
only way to contact either Mimi or her was by calling Allison's
cell.

But these were, at best, stopgap measures. Allison knew there
was really only one thing that was guaranteed to let her stay in
LA, and that was booking something big, something *really* big.

Something like Carlyle.

QUINN WAS SITTING AT LOS BURRITOS EATING FISH TACOS
when Allison called him. It was the little Hispanic girl's regular
day off, but he'd come anyway in case she was covering someone else's shift or something. She wasn't, but once he was there
he realized he hadn't eaten in a while, maybe not since yesterday; he didn't keep track. The little chili pepper charm was in
his pocket, putting out positive juju, when his phone rang and
Allison was on the other end of the line. She sounded weird.
Not that he cared.

She needed to book Carlyle, she said.

Like that had anything to do with him, he told her. Like he
gave a single shit.

He'd gotten a callback for Buddy, hadn't he?

So?

So, she said, she needed to work on the scene with him. "C'mon," she wheedled, but there was an edge of desperation in her voice. "I figure we can help each other." And there was some merit to that. Before he'd moved out, they'd been each other's best scene partner. She told him to meet her at the 7-Eleven down the street from the studio the next day at one o'clock, and to bring his sides.

And even though he was fairly certain it was the wrong thing to do, he showed up. What the hell—he didn't have anything else to do and Jasper had already been headed over the hill.

Just as Quinn approached her, a taxi pulled up to the curb. "Come on," she said.

"What?"

"Come *on*." She took his arm and pulled him toward the taxi. "What, you didn't think we were going to work here, did you?"

She pushed him into the cab, gave the cabdriver Mimi's address, and then settled her tote on her lap, satisfied. "You brought your sides, right?"

"Yeah." He pulled them out of his jeans pocket. He'd folded and folded them into a small, tight square.

"Good."

They didn't say anything else. The taxi pulled up to Mimi's house and Allison handed the driver the fare plus a tip and then led the way up the walk.

"Okay," she said once they were inside, kicking off her shoes. "Do you want a Fresca or anything?"

"No."

"Well, I do." She disappeared into the kitchen and reappeared loudly slurping a can of soda. "Come on." She pulled him into the living room by his wrist and sat on the arm of the shabby sofa in the living room and gave him Carlyle's first line: "*What do you mean, you're not buying it? It's the truth!*"

Quinn moved into the scene self-consciously at first, but then fluidly, channeling Buddy. "*So show me something. If you were a real witch you'd be making something happen!*"

The scene unspooled and filled the room. Quinn hadn't run it in weeks of working with Evelyn. She'd had him working on Buddy unceasingly, but not with the script. She had him doing improv as Buddy, talking as Buddy, reacting as Buddy, and creating situations only Buddy would get himself into and then out of. When Quinn got stuck she'd say, "You should be able to be this character in your sleep, and if you can't do that, we're not done." He could see where she was taking him, too. If he got the chance to audition for Gus Van Sant, he'd know everything there was to know; he'd be able to respond as naturally and automatically and completely as if Quinn had never existed, just Buddy.

Now, as Buddy, Quinn took wing. And though it took her longer, Allison's Carlyle also moved out of her head and into her gut, and they ran the scene over and over and over, working so intently, so in tandem, that an hour seemed like only a few minutes. By the end, the scene had reached such a point of near perfection that they agreed to stop. Overworking a scene could be like putting a hammer to a gemstone. Once you blew it apart, it could be almost impossible to put back together again.

March–April 2007

*T*alent is redemptive. A master glassblower is only incidentally an asshole when his work appears in celebrated installations. Deviant men are declared artists when they write eloquently about perversion; women who smoke cigars are called refreshingly eccentric if they are also celebrated poets. We pardon those with habits, and the better the artist, the more we're willing to forgive.

—VEE VELMAN

Chapter Twenty

EVERYONE AGREED THAT SOMETHING WAS GOING ON WITH Allison. For one thing, Hillary had told Bethy she'd turned off her cell phone, which was previously unheard of. In a spirit of helpfulness, she said, Hillary had turned it on for her once, but Allison had snatched it back and slapped her hand hard and Hillary hadn't touched it again, even though she'd seen on the screen that Allison had twelve new voice-mail messages.

By midweek, when she hadn't been invited to Mimi's house for five days, Bethy hinted after Dee's class that she'd like to come over. Allison shrugged and said she could if she wanted to, which she did, even though Allison disappeared immediately into the bathroom. Bethy went into her bedroom and sat on the bed for a few minutes, but when Allison didn't come out she decided to look at her clothes, which Bethy loved. They were always feminine and made of soft fabrics and pretty colors. Allison hardly ever even wore jeans; a lot of the time she wore floaty skirts and little minis that showed off her legs. Sometimes she let Bethany try on the clothes she liked least, so today, while Allison was in the bathroom—Hillary and Reba were playing a video game in the living room—Bethy opened Allison's bureau drawer and touched her shirts and sweaters. She was about to yell into the bathroom to ask if she could try on a couple of tops when she felt something hard at the bottom of the drawer. Curious, she brought it up: a sock with something inside it—a silver spoon. Allison came out of the bathroom while Bethy was staring at it, and she grabbed the spoon out of her hand.

"That's just like ours!" Bethy said.

Allison quickly put the spoon in her pocket. "No, it isn't."

Bethy looked at Allison in confusion. "Yes, it is, it has the *R* on the bottom. Why do you have one of our spoons?"

"It's *not* your spoon," Allison said again, with the slightest quaver in her voice. "It's from my house in Houston. *R* is for my mom's maiden name."

"You said she'd never been married before, and your name is Addison, so it would have an *A* on it, not an *R*," Bethy pointed out.

"No, I mean it's for her *new* name. Reinhard. That's her new name: Reinhard."

But Bethy could tell Allison was lying. Crushed, she said, "Why would you steal something from us?"

"It's *not*. I *didn't*," Allison said shrilly. "I don't even know what you're talking about. I mean, why would you say something like that? I'd never steal anything. Ever."

"Maybe you didn't mean to," Bethy said helpfully. "I mean, maybe it fell into your purse by accident at dinner or something. That could happen."

"Why were you going through my stuff, anyway? You didn't even ask permission. You're not supposed to just go through someone else's stuff without asking permission."

Bethany was stricken. "I was just looking at your tops, because you always have pretty clothes. I was going to ask if it was okay as soon as you came out of the bathroom. I was going to see if I could try this on." She held up a gauzy blouse.

"No," Allison said, grabbing it out of Bethany's hands. "You can't. You wouldn't even fit in it anyway because you're way too big. You're probably like, what, a size nine? I mean, you'd ruin it." Allison folded the top in elaborate motions and put it back in her drawer. Then she thrust the spoon at Bethany. Bethy didn't reach for it, so it fell and bounced off the floor between them. "Go ahead—take it if you're so sure it's yours. Why would I even want it?"

Bethy stared at her for a minute and then picked the spoon up off the floor and tried to give it back to Allison. "Keep it. I don't even care if it's ours. It's just a spoon."

"I don't want it," Allison said coldly. "I mean, I don't even like it. I bet it's not even silver. I bet it's plate." She pushed Bethy out of the room and closed the door. She must have been standing right there on the other side, though, because Bethy didn't hear any footsteps moving away across the bedroom floor.

Not knowing what else to do, Bethy stuffed the spoon in her pocket and called Ruth and asked to be picked up. While she waited, she sat on the sofa in the living room watching Hillary and Reba playing Halo 2. Allison didn't even come out of her room. When Ruth arrived, Bethy got up and walked out in tears.

"I DON'T KNOW WHAT SHE WAS DOING WITH IT, HONEY, but it's definitely ours," Ruth said, once they were in the apartment and she'd had a chance to take a good look at the spoon. "I noticed it was missing when I washed the dishes and put all the silver back in the box, but I didn't really think anything of it. I figured it had probably been missing for years but we'd never noticed."

Bethy's face was puffy from crying. "Why would she want a spoon? I mean, Mimi has lots of spoons."

"Maybe it reminded her of us."

"But we're *here*."

Ruth sighed, feeling a little sick. "Honey, do you remember that time you took the Lifesavers from Albertsons when you were little?"

Bethy nodded.

"You didn't mean to do anything wrong, you just wanted the candy. So you took it. On impulse. Remember?"

Bethy nodded again.

"Well, I think Allison just took some Lifesavers."

"I didn't see any. I just saw the spoon."

"I know, honey. I'm speaking figuratively. The spoon was *like* those Lifesavers."

"Oh."

Clearly, Ruth wasn't getting through. "You know, if you look at it a certain way, it was a compliment. I know Allison had a really good time with us. I got the feeling that it might have been the first time she'd ever been around a normal family."

"We're not normal."

Ruth smiled. "You know what I mean. We love each other and we like being together and especially now that we *aren't* together that much, we're all really happy when we are. We're a family. I'm not sure Allison has ever had a family."

"That's sad, though."

"Sure it's sad. Not everyone's as lucky as we are."

"Rianne is. She has a nice family."

"She does. But from what you and Allison have told me, not only do I think Allison's not loved the way you are, I don't even think she's welcome. How awful would that be?"

Bethy thought for a minute and then, stricken, said, "Do you think maybe we should adopt her or something?"

Ruth smiled. "Oh, honey."

"No, I mean it. Maybe we should."

"I know you mean it, but life doesn't work that way. And she already has a mother, even though she might not be a very good one. Plus she has Mimi."

Bethany thought for a minute before agreeing. "I think Mimi loves her."

"Do you?" Ruth had her doubts. In LA, she'd begun to think, the difference between love and opportunism was often academic.

"I just hope she won't stay mad at me. I mean, I didn't even do anything—I even told her to *keep* it if she wanted. She's my best friend."

"She'll come around, honey," Ruth said. "Just give her time."

But privately, Ruth wasn't so sure. There had been times in the past when she'd seen in Allison a glint of cold, hard steel that Bethy completely lacked. But before Ruth could get too worked up, Mimi called and turned things upside down.

Like Allison, Bethy had a callback for Carlyle.

They weren't to read too much into this, Mimi strongly cautioned. Joel Sherman was still seeing girls for the first time—including, for example, Laurel Buehl, which was a surprise since Laurel was so old. Nevertheless, Ruth could see that this was extraordinary news. A major feature film by a world-class director! She could feel her heart begin to pound. This was the opportunity of a lifetime, and it might be within Bethy's grasp. That was the thing about Hollywood, Ruth thought, suddenly magnanimous—what seemed like bad luck could change on a dime: you woke up in the dumps and by bedtime you smelled like roses. And Bethy had thought she'd blown the audition! It just went to show that these casting directors were people like everybody else; they saw right through a blown performance to the potential that lay within. And after all, Joel E. Sherman had already cast Bethy once; he'd no doubt heard from the *California Dreamers* set that she was a hard worker, and that she was capable of delivering the goods on cue.

But Mimi was still talking. The callback was three days away, she said; they had some time, so she wanted Bethy thoroughly coached, to which Ruth said, "Well, sure." Mimi warned Ruth one more time that Ruth shouldn't read too much into the callback; sometimes there were three or four rounds before a major role like Carlyle was cast. "We completely understand," Ruth assured her, but from that moment on, with every beat of her heart, she repeated like a mantra, *Oh please, oh please, oh please.*

IN BEVERLY HILLS, ALLISON WALKED INTO GRETA GROBAN'S horrible apartment. The walls were damaged and dirty, like a troupe of little girls had been locked up there and tried to claw their way free. The carpet was grimy—even compared with Mimi's carpets—and a grayish ficus strangled in a pot in the corner. Allison thought that if she had to look like Greta, with her man's haircut and scary eyes, she'd probably just slit her wrists and get it over with.

"Ah," the acting coach said from her seat on the living room's single gray leather couch. "I hope you've arrived ready to work, because you're late. Tell Mimi the next time one of her students is late, I will charge double for the squandered time. Repeat that."

Allison dutifully repeated, "I'll tell Mimi you'll charge double for the squandered time. Whatever *that* means."

"Wasted. It means my time has been wasted."

Allison just shrugged and dug her sides out of her tote. One of the corners was still damp from where Tina Marie had slept on it and drooled. Allison smoothed the pages against her thigh and then straightened her back and shoulders. "Posture!" Dee was always reminding her. "Imagine a string pulling you up from the top of your head!"

"So," Greta said, holding out her hand for Allison's sides. "We begin."

Normally Allison didn't work that hard. She was a quick memorizer and characters came easily to her, plus she didn't really care all that much what some coach or teacher had to tell her. Dee and Mimi and everyone else wanted her to do things in a certain way, but she liked to just do what came to her, instead of planning it all out and having it seem inauthentic and overrehearsed. But today was different, because everything she cared about was riding on booking Carlyle. So when Greta told her to be more vulnerable, be younger, sadder, sweeter, more subtle, Allison did her best. After a half hour, though, Greta abruptly said, "Stop!"

Allison stopped.

"I'm hearing lines from you."

"Well, yeah."

"I don't give a damn about lines. I want to hear *you*—Carlyle. Lines are crap."

"Well, if we didn't do them like a million times, it would probably be better."

"*It.* You see? That's your trouble. You're performing. I don't want performing. I want *being.* Take a moment."

Allison stood there trying to look like she understood at least some of what Greta was talking about, but really it all sounded like the same old garbage. Then she heard Denise's voice in her head, saying in a voice-mail message, "I made him rent me an apartment with a big bedroom, honey, so you could have friends over. See? I'm looking out for my little girl." Like Allison had ever had a friend sleep over at her mom's. Like anyone nice would *want* to stay over with a friend whose mother was a drunk and a stripper. Or with a man who was okay with raping his stepdaughter and then paying her off.

"Okay, I'm ready now," she told Greta with resolve.

"Yes?" Then she noticed that the acting coach was watching her strangely, almost tenderly.

"What?" Allison said.

"You're quite beautiful, you know."

Allison nodded: she knew.

"It is not always an asset. For you, it will be lead roles or nothing, because otherwise you will upstage the actress playing the big one. If you truly want a career—"

"I want a career."

"—then you're going to have to step up. What you've been doing here today is really just so much bullshit. Am I being clear? Yes? Then let's start over. And this time, I want you to break my heart."

An hour and a half later Allison was in a full-body sweat and Mimi had been circling the Beverly Center for what seemed like eternity. Allison paid Greta two hundred dollars in cash—all she had—and poured herself into the car while Mimi was stopped at a traffic light a block away. Tina Marie vacated the passenger seat only long enough for Allison to fasten her seat belt and then leaped nimbly over the gear shift knob— in honor of Allison's homecoming, they'd dispensed with the hated booster seat—and into Allison's lap. Allison fooled with the dog's ears absently.

Mimi looked over: *So?*

Allison slumped, resetting Tina Marie's narrow hips. "I don't know. I'm tired. You know what she's like? She's like pinball, where I'm the ball and she's all those things that light up and boop and spring out at you and stuff and you still end up falling into the trap at the bottom."

Mimi arched an eyebrow.

"Stop. She's *weird*. You know what she kept telling me? She kept saying, 'More from your gut—give me more!' So I'd try that, and she'd say, 'What are you, a parody now?' I don't even know what a parody is. It's some kind of bird, right? What the hell does that have to do with Carlyle, anyway?" Mimi pulled up to a red light and Allison fell against the seat back, nibbling a nail. "See that woman over there?" She took Mimi's face in her hand and turned it toward the far street corner. "She's a man, and she's more feminine than Greta. She's creepy."

"Of course she's creepy. She also gets people on series and feature films."

"Yeah." Allison sighed. "So what time's the audition, anyways?"

"Ten."

"Who's driving me?" Allison figured she'd have to ride with Ruth and Bethany Rabinowitz, since Mimi had told her Bethy had a callback, too—not that Allison could think of a single reason why. She'd be all wrong for the part.

"I'll drive you," Mimi said.

Allison gave a happy little screech. "Really? Oh, you will? Thank you thank you thank you!" She gave Tina Marie a loud kiss on the nose. Both Mimi and Tina Marie looked at her suspiciously. "What?" Allison said.

"Ration your energy. You have a long time to go before ten o'clock tomorrow morning. You don't want to have spent it all before you've even gone in."

"I *won't*," said Allison. "Jeez Louise."

BUT GOOD INTENTIONS OR NOT, AT THE LAST MINUTE MIMI got tied up with an agent, negotiating a contract for Perry, so Allison had to go with Ruth and Bethany after all. And Ruth thought she should have said no, but she didn't. She went to the studio and picked up the girl—she sat in the backseat, making a show of arranging her clothes just so—and drove them over the hill into Hollywood.

"How are you?" Ruth asked Allison via the rearview mirror, trying to sound neutral instead of the way she really felt, which was sad and angry.

"Fine, thank you." Allison adjusted her seatbelt over her shoulder, fussed with the buckle.

"Good." Ruth nudged Bethy a little with her elbow, and Bethy said, "Aren't you so glad we got a callback?"

"To tell you the truth, I can't believe you did. I mean, you said yourself that you blew the audition."

"Well, she must not have," said Ruth loyally. In the rearview mirror, Ruth saw Allison shrug. She willed the girl to say something, anything, to show she would meet Bethy partway, but she just sat there, looking out the car window.

"Why are you still mad at me?" Bethy blurted out.

"I'm not mad at you," Allison said coolly.

"Yes, you are."

Allison shrugged again.

"You're my best friend," Bethy cried.

"Oh, I don't think so."

"You *are*."

Allison arranged her face into a perfect mask and said, "Don't you think it's sad when one person thinks someone's a friend and all the other person was doing was hanging out with them to be polite?"

Ruth could hear Bethy gasp. She imagined herself pulling the car over on the shoulder, ripping open the back door, and giving Allison a very hard slap. Locking eyes with the girl in the rearview mirror instead, Ruth said firmly, "That's enough." Allison's eyes slid away.

They found a parking space almost directly in front of the casting studio—a small act of grace on the Almighty's part, Ruth thought, in compensation for that remark of Allison's. In front of the building some blighted shrubs were dying in a strip of dirt the color and consistency of fired clay. Ruth imagined finding a cup and some water and bringing it back to the dirt along with a trowel and some Miracle-Gro. Maybe she'd do it, if they ever came back here again.

Allison sprinted ahead and Bethy fell back, walking with Ruth.

"Sweetie, don't let her get to you," Ruth said quietly. "This is an important callback and you want to do your best."

But Bethy was on the verge of tears. "I don't understand why she's being so mean. *She's* the one who took something, and we're not even mad about it."

"She's embarrassed," Ruth said. "We caught her doing something wrong. She'll come around, but it'll take time."

"How *much* time?"

"I don't know, honey."

Bethy drooped. "Yeah."

The door was still closing behind Allison when they caught up. Ruth hurried to catch it, putting the flat of her hand reassuringly on Bethy's back as she went through. The girls each signed in. Laurel Buehl was already there. And Ruth recognized Quinn Reilly among the four boys and two other girls who were also waiting. Ruth watched Allison skip across the room to the boy, saying, "Hey!"

She bounced into a seat beside him and chirped, "Hope for a mix-and-match. You and me."

The boy shrugged. He was tall and very thin, as though he was growing too fast for his metabolism to keep up, and he wore purple Converse high-tops as long and flat as clown shoes, baggy jeans held up by a passing thought and a piece of clothesline, and, incongruously, a peach-colored, badly wrinkled, and extremely stretched-out knit golf shirt that looked like it had been given to Goodwill by somebody's father. Ruth remembered hearing that the boy sometimes behaved bizarrely; Allison had once said he'd stripped almost naked at one of Mimi's showcases. There was nothing sinister-looking about him, though; just something forlorn and a little sullen. He leaned his head back and closed his eyes. Within a minute he was snoring softly. Allison punched him in the arm.

"What?" he said.

"You're faking that," she said.

"Faking what?"

Allison punched his arm again and then got up and crossed the room to an empty chair, pulled out her compact, and powdered her nose.

LAUREL AND ANGIE SAT SIDE BY SIDE, LEGS BENT AT EXACT right angles, feet flat on the floor, arms crossed. They often unconsciously synchronized their postures without even being aware of it; they always got their periods on the same day, or at least they had until Angie's chemo had thrown everything off—and even so, they were closing in again, with only a week separating them, down from three.

In a technique she had learned from all those years of pageants to keep herself from getting nervous—after all, she was here against Mimi's recommendation, and for a lead role—Laurel tried to think about something completely unrelated to acting: invitations. Though she'd never even had a boyfriend, she and Angie were planning her wedding with the help of a stack of bridal magazines they kept in a willow basket by the living room sofa. Laurel had a specially designated journal where they were keeping a record of all their decisions. Angie had suggested it two weeks ago, saying the project would be great stress relief. They'd already identified the location (their home church, with the reception in the adjacent rose garden, even though it did overlook the cemetery); the caterer (Beauregard's, the same caterer that had done Angie and Dillard's wedding seventeen years ago—they were toying with requesting the exact same menu, for sentiment's sake); and the style of wedding gown they liked best for Laurel's coloring and body type (a Cinderella style with a tight waist, leg-of-mutton sleeves, crinoline, train, and seed-pearl trim).

"I still think Le Jardin is best," Angie had argued last night about their choice of florists.

"Okay, but I want to keep Lucy Bee in there, too. They make beautiful bridal bouquets. Remember Halley's last year?" Halley Martingale, Laurel's distant cousin, had had a garden wedding the previous year, and it had been lovely.

Angie had capitulated, and Laurel made a note about the florist in the journal. She and Angie, both in their pajamas, had been stretched out on the sofa together, heads at opposite ends but bodies closely connected at the hip like a pair of open scissors. It was Thursday night, one audition away from the end of a long week, during which Laurel had booked and shot the tampon commercial, auditioned for a costar role on *Desperate Housewives* with a callback next week, and shopped on Rodeo Drive for some new clothes for Angie, who wouldn't allow Laurel in the dressing room.

When they'd finished the florist discussion, Angie had laid her head back, closed her eyes, and smiled. "One of the very best days of my life was the day I married your daddy. He was so handsome in his tux and tails, standing there at the altar waiting for me, that I started crying before I passed the third pew. They say that there isn't such a thing as true love, but they're wrong. There's true love in my life every day." Angie sighed. When she opened her eyes, Laurel had tears running down her face.

"You're sick again, aren't you?" she said.

Angie had reached over and taken Laurel's foot in her hand. "Not yet, darlin', but that day may be coming."

"No," said Laurel forcefully. "It isn't."

"No?" Angie had closed her eyes again and smiled faintly. "Well, that's a relief. We still have so much to do."

QUINN SAT BACK, STRETCHED OUT HIS LEGS, CROSSED HIS arms over his chest, closed his eyes, and tried to block out the room, block out Allison, who'd clearly gone off the deep end for Carlyle. Why, all of a sudden, did she care so much? She never had before. It was one of the reasons casting directors liked her—she was relaxed, even indifferent. She'd been brilliant, though; he'd give her that. She'd delivered one of the best acting performances he'd ever seen by her or anyone, there in Mimi's living room where no one even saw her but him.

He tried to chase her out of his mind so he could channel Buddy, be in the moment. This was his third callback, but he hadn't been in LA for more than three years for nothing; he knew not to get his hopes up. Still, even objectively, Buddy wasn't nearly as much of a stretch for him as playing a bornagain Christian on *Grey's Anatomy*, or a teenage assassin on *CSI: Miami*. Relatively speaking, Buddy was a slam-dunk.

Across the room, Allison was admiring her toenails. She kept stretching her legs out and pointing her toes like a ballerina. She kept sneaking a peek to see if he was watching.

Which, in spite of himself, he was.

JOEL E. SHERMAN CAME OUT INTO THE WAITING ROOM AND picked up the sign-in sheet, scanning the list. He looked up after a minute, pretended to be startled by the nine pairs of eyes looking at him, and then smiled.

"Well, well! Let's see what we've got here." He shuffled through the stack of headshots, stopped at one picture, looked up and around the room, and then at the picture again. He turned to Laurel and Angie.

"Why are you here?" he asked Laurel.

"I'm sorry?"

"Who sent you over? Because they shouldn't have. Did you think you'd be reading for Carlyle?"

"Yes," Laurel said faintly.

"Honey, you're way, way, *way* too old."

"I'm only sixteen."

"Doesn't matter. You look eighteen to twenty. Who's your manager?"

"Mimi Roberts."

"That woman is a pain in my *ass*. Okay, look. She shouldn't have sent you. Go home"—he consulted her headshot—"Laurel Buehl. Go home."

"What about the neighbor girl?" Angie said with some desperation.

"Who?"

"The neighbor girl. We heard there was a different character she could play. An older one."

Joel dropped his head in mock despair. "Who told you that? No, don't tell me. I know. She must have forgotten to mention that that role is for an *Asian* girl. Is your daughter Asian?"

"No," Angie said faintly.

"Look, if we change the breakdown and it goes Caucasian again, your daughter can read for it. You can tell your manager that. But I've got to say that right now, I can't see it happening. And here's a piece of free advice: don't call my office in a week or two to follow up. Don't. Because if you do, I'll remember and I will make sure that"—he looked at her headshot again—

"Laurel never, ever auditions for me again. Ever. So don't do it. Don't."

"Yes, sir," said Laurel, stricken. "We're sorry."

But even as Angie and Laurel were leaving the room—Laurel was in tears—Joel had moved on. He picked a headshot off the top of the stack and called, "Betsy Schumacher, where are you?"

A tiny girl bounced up from her chair and spit her gum into a tissue. "*I'm* thirteen," she said. "Just so you know."

ONE BY ONE, ALLISON WATCHED THE GIRLS FILE INTO and out of Joel Sherman's audition room, confident going in, varying degrees of messed up coming out. Bethany went in third, and came out looking glum. From what Allison had overheard—and she'd overheard everything—she'd given an okay audition, but you might as well have vomited in the corner for all that an okay audition was going to do for you, especially when it came to a lead role. Allison was sure she faced no competition there. As far as that went, she hadn't heard any of the girls give a decent read. After half an hour, Allison was the last girl left—her and four Buddys.

In the audition room, seated at a large table, Allison saw a spectrally gaunt woman and a man wearing pink glasses. Allison put her tote down by the door, adjusted her clothes—she was wearing a tweeny pleated skirt and a T-shirt she wouldn't have been caught dead in for any lesser occasion than this—and tried to take a calming breath without looking like she was nervous, which all of a sudden she was. She realized that the casting director had said something to her.

"What?"

"You okay, kid?"

Allison licked her lips. There was a weird humming in her ears. "I'm dandy," she said. "Just dandy."

"Yeah? Because you looked a little pale, there. So okay, go ahead and slate."

As Allison looked into the camera lens and slated, she tried to imagine Quinn reading with her, tried to feel his talent flooding her veins like a transfusion, but it didn't work. She could hear her heartbeat—*Hous-ton, Hous-ton, Hous-ton*—racing away on a rising tide of panic.

"*So show me something,*" Joel Sherman was saying.

"*I am. I'm making us argue.*"

"*Oh, for God's sake.*"

And that's when Allison knew she didn't stand even a glimmer of a chance; it was all slipping away. The gaunt woman was reading e-mail on her BlackBerry, the man was buffing his fingernails on his thigh, and even as Allison was delivering her lines Joel Sherman was shutting off the camera. It couldn't be over; she couldn't let it be over. She blew out a big breath and walked across the room.

"Wait," she said. "Please."

"I'm sorry, honey," the casting director said, capping the camera lens.

She put her hand on his forearm. "*Please,*" she said again, in a whisper only he could hear.

The skinny woman looked up from her BlackBerry.

"Let me do the scene with Quinn Reilly. I mean, he's reading for Buddy, and he's right out there waiting."

"Look—"

Allison was close enough to kiss him. "*Please.*"

He took one step back and caught both of her wrists in his hands.

FROM THE WAITING ROOM, QUINN HEARD ALLISON asking if they could read together—the old building's walls were
thick but the glass transom between the rooms was open—and
he couldn't believe it. She was fucking with his audition, his
chance, his shot with Gus Van Sant. Fucking Allison, man. But
apparently nothing came of it, because the next thing he knew,
Allison was leaving the room like she'd been shot from a can-
non, and she didn't look too good.

She was followed almost immediately by Joel Sherman, who
called him in and introduced him to the people at the table. Then
he started the camera and said, "Go," and Quinn went, with
rage still ringing in his ears. But maybe fury gave his Buddy the
extra edge he and Evelyn had been looking for, because when
the scene was over he knew by the quick, almost furtive way
the producers and Joel Sherman looked at one another that he'd
brought that scene home like a perfectly fired missile.

Chapter Twenty-one

RUTH AND BETHY SAT IN SILENCE IN THE CAR OUTSIDE Joel Sherman's building. Ruth knew without even asking that the audition had been a bust. The child looked like she could burst into tears at any moment, and Ruth was filled with a sudden and disproportionate anger toward not only Allison but also Mimi, who'd conned Ruth into doing her bidding one too many times. Carlyle could have been the opportunity of a lifetime for Bethy, and it had been thrown away. And now, when the best thing for them would have been to cut their losses and run, they were stuck sitting at the curb like a hired car, waiting for the one person who'd most directly ruined Bethy's chances.

"Honey, are you sitting there trying to figure out what to tell me about the audition?" Ruth said.

Bethy nodded mutely.

"It's okay. You don't need to," Ruth told her, and pressed her hand. "I know."

And then came the tears, a torrent of them. When she could talk again, Bethy said, "I just feel like I let you down."

"Let *me* down?"

"I mean, this was for the lead, and I know you thought it was really important and I tried, but they weren't even paying attention. Not Mr. Sherman, but these two other people, I don't even know who they were, and one of them kept looking at her cell phone and then she started *texting* someone. I forgot a line, and before I could make up for it Mr. Sherman just said, 'Thank you, honey, you can go.'"

Bethy cried bitterly, and Ruth started crying, too, and they hugged each other, and then Ruth said, before she knew she was going to say it, "I'm starting to wonder whether we should even be doing this," and by *this* she meant everything. Then Bethy wiped her nose on the back of her hand, and out of habit Ruth gave her a look, and Bethy said, "I'm *sorry*. It's not like I have a tissue," so Ruth fished a crumpled one out of her purse and Bethy took it by the extreme corner, like it was a dead rat, and said, "You didn't already use this, did you?" which was how Ruth knew the worst was over. On the sidewalk a couple of tourists stooped to read the name of the actor whose name was embedded in the star in the sidewalk.

The car door opened and Allison got in. "We can go," she said, and Ruth thought she looked a little shaky as she settled her tote in her lap.

Ruth started the engine, rolled up the windows, and turned on the air-conditioning. No one said a word until they were back on the 101. When Ruth looked into the rearview mirror, Allison was staring out the window fixedly, petting her upper arm under her T-shirt sleeve. Maybe her callback hadn't gone well, either, only she didn't have her mother or even Mimi to comfort her. Despite herself Ruth said, "Honey, are you okay?"

Allison shrugged.

"You don't seem okay," Ruth said.

"No, I am."

Ruth sighed. "Home or the studio?"

"Home, please."

And that was all any of them said until Ruth pulled into Mimi's driveway, except that Allison didn't get out.

"Thank you for the ride," she said, and then, in a small voice without a hint of attitude, she said, "I'm sorry I've been so awful. I don't know why."

"Oh, honey," Ruth said.

"Maybe you could come over sometime," Allison said to Bethy.

"Really?"

Allison nodded because she was crying, and then they were all crying and then laughing about it, and Allison gave them both an awkward hug from the backseat, and with supreme dignity put on her big movie-star sunglasses, climbed out of the car, slammed the door, and waved like anything as they drove away.

ALL AROUND HER, THE HOUSE WAS SILENT. GRATEFUL, Allison closed and locked the front door, went into her bedroom, stripped off her clothes, and stood looking at herself in the mirror. Her mother had had the same size boobs as Allison would probably wind up with—a 34B, probably—before Chet-the-Oilman bought her a new pair a couple of Christmases ago. Allison thought they looked like someone had slipped big, hard doughnuts inside her chest. They came at you suddenly, too. Flat back, no underarm fat, bony chest, suddenly one boob, then nothing over the breastbone, then another sudden boob, then flat over the rest of the rib cage and other underarm. Her mom thought she looked great, though. Ever since she'd gotten them, she hardly ever wore anything except a thong when she was just hanging around the house, especially if Chet was home. Allison thought it was sad, because she didn't look half as good as she thought she did. Her butt was flat and saggy at the bottom; she had a lot of little moles. Allison thought Chet didn't have very high standards. Or maybe he did, and that was why he'd done what he'd done to her in the cabana.

Before him, her mom had been okay with the regular men at the lounge where she used to work. She called it a lounge, but it was a strip club. Allison had known that for years, even though her mother thought she didn't. She used to go into her mom's bureau and closet sometimes when she wasn't home and look at all her stuff. She never tried any of it on, though. She didn't even actually touch any of it; she only used the hangers or a tissue to move it around, as though the clothes were radioactive or coated with poison. There were these clear acrylic shoes about a foot tall, and bikini underwear with no crotches. There were bras that were nothing but a couple of feathers and some string. One of her mom's girlfriends had made it all. Her name was Cynthia, but she called herself Delicious. That's how she'd answer her phone: *Hi, this is Delicious Delight! How can I help you?* She had a laugh like a mule. The year after Allison's mom got her faux boobs, Cynthia had gotten them, too, and the next time she came over to the house she took off her top to show Denise and Allison. "Go on," she'd told Allison. "You can touch them if you want to." Allison hadn't wanted to.

Now she stood in front of the full-length mirror on the back of the bathroom door, watching her reflection raise her arms high over her head. The undersides were crisscrossed with so many cuts, if you squinted a little bit they all ran together. Before Allison had started on them, her arms had been white white white, with blue veins that looked like they were about a millimeter below the skin. Sometimes when she cut there, she'd pierce the veins without even trying. You heard a little pop—or maybe you just felt it—and then they bled for a little while, but not for as long as you'd think, before they clotted. When she did that, she just blotted up the blood with toilet paper and flushed it so no one would see bloody stuff in the wastebasket and ask questions.

Now she turned on the water in the bathtub, got the temperature just right, and poured in some aromatic bath salts she'd bought the other day. Then, while the tub was filling, she dug her box cutter out of the back of a drawer, sat on the covered toilet, and spread her legs wide.

After the first cut, she didn't feel a thing.

THAT NIGHT HUGH WAS WASHING UP HIS MEAGER SUPPER dishes—he'd eaten what he'd come to think of as his white meal: a baked potato, boneless, skinless chicken breast, and steamed cauliflower—when Ruth called for a long talk, something she hadn't initiated in weeks. Apparently there had been some disaster with an audition, though he was a little shaky on the details; and for the first time he detected a pure note of doubt. Mostly he just let her talk. "Of course I understand that she's not going to book everything, I mean, my God, the competition's just overwhelming and there are so many *kids*," she was saying. "But the thing is, you can only hear *no* so many times."

"I know that, Ruthie. I've been saying that."

"Well, I must not have been ready to listen, then. I keep trying to tell myself she's serving an apprenticeship, just like if she were becoming a carpenter or a welder or something, but the difference is, normal apprentices get to *work*, don't they, even if it's at entry-level stuff. I mean, they'd at least get to solder a piece of metal to another piece of metal, or hammer two boards together, you know?"

Hugh smiled and nodded. He suspected it was all a little more complicated than that, but it was best never to stop Ruth in the middle of one of her analogies.

"Don't you *see*?" she was saying, as though he'd been arguing a point instead of quietly clipping his fingernails over the kitchen sink. "It's an impossible system, just impossible," she said. "And she told me she thought she'd let me down. *Me*. And I found that chilling, I really did."

"I can see why," Hugh said.

"And these people they audition for, none of them must have children of their own or they couldn't possibly treat the kids the way they do. Texting someone in the middle of her audition, I mean, really, it's just too much."

"Texting?"

"Bethy said one of the people she auditioned for was texting on her cell phone."

"Oh."

"That can't possibly have been necessary."

"I'd think not," Hugh said mildly.

"Well, I just don't know."

"No," said Hugh, and left it at that. He knew better than to expect the conversation to conclude with any sort of resolution. He had learned a long time ago that you couldn't lead Ruth to a conclusion before she was ready, no matter how obvious it might be to those around her. Her earnestness, her willingness to take on life's hard work herself instead of taking someone else's word for it, was a quality that he found endearing. (His mother, on the other hand, who drew her scathing conclusions directly from other people's folly, had always found it maddening. "What," Helene liked to say, "you have to jump in the river to know you can drown?")

"And you?" Ruth was saying.

"What?"

"How are you?"

Hugh washed the fingernail clippings down the drain. Six months ago he would never have dreamed of clipping his fingernails in the kitchen sink. It was only one of a growing list of ways he was slowly but steadily sinking into domestic torpor, but what was the point of bringing it up? She was agitated enough. So he just said, "My numbers have been good. Manny's pleased."

"Oh, honey. Does the testing still hurt? I can't imagine stick-ing my fingertips all day. Especially with the work you do."

"I'm fine," he said.

"I miss you," she said abruptly, and he could tell she meant it.

"I know, honey; I miss you, too. Is there anything I can do? Should I talk to Bethy?"

"I just dropped her off at Mimi's for a couple of hours. She and Allison have made up. At least that's one good thing."

"Well, sure," he said. "I like the girl."

After they'd said good night, Hugh closely examined the crease in his slacks. Were they too far gone to wear again to-morrow? Probably so. On the other hand, he thought if he put on a fresh shirt to tease the eye upward, he could probably get away with them for one more day.

THE NEXT AFTERNOON, FEELING LIKE AN IDIOT, RUTH inched down Barham Boulevard in a bolus of traffic. Consulting her directions, she turned onto Lake Hollywood Drive and then snaked up the hill. The higher she drove, the more beautiful the houses: mullioned windows and window boxes planted with ivy and lavender, wrought iron detailing, cobbled driveways, and the unmistakable smell of money. Ruth sighed. The psychic had told her that her house was behind a wooden fence.

Ruth found the fence and snugged the car into the curb between a snappy Mercedes coupe and a Nissan Sentra with metal fatigue, which probably belonged to the hired help. She locked the car door, clearing her throat and rearranging Alli-son's beautiful Gucci scarf around her throat. She pushed open a warped door in the fence, half expecting an alarm system to go off, though it didn't; inside, there was a deeply shaded lit-tle courtyard paved in mossy bricks and haphazardly furnished with weathered wooden Adirondack chairs and a table made from an overturned industrial cable spool. Beyond was a screen door, and beyond that was a wooden door, which Ruth opened hesitantly. Nowhere was there a sign indicating that an office lay within. But when she pushed open the door a woman's voice, lightly accented, called out, "Ruth? Come on in and close the door hard, really slam it. It sticks. I'll be ready in a minute." Ruth slammed the door, which didn't quite close. She pulled the last inch to and the door gave in with a splintery sigh.

Ruth expected to find a tacky beaded curtain or smells of burning sage or incense, but in actuality the room was cheerfully neutral: blond Scandinavian furniture, wheat-colored upholstery, bright orange walls, glossy white chair rail and mopboards, wood blinds at the windows. Some kind of noise was playing: ocean waves and seabirds. Ruth had expected the place to be ridiculous, but it wasn't. It was straightforward and reassuring and oddly, even clinically, professional. Ruth couldn't tell if this was the waiting room or—what would it be called?—the séance room itself. She sat on the edge of a stiff loveseat.

"Whew." A tall woman came in rubbing her wet hair with a towel. She looked like a Pilates instructor—blond, fit, mid-forties, laugh lines. She reached into a small refrigerator in a corner of the room and pulled out a container and a plastic spoon. "I'm sorry—my yoga class ran late, and then there was the traffic, always the traffic." She raised the container in her hand like a toast. "Yogurt," she said. "Would you like some? No? I can't seem to get enough of it. What do you think that means?"

The woman was a psychic; shouldn't she know? While Ruth tried to come up with something insightful, the woman sat in a chair, pulled off the container's foil top, and sank in a spoon. Ruth's stomach growled. She was dieting again, and it wasn't going well. There was every possibility that she'd leave here and go straight to Porto's for something big and fat-laden, a brownie or a wedge of red velvet cake.

The woman had evidently said something Ruth had missed, because she seemed to be waiting for an answer.

"I said I'm glad you're here," she said, clamping her spoon between her teeth and reaching across to shake Ruth's hand. "I'm Elva. Elva Morganstern."

Morganstern? Vee hadn't said this was a Jewish psychic. Could Jews *be* psychic?

"I'm a Morganstern by marriage," the psychic said, looking amused even though Ruth hadn't said a word. "My maiden name is Guðjónsdóttir. I'm Icelandic. You noticed the accent."

"How did you know I was thinking that?"

The woman just smiled.

"You know, I'm not really comfortable with this," Ruth said.

"With—?" Elva opened her arms wide, taking in the whole room and, presumably, the activities that happened therein.

Ruth nodded.

"That's all right. A lot of people feel that way the first time they come here." The psychic dropped her yogurt container in a wastebasket. "Thanks for letting me eat my breakfast, by the way. I know it's not very professional. All right, then, let's do this—let's get your payment taken care of. I do ask for it up front, so that will be fifty dollars for a half hour. I take Visa, MasterCard, Discover, or American Express." She took a credit card machine out of the desk. "Or cash, of course, but no one really uses cash anymore, do they?"

Ruth pulled a Visa card out of her wallet. There'd be no fooling Hugh when he saw the statement. She chose not to think about it. The psychic swiped the card and punched in a few numbers very efficiently, as though she could take people's money even in her sleep. Then she smiled at Ruth and said, "Let's go in and see what we can see. Yes, right through there."

They went into an inner room. Ruth half-expected to see some sort of clinical equipment, but instead there was a large potted ficus; a batik quilt showing a river, a deer, and a log cabin; a small blond credenza; a large blond desk; and two comfortable-looking chairs that Ruth recognized from IKEA. Ruth sat in hers and bounced a little. At IKEA they had a display that showed the exact same chair being pummeled over and over by a piston, presumably to show the chair's durability and resilience.

The psychic sat down on a small loveseat opposite Ruth, took a deep, slow breath, and said, "Let's dim the lights. Okay?"

Ruth sat forward on the edge of her seat.

"You're nervous about this, aren't you?" said the psychic.

"I know I'm being silly. Go ahead."

The psychic turned a dimmer switch and the room darkened. Ruth could see a palm tree in the outside yard casting a shadow on the window.

"Now," said the psychic. "Let's see the hand."

"What?"

Elva pointed. "Your hand."

"Oh!" Ruth turned her hand over. The psychic placed it, helpless as a turtle, across her knee and then stroked the palm with her index finger, over and over. The palm began to sweat. It tickled, and Ruth could feel herself on the brink of nervous, hysterical giggles. She cleared her throat. Elva Morganstern smiled pleasantly. "You really *are* uncomfortable with this, aren't you?"

Ruth sighed. "I'm trying not to be."

"You know, a lot of people who come here feel exactly the way you do. And I should come clean." She inclined toward

Ruth confidentially and said, "I can't cure cancer and I won't be sacrificing a goat."

"What?" Then Ruth realized she was being teased. "Oh!"

The psychic settled back, smiling. "Is there anything in particular that you want me to pay attention to?"

"Well, we're here—that is, my daughter and I—so she can act, but I'm beginning to have my doubts about whether it's a good idea. I used to think I knew, but she's only booked one thing in six months, and I gather when she turns fourteen, which is in June, she'll start being at an in-between age where she won't be booking anything, maybe for a couple of years, and yet I don't want to cheat her of opportunities because we are *not quitters,* so if I just had some sense of an *outcome* . . ." Ruth wound down, winded and embarrassed.

"All right. I need to close my eyes for a minute. It helps me gather things up."

Ruth watched the psychic's beautiful Viking bones. Her eyelids were a faint, marbled blue, and beneath them Ruth could see her eyes moving around. That was a little unnerving. What was she seeing back there? When she abruptly opened her eyes, Ruth jumped.

"Well!" said Elva, smoothing her hair like she'd been caught in a high wind. Then she cleared her throat.

"What?"

"Are you stuck—do you feel stuck in place right now? Because I'm sensing that something will break loose for you in the next couple of weeks," Elva said. "There's a different energy. It may be health-related, and it may act like an opportunity of some kind. I sense a fork in the road, a place where you can choose a direction to move in."

"Health-related—is it Hugh, my husband? Because he's diabetic, except we only found out recently, and I've been—well, to tell the truth, I've been *annoyed* with him about it, and now, if something happens to him, it's going to be *my fault* some-how—"

"I don't think so."

"*Bethany?* Oh my God—"

Elva grasped Ruth's hand firmly, as though to keep her from blowing away. "There's no reason to think this is something frightening. It may be something that is, in itself, very minor. All I know is, the energy is different, and it may give you a chance to look at your circumstances differently. It doesn't mean you'll change what you're doing; it may just mean you'll reaffirm it."

But Ruth was busy thinking. "Is it me? Because if some-thing's going to happen to *me*, I'll need to put someone on standby for Bethy, maybe Vee Velman—"

The psychic sighed. "I don't know. No, I don't think so. You know, it's best not to take these signs literally."

Ruth sensed that the woman was getting annoyed, but what did she expect when she was doling out alarming news? "Can't you look again? Maybe a little harder? Maybe if you squint—"

"It really doesn't work that way."

Ruth subsided. So that was it, then; a vague warning about a health issue that could be anything from hives to a heart attack. Ruth felt like she'd put twenty quarters in a gumball machine that had burped out a single misshapen gumball and then died. Fifty dollars, and she felt worse now than she had an hour ago. She could just hear Hugh's patient voice in her head, saying, "For heaven's sake, Ruthie, what did you expect? What you do down there is *our* decision, nobody else's." And he'd be right, of course.

But still.

And just like that, the psychic stood up and Ruth's half

hour was over. She shook Ruth's hand very cordially and Ruth walked out of the room and out of the house and got into her hot car and headed straight to Porto's on Hollywood Boulevard and Magnolia and methodically consumed a chocolate mousse, an éclair, a slab of Neopolitan ice cream, and a Diet Pepsi. Then she called Vee and reported what the psychic had said.

"Don't freak out," Vee reassured her. "I mean, she obviously had low blood sugar, right, with the yogurt thing. So that could make the reception go all haywire, right?"

"It's not TV," said Ruth.

"Well, yeah, but she's getting signals, right?"

"I guess."

"Anyway," said Vee, "you don't know."

"Here's something I do know: I just ate thirty dollars worth of baked goods."

"Ooh. Where'd you go?"

"Porto's."

"Yum," said Vee. "What did you have?"

Ruth told her. "They were good and everything, but I mean, for that much money they should have had gold flakes in them or something. And get this—Bethy's at a class right now that costs a hundred and ninety-five dollars. For three hours."

"The kids' stunt school costs eight hundred and seventy-five each," Vee said reassuringly. "Better?"

"No. I feel just as worried and now I'm about two thousand calories fatter, on top of it."

"Look at it this way," said Vee supportively. "You're now a bona fide Southern Californian."

THE MORNING AFTER THE CALLBACKS, JOEL SHERMAN HAD phoned Mimi Roberts to tell her that neither Bethany Rabinowitz nor Allison Addison would be going any further with

After. That was the language casting directors used to soften the blow: *she won't be going any further.* The fact was, the Rabinowitz girl had never had a shot anyway, he'd just wanted to see what she could do with the role. But Allison Addison was a different story. She had had a shot, so imagine his surprise when the kid had turned into a train wreck.

"I'm dandy," she'd said, though she'd looked like she might pass out. "Just dandy." False and bright as a theater moon. She was stunning, he'd give her that, but she'd been too nervous to hang on to her character. Which was funny, because he hadn't remembered her as a nervous kid, but just the opposite: the last couple of times he'd seen her, she'd been a little too breezy and a little too flip. It had been just as well that at the table, Camilla David had been on her BlackBerry lining up her next lay.

"Look," he'd told Mimi Roberts when she tried to finagle another chance. "The kid choked. And if she's going to—"

"What do you mean, choked?"

"Just what I said—she got nervous. Freaked out. Then she tried to talk me into a mix-and-match so she'd have a scene partner. If she's going to try and direct *me*, what's she going to do with Gus Van Sant? I had to physically walk her out of the room before she finally gave up. Kid must get her way a lot."

He could hear the woman wheezing on the other end of the line, weighing her options.

"Look," he said impulsively. "Keep an eye on her. Something's odd there." Never let it be said that he was a cold and callous bastard. He'd done his bit, run the old storm flag up the flagpole. When he hung up, Mimi Roberts still hadn't said a word.

Goddamn managers.

★

It came as no surprise that Bethany was done. Mimi had guessed that Joel was just trying her out, seeing how she'd do with a part completely different from the one she'd played on *California Dreamers*. Ruth Rabinowitz, of course, had nearly broken down on the phone, so real had been her evident delusion that Bethany had ever had a shot.

But Mimi was deeply disappointed that Allison, too, had been dropped. She had had hopes that the girl might have a real shot at Carlyle. Jumping ahead into a lead role wasn't unprecedented for a young actor with Allison's looks and capabilities. *Unlikely*, yes, but by no means impossible.

But Joel's warning, though chilling, rang true. Mimi didn't know where the girl's mind was these days. She'd been uncharacteristically edgy over the last couple of weeks, alternately agitated and subdued. Except for Carlyle the girl had shown no interest at all in the several costar auditions Mimi had sent her on. She'd been so disruptive in Donovan's last two sessions that he'd taken Mimi aside and told her point-blank that unless Allison could settle down, he'd have to ask her to leave the class. And now she'd fallen apart at an audition, when she'd always been one of Mimi's most rock-solid, reliable actors. You could throw the girl into the deepest ocean and she'd come up with something that floated every time.

Mimi was well aware that Allison was exactly the age when children began leaving the business in droves: they asserted their independence about what they would or would not do, informing the stage moms that they wanted to go to "real" school or that their real ambition was to become a doctor or engineer. Allison might be no exception, though she'd always seemed to have the perfect temperament for a career in the industry: focused without being obsessive, able to let go once an audition was over and move on.

It was five thirty on a Saturday afternoon; the studio was at an uncharacteristic lull. Mimi sat for some minutes, thinking in the quiet. Then she did something nearly unprecedented: she closed and locked the empty studio's front door and picked up the phone to make a call she'd probably been putting off for too long. Allison's mother, Denise, answered on the second ring, and the minute she heard Mimi's voice she said, "Oh, god*damn* it. You were supposed to be my attorney."

"Well, I'm not, but I need a few minutes to talk with you. Can we do that?"

Allison's mother said, "I guess, but I'm warning you right now, if my attorney calls, I'm hanging up on you." Mimi heard the sound of a disposable lighter and the long first inhalation of a cigarette. "So is my kid in trouble?"

"I'm not sure. She's been acting out."

"Isn't that what she's supposed to be doing? I mean, we're paying through the nose for her to be there." She sounded sulky.

"Acting *out*," Mimi said. "Acting inappropriately."

"Oh. Like what does that mean exactly?"

"She's been spending a fortune on beauty products, she's starting to dress like a twenty-year-old, and she's disruptive around the other kids in class. Her head's not in the game."

Denise exhaled straight into the phone receiver. "So what exactly did you have in mind?"

"I don't have anything in mind," Mimi said. "I was hoping you'd have some insights."

"Nope. Not really. Are you still being stalked, by the way?"

"What?"

"Allison told me you had a stalker so everyone's phone numbers and e-mails had to be changed. I haven't talked to her in a couple of weeks. She won't return my calls."

"So she hasn't confided anything in you, then," Mimi said.

"What do you mean?"

"Some kind of problem."

Denise laughed so hard she ended up in a coughing fit. Mimi considered the possibility that she was drunk. "Problems? Allison? What problems could she possibly be having? Why don't you ask me about *me*? Because *I'll* tell you about problems. My husband's been cheating on me and my marriage is ending and I have a fucking lawyer who won't return my calls, and everything in general is just turning to shit. *Those* are problems."

"How much of this does Allison know?"

"All of it, honey. I have no secrets. I've told her she's going to have to come back home, too. She's my only family."

"When did you tell her that?"

"Hell, I don't know—two weeks ago, maybe. Two and a half."

Mimi heard her light up again, and then she heard ice cubes clink in a glass. "Do you know about her cutting?" Mimi asked.

"What do you mean, like skipping school? But she's not even *in*—"

"She cuts herself. With a razor blade."

"Where?"

Mimi had finally gotten her attention: a maimed girl was a devalued girl. "Inside her upper arms, from what I've seen."

"Well, thank goodness. I mean, nobody can see that, right?"

"Did you know about this?"

"I might have seen a little mark or two," Denise said evasively. "Last time she was here. Like she doesn't get enough attention already. It won't scar, will it? Because trust me, that child is going to need every bit of her looks while she's young. You get older and then you've got nothing."

"She's a good actor. She's got that. If she'll straighten out again and focus."

"Well, I really don't see what you want *me* to do. You know, we pay you an awful damn lot of money to take care of her."

Mimi flipped her pen to the back of her desk. It fell over the edge and hit Tina Marie on the head. The little dog gave her an aggrieved look. Mimi closed her eyes briefly. "I'm her manager, not her nanny. You pay me to manage her career, not—" Mimi heard a click on the line: call-waiting.

"Well, my God, *finally*—" Denise said, and then Mimi heard dead air.

Crap.

Mimi sat at her desk, her hand still on the phone, and tried to remember what Denise Addison looked like. They'd met only once, during Mimi's trip to Houston. Just that once, in three years. She had Allison's long, spare build, only in Denise it had hardened into the stringy muscles and tendons that aging women developed when they weighed too little and lived too hard. On Denise, Allison's beautiful features were stark, and her hair had been dry, overprocessed, and hanging in a single lusterless hank halfway down her back. There'd been a tattoo up behind one ear that at first glimpse appeared to be an insect bite or a canker. What had it been? The scales of justice, Mimi thought, astrological sign of Libra—as though cosmic issues hung in the balance, to be decided by this trashy woman who had never been to Los Angeles, never watched Allison on set, never attended a showcase or celebrated an achievement. Admittedly, Mimi had never pressed her to do any of those things. Had it been false pride or a simple recognition of the truth to think that Mimi, though childless, made a better mother? Mimi could still vividly picture Allison as Mimi had first seen her. She'd been luminous, the way some young girls were just before they learned the free-market value of beauty.

Mimi closed her eyes. In their first year together, Allison had loved fixing Mimi glasses of Hawaiian Punch, and as she was pouring she'd sometimes whisper under her breath. Mimi had finally asked her about it and Allison had told her, very casually, that she was reciting the ratio of pineapple rum, 7Up, and Hawaiian Punch that went into a cocktail called Hawaiian Death that her mother had taught Allison to mix. Evidently Denise had thought it was hysterical to use Allison as a bartender when she and her girlfriends got together. She said she also knew the recipes for black Russians, white Russians, strawberry daiquiris, frozen margaritas, and something called Blood of the Innocent.

Tina Marie, always attuned to Mimi's moods, hopped up into her lap, circled twice, and settled. Mimi scratched the bony noggin and labored over what to do. Certainly it would be a mistake to send Allison home to Denise, but it was obvious that something needed to be done.

The phone rang but Mimi let it go to voice mail. It rang three more times, but Mimi ignored it, leaning back in her chair and closing her eyes. Half an hour later, resolved, she packed up Tina Marie, turned out the lights, locked the studio doors behind her, and walked through the stunning late-afternoon heat to her car. Tina Marie minced over to pee near her favorite bush and then they cranked up the car's feeble air-conditioning and headed for home.

ALLISON HAD A BAD FEELING. MIMI HAD NEVER REFUSED TO take her phone calls before. She stripped off all her clothes, got rid of her makeup, put on an old pair of sweatpants and a T-shirt and flip-flops. With her hair pulled back in a careless ponytail and her face bare, she looked closer to twelve than fourteen. She was sitting at the dining room table, where she had a clear view of the front door, and Hillary was sitting across from her.

Hillary was talking, but Allison was concentrating on listening for Mimi's car.

Hillary said, "She must be mad at you. You must have done something."

"Shut up."

"*Did* you do something?"

"Just shut *up*."

Hillary picked at some old nail polish on her thumb. "I could give you a manicure, if you want. You haven't tried that new color you bought yet."

Allison didn't say a word.

"She's probably just returning phone calls and stuff. Or maybe she's talking to one of the casting directors," Hillary said helpfully. "I mean, maybe something wonderful is happening."

Allison laid her forehead on her folded arms. Half an hour ago Bethany Rabinowitz had called and said neither of them had booked Carlyle.

The one thing Allison was certain of was that nothing wonderful was happening.

Chapter Twenty-two

THE LITTLE CHILI PEPPER CHARM HAD BEEN IN QUINN'S pocket for so long, he had created a sensory memory of it, seeing it by feel alone. It warmed him, somehow, to have the charm with him.

He walked by Los Burritos every single day now. The little Hispanic girl was there Mondays, Tuesdays, Wednesdays, Fridays, and Saturdays. She always smiled for her customers, which he liked. It wasn't that easy to smile at strangers and mean it. You had to open up, take risks, expose yourself to injury. But he was learning from her; he was trying to smile at people, too, and mean it, which was a struggle after so many years of holding people off, keeping them away. He even did that with Quatro, despite their growing friendship. Friends were risky; friends could turn. Friends didn't necessarily like you or take care with you; sometimes they only wanted to know you in case you got famous or met someone famous that they might like to know, too. Quatro wasn't like that, though. He fed Quinn excellent food at their dinners out, and he listened when Quinn talked about his auditions and working with Evelyn and how he thought he was getting someplace in his acting that he'd never reached before, a place so deep you didn't even need words. And, at least so far, Quatro listened; and if he didn't understand what Quinn was talking about, he did an excellent job of faking it.

If Quatro was his friend, Quinn thought he might be a little bit in love with Evelyn Flynn. Not in *that way*, of course, be-

cause man she was old; but still, he was in love. He knew she
would leave him one day; he just hoped that day wouldn't be
soon. Unlike Quatro, Evelyn was a cold, hard person, but even
so Quinn sensed that she cared about him and about bringing
him along in a way that Mimi never had. She could be cruel if
he didn't do what she thought he should, though. "Go there,
for Christ's sake!" she'd screamed at him once. "You're standing on the goddamn doorstep. Go! What are you waiting for?"
But here was his problem: if he stepped all the way through the
door, he knew he'd leave her on the other side and be alone.

These two people, Quatro and Evelyn Flynn, were his life-
lines. He almost never saw anyone else now except in acting
class or at auditions; he'd even started staying away from the
apartment if Jasper or Baby-Sue were there, because if they
didn't see him, they couldn't kick him out, which he was sure
they were getting ready to do. He used his time to walk by Los
Burritos and look for the Hispanic girl.

But you can hold off doom for only so long. At the beginning of the third week of March, Jasper ambushed Quinn in
the kitchen, saying, "Hey, man, I'm really sorry about this, but
we're giving up the apartment."

Quinn's heart sank. "Yeah?"

"Yeah." Jasper shook his head sadly, thrust his hands deep
in his pockets. "Baby-Sue and me, we're not making it, man.
We're calling it quits. We gave notice today. We've got the place
for one more month, but if you find a new place sooner, you can
just go and we'll forget the rest of the rent. Okay, guy?"

And what was there to say but okay?

Where was he supposed to go? He was sixteen and a half. No
one was going to rent a place to an unemancipated minor. And
that was *if* he could find a place he could afford on four or five
hundred dollars a month, which of course he couldn't, not in

LA. He was pretty sure Nelson wasn't going to cough up more, though. The latest word from Seattle was that his company was going through tough times, might even be laying him off.

So Quinn had a month. He could ask Quatro if he knew anyone looking for a roommate, but he doubted that anyone Quatro's age would want a sixteen-and-a-half-year-old room-mate, and anyway he wasn't sure he could handle living with a gay guy. Hearing Baby-Sue and Jasper screwing in the middle of the night was one thing, but hearing two guys doing it was something else.

One month.

He put on a leather jacket he'd picked up in a thrift store—it was actually cool outside, plus he liked the fact that the jacket smelled like somebody's father—and left the apartment. He was halfway to Los Burritos when his cell went off in his pocket. He was going to let it ring, but then he saw it was Evelyn.

"Come to my office," she said. She did that: she didn't ask, she commanded. She didn't say why, and he'd learned not to ask.

"When?"

"Where are you now?"

"Santa Monica and Havenhurst."

"Four thirty," she said. Her office was a mile and a half away. No one ever asked how he was going to get someplace. "Can you make it?"

"Sure," he said. What the hell—he was already walking.

WHEN HE GOT TO EVELYN'S THERE WERE FOUR OR FIVE eight-year-olds in the waiting room, plus their mothers or nan-nies or whoever. He'd heard she was casting a spinoff of the American Girl movies for one of the cable channels. She never talked about her work; he knew everything from reading the breakdowns. Baby-Sue was still able to pull up Breakdown Services on Mimi's account so she could see what was being cast. Jasper and Baby-Sue were always sitting around in the kitchen with their laptops open back-to-back, submitting themselves, and Mimi probably didn't even know.

The little girls looked him over for about a fraction of a second and then went back to their Game Boys and video iPods and text messages. One by one Evelyn called them in and gave each one about a minute before turning them loose again. One kid came out crying. Evelyn could be a total asshole.

When the last girl went out—after Quinn had been sitting there for about twenty minutes, which had at least given him enough time to stop sweating—Evelyn followed, turning off the lights, locking the glass front door, and pulling a full-length blind to cover it. She didn't say a word to him, just did her stuff and then indicated with her head that he should follow her back into her office. She pulled a set of sides from her desk drawer and handed them to him. They were from some stage play Quinn didn't recognize. She gave him the first line, and he was supposed to do his in Buddy's character. He tried, but he wasn't feeling it. He was feeling like Quinn, and that was no good.

CHET: Why would you ask me to help you rob
    someone? I mean, why the fuck would I say yes
    to something like that? Come on—would you, if
    you were me?
MARTIN: Yeah, man. I would. I'd do it to help you.
CHET: You're crazy.

"Start over," Evelyn said.

Quinn shook out his hands and flapped the script around for a minute to try to loosen up.

```
CHET: Why would you ask me to help you rob
   someone? I mean, why the fuck would I say yes
   to something like that? Come on—would you, if
   you were me?
MARTIN: Yeah, man. I would. I'd do it to help you.
CHET: You're crazy.
```

"Stop, stop. God," Evelyn said, dropping her copy of the scene onto her desk blotter.

Quinn hung his head.

She leaned back against her desk, crossed her arms, crossed one foot over the other, and waggled it. "So what's going on?"

"Nothing."

She raised an eyebrow.

He looked at her, looked away. "I have to find a new place to live."

"What do you mean?"

"The people I've been staying with gave notice. So I have to find someplace else to live." His voice actually caught in his throat. He hated the way he sounded, like some whiny little kid. He cleared his throat and shrugged.

To his surprise Evelyn softened, looked at him longer than you were really supposed to look at people, like she had x-ray eyes. He stuffed his hands in his pockets, shrugged, looked at the floor, and she said, "I'm sorry," as though she really meant it

"Yeah," he said.

She went around and dug in a desk drawer, pulled out a leather book, licked a fingertip, and flipped the pages. When she'd found what she was looking for, she wrote a name and phone number on a Post-it and handed it to him stuck on the end of her finger. "When we're done here, call him."

"Who is he?"

"A friend. He has a studio behind his house. It's a long shot, but he might be willing to let you stay there."

"Okay," Quinn said, sticking the piece of paper in his pocket. He cleared his throat, blinked hard a couple of times. He'd never lived alone before.

"If it doesn't work out, let me know."

He nodded. She pursed her lips, nodded back firmly, and said, "Can we work now? Because I talked to Joel Sherman this morning. He'll be holding a final callback round tomorrow with six kids, three Buddys, three Carlyles, and then the top four will audition with Gus Van Sant a week from Friday."

He could hear his heartbeat in his ears. "Am I—?"

"Yup." And she cracked the tiniest smile.

"Oh," he said, but it sounded more like a sigh. "Thank you."

She smiled for real this time. "Congratulations."

"Don't say that yet. It'll only mean something if he casts me."

"Honey, it means something just to get this far."

It was the first thing she'd ever said to him that wasn't true. They both knew that getting this far meant absolutely nothing unless you booked it.

WHEN QUINN LEFT EVELYN'S OFFICE HE WENT TO THE Paramount commissary, which looked just like a food court in a mall except that people were all dressed up as doctors, soldiers, beach babes, motocross racers, and old-time ladies in hoop skirts and bonnets, and pulled out the phone number of the guy Evelyn had told him about. Ben—his name was Ben. With his heart pounding he called the number and a guy picked up on the third ring.

"Oh, yeah," the guy said. "Evelyn just told me you'd be calling. You're the kid who needs a place to live, right?"

"Yeah."

"Well, here's the problem, though. I'm going to be moving someone in back there in about a month and a half, soon as he gets back from shooting in Bucharest. They're supposed to wrap in four weeks, but you know that's probably not going to happen, so call it five or six. Even so."

"Yeah," said Quinn. "The thing is, I'll be okay where I am now for another three or four weeks. It's for after that."

"Oh. So that won't work," Ben said, and he sounded like he was sorry.

"No," Quinn said. "But anyway, you know. Thanks."

To distract himself—hell, to keep from crying—he bought himself a Coke and an ice cream sandwich. Once he'd finished them and felt like he had pulled himself together, he called Evelyn and told her what the guy had said.

"Okay," she said and got off the phone. It was almost worse than if she hadn't offered to help in the first place. He guessed he was on his own again. He threw away his trash and headed for home. Only then did he really think about the fact that he was still in the running for Buddy. A one out of three shot. What had he been thinking of, moping around about stupid Jasper and Baby-Sue? He had a whole month to find a place to live. Something would come through. He'd walk by Los Burritos and see if the Hispanic girl was still working, even though it was pretty late, eight o'clock. At least it would give him something to look forward to during the long walk back.

EVELYN SHUT DOWN HER OFFICE RIGHT AFTER QUINN LEFT and put her things in good order. She was fastidious in her professional as well as her personal habits, feeling that clutter was a wasteful time-sink—in a lifetime, how many hours would you throw away, searching for things you could have located very handily if only you'd had a system? She knew she had a reputation for making lightning-fast casting decisions, but it was only because she had done her homework. She knew the kids she'd be seeing, she didn't waste her time seeing people she knew were never going to work out, and she could spot the standout, the rare gem, at a thousand paces.

Thus Quinn Reilly.

Evelyn was working him like a thoroughbred racehorse, leaning and firming up his acting chops, honing Buddy with the precision of a master craftsman. And what was happening before her eyes—not that she'd tell Quinn this—was an extraordinary transformation. He'd arrived on her doorstep with all the drive and all the talent she needed in an actor in whom she planned to invest time—and she rarely invested her time—but with blunt edges and sloppy habits, going for the cheap emotions, the guaranteed attention-getters, instead of digging for subtlety and nuance. Now, seven weeks after they'd started working together, Quinn had honed his acting skills into a thing of beauty. She had never known an actor who slipped into character with such ease, which was ironic given the hair-trigger personality of Quinn himself.

If Gus Van Sant, with whom Evelyn had never worked (though of course she knew him; she knew everyone), was truly willing to gamble on an unknown actor, Quinn would bring everything he needed to the table. Everything. And she'd already told this to Joel Sherman, who'd given her his promise that he'd get Quinn in front of Van Sant no matter what. She'd believed Quinn was ready, but now there was this damned housing thing, which had obviously brought him down. Evelyn, at that age, had been a coddled day student at Miss Porter's School in Farmington, Connecticut, learning to be a young woman of accomplishment and grace.

Very few people in LA knew, because she made a religion

of keeping her private life private, that Evelyn had a son. He'd been born thirty-three years ago with severe cerebral palsy that included mental retardation, and she'd committed him to an institution outside of Fresno when he was five. Never married—the father was a man of no consequence—Evelyn had had to put in ridiculously long and unpredictable hours even then, though she'd been a talent agent in those days, not a casting director. It had been a wrenching decision, though an absolutely necessary one (though of course her mother had disagreed). Evelyn saw him only occasionally. Though the caregivers at the facility assured her he knew who she was, she doubted it. He would look at her dully, drooling onto a diaper fastened around his neck like a bib, when she laid out the visit's gifts—chocolates, a new picture book, a bouquet of exquisitely expensive flowers—on the tray fitted to his wheelchair. She had no idea whatsoever what to talk about, or whether to talk to him at all. Sometimes she wheeled him onto the facility's lawn and let the Canada geese settle all around him, lured by a small bag of breadcrumbs she always brought along. The birds, unlike Evelyn, clearly made him happy. He'd kick and moan in guttural enthusiasm as she put a small handful of breadcrumbs into his spastic fist and helped him turn the hand over and sprinkle them as far from his chair as was possible, which was to say within inches of the wheels. The birds would gather around him in a honking crescendo, and Evelyn and Bruce—that was his name, Bruce—would watch them eat. It was always a tremendous relief when the visit ended and she could climb into the sanctuary of her beloved Mercedes and return to her life. Over the years she had visited less and less often. The nurses had finally admitted that Bruce was often agitated after her visits, and it was hard for her to find the time.

Now she had this Quinn, a boy who had everything her

own son lacked, even if he was clearly grappling with a difficult temperament. Evelyn had learned a long time ago to cloak her heart, but she could and would champion him professionally. The problem was, if he was worried about his housing situation—and who could blame him, at his age—he could blow the greatest opportunity he might ever have, an opportunity that could radically change his destiny.

Evelyn also believed that Quinn was her last best hope for playing a formative role in the early career of a talented actor, never mind *the* most talented young actor she'd ever met. She knew Joel Sherman wanted a legacy, too; they'd talked about this, agreeing, based on Evelyn's assurances, that they would not only call Quinn back, but put him with two other actors of very different styles and profiles, leaving Quinn to shine. If he wasn't chosen, it would be because Van Sant had had something radically different in mind, in which case Quinn could be god-like and still not book the part. But she couldn't imagine the director turning the boy down, if Quinn was on his game. His Buddy was high-strung, angry, grief-stricken, and raw. He took Evelyn's breath away, and Joel had seen exactly the same thing.

But when halfway home her cell phone had gone off and Quinn told her Ben was a no-go, he'd sounded on the verge of tears. She told him she was about to lose her phone reception going through Coldwater Canyon, but what she really wanted was a little time to think.

Because there was, of course, another possibility.

She lived in Studio City, in a tranquil little neighborhood of single-family homes with established jacarandas and oaks and dense rosebushes along white picket fences, attended to during the day by highly regarded gardeners. When she'd been looking for a house—how long ago, now, twenty-four years, twenty-five?—she'd thought her mother would come to live with her and so, with that in mind, she'd chosen a spacious single-story house with a tiny cottage behind it. Her mother, as fate would have it, had died of a brain aneurysm in her own living room in Connecticut, right in the middle of a rubber of bridge, but Evelyn had gotten attached to the place by then and had kept it. She had no more than to walk in the front door to feel her blood pressure drop, soothed by the soft mauves, grays, and buttery yellows she'd used everywhere. Her walls were hung with fine art—she was partial to abstract paintings and sculpture, and owned a modest collection of lesser Rothkos—and all her windows were treated with sheers for privacy and light. It was her sanctuary, her haven and refuge, and she had never shared it with another living soul.

But now she decided that, if necessary, the boy could stay in her cottage, a spare five hundred square feet including a neat Pullman kitchen, a single bedroom, and a bath. If he booked Buddy, he'd be on location in Portland, Oregon, right away, and staying for a good three months, during which time she could find him a more suitable place to live. In the meantime, she would make it clear that under no circumstances could he be in her house without her express invitation or permission. Even so, the thought of actually inviting a young person onto her property frightened her. She'd developed an entire lifestyle around safeguarding her isolation. She had no close circle of neighbors and acquaintances; she didn't spend long, pleasant weekend afternoons in her garden sipping drinks with old friends or family members. Did she really want a boy in her backyard? She gathered that he was relatively independent, and that he had adequate spending money for food and incidentals. The San Fernando Valley had a usable bus system, as she understood it, and of course he could ride over the hill with her, which would give him a jump-off point to Hollywood, West Hollywood, Century City, and Beverly Hills. And it would all be temporary.

If she had to, she would take him in.

Chapter Twenty-three

AT THE END OF THE MIX-AND-MATCH SESSION FOR BUDDY and Carlyle, Joel E. Sherman shook a couple of Tums from the bottle in his top desk drawer, chewed them ruminatively, and reviewed his options. The problem, as he saw it—and the producers knew it, too—was that the chemistry between his top picks for Carlyle and Buddy sucked. No matter how he'd put them together earlier in the afternoon, the same crappy, flat energy sat over the room like a toad.

So he went back over his choices yet again, even resorting to the kids he'd eliminated in the last round of auditions, to see if there was something he was missing. The Rabinowitz girl was a good kid, and cute, but of course she was no more capable of holding down a feature film than somebody right off the street. He'd keep her in mind for something else, maybe some small part, but that was it.

And then there was Mimi Roberts's other girl, Allison Addison. She might have been in contention before her callback, but even if that day had been an aberration and she turned to gold the next time, he'd never feel comfortable about hanging a movie from her shoulders. And he couldn't recommend someone he wasn't comfortable with. No, whatever she was working through, he didn't want to be part of it.

And then there were the Buddys. His first pick was, still and absolutely, Quinn Reilly. But was the kid a solo act? Joel had certainly seen it before: you got an actor who had all the chops in the world in monologues, actors so strong they took your breath away, and then you put them in a scene with other actors and, presto, they turned to shit. He'd learned the hard way that when that happened, there wasn't a thing you could do about it. If that was the case here, he'd have to cut the kid loose. And if he cut the kid loose he was fucked, because he didn't have any other Buddy he felt certain could do the work. No, he'd have to start all over again for *both* roles, and that would probably mean releasing breakdowns in New York and San Francisco and Atlanta, and that would cost a fortune, both in terms of time and money. Plus Van Sant's production window was tight and getting tighter by the hour: he wanted to start shooting in five weeks.

Then suddenly—and this was what he loved about himself—he came up with an idea from something Evelyn Flynn had mentioned to him on the fly. It would require Van Sant's buy-in because she didn't fit the breakdown, but if the chemistry worked the way Evelyn had described it, it was at least worth showing the director what he had.

"Hey, Lisa!" he yelled out his office door.

His latest skinny casting twit hollered back, "Yeah? What?"

She was probably too weak from anorexia to get up and take the ten steps to his office. He let it go. "Get Esther Stein at William Morris on the phone!"

Three minutes later he was explaining to the agent what he was thinking. Esther agreed: the girl was a doll, an absolute *doll*, and she had the chops to carry off the part. Did he want to see her reel? Nah—he could watch her demo online, but he'd seen her work before and anyway a reel wasn't going to tell him if she could work with Quinn Reilly. So he set up a meeting with the kid for later the next day, never mind that it was Saturday and he didn't work on Saturday, and then he yelled again and this time the skinny twit scared up Evelyn Flynn. Not only was she managing Quinn Reilly, but she was a damned good casting director, and if she thought he was crazy, he knew she'd say so.

She didn't say so. What she said was, "What time do you want him?"

THE NEXT MORNING THERE WAS A POLITE KNOCK ON HIS door and a small girl appeared. She was exactly the way Joel had remembered her: heart-shaped face, big, serious green eyes, freckles, hair the color of a copper penny, strong widow's peak. He'd never been able to resist a widow's peak.

"Hey, come on in. It's good to see you, kiddo." He came around his desk and gave her a hug. "Is your mom with you?"

"She's in the car."

Another sign that the gods were smiling: a good mom knew her place, and in Hollywood a good mom was rarer than hen's teeth. "Yeah, good. Did Esther tell you what we're doing?"

The girl nodded. "I only got the sides an hour ago, though, so I'm not off-book yet. I hope that's okay."

"Yeah, no problem." God, but you had to love this kid. Eleven years old and she was already more professional than 98 percent of the adult actors in LA. He found his copy of the sides. "I'm not even going to put you on tape right now. Let's just run through it."

So they did. And when they'd finished, he had goose bumps, actual goose bumps. She was a couple of years younger than the breakdown called for, but in his opinion—and his opinions were rarely off the mark—she could handle the part, if Van Sant was willing to go younger. And if there was chemistry.

God, let there be chemistry.

★

QUINN WAS WAITING ON THE STEPS OUTSIDE BABY-SUE'S apartment building when Evelyn Flynn pulled up. He held the usual headshot and résumé.

"I doubt you'll need that," she said. "I think he knows who you are." He looked over to see if she was teasing him, but he couldn't read her. Even after all the time they'd spent together— and it was hours and hours and hours—he still didn't know a damned thing about her.

"So who am I reading with?" he said.

"That shouldn't make any difference. And evidently Gus Van Sant won't be there—this is just for Joel."

"Yeah, but is it someone I've read with before?" She didn't answer, and he decided to keep his mouth shut. If she didn't want him to know, she must have her reasons. Besides, she looked like she had a lot of things on her mind, and he wasn't necessarily one of them.

"Remember that this is for chemistry," she said when they were a block from Joel Sherman's office. "He already knows you can act. What he isn't convinced of is whether you can act *with* somebody. So you're going to have to prove it. And I probably don't need to say that even if you do, you're a hell of a long shot, so don't fuck up."

She pulled her car up to the curb and let him out. Just before he slammed the door she said, "Hey."

"Yeah?"

"You know this one matters."

"Yeah," he said. "I know."

"Call me when you're done, and I'll come pick you up." He shut the door and she drove off without looking back.

Inside, he found Joel Sherman sitting at his desk talking to someone. She turned around, and he saw it was Cassie Foley. They couldn't be considering her for Carlyle, though—she was two years too young. But maybe Evelyn had talked the casting director into bringing her in to read with him anyway so he could see how Quinn worked. That would be a huge break for him. Even if he passed the test, he'd still have to audition well with the real Carlyle, and for Gus Van Sant, but he was pretty sure he could do that no matter who it was, if he thought they'd cast him. *If they cast him.* For the first time, he actually thought that.

If.

If!

JOEL SHERMAN GOT ON THE PHONE AS SOON AS THE KIDS were gone. It had been a great read; his hunch had been right on the money. He tried not to think about the fact that he was about to propose something that would fundamentally change the way a world-class director like Gus Van Sant looked at his characters, even coming from a casting director of Joel's stature and reputation. Interfering with the Vision, and all that crap. Better not to think about it. "Yeah, it's Joel Sherman. He around?"

But it turned out that he was not around; he was already in Portland scouting locations. Joel checked to see if he'd be there long enough for Joel to actually fly up there in person with the tape he'd made of Quinn and Cassie, but he wouldn't; he'd be coming back to LA in the morning, after a week out of town. Joel didn't think he should wait that long, knowing he'd be competing with everybody else for the director's attention. So he took a deep breath and closed his door so the skinny twit couldn't eavesdrop on him if it didn't turn out well.

"I'm putting him on," somebody said on the other end of the line, and then there was Van Sant.

"Yeah, Joel Sherman here. Listen, I want to run something by you."

"Go."

And so Joel laid it out: Quinn Reilly and little Cassie Foley and her widow's peak and freckles and his little-boy-lost quality and suppressed rage and her sweet charm and old-soul depth. He talked and talked, but when there was still nothing coming back at him, not a single word, he ran out of steam and just stood there, looking out his office window at a bum pawing through a trash can on the other side of Hollywood Boulevard. He'd probably been an actor once. "Hello?" he said.

"Yeah, okay," Van Sant finally said. "I'm willing to consider it. That's all I'm going to say until I see the tape. I'm going to put Sybil on, so she can tell you how to get it online or whatever so I can take a look at it tonight. I'm open, though. Okay? Yeah. I'm open. Here's Sybil." And there she was. Joel had the skinny twit pick up, because he didn't know a thing about uploading and downloading and photo buckets or whatever the fuck you were supposed to do, and he had no desire to learn it. That's what he paid her for. From the sounds of it, they worked something out in a minute, minute and a half, and then she was off the phone and he was having an attack of delayed sweating.

"No prob, boss," she yelled at him. "I just need the disk." So he popped out a tiny CD—Jesus, how much smaller could they get before you were recording on Cheerios?—and took it to the desk out in the waiting room and she smiled at him nicely and said thank you. If she got this done right, he might give her a raise so she could take more acting classes, maybe put on a little weight.

Back at the window, he could see that the bum had moved on down the street to the next garbage can. Who knew why an actor's career lived or died? Sometimes it was just a bunch of unrelated things lining up: who smiled the right way at the right moment at the right person in the right frame of mind to say yes. That same smile, ten minutes earlier or later, and instead of having a star on the boulevard you'd be picking soda cans out of the trash. It was a killer world out there. Despite his many, many successes, if he'd known, when he was just starting out, all the things that he knew now, he'd be selling shoes in his grandfather's store in Pocatello.

WHEN GUS VAN SANT GOT BACK TO LA, HE WANTED TO see Quinn and Cassie right away. If he didn't feel they could anchor the movie, he'd told Joel, who'd told Evelyn, he was prepared to open the casting call to nonactors. He often worked with what he called naturals, nonprofessional kids who could read fluently and had a natural ease in front of the camera. And if they did that, it probably wouldn't be cast in LA at all, but in Portland, Oregon, Gus's hometown, where most of the movie would be filmed because Gus thought soundstages made movies feel inauthentic.

Quinn and Cassie had exactly one shot. Evelyn had already told Joel that she'd worked with Quinn so he'd have the character down without sounding stale in a cold read. She knew Quinn was ready.

Evelyn picked him up at his apartment at one thirty. She was relieved to see that though shabby, his clothes were clean and his hair freshly washed. They said very little on the way to the audition. Quinn seemed to be in a good frame of mind, though nervous; as she drove, he drummed on his thigh in the supremely irritating way that every teenage boy seemed compelled to do. She let it go, pulling up in front of Joel's office and letting Quinn out before dealing with the car. She looked at him, he gave her a curt nod, and then he was out and gone. They both knew exactly what was at stake.

By the time she parked the car and got upstairs, the wait-

ing room was empty except for a small, curly-haired woman
marooned on one of the heavy wooden benches. She smiled at
Evelyn and said, "Are you with Quinn?"

Evelyn nodded. "You're Cassie's mother?"

The woman affirmed that she was, but she seemed as disin-
clined to talk as Evelyn was. They were both trying to overhear
what was going on in the next room. There was laughter, but
the voices themselves were too low to hear clearly. Then chairs
scraped across the floor, and in another minute Evelyn could
hear them reading from the script. She identified it as the scene
in which Carlyle and Buddy explained to the grandmother that
they'd had the household's landline cut off that morning at the
mall, since they both also had cell phones. The grandmother
arcs from anger to grief, saying she'd called that number every
day since her daughter died so she could hear her voice on the
message, and now, by disabling the phone line, it was as though
they'd killed her. Buddy loses his temper and storms out of the
kitchen and then the house, leaving Carlyle to cope alone. It
was a pivotal scene, and a great opportunity for Quinn to rapidly cycle through a range of emotions. The kids read the scene
a number of times, presumably on Van Sant's redirects. Then
it got quiet for a few minutes and all Evelyn could hear was a
single low voice murmuring. Abruptly, chairs scraped against
the floor again, the door opened, and Quinn and Cassie came
out. Both were flushed.

Joel appeared in the doorway just long enough to say,
"Thanks, guys. We'll be in touch." He gave Evelyn an unreadable look and then closed the door.

Cassie's mother gathered up Cassie's backpack and iPod and
led her out into the hallway with a gentle hand on her shoulder.
Quinn and Evelyn waited until they heard the woman's heels
fade away down the marble stairs.

Evelyn looked at Quinn, and Quinn looked at Evelyn with a shrug. Without a word, they went into the hallway and down the stairs and out onto the street to the car. They could just see Cassie's mom pulling away into traffic.

In the car, Quinn finally said, "I think it went okay."

Evelyn started the car, but she didn't go anywhere. "Good."

"I mean, I think it went okay."

"Good," Evelyn said again. "Did he say anything?"

"No. Just what you heard. They'll let you know. I mean, he didn't seem excited. Van Sant didn't. He gave us a bunch of re-directs, but he only had us read the one scene." Quinn thought for a minute. "But a couple of times he said, 'When we work together.'"

"*When* we, or *if* we?"

"No, it was definitely 'when we.'"

Evelyn looked over at him. He looked back at her. "That could be something," she said.

"I know."

"How did Cassie do?"

"She's great. She was great."

"Did he tape you?"

Quinn nodded.

"Then he probably wants to see how you look on film before he makes up his mind. He'll talk it over with Joel, too, try to find out more about how you work, what your range is. And he'll probably talk it over with the producers."

"Yeah."

"So now we wait," said Evelyn, pulling into traffic. She, of all people, knew the dangers of second-guessing. The idea was to move into a state of serene suspension until the call came. How often had she been on the other side of the table? She'd forgotten how much harder it was when you weren't the one in control.

"So where do you want me to drop you?" she asked Quinn.

"Oh," he said. "The apartment, I guess."

EVELYN TOOK A WORK CALL, AND THEN ANOTHER, AND then they were back at Jasper and Baby-Sue's. She didn't even get off the phone as Quinn got out, just lifted her hand in farewell and kept talking. She could be a real dick. But just as she drove away, she winked.

Almost immediately, as he headed over to Hazlitt & Company to see what Quatro was doing, she was on the phone. "He wants you to go bowling," she told him.

"What?"

"He wants to take you and Cassie bowling. This afternoon at four." Just under an hour from now.

"Why?"

"Probably so he can get to know you both a little better in a place where you'll be more relaxed. I think it's a great idea."

"I suck at bowling."

Evelyn laughed. "He's not recruiting you for a league, honey. He's just trying to find out who you are."

Quinn heard his pulse in his ears. Gus Van Sant wanted to go bowling. "Can Cassie make it?"

"Of course she can make it. So can you. He's going to meet you at Pinz in Studio City at four o'clock. Can you get there on your own? It's on Ventura Boulevard."

"I don't know. Yeah, probably. If I can't find a ride, though—"

"You can call me if you have to. Do you know where Cassie lives? Maybe they can take you."

"Yeah." Quinn just stood there on the sidewalk for a minute, stunned. Gus Fucking Van Sant wanted to take him and Cassie bowling.

"Good for you, honey," Evelyn said softly. "Good for you both. Just relax and have a good time."

"Yeah," he said—like that was going to be possible.

"Strike out, or whatever you do when you bowl."

"Yeah. Okay." Then, just as she was about to get off the phone, he said, "Wait—Evelyn?" He realized he'd never called her by her name before.

"Hmm?"

"Thanks. I mean—thank you."

"Don't thank me yet," she said. "Just be yourself. And if you can't do that, be Buddy."

AT HAZLITT & COMPANY, QUATRO WAS WORKING ON A client, a young guy—probably an actor, given the safe haircut Quatro was giving him. Quatro caught sight of him in the waiting area, said something to the client, and came up.

"Hey, you okay?" he asked Quinn. "You look a little weird."

"I'm going bowling with Gus Van Sant," Quinn said, and broke into a grin. "Gus Frickin' Van Sant."

"Get the fuck out!" Quatro cried, pounding him on the back.

"Me and Cassie. At four."

"No shit!"

"No shit."

Quatro shook his head. "Wow."

"Whew," Quinn said. "Do you think I should wear something, like, special? What are you supposed to wear when you go bowling, anyways? I *suck* at bowling. I haven't even been since I was a kid."

"You're still a kid."

Quinn gave him a look. "I mean, are there, like, bowling clothes you're supposed to have or whatever?"

"Only the shoes, and trust me, no one normal owns their own bowling shoes—you can rent them there. Just make sure you're wearing clean socks with no holes."

Quinn nodded. "I'm glad Cassie's going," he said, because he was. She'd know what to do. She was just a little kid, but she was much better at people stuff than he was. She had a great laugh, too, one of those belly laughs that makes you laugh, even if you don't know what's funny.

"Okay, bud," Quatro said, grinning. "Knock 'em dead. I better get back to Mario Andretti, there."

"That's not really Mario Andretti," Quinn said doubtfully.

"Nah, just a guy who likes driving race cars and wrote a book about it." He clapped Quinn on the shoulder. "Call me later and tell me everything."

Quinn watched Quatro walk back to his chair and say something to the client. The guy looked up to the front of the salon at Quinn, and Quinn cracked a smile. *Gus Van Sant.*

His cell went off again as he was walking out the door. It was Cassie. "My mom says do you need a ride? We can pick you up. You live in West Hollywood, right? Because we're over here on La Brea."

Quinn gave her the address of Los Burritos and said he'd be waiting in front in ten minutes. To the best of his recollection, he was wearing good socks, and if he went back to the apartment he'd just get nervous. More nervous.

THE LITTLE HISPANIC GIRL WAS WORKING, WHICH OF COURSE he knew because it was Saturday. He'd been afraid she'd be on a break or called in sick or something, but she was right there, talking to a woman and her daughter in Spanish. He stood in her line, hoping she wouldn't take too long because he only had maybe five more minutes. If she smiled at him, it would be a good luck sign. As always, he had the little chili pepper charm in his front right pocket.

She got through with the mother and daughter and looked up at him. He was pretty sure she recognized him. "*Hola!*"

"*Hola,*" he said. "I don't really know how to say anything else, though."

"Okay."

"I'm going bowling." Then he pantomimed bowling, in case that wasn't in her vocabulary, because why would it be?

She smiled. "Yes?"

"I mean, I'm going bowling with somebody really important."

"That's good, then."

"*Sí.*" Quinn could feel the guy in line behind him getting restless. "I guess, can I get a Pepsi, *por favor?*"

"*Grande?*"

"*Sí, grande.*" She smiled like he'd done something amazing instead of saying something even Hispanic preschoolers knew. That was okay, though. He could feel himself blushing. She filled a cup with soda, put the lid on carefully, and then took the straw out of its paper wrapper for him and put it in the cup before handing it over. It was a strangely intimate thing to do. He was pretty sure she wouldn't do that for most people. "*Muy bien,*" she said. "*Buena suerte.* Means good luck."

He put the money in her hand instead of on the counter, and she closed her fingers over it. "*Muchas gracias, señor.* Thank you." She smiled and he thought, for the millionth time, that her family must have a wonderful life with someone like her in the house.

He took his soda and went out onto the sidewalk. Cassie and her mom were just pulling up; Cassie opened the back door for him from inside, and he climbed in beside her.

"Hi, honey," said her mom. He felt silly sitting behind her, like she was the chauffeur. Little kids sat behind their moms in a car, though, so he knew why Cassie had just assumed he'd sit back there, too. It was okay.

"I gave Cassie enough money for both of you to bowl a couple of games and rent shoes. I'm sure he won't let you pay, but just in case."

"Oh," said Quinn. "Thanks." He hadn't even thought about what it would cost to bowl. After paying for the soda, he had four bucks on him, maybe five, plus some loose change.

"I think it's wonderful that he wants to get to know you both a little better." She met Quinn's eyes in the rearview mirror. She had a nice, worn-out-paper-bag kind of face. "Cassie said she thought you'd done a good job at the audition," she said. "Did you think so?"

"I don't know. Yeah, probably. I couldn't really tell, though."

"I thought he liked us," Cassie said.

"Enough to take you bowling, anyway," her mom said.

"I have a new game," Cassie said, offering Quinn her Game Boy. "Do you want to see?"

"That's okay," Quinn said. "I'm kind of nervous."

Cassie shrugged and went back to her game. "Okay."

He didn't say anything for the rest of the ride and neither did Cassie or her mom. The traffic in Laurel Canyon wasn't too bad, and they were over the hill and at the bowling alley on Ventura Boulevard in Studio City a full ten minutes early.

"All right, you guys," Cassie's mom said. "Hop out. Cassie knows to call me when you're done. I'll be doing some shopping in Sherman Oaks. Okay?"

"Okay," said Quinn, and then he remembered. "Thank you for the ride and everything."

"Break a pin," Cassie's mom said, and drove away smiling.

Chapter Twenty-four

THE DAY AFTER HER CONVERSATION WITH DENISE ADDI-son, Mimi left Reba and Hillary at the studio, telling them she was running Allison to an audition. Instead, she drove to the Good Earth on Ventura Boulevard—she hated the place, but it was a nod toward Allison, who loved it—and asked to be put in a booth by the window toward the back.

Allison ordered a soy shake and egg white omelet; Mimi ordered a cup of coffee and eight-grain toast. It was mid-morning and no one much was around. She stirred a packet of real sugar into her coffee—at her weight, fussing over the extra twenty calories was laughable—and watched Allison nervously exam-ine a switch of hair for split ends. Fortified by coffee, Mimi began.

"All right," she said. "Here's the deal. I'm going to give you a full studio scholarship"—there was no such thing, but Allison wouldn't know that—"which means your mom won't pay for you to stay with me anymore. You'll drop out of acting for a year—no auditions, no classes, *nothing*—and you'll go to real school, instead. There's a charter high school for the arts in Van Nuys that'll take you next fall. If you don't maintain a B aver-age at the end of the first semester—and I mean a *B*, not a B minus—you'll be on a plane to Texas the next day. You'll be tutored once a week until you're sixteen so you'll be ready to pass the proficiency test and get your legal eighteen. If you don't pass the CHSPE by your second try, we're done. You'll get one hundred and seventy-five dollars a month as allowance, period.

No Beverly Center shopping sprees, no credit cards, *nada*. And you'll be paying for your own movies, snacks, and whatever else. You can go back to Houston any time you want, but as long as you stay with me, the rules don't change and nothing I've said is negotiable."

Their waitress slid Allison's omelet and soy shake in front of her, and handed Mimi her toast with a basket of organic butter and jams. Mimi waited until she left before she went on.

"I've also told Hillary's and Reba's parents they'll have to find someplace else for the girls to live, if they're going to have them stay in Hollywood. I'm not going to house anyone anymore."

"Except me."

"Except you."

Allison watched her with absolute concentration. "What about boot camp?" The summer session was due to begin in seven weeks.

"I'll have the parents pay studio families to house their kids. I'm not going to change anything during the day."

"I know, but will I get to do boot camp?"

"You won't participate, no. You'll be working for me, to help me run it. I'll pay you five dollars an hour. Depending on your behavior and how hard you work, I may or may not let you do social things with them. You're going to have to earn that."

Mimi spread butter, put a clot of jam on her toast. She'd expected Allison's face to brighten, but it didn't. Instead she said, "She won't let me. She wants me to come home."

"She did, but now she's agreed to do this."

"Why—"

Mimi held up her hand. "I'm not done yet."

Allison watched her.

"If and when you go back to acting, I'm going to take a

manager's fee of twenty-five percent of everything you earn until you're eighteen—*really* eighteen, not legal eighteen—and I'm going to have you and your mom both sign a contract saying so. It'll reimburse me for your room and board. If you book a series, it'll add up to a lot of money. If you can focus again, it'll happen. If you can't, once you're eighteen you're going to be on your own."

"What if she changes her mind?" Allison asked.

"I don't think she will."

"How do you know?"

"I just do." In fact, Mimi knew because the terms of her deal with Denise weren't quite what she'd laid out for Allison. Mimi wasn't just giving Allison a free ride to live with her. Mimi was actually *paying* Denise to let Allison stay with her. It wasn't much, but Mimi had set the figure high enough that Denise would be reluctant to do without it, once she'd started receiving it. Call her a cynic, but Mimi was an absolute believer that money was the ultimate motivator, at least for a woman like Denise. "And if we have to, we can get you emancipated. That's it," Mimi said.

Across the table, Allison started crying.

"What?" said Mimi, handing her a napkin.

Allison blew her nose.

"Talk to me," Mimi said. "This is the time to put everything on the table."

"You're going to keep me," Allison said.

"Yes, I'm going to keep you."

"I didn't think you would."

"Why would you think that?" Mimi said. "Of course I'm keeping you."

"You made Quinn go."

"You aren't Quinn."

"I'm ready to go home now," Allison said, even though she hadn't touched her food. "Can we go home?"

"Yes," Mimi said. "We can go home."

THAT NIGHT, ALLISON GOT INTO BED AND JUST LAY THERE, looking at the ceiling. Fat Reba was snoring; Hillary kept turning over and over and over. Allison saw a vision of herself tiptoeing up to each one of them with a big fluffy pillow in her hand and suffocating them. She might just do it. Not really, though.

From Mimi's room she could hear Jay Leno doing his *Tonight Show* monologue. She threw back her covers, put her slippers on—lovely satin mules with feathers over the insteps, bought on sale at Neiman Marcus—and click-clacked across the wood floors of the hall and living room and stood in Mimi's bedroom doorway—which, strictly speaking, was forbidden.

Mimi was sitting up in bed in a pair of men's pajamas. She looked tired and disheveled. Tina Marie was snoring on the foot of the bed.

"I can't sleep," Allison said.

"It's early." It was, at least by household standards.

"I know, but I'm *tired*."

Mimi patted the bed and moved over to make room for Allison. Allison slipped under the sheets, fluffed one of Mimi's extra pillows, and propped it behind her. They watched Leno for a few minutes. Allison didn't get any of the jokes, but she didn't really care. It was just nice to be sitting here. Safe. She wondered if Jay Leno knew what an ugly man he was. If she were that ugly, she probably wouldn't even want to be an actor, because someone like her was going to sit there in a theater in the dark and think how bad she looked up there on the screen. She snuggled deeper into the pillows, pulled the comforter higher, and closed her eyes. She could probably go to sleep now, here, in Mimi's room, listening to the studio audience laugh about things that didn't matter.

"Show me your arms," Mimi said.

"What?"

"I want to see your arms."

Allison crossed them over her chest. "Why?"

"I want to see if you're still cutting."

Allison sat still for a minute. Then she uncrossed her arms, which she hadn't worked on in a while—because she'd moved lower, but she wasn't about to say that—and which were starting to heal. She held them out in front of her and turned them over. Even so, she could hear Mimi suck in her breath.

"My God," Mimi said. "What were you thinking?"

Allison put her arms away. "I don't know. Nothing." Which of course wasn't true. She'd been thinking about everything— Bethany's betrayal, Chet-the-Oilman's rape, her mother making her come back to Houston, her failure with Carlyle.

"Doesn't it hurt?"

Allison shrugged. "Sometimes. Not usually."

Mimi shook her head. "You know they'll scar."

"No, they won't. They're just little cuts. They don't go very deep."

"Oh," said Mimi, "you'd be surprised."

EVERY FRIDAY NIGHT, HUGH AND HELENE SHARED A POT roast or brisket dinner. Tonight they had eaten over a vigorous discussion of just how much of an idiot George W. Bush was. Hugh put him at nine point five on a scale of one to ten; Helene was inclined to go easier on him because he wasn't, after all, an especially *bright* man, which wasn't his fault. His parents should have known better than to encourage him to pursue a career for which he was so clearly ill-suited. Then, while Hugh was forking up a potato, she said, "Hanummf."

Fork poised in midair, he and Helene had exchanged identical alarmed expressions.

"What?" Hugh said.

"Peaninomoffn," she said.

"Smile for me, okay, Mom?"

And with effort she mimicked a smile—or, more accurately, her left side mimicked a smile. Her right side sat the little exercise out.

"Okay," Hugh said, jumping up from the table, pressing the kitchen's emergency button, and then immediately dialing 911. Helene continued to try to talk, tears of frustration streaming down her cheeks, until Hugh finally grasped her hands and said, "It's all right, Mom. We'll take care of this. Okay? We'll take care of this. Just try and relax now. Help's only a couple minutes away."

THE NEXT MORNING, AT THE ALAMEDA EXTENDED STAY Apartments, Ruth's phone went off while she and Bethy were getting ready to go to a commercial audition for bathroom tissue. Ruth was groggy even though she'd been awake for hours; she and Hugh had been on the phone until late last night, talking quietly in the courtyard so she wouldn't wake up Bethy. He'd called from the hospital, exhausted: it looked like a stroke. Ruth's first thought had been, *So that's what the psychic meant,* followed, to her lasting shame, by, *Thank God it wasn't me or Bethy.*

Now, dreading the worst, she searched for her phone. Bethy found it first, buried at the bottom of Ruth's purse. Instead of Hugh, though, it was Allison, asking for Ruth.

"Do you think you guys will be at the studio later?"

"Probably not," Ruth said. "Bethy's got an audition."

"Could you come, though?"

Ruth sighed. "What do you need, Allison?"

"No, I don't need anything. I have something to tell you guys."

"Oh?"

"So I was hoping you were going to be here."

"All right," said Ruth. "We'll try, but I can't promise."

"Thank you," said Allison, and Ruth thought she hadn't heard that voice in a long time. *Thank you for letting me stay with you.* She didn't have the energy for the child right now, though.

As soon as Ruth got off the phone it rang again, and this time it was Hugh. Ruth put the phone against her chest and said to Bethy, "It's Vee, honey. I'm going to take it outside."

"She's having seizures," Hugh told her now. "They don't know why, so they're doing an MRI. It may not have been a stroke at all."

Poor Hugh. "Where are you now?"

"In the waiting room at Swedish. I had Margaret cancel all my appointments."

"I'll come home."

"Not yet. Let's see what it is first. We could already be past the worst of it."

He didn't sound like he thought they were past the worst of it, though. He sounded like he was preparing himself for more bad news. "I'm so sorry, honey," Ruth said.

"She's scared."

"Of course she is," Ruth said.

"So am I."

"I know."

"Well," he said. However ambivalent Ruth's own feelings about Helene might be, Hugh was utterly devoted to her.

"Call as soon as you know anything," she said. "Bethy has an audition for toilet paper, but I'll keep my phone turned up."

"Toilet paper," Hugh said.

"Charmin. I know."

She could hear him sigh. "All right. They said we probably won't know anything for at least a couple of hours."

"Well, I'll stand by. I love you, honey. Tell her Bethy and I are thinking of her every minute."

"You haven't told her, have you?" Hugh said.

"No. Not until we know more. But your mother doesn't have to know that."

After Hugh had hung up, Ruth just sat there looking stupidly at the cell phone in her hand and thinking about how, in a single moment, everything could change.

Bethy was standing at the threshold of the closet when Ruth let herself back into the apartment, looking at her clothes. "What do you wear to an audition about toilet paper?" she asked.

"Who knows," said Ruth. "Who cares? I say just wear a nice T-shirt and jeans. Look like a nice middle-class kid who takes pains with her hygiene."

"I don't even know what that means," said Bethy.

"It means it doesn't matter." Ruth took a clean purple T-shirt out of the bureau and handed it to Bethy. "Isn't their logo lavender?"

Bethy shrugged, turned her back on Ruth, and changed. "What did Allison want?"

"She wanted to know if we were going by the studio today."

"I wonder why? I mean, except for in the car the other day she hardly even talks to us anymore."

"We could swing by, if your audition's on time. She said she had something to give to us."

"Whatever," Bethy said.

IN THEIR BEAUTIFULLY APPOINTED APARTMENT AT THE
Grove, Angie was stretched out on the living room sofa, feeling
like roadkill and watching the little Roomba vacuum go around
and around. It was an early model, and its sensors hadn't been
perfected yet. As she watched—her head aching—it made an
abrupt and unwarranted right-hand turn straight into a wall. It
should have turned itself around again but it didn't; it just kept
straining against the wall.

Through half-closed eyes, Angie looked at her daughter
puttering in the kitchen and wondered what she'd look like
at thirty-five. Angie would have liked to see that—she would
have liked that more than anything. But it was getting easier to
picture Laurel's life—and Dillard's, for that matter—without
her in it. The thought used to flatten her—Laurel's wedding,
the birth of her first child, her laugh as it would sound when she
was fifty. Now, when she thought about the future, she got only
a quick, powerful kick to the gut. One day, probably when she
was closer to dying, she'd be so aware of their going on without her every single minute of every single, final day that there
wouldn't *be* a moment when she had to remember all over again
that she was dying. Maybe that would be easier.

IN THE KITCHEN AS SHE WAS PULLING TOGETHER A CHEESE
and bread and crudités tray that would pass for dinner, Laurel
drifted through her favorite beauty pageant memories. Angie,
dressing her up in a princess dress, patent-leather pumps, and
a stiff itchy slip, high ponytail and spangles in her hair. Angie,
stroking on Laurel's lipstick from Laurel's own little makeup
case, applying mascara and blusher and saying to Dillard, "Isn't
she a little angel girl? Oh, take another picture, honey," and
Dillard kneeling down on hotel lobby carpeting from Alabama

to Tennessee to squeeze off shot after shot with his professional-quality, auto-wind camera. Angie, saying the same thing to her at every pageant, as Laurel waited in the wings: "Show the Lord you're listening." The first time she said it Laurel asked her what she meant, and Angie said, "He has blessed you with beauty inside and out. He has big plans for you, honey, and if you're listening to Him, He'll help you excel at whatever you do."

So Laurel had smiled for the Lord and the judges, had learned to dance and sing and comport herself in a way that was both poised and vivacious. And over the years she *had* excelled on the pageant circuit, winning Little Miss titles in her town, county, and, almost, her state, where she'd been second runner-up. So when Angie got sick, Laurel had felt she could rightly ask a favor of the Lord in return, and find that *He* was listening. She had put in years of unceasing toil by then, not only in pageants but also in acting classes, talent competitions, and promotional events at shopping malls and for civic groups. In Hollywood she had sung songs about boxed macaroni, praised the superior quality and durability of paper towels, and eaten chicken and hamburgers and chocolate chip cookies with a glad heart because surely these would prove her godliness. Theatrically, she'd finally booked a four-line role on *CSI*; a one-liner that had later been cut on *Unfabulous*; and, her crowning achievement, a flashback that was almost heartbreakingly poignant, though silent, as a young Francine on a made-for-TV movie, in which she, as Francine, walked down a country lane and into a flowering apple orchard with her father, who would soon lose his life on the battlefields of France during World War II.

In all, in eight months Laurel had booked more jobs than anyone else in the studio: eighteen commercials, infomercials, industrials, and PSAs, as well as the three theatrical roles. And she showed no signs of slowing down. The more sallow and exhausted Angie looked, the more Laurel forced herself to bloom.

On every set, in secret, she'd asked the PA whether Angie could have the most comfortable chair, the dressing room with a couch, the one closest to the bathrooms, because she was terribly sick. She varied the explanation, saying Angie had kidney disease or congestive heart failure—things that were clearly serious without being contagious, though she never once said cancer. And the PAs always came through, especially in the last months when all you had to do was look at Angie to see that something was very wrong. Oblivious, Angie constantly marveled that people treated them so nicely on set, always arranging the schedule so Laurel was one of the first actors to be signed out at the end of the day. Angie never once caught on, a fact that Laurel was more proud of by far than any of the work she did for the camera.

She'd felt certain, given all she had done, that He would hear her.

But in the last month she'd watched Angie become more and more exhausted, and though her mother thought she was keeping the terrible bruises on her arms and legs covered, Laurel saw them every night after Angie fell asleep, because she checked on Angie at midnight—set an alarm for that express purpose—and pulled up the covers, smoothed a pillow, listened to her mother's breathing. And the bruises leaked from beneath sleeves or pant legs until they began to run together. Still, Laurel had hung on to hope, had tried to convince herself that this didn't necessarily mean that Angie was dying.

Except, of course, she *was* dying, and it mattered not at all that they weren't nearly ready.

And that was a bitter, bitter pill. That was the Lord's slap, His disapproving judgment, not only of Laurel but at Angie's expense. Angie was dying because Laurel didn't know how to do the Lord's bidding. Trying, evidently, didn't count.

So when Mimi Roberts called and told Angie that Laurel had booked a small role in *After*—as a pious girl whose sole contribution to the movie was to tell Buddy that at least his mother was joyful because she was in heaven—Laurel began to scream. She screamed and screamed until Angie called 911 and they gave Laurel massive doses of Valium and when she finally stopped screaming, she told Angie she was done. And nothing Angie could do or say would change her mind.

BETHY'S AUDITION WAS ALL THE WAY DOWN IN SANTA Monica at Westside Casting Studios, which Ruth hated because it meant they had to take the 405, highway to hell. Ruth and Bethy arrived twenty minutes late because they'd been hungry, said screw it, and stopped to grab a burger at a McDonald's a couple of blocks away. The studio waiting room was full to bursting with African American girls. Something was up. They were trying to decide whether Bethy should even bother to sign in or just call Mimi, when a casting assistant with ear gauges and crazy, shoe-polish-black hair hurried over shaking his head.

"Wait, wait, wait. Please don't tell me you're here for Charmin, because the ad agency's going in a different direction. Didn't your agent tell you? We called everyone this morning."

"*Crap,*" said Ruth.

But the casting assistant was already rushing away. "Next group, please, where are you?" From across the room Ruth watched him say to some of the girls. "No, there should be only four of you. No, *four*. You're five. One of you is in the wrong place." He culled a girl from the group and ushered the rest into the audition room, where, from the sound of it, they were being asked to burst into song. Ruth looked at Bethy and Bethy looked back and they shrugged their shoulders and walked out.

Ruth called Mimi from the car. "So did Holly call to tell you the toilet paper commercial call was for black girls? Because we just got down here and unless Bethy can suddenly pass, we're fucked."

"Let me call Big Talent," said Mimi.

Ruth sighed. "What's the point? Crap, crap, *crap*! It just took us two hours to get here, and it's going to take us three hours to get back because it's rush hour."

"*C'est la vie,*" said Mimi.

"Whatever," said Ruth. Normally she'd have been livid, but at least they'd had something to do while Ruth waited for her cell phone to bring them more bad news from the north.

AN HOUR AND THREE QUARTERS LATER, THE CALL CAME.

"She has a mass," Hugh told her. She and Bethy had ground to an absolute standstill eight miles short of the 101.

Ruth felt her chest get heavy. "What does that mean? Does it mean cancer?"

"We won't know until they go in."

"So they're going to operate."

"They already are. They took her into surgery half an hour ago."

"Oh, honey," Ruth said.

"What's going on?" said Bethy.

"Hush," said Ruth.

"We should know more in a couple of hours."

"*Damn* it. All right, well, let me know as soon as you do."

"Mom, what's going on? Is Daddy all right?"

So while they crept toward the 101 at two miles an hour in heat so high that it could take your breath away if you didn't

have air-conditioning, Ruth told Bethy about Helene. She tried
to sound chipper and hopeful but Bethy, who had always been
able to sniff out a rat, burst into tears and refused to be consoled.
Ruth let her cry it out. Then she started to talk, and she didn't
stop until they'd reached the 101 about half an hour later. She
talked about how hard it was on Hugh to have them here; and
how, even though he loved them and missed them, he didn't see
any way that selling his Seattle practice and coming to LA made
financial sense; and how there was Helene to think of now, too.
She talked about how much it was costing them to live in LA,
and how much harder it was to book things than they'd ever
imagined, even though Bethany was an astonishingly good actor whom Hugh and Ruth were so proud of there weren't even
words. She talked about what diabetes really entailed, and how
a diabetic's outlook was as important as his medical care, and
how Hugh was trying very hard to take good care of himself,
but still. She talked about how Bethy was missing a lot of what
being a teenager was all about—school plays and pep rallies and
going with friends to the mall and, later on, proms and dances.
By the time Ruth merged onto the 101, she realized what she'd
just done with no forethought whatsoever: she'd made a case—
a well-thought-out, articulate, *compelling* case—for leaving this
place behind and going home. *Really* going home. And the more
she talked, the calmer Bethy became, and *that* was the first thing
that had really surprised Ruth in days.

"Talk to me," she said.

"About what?"

"What do you mean, about what? About everything I just
said. About the idea of going home. Does it upset you?"

Bethy nibbled on the end of a lock of hair. "Not really."

"No?"

"No. I mean, not if Daddy needs us. And Nana."

"But this is your dream, honey. I know that."

Bethany shrugged. *Shrugged.*

"No?" said Ruth.

"No. I mean, yes. Yes, it's my dream. But if Daddy and Nana need us at home, we should do that."

"Don't you want to think about this? It's a huge decision."

"That's okay," said Bethy, and Ruth could tell she meant it. "I mean, I know this was exciting and stuff, especially at first, but it's not like I thought it would be. I thought I'd be working all the time. And I miss, like, everything. I mean, I miss having real friends and stuff. School."

"Honey, if we go home now, we might never come back."

"Yeah." Bethy shrugged again, looking out the window. "That's okay, though. Hey, can we do Bob's for dinner?"

And just like that, with exactly that little anguish, it was over—Hollywood, LA, everything. Damned if they hadn't hit the psychic's fork in the road and known all along which way to go.

THE ONLY CAR IN THE STUDIO LOT WAS MIMI'S. BETHY folded her arms across her chest and said she'd wait in the car. Ruth started to argue with her and then, abruptly, she gave up, putting all the windows down and saying, "If you stop sweating or you get light-headed, honk the horn immediately, and I mean immediately, because it'll mean you're getting heatstroke."

"I won't get heatstroke," Bethy said.

Inside, Ruth was greeted by Tina Marie and then by Allison. The little dog, apparently unmoved by the smell of Ruth's shoes, returned to Mimi's office leaving a trail of piddle behind. "Tina Marie!" Allison called after her. "You come back and clean that up!"

She looked at Ruth, looked away, took a deep breath, and

said, "I miss you and Bethy. Like, a *lot*. I know I did a bad thing. I don't even know why I took it, and then I lied about it. I'm really, really, really sorry."

"The spoon? Oh, honey," Ruth said. She pulled Allison into a hug. "Thank you. I know this was a hard thing to do. We've missed you, too." And to her surprise, Ruth meant it.

"I *know*," said Allison.

Ruth coaxed her into going out to the parking lot and talking to Bethany while Ruth poked her head in to see Mimi—who was, of course, on the telephone. She signaled for Ruth to sit in the visitor's chair and hung up a minute later. "Is she still going back to live with her mother?" Ruth said, gesturing vaguely over her shoulder to indicate Allison.

"No," said Mimi. "She'll be staying here."

"Oh! Well, that's good, then," Ruth said. "Listen, I'm probably going to have to go back to Seattle again. My mother-in-law's having some kind of medical crisis. We don't know much right now, but whatever it is, it's not good."

"You've been having a tough time," Mimi said, which was the closest thing to kindness she'd ever shown Ruth.

For a minute, Ruth felt incipient tears. She concentrated on breathing through her nose until the feeling passed. "It's being so far away—it makes everything turn into such a bigger deal. Anyway, here's what I wanted to ask you. If we went home—I mean Bethy, too—would it be that bad?"

"What do you mean, if you go home? You mean for the summer?"

Ruth nodded vaguely. "Well, or for, you know, a break. To reevaluate."

"That's up to you. Bethany's turning, what, fourteen?"

"In June."

"Yeah. If you're going to take a break, this is probably a good time to do it, with summer coming up. Episodic season's over, and feature films are pretty much cast already."

"So it wouldn't hurt her chances."

"I can't tell you that."

"Okay," said Ruth, standing.

"Just let me know what you decide," Mimi said, already turned back to her computer. "Let me know and let Holly know, so we can book her out."

"Yes, ma'am," said Ruth.

Out in the parking lot, Allison was leaning way in their car window, talking to Bethany. By Allison's body language Ruth gathered that things had gone well between them. When the girls saw her, they talked her into taking Allison with them to Bob's for dinner, where they chattered like magpies right through dessert, giving Ruth a racking headache. The shy waiter was nowhere to be found, which was probably just as well since Ruth had a consuming desire to tell him about Helene and the decision she and Bethy had just made to go home. Like he'd miss them. Like he even *recognized* them. Would anyone miss them? Yes—Vee Velman. After dinner Ruth dropped the girls off at CityWalk for a movie, pulled up a rickety patio chair by the apartment's scummy pool, and dug out her phone.

"Okay, here's the thing, and it's creepy," she told Vee. "Your Viking psychic got it right. My mother-in-law's in the hospital with some kind of brain tumor. I'm going to have to go home again." She watched leaf debris, a plastic water bottle, and half a potato chip bag scud across the pool in a light breeze.

"See, I *told* you," Vee said. "I told you she'd have something for you."

"I don't see that it's done me any good, though. I mean, it's not like I could warn Hugh or Helene. All it did was make me crazy, and now this."

"Sure," said Vee. "That's a bummer. So do you want Bethany to stay with us this time? When are you leaving?"

"Tomorrow," said Ruth. "But here's the thing: we might not come back."

"Really?"

"Really." And as Ruth said it, she realized she meant it. "It's just too hard. We thought she'd be working a lot more. I mean, she's only booked the one costar role. Not even a commercial. In eight months. Hugh's sick and he misses us, and now there's this thing with his mother. . . ."

"But it can go like that," Vee argued. "Hell, they can go *years* with nothing, and then, bam! They book something huge."

"Or they can just go for years with nothing."

"There is that."

"No, I think we're done. Helene needs Hugh, and Hugh needs me."

Vee was silent for a minute. "So does Bethany know?"

"Yes."

"Was she okay with it?"

"You know, to tell you the truth I think she might be secretly relieved. There's been a lot of tension at the studio with one of her friends, even though that seems to be over for now. And some of the other families are starting to leave for the summer, so it'll just get lonelier and lonelier."

"Don't forget Clara."

"I know, but you guys are too far away to see often, plus Clara has her own life. She doesn't need Bethy dropped on her." Ruth picked a piece of hair off her pants. "This is *so* not what I expected."

"LA never is," said Vee.

"I don't know—we might end up coming back when Bethy's legal eighteen. Then maybe she'll have more of a chance."

"Sure," said Vee, but they both knew they didn't believe it. "So anyway, call me sometimes. I'll call you."

"I will," said Ruth. "I'm going to miss you."

"Are you crying? Why are you crying?"

"It was such a nice dream," said Ruth, and then she was sobbing. "I was so sure it was going to be—I don't know what. *Phenomenal*. And all we've really done was press our noses against the glass."

Vee made a sympathetic noise.

"I'm going to hang up now," Ruth said. "I'm embarrassing myself."

"Okay," said Vee. "Love you, babe. Safe travels."

"Yeah," said Ruth. "I love you, too."

To herself, once she'd gotten off the phone, she muttered, "Well, *that* was god-awful," because it had been—unexpectedly so. She'd had no idea she would be so emotional about pulling up stakes and going home—far more emotional than Bethany was, when it should have been the other way around. Could this have been *Ruth's* dream, all this time? Might Bethy have just been going along with it? Maybe Ruth had wanted it for herself, recognition by proxy; maybe she was no better than every other stage mom who was compensating for a hollow core by filling it up with someone else's prospects.

Or maybe that was all just so much crap.

She went back to the apartment and finished packing, then ran a load of food, laundry detergent, and odds and ends to the studio for anyone to take home who could use them. She was relieved that Mimi wasn't there. Mimi hadn't seemed either disappointed or surprised that they were going. Maybe what she'd been surprised about was that they'd lasted this long. Ruth knew she'd had unrealistic expectations, and that Mimi was leery of that because it had a tendency to blow up in her face.

It hadn't seemed to matter that they'd been earnest and done everything she'd asked them to do. In fact, it was possible that their earnestness—which really amounted to colossal naïveté—had worked against them. Mimi tended to lean toward the realistic ones, the ones who were bracing for the long haul, the ones who were settling in, making lives here as well as careers. They'd never done that. They'd never even made the distinction, until now.

Chapter Twenty-five

CASSIE WAS THE ONE WHO DELIVERED THE NEWS. SHE TOLD Quinn that when she couldn't reach him by phone she asked her mother to drive her to his apartment building, and then wait for him to come back from wherever he'd been—which was Hazlitt & Company, getting his hair trimmed. When he saw her on the steps his heart began to pound. Why would Cassie be there with *bad* news? She wouldn't be.

"Guess what?" she said, and then she actually *waited* for him to say, "I don't know—what?"

"We booked it," she screamed, and jumped straight up into his arms. He hugged her tightly and spun her around in mid-air. "We both did!" she screamed. "You're Buddy and I'm Carlyle!"

He couldn't imagine that anything would ever again feel as good as this moment did, right now. He'd booked the lead in a feature film being directed by Gus Van Sant. *Gus Van Sant!*

Cassie's mom got out of her car and gave him a big hug. "Congratulations, honey," she said. "You two are about to blast off for the moon."

EVELYN DROVE UP TO THE CURB AS CASSIE AND HER MOM drove away. She got out without even turning off the ignition, and she was grinning.

"Son of a bitch," she said.

★

An hour and a half later Jasper was loading up the bong again, but Quinn could still tell he was majorly pissed off that Quinn had booked the movie. Lightning doesn't strike twice. Not that Jasper had been in the running for *After*; it was more of a cosmic thing. Statistically hardly any unknown actors landed leads, never mind in a major film. Maybe one out of the zillion actors in LA. Since Quinn was that one, Jasper was fucked. It made sense.

And it was *Gus Van Sant*!

Oh, man.

They'd smoked a ton of weed in twenty minutes and you'd think that would have mellowed him out, but Quinn couldn't sit still. He wasn't ready to tell Mimi his news yet—she wasn't his manager anymore anyway; fuck her—and Evelyn Flynn already knew. He tried to think about who else to tell who'd give a shit. Not his family; not Nelson. Rory, probably, but that meant calling the house and he wasn't up for that. He grabbed his wallet and told Jasper he was going out, and when he found himself on the street—and it was a great street, he was suddenly in love with it—he turned right. Toward Hazlitt & Company. Quatro would be happy for him. Quatro wasn't an actor.

The place was packed—clients were sitting at every single station. Quinn stood in the reception area for a minute or two, watching Quatro work with a client who looked vaguely familiar—a character actor? Someone Quinn had auditioned with once? Then Quatro spotted him in the mirror, said something to the client, and came up to the front.

"Hey, buddy. Everything okay?"

Quinn just looked at him with an uncontrollable grin.

"You got it, didn't you? You fucking *got it*?" Quatro gave a huge war whoop and grabbed Quinn's arm. "Holy shit, man!

It's Gus Van Sant!" He started laughing and Quinn started laughing and they couldn't stop.

The salon was riveted.

Quatro finally yelled, "This man has just booked the lead in a major movie being directed by *Gus Fucking Van Sant*!"

The place erupted into clapping and whistles and whoops.

"Oh man, oh man" said Quatro, clasping Quinn in a bear hug. "I am so proud."

And then Quinn was crying and he had no idea why because he'd never felt this way in his whole life, not even close.

"I'll tell you exactly why," said Quatro. "It's joy, buddy. It's pure, unadulterated joy."

EVELYN FLYNN TOOK HIM TO NOBU FOR DINNER. THE GUY at the front recognized her, and they had a little how-are-you-you-look-great kind of moment, and then they followed him to a table in the back that was pretty much surrounded by potted plants—for privacy, was Quinn's guess. Jennifer Aniston was sitting at the next table over.

Evelyn turned away menus and ordered for them both from a waiter who looked like Forest Whitaker when Forest Whitaker was still fat. Evidently Quinn was getting steak. He wondered what she'd have done if he were a vegetarian or a vegan or something—not that he would be; he loved meat. She'd probably have told him to eat it anyway, and he probably would have done it.

Quinn knew his life was never going to be the same. And he knew he owed that to Evelyn Flynn, who was breaking a piece of crusty bread into smaller pieces and dipping them in a little pool of olive oil like it was just another day.

"So?" she said.

"On top of the world."

She smiled. "You should be. You've been given a tremendous honor. *And* a responsibility. Don't ever forget that. This man is balancing his reputation on your shoulders."

"Yeah," he said, even though he'd never thought about that before. Then he worked up some courage. There'd been something he'd wanted to know from the beginning, only he'd never gotten up the nerve to ask her before. "Why did you do this?"

"This?"

"Me," he said.

She thought for a minute. "When you act, it transforms you. You have the ability to disappear inside a character. That's a gift—hardly anyone can do it. You can."

"Haven't you ever wanted to be an actor?"

She smiled. "Not even a little bit. My talent is recognizing talent and knowing what to do with it when I've found it. I'm very, very good at that."

"Can I still work with you?"

"You'll have one of the best directors in the business. You need to work with him."

"I'll see you sometimes, though. I mean, will you come to the set sometimes once we're back in LA?" Despite Van Sant's feelings about soundstages and inauthenticity, Quinn had already been told they'd be doing some work here after all.

"Oh, you'll see me now and then," she said smiling. "But you won't care very much."

"Are you kidding? Yes, I will."

"Not in a few weeks. Not once you're working. Because I guarantee you this: you've never worked as hard in your life as you're going to be working on this movie."

Their steaks arrived and they ate and drank and then she

drove him home, which was still Jasper and Baby-Sue's apartment. When he was about to get out of the car, she put her hand on his forearm. It was the first time she'd ever touched him. Then she let go.

SHE TOOK THE LONG WAY BACK HOME TO STUDIO CITY, driving uncharacteristically slowly; normally she kept her speedometer at between ten and fifteen miles per hour above the speed limit and saw traffic tickets as a necessary evil, but tonight she felt strangely melancholy. This was the difficulty of allowing a client into your heart. You could go only so far with them before you crossed a line into the inappropriate. She had already begun engineering the hand-off to a full-time manager who could mother him and counsel him and shield him and coach him and find him decent housing in LA while he was on location. If there were a couple of weeks between the loss of his apartment and leaving to shoot on location, she would still let him stay in her guesthouse, but in the end, and possibly as a cosmic nod to her unprecedented willingness to breach her solitude, it appeared that she might not need to house Quinn after all. She didn't know how she felt—oddly let down as well as hugely relieved. In the long run, she'd move on and so would he. And that wasn't the worst thing she could think of. The worst thing was to get so attached to a boy like Quinn that you mistook symbiosis for love.

IN HOLLYWOOD, DILLARD BUEHL BACKED THE HUMMER up to the freight door at the Grove. The day before, he'd hired a couple Mexicans to help him move out the big furniture: the couch and club chairs and beds and bureaus. Angie hadn't let him hire a moving company; she said they needed to keep their expenses down, now that she was going to be needing care. Even hospice wasn't free. So he'd be driving the truck cross-country himself; Laurel had gotten her license a week earlier so she could help Angie with the Hummer. He didn't like the thought of either one of them driving, but Angie had been in-sistent: she didn't want to get sicker a moment before she had to. That day was coming, but she'd be damned if she'd meet it halfway. Until then, she told Dillard, she'd drive.

Dillard had offered to close up the Atlanta house and come live with them in LA so Laurel could keep working on being a star. But the girls said no, that Laurel didn't want a Hollywood career anymore, and Angie already had an appointment with her oncologist in Atlanta. It was time to go home. He guessed she needed to feel like she was in control; the best thing he could do for her and for Laurel, she told him, was to do exactly what he had always done in summer: boil and sell peanuts. He didn't particularly want to do that, now that he knew why Angie had looked so bad the last time he'd seen her in LA. But he'd do it like she'd asked him to, because there wasn't anything else he could do for her. Later, yes. But not now.

He brought down several loads of bedding and the last of the odds and ends—framed posters, the Roomba, an oasis of potted plants that they'd be giving to Mimi for the studio on the way to dinner. They'd stay at a hotel tonight, so Angie could get a good night's sleep before setting out tomorrow.

When they drove up, Mimi and Allison were waiting for them in the studio parking lot. Dillard pulled in as close to the studio doors as he could, because some of the plants were heavy and he wasn't as young as he used to be. They all climbed out—Angie too—and started pulling out urns and pots and tubs full of greenery. Angie had a green thumb, as it turned out, and the plants had thrived under her care.

"You better not kill them," she told Mimi. "I'll be checking on you." Mimi had smiled—wanly, Dillard thought—and held out her arms for a hug. Angie and then Laurel embraced her. Just eight months ago they'd stood in this very place and speculated about the first movie that Laurel would star in. But even then, Angie had known about the cancer, and Laurel had, too. He couldn't understand that, how they'd been able to be so festive.

Because they'd chosen to be, Angie had told him. Because they were that strong, Dillard thought. He hoped they'd be able to teach him that as they went along, because they were clearly built of tougher stuff than he was.

Allison gave Angie a hug first, and then Laurel, and for a minute the two girls clung to each other.

Mimi took Angie's hand briefly and said something too low for Dillard to hear but that made Angie smile, though sadly; and then they released each other and Angie made a beeline for the car. Even for her, strength could get you only so far. Dillard had to look away. Usually when you said a difficult goodbye you could comfort yourself with thoughts of something pleasant that lay ahead. But he couldn't think of a single thing to look forward to without fear and dread. Angie was dying and he was not and there wasn't a thing he could do to reverse the roles or change the outcome. But Angie had told him very firmly that there wasn't going to be a funeral before she was gone. She wouldn't put up with that. And he guessed she was right.

Now he shut the Hummer's heavy door behind her. They lifted their hands to Mimi and Allison and some of the other kids who'd come out to the parking lot as they pulled away.

SLOWLY, SO LAUREL WOULDN'T NOTICE, ANGIE OPENED her hand to see what Mimi had put there. In her palm was a single clear glass marble.

IN WEST HOLLYWOOD, QUINN REILLY STOOD JUST beyond the patio at Los Burritos, wavering. He'd be leaving for Portland in the morning—Gus, anxious to get going, had moved the production schedule up so they could start shooting two weeks earlier. He and Cassie and her mom, Beverly, would be driving to LAX at four a.m. He'd already said good-bye to Quatro, who'd given him a camera as a send-off gift.

"You better take pictures every damn day and e-mail them back to me," he'd said, coming to the front of the salon to give Quinn his gift and pull him into a close hug, pressing his head against Quinn's head like a kiss. "I'm going to miss you."

"Me, too," Quinn had said, and he meant it. Quatro had been the beginning of all the good things that had happened to him in the past nine months. Quinn had made him promise that he'd come to Portland for a visit before the shoot was over.

The other good thing to come into his life—besides Gus and *After* and everything he still had to look forward to—was the little Hispanic girl. So now he stood on the sidewalk in front of

Los Burritos, nervous and undecided, watching her wait on a tiny, dark-skinned man who looked like he'd come from somewhere high in the Andes. There wasn't anyone else in the place, so when she handed the man his change Quinn took a deep breath and went up to the counter.

"*Hola!*" she said brightly. "*Cómo estás?*"

"*Bien, gracias—y tú?*"

"*Bien.* Your talking is much better."

"You're a good teacher," he said. He could feel his face heating up the way it always did.

She smiled shyly. She'd told him her name was Marcela. He thought that was pretty. "What would you like?" she said.

"No, nothing. I brought *you* something."

She looked at him uncertainly. He pulled his hand out of his pocket and opened it. The little chili lay on his palm.

"Oh!" she said. "It's very pretty. *Muy bonita.*"

He extended his hand. "It's for you."

"Me?"

He pointed at her little chili earrings.

"Ah!" Her face lit up. "To go together. *Muchas gracias.*"

To go together. He liked the way that sounded. Then, though he hadn't planned to say anything, he told her, "I'm going away for a few months."

"Yes?"

"I'm doing a movie. I'm the lead in a movie." His face was probably beet red; he felt stupid saying it, even though it was true, because it sounded like a lie. "Gus Van Sant is directing it."

"That's good?"

Quinn nodded.

"Oh! Good, then." The girl closed her hand around the charm. "Then I'll know why I don't see you."

He nodded, but then he had no idea what else to say, so he just turned around and started to leave.

"Wait," she said. "*Tu nombre?* What's your name?"

"Quinn."

"Quinn?" She pronounced it like *queen*, but he didn't mind. "Quinn what?"

"Quinn Reilly."

"Okay. I watch for you."

Then someone came up behind him, and just like that it was over. She tucked the charm into the apron of her uniform and smiled at him and he ducked his head because he didn't know what his face should be doing and then he was back on the sidewalk, excited and relieved.

He wondered how he'd feel about leaving LA. He'd been here for four years. And now he was going to be someplace new, even if it was just Portland, doing something he'd dreamed of every single day for years. By the time he came back here, he wouldn't be the same actor anymore. He probably wouldn't even be the same person.

He shoved his hand deep in his pocket. It felt empty without the chili pepper charm. He was glad he'd given it to her, though. Maybe she'd be wearing it the next time he saw her.

That would be nice.

IN VAN NUYS, ALLISON MADE WINGS OF HER ARMS AND soared around Mimi's living room. "Look at me—I'm flying!"

They'd been sitting together in the living room, where Allison was watching *Saturday Night Live* while Mimi went through the day's breakdowns on her laptop. Tina Marie was snoring in her basket across the room. Allison had offered to make them a snack, taking wing on the way to the kitchen. Mimi just shook her head. The girl had been in high spirits ever since Mimi had laid out her new life. Far from objecting, she had settled into a state of almost manic proactivity. She'd wanted to register for school right away, though the new school year wouldn't start for months. She'd cleared out all her monologues, sides, résumés, headshots, and even her Mimi Roberts Talent Management tote bag; and when Mimi told her that wasn't necessary, Allison had pointed out that she was on hiatus, wasn't she? Why would she need that stuff? And of course she was right.

Last week she'd helped Reba and Hillary pack their things to ship home, since neither family had found the girls housing. The night before they left LA, Allison and Mimi had taken them out for dinner at the Olive Garden—Reba's favorite restaurant, based on the bottomless breadstick basket—and as a farewell gift Allison presented each of them with a scrapbook full of head-shots of all Mimi's clients, plus little goodie bags with snacks to take on the plane. Once they were gone, she cleaned the bedroom and bathroom until the porcelain and chrome shone; organized her closet by color and outfit; and then turned her attention to the rest of the house. At least she could hire herself out if Hollywood failed her, Mimi thought wryly. In Holly-wood, good housekeepers were always in demand.

"Look at me, I'm flying!" Allison soared out of the living room and into the kitchen. Mimi smiled and went back to work.

IN SEATTLE, RUTH PASSED BY BETHANY'S ROOM WITH A stack of warm folded towels and saw her sitting on the end of her bed, gazing out the window at the apple tree in their neighbor's yard.

"Are you okay?"

Bethy nodded. "It's weird, though. Doesn't it seem like we were never there at all?"

Ruth thought about the mute testimony of their depleted bank account, but she knew what Bethy meant. "Do you miss it?"

Bethany nodded thoughtfully. "Sometimes."

Ruth still missed it every day, even after being home for three weeks. She missed Vee and Bob's Big Boy and the gentle waiter whose hand she'd once taken, and feeling that at any moment their lives and prospects could change, and always for the better. She even missed Mimi. She was surprised at how often she heard the woman's voice in her head. Mimi Roberts was a survivor, someone who'd learned to adapt and even flourish in Hollywood's toxic environment. Except for Allison, the rest of them were gone: Quinn was in Oregon filming; Hillary and Reba were at home with their families; and Laurel, Angie, and Dillard were in Atlanta. They'd heard that even with aggressive chemo, Angie wasn't expected to live more than four or five more months.

"I miss Allison," Bethy said. "I'm glad she's coming to visit." They'd agreed she could come to Seattle and stay with them for a couple of weeks in August.

"Have you heard from her lately?"

Bethy nodded. "She said this year's boot camp kids are total losers. She has to help Mimi with the little kids' classes and stuff—she isn't even doing any of the workshops. She says it's okay, though, because she's done boot camp like a million times. Mimi's taking her up to Big Bear for a week, and then she's going back to see her mom. She says she doesn't want to go, but Mimi's making her. It's just for a couple of days, though."

"Well, I'm sure she's looking forward to seeing her mother."

Bethy just shrugged. "She says her mom doesn't even care if she comes or not, now that she's rich and divorced and stuff."

"I'm sure it's not that simple," Ruth said, thinking, though, that it probably *was* that simple. She wasn't as naïve as she used to be. She had assumed that since she and Vee Velman had been mainly telephone friends even in LA—they'd probably seen each other in person only six times in all those months—they would just carry on in exactly the same way even if Ruth was in Seattle. But although they'd talked a few times since Ruth had been back, the calls had been short and surprisingly empty, and Ruth could see that in another call or two the friendship would just peter out, one more relationship based on shared circumstance. It was a shame, but Ruth understood it.

Bethy had moved on. "Rianne broke up with her boyfriend," she was saying.

"Again?"

"Yeah, but she says this time it's for good. So we were thinking we might go to Belle Square later, if that's okay with you. She said her mom would drive us, if you can pick us up."

Ruth nodded. "I'm glad you're friends again."

"Me, too."

"Do the kids here know you've been on TV?"

Bethy shrugged. "Nah."

"But don't you want them to know?"

"Not really." Bethy looked away, out the window.

"Why not?" Ruth cried. "You've done something absolutely amazing."

Bethany picked at a slub in the fabric of her bedspread, and then Ruth finally got it: who wanted to be different at fourteen?

Ruth turned to go down the hall, calling over her shoulder, "Just let me know when you're leaving and what time you want me to pick you up."

She stowed the towels in the hall linen closet and then headed for the back bedroom. Helene Rabinowitz would be going home from the rehab center tomorrow, finally, with her brain largely intact, and Hugh's diabetes was under control. Last night Ruth had ordered twenty pounds of clay and told Hugh that she planned to start sculpting again. He'd kissed her on the top of her head and said, "Good for you, Ruthie. I know this isn't easy." And it wasn't. But last night she'd begun to clear out the back bedroom, where their things were still sitting right where they'd left them three weeks ago.

She pried open a lid and found extra headshots and résumés, books of monologues, folders filled with sides, Bethy's Mimi Roberts Talent Management tote bag, and clothes she and Bethy had bought especially for auditions—artifacts from a lost civilization. She felt a sudden sense of vertigo: Had they really done all this? She pulled out a long feather boa Bethy had used as a prop for some of her headshots, and then, running her hand around the bottom of the box, she felt the frames of a lens-less pair of glasses. She pulled them out and put them on, thinking they would make Bethy laugh. Or maybe they were capable of magic, of opening a portal through which they could go back. But no. They were just cheap plastic sunglasses frames, slightly warped from sitting in the hot car. She could never go back there again and neither could Bethany. Angie would be dead and the rest of them would be older, and Ruth would step back into her life and her marriage and the steady hum of ordinariness, and eventually that would be enough.

"What are you looking at?" Bethany said from the doorway. "They don't even have lenses."

Ruth turned to Bethany and smiled. "I know," she said. "I'm seeing you."

WORKS BY DIANE HAMMOND

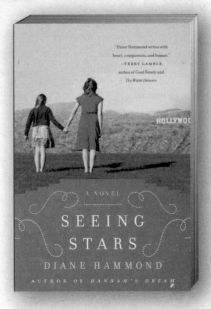

HANNAH'S DREAM
A Novel

ISBN 978-0-06-156825-1 (paperback)

"Irresistibly touching, delectably uplifting, Hammond's understated yet gargantuan tale of devotion and commitment poignantly proves that love does indeed come in all shapes and sizes."
—*Booklist* (starred review)

"Featuring a cast of endearingly quirky characters (notably, an elephant named Hannah), this charming story enchants and provides a nice balance of lighthearted and poignant moments." —*Library Journal*

SEEING STARS
A Novel

ISBN 978-0-06-186315-8 (paperback)

Ruth believes that her daughter Bethy is a terrific little actress. And if Bethy wants to leave the Pacific Northwest for LA and a merry-go-round of auditions, classes, and callbacks—well, Ruth will lead the way. Hollywood, of course, eats people like Ruth and Bethy for breakfast. Surrounded by other aspiring child stars, stage mothers, managers, and talent agents, Ruth and Bethy will discover just how far they can go, and maybe just how far they want to.